Book
of a
Thousand Days

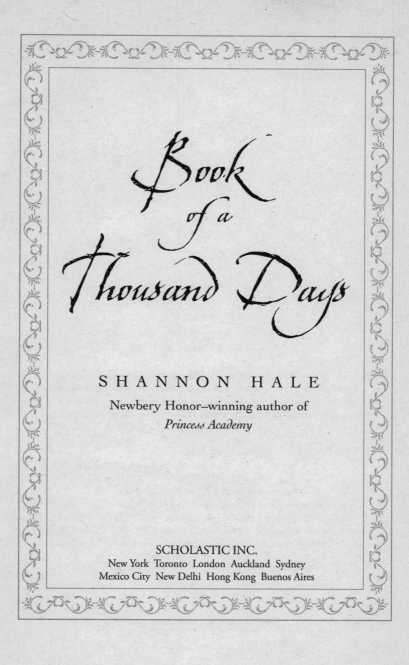

Book of a Thousand Days

SHANNON HALE

Newbery Honor–winning author of
Princess Academy

SCHOLASTIC INC.
New York Toronto London Auckland Sydney
Mexico City New Delhi Hong Kong Buenos Aires

ISBN-13: 978-0-545-08806-0
ISBN-10: 0-545-08806-2

12 11 10 9 8 7 6 5 4 3   8 9 10 11 12 13/0

Printed in the U.S.A.   40

First Scholastic printing, April 2008

Typeset in Cochin

FOR VICTORIA

To the girl and the geese nine others said, Nay!
But you poured me some tea and asked me to stay
And built me a cottage at Bloomsbury Place
With pillows on chairs and sun on my face.
Our fifth together is me hugging you;
May dozens more follow before we are through.

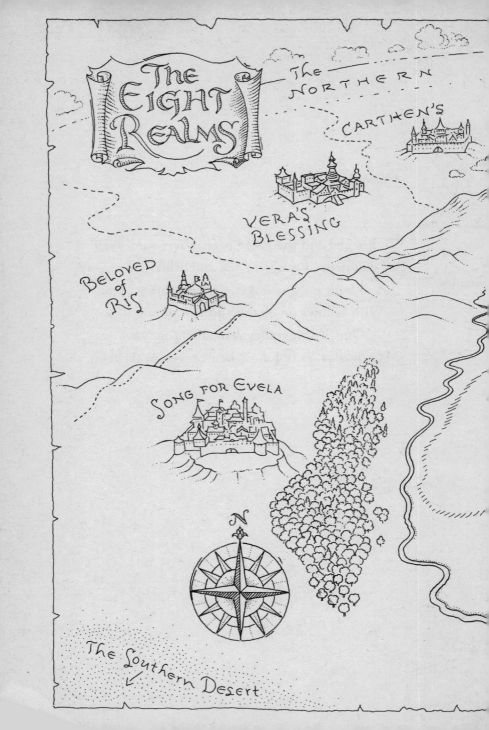

WASTE

PRAYER

PRIDE of
NIBUS

The
Sacred
Mountain

GODA'S SECOND GIFT

The
STEPPES

THOUGHTS of UNDER

TITOR'S GARDEN

A book of thoughts kept by Dashti,

a mucker and a lady's maid,

Containing an account of our seven years

in a tower and our adventure thereafter

PART 1

The Tower

Day 1

My lady and I are being shut up in a tower for seven years.

Lady Saren is sitting on the floor, staring at the wall, and hasn't moved even to scratch for an hour or more. Poor thing. It's a shame I don't have fresh yak dung or anything strong-smelling to scare the misery out of her.

The men are bricking up the door, and I hear them muttering and scraping cement. Only a small square of unbricked sky and light still gape at me. I smile back at its mean grin to show I'm not scared. Isn't it something, all the trouble they're going to for us? I feel like a jewel in a treasure box, though my lady is the—

My lady suddenly awoke from her stupor and sprang at the door, clawing at the bricks, trying to shove her way out. How she screamed! Like an angry piglet.

"Stay in!" we heard her honored father say. He

must have been standing near the opening. "Stay until your heart softens like long-boiled potatoes. And if you try to break your way out, I've told the guards to kill you on sight. You have seven years to think about disobedience. Until you are meek with regret, your face turns my stomach."

I nearly warned him that such words would bring him bad luck and canker his own heart. Thank the Ancestors that my lady's fit stopped me from speaking out of turn. When I pulled her back, her hands were red from beating at the bricks and streaked with wet cement. This isn't exactly a happy-celebration morning, but I don't see what good it does to thrash about.

"Easy, my lady," I said, the way I'd speak to a feisty ram. It wasn't too hard to hold my lady back, even squirming as she was. I'm fifteen years, and though skinny as a skinned hare, I'm strong as a yak, or so my mama used to say. I sang the calming song, the one that goes, "Oh, moth on a wind, oh, leaf on a stream," and invites the hearer into dreaming. I feared my lady was so angry she wouldn't heed the song. But she must've been eager to sleep, because now she's snoring on my lap. Happily the brush and ink are at hand so I can keep writing. When you can't move, there isn't much to do but think, and I don't much want to think right now.

Sticky sobs shake my lady even while she sleeps. My own eyes are heavy. Perhaps it's the darkness making us so drowsy. Goda, goddess of sleep, keep us tonight.

Day 2

It's quiet and as dark as night, our only light a quivering candle. The door is bricked solid. From time to time I hear voices, so I suppose the guards remain outside.

Goda heard my prayer last night and did let us sleep until morning. I know it's morning because I peeked through the dump hole. That's a tiny metal flap that opens just enough to empty our chamber pot and wash water on the ground outside. It looks like this.

When I push it open, a lip of brick wall prevents me from looking straight out, but I can see the ground five handspans down. Very thoughtful of her honored father, I think, to design our prison such, so we have a way to throw out our waste and don't have to breathe foul air for seven years.

This tower used to be a lookout tower, standing as it does on the border between Titor's Garden, which is her honored father's land, and Thoughts of Under, which is the realm to the east. The upper story was the lookout, but the windows are bricked blind now. Too easy to escape from, I suppose, or else her honored father hopes to crush her spirits with darkness. The upper floor is my lady's chamber. The air is best there because tiny slits in the bricks let fresh air slink in. If I press my face to a certain slit, I think I can see blue that is the sky. Or maybe I'm just seeing shadows.

The middle story is our kitchen, with hearth, pots, table, and one chair. Stacks and stacks of wood line the walls, and my own straw mattress keeps the floor company. A ladder descends into the cellar. It looks something like this.

And here's the bit that makes me tremble with delight—in our cellar there is a mountain of food! Barrels and bags and crates of it. And we have a fine well dug right in the cellar floor. My lady is napping in her chamber, so I just came down here to look at the food. Seven years' worth. Such a thing I never imagined. Even though I can't see the sky, it's hard not to want to dance about, knowing that for seven years at least I won't starve. That's paradise for a mucker like me. How my mama would laugh.

Day 6

I've been much occupied these past days, learning the ways of our tower, counting sacks of flour and rice, barrels of dried and salted mutton, figuring how much we may eat each day and last for seven years. It's useful knowing my letters and numbers so I can write down the figuring. We've boxes of candles and a stack of parchment, surely enough to keep me writing for seven years.

These are the meals I've cooked these last days:

Breakfast — warmed milk with sugar, eaten with flat barley cakes. Each morning the guards knock on the metal flap and hand up a horn of fresh mare's milk. First thing, I splash a drop of milk in the north corner, facing the direction of the Sacred Mountain, and say my prayers. By tradition, I should dribble the milk on soil, not stones, but it'll have to do since the metal flap faces south.

Dinner — dung cakes. That's what we muckers call them, though I don't use that crude term around my lady, of course. They're made of salted meat (simmered long to soften) and onions, wrapped in dough and cooked on coals. That's how we used to eat them with Mama, only here I get to add spices — cinnamon and peppercorns! Two times before the tower I'd eaten spiced food, but never had I reached my own hand into a barrel and touched the raw powders and seeds. Someday when I leave this life and my soul climbs the Sacred Mountain, I imagine the Ancestors will be too beautiful and bright to look at, but their skin and breath will smell of peppercorns and cinnamon, anise, cardamom, and fennel. Heavenly, it is.

Supper—rice and dried peas, boiled with milk and raisins, and sweetened with a pinch of sugar. Delicious. My lady says she's used to eating the large meal at night instead of midday, but that makes no sense to me. She didn't order me to change the dinner and supper order, so I'll keep it the same.

These past meals have been as hearty as I ever had, and if being a lady's maid means I get to eat the same food as my lady—with spices even!—then you'll never hear me complain.

Sometimes to get her through a long day, I give my lady a mess of dried fruit or a slap of cheese. Even so, she swears she's starving. The mouth grumbles more than the stomach, my mama used to say. My lady can't really be hungry—I think she's just sad to be imprisoned away from her love and hoping that the food will fill her up where her heart breaks.

But so much food! Each day we eat three times, and I roll around on my mattress at night and laugh into my arm and pray to my mama so she knows I'm doing fine.

Day 11

It occurs to me I ought to relate the why behind our imprisonment. And at the moment, with dinner eaten and cleaned up, washing done, and my lady resting, I've nothing more to do but stare at the candle flame. It tosses and bobs like a spring foal and sometimes I find myself staring at it so long, the flame is all I can see for an hour after. But now I'll write.

I came to the city of Titor's Garden only one year ago. My mother, the Ancestors bless her, died from the floating fevers that take people in the summer. I was alone, my father dead when I was a baby, and my brothers gone to make their world way when I was a girl of eight and still in two braids. I wear one braid now, though still long down my back. My lady wears her braid pinned up, though she's not married and just one year older than me. I suppose she has the right to do her hair how she pleases, her being gentry and all.

Anyway, with my mother passed to the Ancestors' Realm, I made the long walk from the summer pastures to the city, hoping to find work. The city had too many people for my mind. Where do they all sleep? How do you feed so many bodies? My head hurt trying to reason it out. I found the house of chiefs soon enough and purchased employment with my last animal. A thin woman people named "Mistress" had me stand before her and tell what skills I had, declaring at the end that I would be of best use working in the stables. When she rose from her chair to show me the way, she winced and rubbed her back.

"Have a pain there, Mistress?" I asked.

She didn't answer. I suppose it was right nosy of me to speak up like that, but I thought I could help her, and why sit quiet when you can be useful? So I said, "I might help that pain, Mistress, if you let me."

She didn't argue, so I put my hand on her back and I started with the song for body aches, the slow, sliding tune that goes, "Tell me again, how does it go?" and then twined into it the hopping tune for buried pain that goes, "Berries in summer, red, purple, green."

She stretched when I was finished. "You're a mucker, then? I've heard of the healing songs but never thought much about them." She looked at me thoughtfully, then set in on any number of queer questions.

"What is the proper remedy for a lady in fits?"

"Make her drink warm milk and rub her back," I answered easily enough.

"Show me a straight stitch."

9

And I sewed a line straighter than the finger of Ris, god of roads and towns.

"Let me see your hands," she said, and checked them for calluses. "Mmm-hmm. And your mucker mother taught you all the healing songs?"

"I don't think a body can know them all, but I know the useful ones, like the song for helping a mare birth a foal and the song to get a she-yak to stand still for milking—"

"No, no, I have no use for horses and yaks. The songs for aches of back and belly and head. Like you just sang for me."

"I know dozens, I guess."

"Then I'm going to make you a lady's maid for the most honored house in Titor's Garden. Our lord's second daughter, Lady Saren, she's bound to need a fresh maid by the time your education is done. She certainly seems to go through them quickly."

Mistress sent me to an old man named Qadan, who lived beside the house of chiefs. I cooked and cleaned for him, and in the afternoons, a group of hopeful scribes joined us for lessons in reading.

"As Lady Saren's maid you'll need to know your letters," Mistress had said. I didn't know then why this is so, but I do now—because unlike most gentry, Lady Saren herself doesn't know them.

What a strange and wondrous time it was, eating two big meals every single day, sleeping by a fire always lit, and learning the secret language of ink strokes. On days when I finished chores and errands early, Qadan taught me sketching. I was so busy and my belly so full, I would fall asleep even as I was falling into bed.

But some nights, when I tossed on my mattress, awake and staring at nothing, the sorrow would strike me. Quiet there in Qadan's dark house, my heartache felt like a river, and I was sinking into it, carried away fast in its coldness. That's the best way I can explain it, and what I mean by it is, I missed my mama.

Sometimes Qadan threw candlesticks at us when his back pinched him sour, but mostly he was a good teacher. He said the best way to practice writing was to keep a book of thoughts. The first one I wrote in was left behind in our rush to this prison. I found this blank book of stitched-together pages among the parchment and inks, and I asked my lady if I might take it for my own. She had no use for it.

It seems a bit of a laugh now, all that time spent learning and now I find myself in a tower with no occasion to write my lady's love letters or keep her books. Instead I'll record the details of our confinement, so when the seven years are over and the lord's men pound through the walls, if all they find is a delicate lady and her humble maid shriveled like old ginger roots from lack of sun and air, they'll know somewhat of our happy time still breathing.

Though my lady doesn't sound happy. She's thrashing on her mattress again. I wonder, is it in the gentry's nature to suffer so? Could the Ancestors give gentry beauty and perfection, food and large houses, and a world to do their bidding, and yet curse them with wretched sorrow? My poor, poor lady.

I had best go see to her now and finish my account later. There will be, I'd guess, plenty of time to do so.

Day 13

While I was washing up tonight, my lady fell asleep on my mattress, not wanting to climb to her chamber. She wears fashionable shoes with the toe long and curled toward her ankle, which are certainly pretty but do make it difficult to clamber up ladders. It wouldn't be proper for me to sleep on her mattress, so I'll finish my story before making my bed of the grain sacks in the cellar. The Ancestors bless her.

After one year with Qadan, Mistress had me take the oath of a lady's maid. I cut my finger, splashed drops of blood toward the north and the Sacred Mountain, and swore to serve the gentry and my new mistress however the Ancestors saw fit.

"But I'm still a mucker, right?" I asked.

"You'll always be a mucker," said Mistress.

I was relieved. I know muckers are the simplest of commoners and becoming a lady's maid is a right honor, but I couldn't give up the wild steppes forever, couldn't turn my back on Mama and all she taught. I feel like a mucker from the ends of my hair to the mud of my bones.

After the oath, Mistress escorted me to the city's center and left me at the lord's house. It was near as beautiful as a mountain in autumn with its three-tiered roof covered in red and green enamel tiles. Inside was less welcoming—grand and cold, the floor stones seemingly cut from ice. Everyone was running around, women were wailing, men were yelling. At the time, I thought it was always that way. I hadn't heard yet of the trouble.

Hours I spent sitting in a corner, waiting for someone to be sensible. I could see myself in a mirror, and I stared and thought how plain I looked in my mucker boots and working clothes inside a gentry's house as fine as sugar. I'll sketch it from memory, so it won't be just right.

No one paid me the least mind, and though it wasn't proper, I decided I'd find my new mistress myself. Ancestors forgive me, but what else could I do? I was of no use to anyone just sitting there.

Errand boys rushed up and down corridors, maidens sulked on benches. Some wept. When I asked for directions to Lady Saren's chamber, no one questioned why I wished to go there.

I entered the chamber slowly, squinting. I'd never met any gentry before and was worried that the glory of the Ancestors might be so bright inside her, it would burn my eyes. I was a little disappointed then to find my lady looking much like anyone else, still in her white sleep clothes, her hair in a braid with half the hair poking out. Her eyes were puffy and red, her nose wet, her feet bare. She sat on her bed, alone, straight as a tent pole.

The first thing I wanted to do was comb her hair straight and plait it tight, dress her and set her up like a proper lady, let the glory of her divine ancestors shine in her properly. But I had to stand there, quiet, and wait for her to look up and see me. It isn't allowed for a commoner, of course, to speak to gentry first.

The flats of my feet were aching by the time she saw. And in all that time she hadn't moved.

"Who are you?" she asked. There was something about her manner that reminded me of a little girl, though I learned since that she's sixteen years.

"My lady, I'm Dashti. I'm your new maid."

"You can't be, they're all hiding from me because they don't want—" She considered me. "What is your name?"

"Dashti, my lady," I told her again.

She hopped off her bed and grabbed my wrist, but tight. Her swiftness and force startled me. "Swear you'll serve me, Dashti. Swear you won't abandon me. Swear it!"

"Of course, my lady, I swear." I didn't know why she grabbed me and yelled. I'd already taken the oath and learned to write letters and everything.

"All right," she said, wandering around the room as if looking for something. "All right then."

I led her back to the bed and had her sit while I combed the muddle of her hair and bound it in a braid, every hair crisscrossing so the smarts wouldn't wander out of her head. She scarcely moved as I washed her face and hands and underarms and feet.

I looked in her wardrobe for clothing and found two dozen deels. They were like the long-sleeved robes over tunic and trousers that any commoner wears, but they resembled my own deel as much as a worm resembles a snake. Before coming to the city, the only cloth I'd seen was leather, fur, or felt. Qadan taught me the names of other cloths—brocade, satin, damask, silk. My lady had them all, I'd dare guess, and embroidered and fine, layers stitched upon each other, trimmed and as colorful as a summer sunset. You must think I fib, claiming any person could have such clothes and so many, but I swear by the eight Ancestors that I speak true as truth.

When she was dressed and combed and cleaned, the beauty that is Lady Saren really began to show, and I think she felt it, too. Once she even said, "Thank you, Dashti."

Those words made me feel combed and cleaned myself.

Then her honored father entered, and she stiffened and began to whimper as if fighting off a fit of sobs. He had one crooked leg. This surprised me fit to staring. I don't mean disrespect, but I'd always thought that gentry would be formed and perfect of limb, lovely and radiant, being the offspring of the Ancestors. But truth be, if her father had worn common clothing, I might've thought him a mucker. Either the Ancestors want it this way, or else Under, god of tricks, was deceiving my eyes.

"Still bleating about it, are you?" said her honored father. He was a man too small for his voice. "Titor and his dogs, girl—it's your mess. Crying about it is like rolling around in your own filth."

He watched her for a moment, and I swear by Titor *and* his dogs that there was a touch of sympathy in his eyes. I'd have sworn it on my mother's memory till he up and slapped her face. It didn't make sense, as though he slapped her more from duty than anger.

Mama used to say, "Hitting is the language of cowards and drunkards," and here a member of the honored gentry struck his daughter for crying.

"What's this thing here?" he asked, looking at me now, taking in my rough boots, my wool deel, my leather sash. "Why is one of your maids dressed as a mucker? Are you a mucker? Answer me, girl."

I answered him. "Yes, my lord, I was born on the steppes, and when I came to my lord's city last year I—"

"That's enough, I don't want the whole story. You're nothing to look at, are you?"

I thought that was a useless question. I'm right aware of the red birth splotches on my face and arm, not to mention my dull hair and lips thinner than the edge of a leaf. Mama said that beauty is a curse for muckers. She once told me about Bayar, her clan sister, who looked like Evela, goddess of sunlight. And what happened to Bayar? A lord fell for her beauty, got her with child, then left both girl and baby in the mud and never returned. That's gentry's right, I guess, but it was a bit hard on Bayar.

"I remember now," my lady's father said with a *humph*, "Mistress Tolui said some mucker girl was coming from Qadan's. What a hell you walked into, though it can't be worse than your own home. Muckers survive on grass alone, just like sheep, isn't that right?"

"Well, my lord," I said, not sure how to contradict gentry, "we—"

He slapped his daughter's face again, suddenly and with no cause, like a snake striking. The sound of her cry was sharp and sad enough to break a bird's wing. It was then that I began to understand my lady—I think she must've lost her mother long ago, before she was old enough to learn how to comfort herself.

"There she goes again!" he said, his big voice booming out of his small head. "She'd gone quiet, and I've grown accustomed to her crying. Bawl all you want, wench! No one will hear you alone in the tower."

At that, she forced her tears to stop and looked right back at him, as brave as anything I've seen. "I won't be alone," she said. "My new maid is going with me."

"Is that what you think?" He was rummaging through her wardrobe, pulling deels from their hooks and tossing them onto the floor. "You don't deserve a maid, and I won't force one to attend you. So let me hear the maid say she's willing to go."

My lady was clinging to my arm.

"Go where?" I asked.

Her father laughed. "Now I understand." He took hold of one of the deels and ripped the sleeves off. "I, her honored father, have arranged an enviable match with Lord Khasar. He is the lord of Thoughts of Under, the most powerful of the Eight Realms. And does my daughter thank me? And appreciate her responsibility to form this alliance? No, she declares she's promised herself to Khan Tegus of the lesser realm Song for Evela. She refuses to marry Lord Khasar. How's that for gratitude? I'm sending her to a watchtower shut up as a prison and we'll see if seven years beneath bricks won't kill her rebellion. So say it, mucker girl, will you lock yourself up with this disobedient child?"

My lady was squeezing my arm so tightly now, my fingers felt cold. One of her cheeks was pink from his slap, her brown eyes red from crying. She reminded me of a lamb just tumbled out, wet all over, unsure of her feet and suspicious of the sun.

She'd be alone in that tower, I thought, and I remembered our tent after Mama died, how the air seemed to have gone out of it, how the walls leaned in, like to bury me dead. When Mama left, what had been home became just a heap of sticks and felt. It's not good being alone like that. Not good.

Besides, I'd sworn to serve my mistress. And now that her hair was fixed and her face washed, I saw just how lovely she was, the glory of the Ancestors shining through her. I felt certain that Lady Saren would never disobey her father lightly. Surely she had a wise and profound reason for stubbornness, one blessed by the Ancestors.

"Yes," I said. "I'll stay with my lady."

Then her father up and slapped me across my mouth. It almost made me laugh.

I'm right proud of myself for remembering so much! Maybe I got a few words wrong, but that's so near how the conversation went, I'm going to call it truth. My hand aches from writing and my ink grows thin from watering, so I'll finish for tonight.

Day 14

As my lady didn't budge from my mattress last night, I slept as I could on the sacks of barley flour in the cellar, but squeaks and scratches kept nipping at my dreams. When I woke from a nightmare and sat up, two tiny eyes stared back.

A rat. And where there's one, there must be more.

This makes me count numbers and rub my forehead. There's seven years of food for my lady and her maid. We don't have enough to spare for a family of rats. I found four sacks of grain with holes nibbled through and counted six tallow candles missing from a box. What if they eat more? A lot more? How will we survive seven years with rat-spoiled food and no light?

Day 19

Little time for writing these past days. When I'm not washing and cooking or singing and caring for my lady, I sit in the cellar with the broom and swat at anything with eyes. There are a dozen rats at least.

I don't have arsenic to make rat bread, so I fashioned a trap the best I could. Among our supplies I found some nails, as long as my finger and sharp, too. I drove them up through the lid of a barrel then lay atop the nails a piece of parchment. It looked a solid object to me, and to the rat as well, I suppose. Here's how it must've been:

I found it this morning, its body stuck inside the spikes with one nail up through its chin. I won't show it to my lady, save her. She is already feeling ill. I sang the song for stomachache but she grew tired of the melody and sent me away. I hear her upstairs rocking on her bed.

Sometimes I think there's something not quite right with my lady. She seems sad, but when I sing the song for sadness, she doesn't respond. Nor does the song for clear thoughts make her think straight. I guess a couple of songs just isn't going to be enough for whatever ails her. Mistress chose me because I know the songs, and now I begin to realize that my duty with Lady Saren will be more than just keeping her fed and clean. Perhaps the Ancestors sent me to heal her.

But what ails her? Could it just be she's that heartsick for her love, Khan Tegus? I can't wrap my thoughts around how deep their love must be. It's too high above me. It's surely a powerful love that bids a girl brick herself away from the Eternal Blue Sky for seven years. I once liked a boy named Yeke with kind eyes, but I wouldn't have given up the sun for him. Her khan must be such a man from legend, a man formed by Evela, goddess of sunlight. Perhaps if I looked at him, I'd have to squint. I'll ask my lady.

Later

My lady doesn't recall squinting.

Day 27

Not only have I been unsuccessful so far in healing my lady, she seems to have worsened. She spooks at sudden noises, like the wind getting hooked in the chimney or the wood floor whining under my feet. She startles and cries out as if each new sound were a cold hand grabbing her from behind.

Today while she lay upstairs, I heard a voice shouting outside, and I thought, Ancestors preserve us, but my lady's not going to like that. Sure enough, she poured herself down the ladder so fast, she fell to her knees at the bottom. Not waiting to stand again, she crawled to me and clutched my legs.

"He's here, Dashti. Do something! He's here!"

I didn't know who she meant. I was certain the voice had been one of the guards who circles our tower, and I told her so.

"No, it's him, it's him."

"Who, my lady?"

"It's Lord Khasar." She stared at the walls as if expecting them to fall down around her. "He'll be furious that I refused him. He won't give up. I knew he wouldn't. In this tower, I'm a tethered goat left out for the wolf, and now he'll take me and marry me and kill me."

I held her and sang to her and let our dinner burn on the fire, and all the while she shook and cried dry tears, her mouth hanging open. I've never seen a person cry like that, with real fear. She made my blood shiver. I wish I knew what ails her, but perhaps it's too soon. Mama used to say, you have to know someone a thousand days before you can glimpse her soul. When the chill in the stones told us it was night, my lady's grip relaxed. She was so tired from shaking, she fell asleep on my mattress. I guess I'll be sleeping in the cellar with the rats.

I wonder what it is about Lord Khasar that makes her tremble fit to come apart at the joints. And I wonder if he really will come for her. But there's no sense in worrying about it. If he does come, we've nowhere to run.

Day 31

A few minutes ago we heard a voice. I dropped the robe I was washing and hurried to my lady, who clasped me so tightly around my neck I couldn't talk.

"It's him, it's him," she muttered, hiding her face in my neck. "I told you! It's Khasar and he's come back."

But then I really listened. The voice became clearer, and I heard it calling in a hush, "Lady Saren! Can you hear me? It's Tegus. My lady, I'm so sorry."

I gasped. "My lady! It's your khan—it's Khan Tegus!"

She stared at the wall. I expected her to run forward and cry for happiness to hear his voice, but she didn't move. Even now as I write this, my lady sits on my mattress, hugging her knees to her chest. And her khan continues to call.

"Go to him," I say. "You can talk through the flap."

But she just shakes her head.

Later

I'll do my best to remember exactly how it went.

It didn't seem right to keep her poor khan calling, his voice rasping in an effort to whisper and shout at once. Someone should answer at least. I fetched a wooden spoon and lodged it against the flap to hold it open.

I was just about to speak when my lady leaped at me, covering my mouth with her hand.

"What will you say?" she whispered.

"What would you like me to say?" I asked under her fingers.

My lady removed her hand and started to pace and fret and rub her head. She looked as if she'd like to run away, had there been anywhere to run. My poor lady.

"Say you are me."

"What? But why, my lady?"

"You are my maid, Dashti," she said, and though

she still shook like a rabbit, her voice was hard and full of the knowledge that she's gentry. "It is my right to have my maid speak for me. I don't like to speak to someone directly. What if it isn't really him? What if he means us harm?"

"But he'll know my voice isn't yours, and if he knows—"

My lady raised her hand and commanded me to obey on the sacred nine—the eight Ancestors and the Eternal Blue Sky. It's a sin most gruesome to play at being what you're not, and worse than sin to be a commoner speaking as a lady, but what could I do when she commanded me on the sacred nine? She is my mistress and an honored lady besides. I never should have argued. The Ancestors forgive me.

"Khan . . . Khan Tegus," I said through the hole. I stuttered hideously, my words mimicking my scattered heartbeat. "I'm here. Sss—Saren."

I could hear him come closer, and by moonlight, I saw the tip of his boot step on that patch of ground beneath the flap. I thought to be grateful rain had come that morning and the ground was clean.

"My lady, I am so sorry. I came to Titor's Garden to reason with your father, but he wouldn't attend me. His message said only that you are to wed Lord Khasar or no one. I've counseled with my war chief and he says if we attack your father outright, we have a good hope of winning, but we'll incur terrible fatalities on both sides. I thought . . . I imagined you wouldn't want me to do that. I would hate to face your own father and brother in battle."

"No, of course not," I said. His voice sounded so sad, I tried to think of something to cheer him. "Don't worry, we have loads of food, even five bags of sugar and enough dried yogurt to keep a sow and all her sisters happy."

Her khan laughed, sounding surprised to be laughing at all. "That's good news."

"Isn't it? We've fifteen bags of wheat flour, twenty bags of barley, forty-two barrels of salted mutton . . . well, you don't want to hear all about our food."

"And why not? What's better than food?"

"Exactly!" I thought her khan showed good taste and was much more interesting now that his voice had ceased to be so plaintive. "But how are you able to talk to us? Do our guards know you're here?"

"They're asleep," he said. "My men are camped in the woods near here, and I've been watching for hours until all your guards went into their tents to warm themselves. The night's pressing cold. A guard may peek around again, so I shouldn't stay long, but I'll return tomorrow. Is there anything that you need?"

What did my lady need? Sunlight, starlight, fresh air. I said, "Something from outside, perhaps? A flower would be lovely to see."

"A flower? I thought you might want something more than that."

I didn't want to complain about the rats, I wasn't sure if gentry would, so I just said, "We have plenty of food and blankets. We're fine."

"I'm relieved. Farewell until tomorrow, my lady."

"Farewell. . . ." I found I didn't dare say "my lord" in return. It was too much a lie. He is *her* lord, *her* khan. Feeling as though I had swallowed a great lump of knotted rope, I brought in the wooden spoon, letting the flap clank shut. Immediately I knelt facing north and prayed, "Ancestors, forgive me, Dashti, a mucker, for lying in words and deeds."

I said it aloud and hoped my prayer would prick my lady a little, so next time she'd speak to her khan on her own.

Why is she so afraid? It makes no sense. She gets worse every day, I think. Perhaps she's tower-addled. I'll go comb her hair and sing the song again for setting a person's brains straight, the one that goes, "Under, over, down, and through, light in the big house, food on the table."

Day 32

He came again last night, whisper-shouting, "My lady! My lady!"

That's not me, so I didn't answer. I stayed on my mattress, mending a stocking, wishing on each stitch that my lady would go speak to her khan herself.

"My lady?" He tapped on the metal flap. It can't be opened from the outside. *Rap, rap, rap.* "Lady Saren? Are you all right?"

At last she arose from our one chair and stood before me. I kept stitching, praying she would act.

"Speak with him, Dashti," she said.

"Please, my lady . . ." I shouldn't have argued, Mistress would've scolded, but better to be scolded than hanged on the city's south wall. In the city, I learned that's where they execute those whose crimes are so rotten they'd have no hope of ascending into the Ancestors' Realm. The south wall. The wall farthest from the Sacred Mountain.

My lady offered me her hand. How perfect her hands are! I've never seen skin like hers, so soft, no rough spots on her fingertips, her palms like the underside of calf leather. She'll be made to touch nothing harder than water, so I swore by the eight Ancestors and the Eternal Blue Sky. And if what she commands leads my head into a neck rope, then so be my lady's will.

I spoke a prayer in my heart—*Pardon me, Nibus, god of order.*

She sat on my mattress while I lodged the wooden spoon beneath the flap.

"I'm here," I said. I could see his boot in the puddle of moonlight. It was brown leather, double stitched. It would take a mucker a week to make one of those boots.

"I didn't wake you?" he asked.

"Oh, no, I never sleep. . . ." I was going to say that I never sleep until my lady does, but I stopped myself.

"You never sleep?"

"No, yes, I do, I just, I mean . . ." I don't know how to lie to gentry.

"That's a shame. I'll say some prayers for you to Goda, goddess of sleep."

His voice went dry. I knew he was teasing me, so I said, "And I'll pray for you to Carthen, goddess of strength. Your ankles look too skinny to carry you." They didn't, of course, but accusing one of having skinny ankles is a friendly insult among muckers, and it felt so natural to say.

I could hear the smile in his voice when he said, "I'll wager it'd take three of your ankles to make one of mine."

"Not a chance," I said. "I have sturdy ankles, strong as tree trunks."

"Show me, then."

So I did. I was wearing a pair of my lady's older slippers, the kind with the toe curled up prettily, so I was proud to let him see my foot when I lowered my right leg through the flap down to my knee. I could feel her khan press his own leg against mine, measuring our ankles together.

"Hmm," he said, "I hate to contradict, my lady, but I think my ankle puts yours to shame."

"Not a chance. And it's not a fair comparison, as you're wearing boots." I was giggling. I couldn't help it, it was so ridiculous, my leg down the dump hole to prove I had sturdy ankles, her khan measuring them, and my lady surely wondering if we're insane. And then when I tried to lift my leg back up, I got stuck, and I felt his hands unhook the tip of my slipper from a metal catch and help raise my leg. He was chuckling by now, too.

"Oh! I brought you a gift."

He lifted something. He used both hands as one does to show deep respect. I thought how he must have had to kneel on the ground to do so. I thought how no one had ever offered me something with both hands before.

It was a pine bough. I reached down and took it. His hands were cold and rough, and I wished I'd had gloves to give him. I thought to hold his hand and sing the song for warmth, but that wouldn't do at all, a mucker holding gentry's hand, and him thinking me his betrothed lady. Not at all.

"You asked for a flower," he said, "but in autumn there's little to choose from. Besides, I think pine boughs smell better, don't you?"

I smelled it like I was starving and the odor alone would fill up my belly. My head got dizzy with memories of Mama and being cold and cozy.

"It smells like the winter nap," I said, longing for some truth to tell. "Midwinter every year, my mother would decorate our . . . our home with pine boughs, cracking the needles to get the richest smell, then we'd curl up in blankets and take our winter nap, five days of no food but milk, sleeping on and off all day and night, like the burrowing animals do."

"That sounds strange and lovely and wearying, too. Is winter nap a common custom in Titor's Garden?"

"Common enough." I didn't say that it's common for muckers. We do it as a prayer to Vera, goddess of food, to help us through another year, and we do it because at midwinter there's not much food for the having anyway. I don't suppose my lady needed a winter nap, with her honored father's cellars full of grain.

"In Song for Evela, our midwinter rite is just the opposite. All folk come together under my roof and eat and eat and eat. Enough cakes, apples, mutton, and raisin rice to last a year! Sometimes it feels good to feast until it hurts."

"You feast with muckers, even?"

"What are muckers?"

"The folk that live on the grassy steppes in ghers—those are felt tents they make themselves."

"Are they herding folk?"

"That's right. The steppes of Titor's Garden are too hard for farming, rocky and windy and rough. Muckers do work when work is sent out from the city folk, and the rest of the time they travel with the seasons, herding sheep, horses, reindeer, yaks."

"May I say something? Will you be offended?"

"No . . . ," I said, though I was thinking, He knows I'm a mucker!

But then he said, "Your hand, when you took my pine bough, I saw—your hand is beautiful."

I tucked my hands under my arms and looked

at my lady. She was staring at her own hands and frowning. All I could think was, thank the Ancestors that I took the bough with my right hand and not my left, which bears the red birth blotches.

"You've gone quiet," he said. "I've offended you. I'm sorry."

For some reason that got me laughing.

"What's funny?" he asked, even though his voice hinted at laughing, too.

"My hand—you thought it was beautiful! And then you thought I'd be offended. . . ."

My heart is beautiful, Mama used to tell me, and my eyes, but never my blotchy face, never my browned and callused hands. If next to my own he'd seen my lady's pale, smooth hand. . . .

"Don't stop laughing!" he said, and he started to say things to get me to laugh again, telling a story of how he was once riding a horse that stopped suddenly, sending him flying off the saddle to land headfirst in a barrel of water. He wasn't satisfied that I was truly laughing then, so he sang the silliest song I guess I've ever heard. It was about a bodiless piglet, and I remember one verse of it because it repeated several times:

This morning I found a piglet,
grunting beside my bed

This piglet, she had no body —
  she was only a head!
She rolled about while squealing,
  moving by snout and by jaw
Happily snuffling for treats
  without use of hoof or paw.

My lady even smiled, which made me feel fat with goodness. He did keep us laughing until fear of the guards was eating at him. Then he sent up a bag of fresh meat, raw and still warm.

"From an antelope my war chief slew for you. He's fierce with an arrow. I wish I could claim I'd slain it myself, but my clumsy shot went wide. I thought fresh meat might make a pleasant change."

"Oh, Khan Tegus, oh, my lord," I said, and that's all I could say for a few moments. "We have salt meat . . . but fresh, it's a difference, isn't it?"

"I'll say! Eating salt meat, you have to drink so much for your thirst, there's no room in the belly for food."

"And we have salted everything here — vegetables and meat and cheese and cracker bread. Though I'm not complaining, please don't think. The food's wonderful, as long as I can keep the rats out."

"There are rats?"

I hadn't meant to grumble, but there was this little pressure inside me, pushing inside my chest, urging me to confide some truth to him. "We've a plague of rats in the cellar. We swat at them and even got one in a trap, but I'm afraid my . . . my maid won't have enough to eat, after a time. My, uh, my father brought us so much food, but not enough for the rats, too."

"Your voice is tilting down, my lady," he said, "and I guess that you're frowning. You're worried. I should go now before the guards return, but keep the rats out of your hair tonight and I'll return tomorrow."

He left.

I don't have anything else to write, but I don't want to put down my brush yet. I want to keep all that happened, the feel of the evening still thick in my head, the sounds of his words awake in my ears, twitching pleasantly inside me. I'd guess I'm tower-addled and talking to someone from outside just made me wistful. That's all. That's why I feel this way, twisting and floating, as though my heart is bigger than my chest.

I do like the world quite a lot. Nothing more to say, so I'll draw.

Day 33

It must be past midnight now, but I'll write till morning if I have to. I don't want to forget a word.

Her khan came again. When I heard him calling,
I didn't wake my lady, who was asleep upstairs.
Should I have? Or was it right to let her sleep? And
asleep or not, should I have ignored him and refused
to continue the lie? Ancestors forgive me, in the moment I didn't think twice. I just opened the flap and
let his voice come in.

"Did you sleep well last night?" he asked. "I might
take offense if you went ahead and slept with rats in
your hair, after I specifically warned you against it."

"I slept well," I said, laughing. "Sleep is always
sweet."

"Not all would say that. You're an antelope who
bounds through life, I think. Here you are, locked in
a tower and laughing still."

"You make me laugh."

"Why is that?"

"I can't say." And I couldn't. Why do his questions
make me laugh?

"I think I'd like to make you laugh all day long. If

I could take you out of here, I'd hold a feast and a dance, and see you bedecked in a silver deel, laughing and bounding about."

"Why silver?"

"Because in the dark, your voice sounds silver."

My face burned feverish hot, so hot I thought I might die of the mud fever at once, but the feeling eased as I kept talking.

"That's a pretty thing to say." I forced my tone to sound light. "I wish I could think of pretty things to say, too, besides that your ankles are skinnier than a jackrabbit's ribs."

He cleared his throat. "It's just the cut of these boots, I assure you. And no excuses, my lady. You've had a flowery tongue in your time. Don't you remember our first letters?"

"It's been so long," I said, unhappy with the lie. "What did I say?"

Her khan chuckled. "Before coming here, I looked over all our letters, and the early ones, when you were thirteen and I fifteen. Well . . ."

"They were fairly ridiculous, weren't they?"

"In truth, you weren't so bad—more formal. You're very different to speak with in person. But I found some drafts of letters that I sent to you, and in one I wrote something akin to, 'When I think of you, my heart melts like butter over the bread of my stomach.' I thought it was very poetic at the time. Or in another letter I wrote, 'You are like a shiny red apple with no worms.'"

I wanted to be respectful of his first words of love, but trying to hold in the laugh made me snort like a camel, and then he snorted, so laughs came rumbling out of me. We were trying not to laugh, of course — I didn't want to wake my lady and he didn't want to wake the guards, but that made it even harder to stop. How my side ached! I wheezed and said I couldn't breathe, which made him laugh harder, which in turn made me laugh harder because, truth be told, his laugh sounds like a yak's grunt. I told him as much, which was a mistake, because that brought up his laugh anew.

Can I describe what it felt like to sit in the dark, laughing with her khan through a bricked wall? The hard grayness lifted out of me like the bones from a fried fish. I felt strong enough to float, warmed as if by sunlight, my bones thrumming and my skin tingling. My mama used to say that the mightiest of the healing songs was a good laugh.

When we'd calmed down and I'd wiped the tears from my face, we sat in silence. I leaned against the wall, resting my head on the bricks. I could see by the angle of his boot that, outside, he was doing the same. It was almost like touching.

"My jaw hurts," I said.

"I can't stop grinning. Some of my warriors are watching for the guards a few paces off, and they're sure to think I've gone crazy."

"Maybe you have, did you think of that? You certainly sound crazy, laughing like a wild dog."

"Careful with the accusations of insanity, oh my lady whose home is a tower with windows of brick, all for the sake of some skinny-ankled, laugh-prone boy of a khan."

"If a lady is crazy to be bricked up in a tower, then what is a khan who sits outside to laugh with her?"

He sighed and groaned at once, the sound of his smile gone. "I'm sorry I can't break you out. I can't believe you don't despise me for it."

"Stop that. What's bothering you? I mean, besides this tower? I can hear your voice is tight, you've got an ache somewhere, nagging at you."

"How did you know? Yes . . . you're right. It's my leg. I was injured at sword practice last year. When I stand for a time . . ."

"My maid, she's a mucker girl, she knows the healing songs."

"The healing songs?"

"What a large world it is if there are people who never heard of the healing songs. Here, I'll have her sing to you. To work right, she should be touching your leg. Just you touch the leg yourself and listen, and close your eyes."

I crouched by the hole, down low so I was as close to him as I could be, and I sang the song for old injuries and wove it with the song for strong limbs, singing up with the coarse chanting of "High, high, a bird on a cloud," and singing down with the low swinging melody of "Tell her a secret that makes her sigh."

When I stopped, he was quiet for a good long moment. I could hear his breath, up and down like a bird's wings flapping.

"Thank you, my lady's maid," he said. "That was . . ."

He didn't finish, leaving me wondering. Some say hearing the songs makes them tickle inside, some say they feel as if they've suddenly gone hot to cold or cold to hot. Some say it's like dreaming while awake, or swimming while dry. I wish I knew how it felt inside her khan.

"My lady's maid, where did you learn such things?" he asked.

I gasped and bit my knuckle and wished I were

smarter than I am, but then I thought to say, "My maid is shy. She's a mucker and thinks she shouldn't speak to gentry, but she's grateful her song helped you."

"How does that work? I mean, the songs sing about birds and secrets and sighing, not about healing, nothing like the conjuring words of the shamans."

"What the words say doesn't matter. The sound of the words and the sound of the tune together speak a language that the body can understand . . . or so I've been told by my maid. The body wants to be whole, and when you sing the right sounds, you're reminding it how to heal itself."

"Can muckers heal? Does she have the power to stop blood flowing and stave off death?"

"Oh no, only the Ancestors have power of life. The healing songs just ease suffering, whether of body or mind. Times I've seen a man who'd decided to die, and a healing song changed his mind and let his body fight the disease off. I—my maid, she's never per-formed anything so grand. Though her mother has."

I could hear him move around, as if getting more comfortable, and lean his head closer to the hole.

"Keep talking, my lady. Your voice makes me want to stay and stay."

I lay down, resting my head on my hands, facing his voice. And I spoke. I wished I could whisper true things, about my mama, about the day my brothers left, about how a rainy spring makes the steppes grass so green you wish you were a yak so you could eat it. But I was being my lady, so I hid inside stories. I told the legend of how the Ancestors formed commoners from mud so there would be people in the world to serve their gentry children. He told me another that I'd never heard before, how Goda, goddess of sleep, took the form of a raven and first brought night to the world so all could rest. I would write down the exact tale here if I could recall it, but already some of his words slip away. All I remember for sure about that part of the conversation is I felt like I was riding a fast mare and I was sleeping in a warm blanket, both at the same time.

From outside, we heard a dog howl.

"That's a guard dog." His voice got a spice of anger in it. "Why do they have to come back so soon! Why don't they give us another hour of peace?"

I would've liked another hour myself.

"Listen," he said, "I am going to break you out. I'll come tomorrow night. I have enough warriors with me to kill the guards—"

"No, my lord, you can't just kill the guards!"

"Then we'll drug them somehow, and when they're sluggish and sleeping, we'll break down the—"

"No! Listen. My honored father is terribly mean,

he'll know it was you, he'll come after you. It'll be war between Titor's Garden and Song for Evela, sure enough. And if Lord Khasar hears you've taken us . . . he's a beast, I've heard. You don't want a war with him. We can wait for my . . . my father to soften. He's bound to let us out sometime, and meanwhile we're safe here." I believe that. Having now spent weeks in the darkness, I don't think her father will truly leave us here for seven years. No father could do that.

"But no, I . . ."

Her khan paused. He knew I was right. We couldn't start a war over a tower, not when my lady and I were alive and the cellar more full of food than of rats. The Ancestors bless him for hoping otherwise.

"It's all right, my lord. We'll be fine enough. We will."

"But my lady—"

"Just tell me, what's the sky look like tonight?"

Her khan sighed as if he were going to argue more, but then went quiet, and I imagined him looking up, squinting, waiting for the right words to fall into his head.

"The air is so clear, it shivers," he said. "All the stars are out, every one, even the babies. It's so bright with stars, the blacks of the sky look a dark, dark blue."

I could see it just like he said it.

"My lady." His voice was soft, as though there were no wall, as though he were right beside me. "I should return home. There's been unrest lately, Lord Khasar making threats and the like. I'll come again as soon as I can, and we'll see then if it's time to knock down this wall."

I said, "That's fine," though I didn't want him to leave. But I was speaking for my lady, and I spoke as I thought gentry would. "Your people should come first."

"I have a farewell gift," he said, a touch more brightness in his voice. "My chief of animals came on this journey, and she brought some companion animals along with the horses and yaks. When you mentioned your trouble with rats . . ."

I heard him call lightly to someone, then her khan's bare hand came through the hole, raising up something furry that mewed.

It was a yearling cat, long and lean, pale gray with green eyes. I put my face in its neck. It smelled of wind in the grass, of riverbed clay, of the world. I wanted to give him something in return, so I unhooked the neck clasp of my deel and shivered out of my shirt. It's just an undershirt, but it's what I wear closest to me and seemed the kind of a gift Lady Saren should offer her betrothed. Things worn closest to the skin, to the heart, carry the scent of a person, and of course, scent is the breath of the soul.

I leaned down, giving him the shirt. He took it, and took my hand, too. His hands were warm today, rough on the palms like well-used leather. And so much larger, my own hand nearly disappeared into his. He didn't say another word, but I felt different, as though he had sung to me the song for heartache, the one that goes, soft and slow, "Tilly tilly, nar a black bird, nilly nilly, there a blue bird."

Day 35

It's been two days since her khan left. We'll have the rest of his antelope meat tonight. I hope he has a safe journey.

I named the cat My Lord.

Day 39

I'm in love! My heart's so light it floats and carries me so my feet don't walk. I sing all day and I don't mind the washing, and that's how I know I'm in love. Completely smitten with My Lord the cat.

He's like a naked beech tree, sleek and gray. He's prettier than a morning sky and knows it, too. I shouldn't encourage him but I can't help it, and tell him all day long, "You're the prettiest cat in the world, My Lord, you're smarter than a dog and faster than a bird." I give him all the best bits from my dinner. Whenever I'm not singing to my lady's hidden ailment, I'm slathering the cat with songs.

My Lord has already killed three rats and I haven't heard so much as a good morning from the rest. And at night, do you know where he sleeps? With Dashti the mucker. The only cats I've known were so mangy their fur was half gone and they wheezed like startled snakes. But My Lord is gentry among beasts, a khan of cats.

And he always knows when it's day. Times there are when I wake thinking that it's morning, only to peer out the flap and see darkness thick as stew. Time makes no sense in a dark prison. But My Lord the cat knows the time. As soon as it's morning, he stands on my chest, touches his cold nose to mine, and breathes on my lips.

I'd ask my lady if she'd prefer My Lord to sleep with her, but Titor, god of animals, himself can't force a cat to change his mind. Besides, it might not be proper to share a bed with a cat, she being an honored lady and all.

Day 48

Two weeks since her khan left. I asked my lady how far to his home in Song for Evela, and she thinks it'd take about two weeks, so perhaps he's already home.

Today I find myself remembering one night as a little girl, when our gher was still full of family, and a traveling shaman stayed the night. It's good luck to offer any stranger one night under your felt roof, but doubly so for a shaman. How excited we were! I remember watching the shaman with wide eyes and doing my best to blink as little as possible. If he turned into a fox, as I'd always heard shamans can, I was determined not to miss the sight. The shaman didn't transform that night, but he told us stories of the Ancestors and what they willed us to do in order to enter their Realm one day. And he told us how gentry were the children of the Ancestors, how it was a commoner's privilege to serve them. It was the first I'd ever heard of gentry.

Many times after that night I liked to lie back and imagine what the gentry might be like—skin that glows like a candle, eyes shining with the wisdom of the Ancestors. Sometimes I actually thought they might have tails like foxes or butterfly wings. Then meeting Lady Saren and her father . . .

But now I've spoken with Khan Tegus, and though his hand didn't glow or anything, there was something in his voice, in his words, that was different than anyone I've ever known. The mark of the Ancestors must be in him, stronger than in some gentry. Maybe that's why his title is khan instead of just lord. I'll ask my lady.

Lady Saren told me a story tonight while she petted My Lord the cat. How many things she must know!

She said that the Eight Realms were once united under a Great Khan, and the seat of his power was Song for Evela. Now all the realms have their own lord or lady rulers, but in memory of the Great Khan, the ruler of Song for Evela still carries the title of khan. I asked her how she knew, and she said all gentry families keep the history of wars and marriages and so on. Such a thing as history never occurred to me before.

Day 73

It's fully winter now. There's a rim of ice on our well that I have to crack with the bucket. Each time I open the metal flap to the outside, I get blasted by cold. The wash water freezes as I pour it on the ground, and afterward I spend several minutes before the fire just to get color back in my hands. This time of year, it's too cold to snow. High winter out-of-doors is death as sure as a knife in the chest, and a winter's funeral brings bad luck to the whole clan.

I'm a mucker, so I thought I knew winter, but from inside this tower I've learned something new—the winter wind has its own voice. Autumn wind has a gusty warmth to it and a lower tone as though it sings from deep in the belly. The winter wind screeches around the tower, singing the high harmony, its voice sharp with ice. My lady isn't fond of that sound.

A few days ago, I carried her mattress down to the main floor and shut the door in the ceiling so we keep in more of the fire's heat. I think even the Ancestors understand that in winter, a mucker maid and a lady must sleep side by side.

Surely her khan won't return until after winter. Spring seems as far off as the Ancestors' Realm.

Day 92

Yesterday smoke was filling our room something awful, and in a locked tower, air filled with smoke would kill us right quick. I rolled up my lady in all our blankets before I smothered our fire. In the time it took me to clean out the blocked chimney, my jaw was hammering and my fingertips turned blue. I relit the fire and shivered on my mattress until the room warmed again, there being not a spare blanket for my shoulders.

This winter, Goda, goddess of sleep, must have made Evela, goddess of sunlight, awfully drowsy. No memory of sunshine hangs in the air. Everything feels gray and hard and dark. I guess that might make me bitterly sad, but right now, My Lord is asleep on my lap.

Day 98

The guards only bring our daily milk every two days now, sometimes three. In the cold, they must stay in their tents, keeping the fire going nice and toasty, venturing out only to milk their animals and make yellow ice.

To help our milk last three days, I add water. It wouldn't be proper for my lady to drink plain water, as if she were poorer than poor. Even Mama and I always had milk to drink.

Day 122

Little to record. I wash, I cook. I stoke the fire. Whenever the wind moans, my lady shivers as though she feels it on her skin. She's refused to bathe for weeks, but this morning I insisted. When I dunked her hair into a bucket of water, there was a powerful scent, reminding me of the time my brothers' reindeer fell into a stream.

Today, for the first time, I couldn't enjoy the spices in the food. It was as though I couldn't taste them. I can't say why that was.

Still, My Lord the cat is so beautiful.

Day 141

The middle night. I just woke after a dream, though it was the kind of dream that's more memory than imagination. I saw again the last night her khan was here, the sight of his hand lifting up the cat. And then I saw what I gave him in return. I hadn't thought of it again since that night. The memory jolted me awake.

I gave her khan my shirt. Ancestors, there was a basket of washing right by my mattress. I could've seized one of my lady's own shirts. He would've inhaled her scent, the breath of *her* soul. Even though there was something else at hand, I chose to give him my own garment.

Why didn't the Ancestors strike me dead? After such an offense, I'd think they wouldn't permit this mucker maid to remain breathing. Perhaps they only ignore me because I'm shut up in this tower, cut off from the gaze of the Eternal Blue Sky. Perhaps if

I ever step out of its shadow, I'll be struck in the instant and crumble into a heap of ash.

Day 158

This morning, we . . . I'm shaking still. I didn't realize until I put the brush to paper. If My Lord the cat weren't on my lap, I don't know that I could be calm enough to write at all.

This morning, we heard voices outside. Now that it's warm enough for the sun to burn holes in the icy ground, we've begun to hear our guards again, chatting as they walk around the tower and occasionally shouting saucy things at us. But these voices were new. One was so deep and loud, I felt it in the stones of the tower. I felt it in my bones.

I was darning my lady's stockings by the orange light of the fire, and my lady was lying on my bed, teasing My Lord the cat with a stocking too holey to save. When we heard the new voices, she sat upright, like a fawn stops grazing when she hears a hunter's step.

"Is it your khan, do you think?" I asked. "Back already?"

My lady didn't answer. She's so often spooked,

I didn't realize that this time she was truly terrified, so badly that she couldn't speak or move.

I left my sewing, fetched the wooden spoon, unhooked the flap, and jammed it open.

"Don't, Dashti," she said too late, just as a hand shot up the hole and seized my arm.

I screamed, I think. The hand was covered in a black gauntlet, the wrist trimmed in metal spikes. It was not her khan.

"Do I have her?" said the voice low enough to grumble in stones. "Do I have my lady?"

"No, I'm sorry, no, no," I said.

"Who is this?" He shook my arm.

"I'm Dashti. I'm my lady's maid. I'm the mucker maid."

He laughed as if I'd just told a wicked joke. "Yes, I know muckers. There are hundreds of the ragged folk wandering the steppes in Thoughts of Under."

He let go, and I pulled my arm inside.

"Put your arm back!" He yelled so loud, the cat screeched.

I didn't want to. Ancestors, I wanted to crawl under my mattress. He may have a voice like an earth rumble and put my lady in the fear shakes, but I recognized the command of gentry, and I must do what he says. I lowered my arm back down the hole.

He didn't grab me again, just tickled his gloved fingers against my fingertips. He was chuckling, lower than his voice. Then he slapped my hand against the wall. It stung like a log full of hornets.

I pulled my arm up, but he said, really slowly and sweetly like I was his favorite lamb, "Back down, Dashti the mucker maid."

Again I lowered my hand, and again he slapped it against the wall. I left it there, and I was crying, but not just because it hurt, I think. The next time he slapped, my lady grabbed me under the arms and pulled me away from the hole. We fell back on my mattress.

"Stay here," she said.

I stayed. After all, she's my own mistress. Let that black-gloved lord growl and yell all he likes, I'll obey her first.

"It's him. It's Lord Khasar," said my lady.

And I stopped wondering why she refused to marry him.

"Are you in there, Lady Saren? Do you believe you're hiding, stashed in a tower all the world can see? You're not very good at the hiding game. You never were."

I wish I could write that my lady stood tall, that she declared she would never love him or bow to him or tremble at his voice, let him do his worst, or somewhat of that bold kind of talking. I saw her show a bit of courage to her father once, but at Lord Khasar's voice, she covered her face and cried so hard she squeaked like rusted hinges. I'm sorry for her, I am, but sometimes I think crying's done for and it's time for doing. If only I knew what ailed her, perhaps I could help, but I guess there are corners and folds of my lady's soul that I'll never see.

I sat with her, put one hand on her belly and one on her back, and sang the song for bitter sorrow, the one that goes, "Darker river, blacker river, faster river, pulling me." I sang while Lord Khasar spoke. She calmed some. I didn't dare go pull the wooden spoon and shut the flap. He couldn't touch us, safe here in the center of the room, but his voice slinked in like smoke. Not even in the cellar under sacks of barley would we be able to hide from that sound.

These are the sorts of things he said.

"Your father hobbled to Thoughts of Under to see me, whining like a girl in two braids. He told me, 'My daughter awaits you in the watchtower on the border of our lands. Knock down the walls! Take her, bound and gagged, I care not. She is refuse to me till she bends her will to your own.' He spoke grandly, but his knees shook. Do your knees shake, my lady? I don't trust a man who fears me, and all fear me.

Do you fear me, my lady?" He laughed heartily at that.

"I remember your eyes when we first met. You were eleven years old? Twelve? Your eyes were as dull as a cow's, but you looked lovely dressed in silks. You still do, don't you, my jewel? You are beautiful adorned in gold, so who cares about your dim eyes?

"And I remember how your eyes changed after sleeping one night in my house. You no longer had cow eyes, but mouse eyes, rabbit eyes, the wide eyes of prey. How much I enjoyed that night, I really can't express. Besides you, there's only one other person still living whom I've allowed to see me feeding. I hope you feel that honor, Lady Saren. I trusted you with that secret because I know you'd never dare tell."

Here he laughed with a dark, dry rasp, and I wished I knew what he was speaking about. My lady lay on my bed, one arm wrapped around her face, the other clinging to my waist, her entire body quaking.

"That's when I wanted you as my own. I told your father then that you would be my bride. But I won't knock down this tower for you, not today. I won't force you out yet. I'm having too much fun."

His voice was nearly a whisper, and yet we could still hear. "The day will come when you will choose me over the tower. Knowing what you know, you will still choose me. I hunger for that day."

Then for some time, silence.

I think he'd been gone a long while by the time we could sit up and breathe. My lady still clung to me. I was too shaken to sing anymore, my voice felt sticky and my heart clattered about, so I held her till she could stop shaking, too.

"You'd met him before, my lady? You knew his temperament, that's why you refused to wed."

"Yes," she said. There were secrets laden in that word "yes" that she didn't explain. I could feel it, and it made me afraid.

"His voice is heavier than lead," I said. "And he slaps harder than your honored father. Do all gentry slap people? I suppose it's a noble's right, but I wonder, your khan doesn't seem like to slap."

"No," she said. "I chose him because I thought he was safe."

She was so beautiful as she said those words, even with the red eyes of crying. She made me believe she could choose whomever she wanted, and the poor man would have no choice but to fall in love with her, too. Perhaps even Lord Khasar was in love with her, in his own way.

"Did Khan Tegus make you laugh?" I asked.

She shrugged, and I realized I'd never heard her laugh. She pulled her knees up and stared at the fabric of her deel stretched tight between them. She took a deep breath and I hoped, hoped, hoped it meant that she was going to talk more. It's so rare with my lady. I don't know if she was always a quiet one or if her will to speak has been smothered by the tower darkness. When she opened her mouth, I had to suppress a sigh of contentment.

"After my father and I spent time at Lord Khasar's house, after I saw what that man was, I thought to betroth myself to someone else before Khasar officially asked. I knew he would ask, as soon as I turned sixteen and was of an age. I chose Khan Tegus. He was on friendly terms with my father and I thought him gentler than most. We wrote letters for years. I told my maid Qara what to say and she wrote for me. Qara was my best friend. When my father condemned me to this tower, she ran away."

My lady's eyes were empty as she spoke. I shivered, imagining being a child in that large house with floor stones that look to be cut from ice instead of passing winter nights in a snug gher. To be raised by a fierce lord who slaps instead of by a mama who sings.

This was the most my lady had ever confided in me, and I longed to keep her talking. "How did you first know you loved Khan Tegus? Did you—"

"I'm tired," she said and climbed the ladder to bed.

And that's how it is with my lady. Sometimes we share a few words about the food or My Lord's prowess with the rats or the cold that burrows between bricks, but let me broach the topic of her khan, or black-gloved Lord Khasar, or her father and his house, and my lady is suddenly as tired as a weeping willow in full leaf.

My Lord the cat is asleep on me or I would've ended my account and gone to bed long ago. His purring shakes my lap but steadies my hand.

Day 160

The guards generally don't speak with us. Sometimes they shout at us, but they don't expect a response. Times I've asked them for news of the world, for fresh meat, for anything. Even knowing they'll say no, it's a thrill to holler through the hole and know that another person hears my voice and might answer. Her honored father must have warned them sharply to leave us well alone, but this morning I got one to speak.

I held open the flap to dump the wash water and splashed someone's boots.

"Watch it, now!"

"Sorry," I said, not afraid, for I knew the voice as belonging to one of our regular guards. "Is he gone?"

"Lord Khasar? Yes, gone two nights ago, thank the Ancestors."

"Did he hurt any of you?" My hand still smarted from the bashing and made scrubbing my lady's stockings and unders no pleasant task.

"Not much," he said.

It was more than he'd spoken to me in all our tower days, so I risked more questions.

"Can you tell me, what does the sky look like today?"

"Sky? It looks like a sky."

"Is it blue?"

The guard snorted. "It's always blue."

But he's wrong. Though we call it the Eternal Blue Sky, I know that sometimes it's black, sometimes white, sometimes yellow, pink, purple, gray, black, peach, gold, orange, a dozen different shades of blue with a hundred different kinds of clouds in thousands of shapes. That's what makes it so wondrous. If the guard couldn't see that, I wouldn't bother to explain.

"What of the world?" I asked. "Is there news from Titor's Garden? From my lady's family?"

The guard laughed like a horse snorts. "I feel like I'm talking to the dead. You're not coming out of that tower, miss, not unless that lord from Thoughts of Under breaks you out, and then he'd snap a maid's neck and toss her to the dogs, more than like. Enjoy your brick room and don't worry about what's outside. Nothing here belongs to you anymore."

He was laughing when he said it, but I could read his voice plain as my own letters — he was sorry for us, and he was sorry for being sorry.

They weren't nice words he said. He could've lived a good life and died never having made a person feel rubbed down to bones and too sad to hold together. Still, it can't be an easy thing, guarding two girls who've been thrown into the rubbish heap of Under, god of tricks. I think he laughs because he doesn't want to hurt for us.

While he was still close enough to hear, I sang the song for stone hearts, the one with the bristling tune that goes, "Chick tight in a shell, wings up and away." He listened some, then walked on.

Day 162

Spring's here, the first breath of it anyway. The stone floor is not so cold at night, and the air coming in from outside, which used to smell like a hole dug deep, now smells like blue sky. My Lord senses the change, too. He's friskier, wants to jump and play, and I exercise him with stockings and bits of salt meat.

I thought my lady's mood might change with the season, but she's still the same, her back rounded more than straight, her eyes dim. I try new songs on her, I combine songs. Though sometimes her temper lifts, the change never lasts long. But I'm mucker stubborn, and I'm determined to discover her ailment.

A fresh breeze just found its way up the dump hole. I wish I could see the buds on the trees, just trembling to open and be leaves, and hear all the honeybees out and buzzing, so happy to be free of their winter hideaway they're like to burst.

Day 180

I would write more if I had something to say. I'll draw here the profile of my lady as she stares at the wall. She's been sitting in silence since dinner, and it's nearly time for supper.

Day 223

This past week I was wishing for something new to happen so I could have a reason to write. It's bad luck to make a vague wish like that, because Under, god of tricks, is bound to grant it with something unpleasant. And so he did.

Lord Khasar returned today.

"I'm back, my lady, my love!" He shouted heartily, as though he called all the world to dinner.

"I wish I could hit him," said my lady. "When I think of him, I want to punch him with all my strength. I wouldn't care if he hit me back, if only I could hit him once, hard, between the eyes."

That sounded like a very nice plan to me.

There was a knock on the flap, and we took a step back.

"Go away," I said. "My lady doesn't want you. Leave us be!"

There was some clanking and scraping, the noises seeming to come from all around us. We stood in the center of the room, I holding my lady's hands. Then with a shriek of metal, the flap tore right out of the bricks. My lady screamed and jumped back against the far wall.

"If you don't open up when I knock, I'll have to tear down the door," said Lord Khasar. His voice echoed up in our tower, loud as thoughts. "Come give me your hand, mucker maid."

"Stay, Dashti," said my lady, the Ancestors bless her.

Lord Khasar laughed in his way, low and loud. "Is it time to come home yet, Lady Saren? Are you well pickled in this barrel? Shall I break you out?"

"Tell him no," I whispered. My lady wouldn't speak.

"Nothing to say? Then perhaps I should burn you out," he said.

Something flicked up the hole. I didn't see where it landed till the smoke started. My mattress was on fire. I leaped at it, stomping on the burning straw. Then another fiery chip shot into the room, and another. More and more rained down with near-silent ticks. Some fizzled on dry stone, but others found cloth, wood, and straw, and set in to smoke or burn. My lady ran with me, stamping at anything bright. If fire took hold, we'd cook in this stove of a tower long before a wall could be knocked down.

All I could think was out, out, out, as I ran and stomped and slapped. My lady began to scream hysterics and pound at the bricks, and I was left to fight the little fires alone. My breath was scraping hard in my throat and the smoke made me want to vomit.

"Behind you!" she shouted, pointing. A washcloth was burning hard right by the stack of wood, and if the wood caught fire, we'd be rabbits in the pot, no question. I flung myself at the rag, rolling over it to squash the flames.

I was aching and sweating when the fire chips stopped coming. My lady collapsed on my partly charred mattress, her eyes staring at the ceiling. I don't know if we'd fought the smoke and flames for minutes or hours, but I guess I never felt so scared in all my life.

"I wish I could have witnessed that dance!" said Lord Khasar. What a horrid sound his voice is, how greasy black his every word. "But you will dance for me yet, my willow flower. Will it be tonight? Tell me now, Lady Saren, because I won't come again until your seven years are over. Will you choose six more years in this dungeon or the rest of your life in my house? My house where you will have ten lady's maids and ten times that many deels, fresh food, warm baths, a large room with five windows and a door to the garden. A garden, my lady, rimmed with flowers in the summer that will bow to your beauty. And the only cost is," here his voice went very dry, "you will share that house with me."

His voice had become both softer and louder. I guessed his face was right up under the hole where the flap used to be.

My lady's chamber pot stood by my feet, waiting for disposal. Well, my lady stood up, tore off the cover, and dumped it down the hole with a slosh and a splash. All her waste, both the liquid and the muddy kind, must've spilled onto his face, right into his open, shouting mouth.

He hollered, and rightly so. We held so still it hurt, but we haven't heard Lord Khasar's voice since. Never have I felt prouder to be maid to Lady Saren.

After a few moments, I giggled. My lady giggled. Then we lay back together and laughed in a tight way, as though we actually cried.

Later

There's howling outside.

My lady is curled up in the center of the room. She won't speak to me. I lay beside her and sang the lulling song for comfort, the one that goes, "Trails of poppy, poppy, poppy," but a song of healing can't help if the person won't will it. Right now, I guess, she needs to be terrified. I don't want to be. I hoped writing would help.

There's another howl. Why does that sound dance like fingernails down my back? I've heard wolves call out before. When my family kept sheep, a howl was a useful noise, a reminder to gather in any of the herd we didn't want to lose that night. And if a wolf got too near, my brothers would sing the song of the wolf, a baying tune that made the wolves want to howl back but also invited them to leave us be. And they always did. There are far worse things than wolves.

My Lord the cat is sitting on my lap. The hair on his neck is up straight as trees, and he mews hard at each howl. The sound is getting closer. With the metal flap torn off, I can see it is black night outside. I should put some kind of cover there, but I don't dare get closer.

Something's happening. There's no more howling, only snarls. The guards' dogs were barking fit to burst, but now they've gone quiet. I hear our guards shouting one at another, I hear one of them scream. There's another. Ancestors, there's another scream. What's happening? It doesn't sound like battle. It sounds like nightmares.

My lady still trembles. My Lord the cat is hissing. I stroke him and sing. I wish someone would sing to me. There's a scream again, just outside the —

I write from awful silence now. I was interrupted before by a cry for help, so close, right at the mouth of the hole, so I crept closer to see if I could give aid.

Of a sudden, the jaws of a wild animal shot up, growling and snapping at me. A wolf, I think, but enormous, and its mouth was smeared with blood. Did it come from the woods? Or is it possible Lord Khasar breeds wolves to be blood hungry for battle?

I fell back on the floor and tried to scoot away. It couldn't get in, it was much too large, but its mouth drooled and snapped at me, the nose sniffed the air as if hunting.

Then, too late, I saw My Lord crouched, preparing to pounce.

"No!" I shouted and leaped forward, trying to hold him back, but I missed. My Lord jumped at the thing, snarling and shrieking. Both animals disappeared down the hole. I heard horrible growls from the beast, and a yelp from the cat. But not a cry of pain, I think. I hope. Oh, my cat, my sleek gray cat.

All was quiet again. My lady didn't weep, she just stayed in her ball, shaking. I ran back and forth, trying to comfort my lady and returning to look for My Lord at the hole. Nothing in the world seemed alive but me, and I didn't much want to be.

Many aching minutes later, I dared to get close to the hole. I feared those snapping wolf jaws or that black-gloved hand, but I placed myself near enough to call out.

"Is anyone there? Hello? Please answer."

I heard nothing from the guards. They don't always answer, perhaps they ran off or are hiding. Perhaps.

Please, Titor, god of animals, please keep My Lord the cat. Please keep him safe.

Day 224

No sign of My Lord the cat. No sound from the guards.

Day 225

My Lord hasn't returned. I wait by the hole and I call. Still no sound from our guards.

Day 231

My Lord the cat used to make a little hiccup sound in his throat whenever he jumped onto the table. His favorite treat was cheese. When he attacked a rat, he was deadly fast, going straight for a fatal bite on the back of the neck. When he ate the rat, he was meticulous, finding his favorite bits first, spending hours to consume the whole. When he was deep asleep, he sometimes meowed, a sound of total contentment. I didn't mind waking up to that noise, not a bit.

Day 236

My lady says My Lord is gone, killed by Khasar.

"Why would Lord Khasar kill a cat?" I asked.

"I know things," she said. "People think I'm not smart, but some things I know."

She wouldn't tell me what she knows. Sometimes I feel lonely with her sitting right beside me.

And where are the guards? They haven't brought milk since Khasar was here. Maybe they're all right and just ran home to the city to report to my lady's father. I hope they come back soon. Without fresh milk, I've had to mix dried yogurt into my lady's water. It's clumpy and tastes sour, but at least she won't have to drink plain water.

And worse news—the rats are back. Just a few days without a cat and already they return. I hear them scratching and yipping and rustling down there. I set up more traps, but they avoid them. The washing isn't done and we had a cold lunch because I stay hours in the cellar, trying to smack rats with a broom.

I think My Lord the cat must be fine. He'll come back soon.

Day 240

My lady offered to sit a spell down below combating rats so I could warm my hands and make dinner. It seemed a task not fit for gentry, and when I protested, she insisted she'd do it. I supposed if she was willing, then it would be all right.

When the meal was laid out on our little table, I called her up from the cellar. My lady climbed the ladder and made straight for the upper chamber.

"I don't feel well," she said. "I'm going to bed early."

"Let me come sing to you," I offered. But she refused.

When I returned to the cellar for more rat swatting, I found the culprit of her illness — my lady had eaten half a bag of sugar.

Day 245

Every day, my lady says she will take a turn whacking rats, but really she's down there eating. Rats squeal and skitter around her, and I hear her lips smack, smack, smack.

Day 268

She's devoured our dried fruit, every crumb, and all the sugar's gone but dust. Now she's demanding I soak more meat overnight, cook larger meals and more bread. I tried to argue once, but she raised her hand and commanded me to obey on the sacred nine. So I do. Though I grumble enough to put any piglet to shame.

Six more years, and not a grain of sugar. Six more years and no fruit, fresh or dry.

Later

It appears she also ate the last wheel of cheese. The rats will be heartbroken.

Day 281

Last night or morning or whatever time it was, I sat by the fire taking out the seams in my lady's clothing and stitching them back up broad. Since she's taken to eating, she's rounder than before.

I told her, "My lady, our food supply's in peril. We have to be careful."

"It doesn't matter," she said. "We won't last seven years anyway."

That made us both quiet. She stared at the fire for so long, I wondered what thoughts rode the flames in her vision. Then she asked me, "Dashti, would you have married Lord Khasar?"

"No! I'm a mucker, I couldn't marry a member of the gentry."

"But imagine if you were me, would you?"

I tried to imagine. Even how he slaps hands and flicks burning chips into our tower, even though his voice makes my stomach spin, would I marry him to escape this coffin? After falling in love with her khan, would the thought of being with any other man make me weep and tangle my hair? Would I have chosen to lock myself up for seven years and even die from darkness? I tried to imagine, but it made me dizzy, and I couldn't keep my eyes on the stitching. *Stop.* Just thinking of a commoner marrying gentry is a gross sin of the kind that could get me noosed on the city's south wall and never welcomed into the eternal Realm of the Ancestors. She's wrong to make me think it.

My only reply was, "You do what you think's best, my lady. If you'd rather wed Lord Khasar than be in this tower another day, I'll stay with you all the same."

I didn't want to say that, but I did, and I meant it. I'm her lady's maid, I swore an oath, and I'll serve her till I die.

She smiled, and I saw her cheeks dimple for the first time since we met. What a sad little bird she usually is, how she droops and moans when she could be as brilliant as the sun. Sometimes I forget that she's gentry, that her blood is divine. But when she smiled, I remembered—she is as beautiful as light on water.

She looked back at the fire. "I know I should have married Lord Khasar. I was born to marry. That's my only purpose."

"That can't be, my lady."

"My father told me so when I was small enough to sit on his knee. My older sister, Altan, she'll be the lady of the realm after my father. I have an older brother, Erdene, who will rule if Altan were to die. I'm the third child. I used to dream I'd be chief of animals one day. I like animals. But my father said I'm too dull-witted. And besides, I'm gentry—any commoner can be raised up to be a chief. But the third child of a ruling lord is only fit for marrying off to other gentry."

I could tell by the way my lady stared at the fire that

she was done talking, so I sat by her, quiet, and thought about what she'd said. Her sister's name, Altan, means *golden* in the naming language. Gold is the color of the gentry, and it seems a right name for the lady of a realm. Erdene means *jewel*, another noble name. Saren means *moonlight*. I wonder what her mother thought when she named her moonlight, the dim light that keeps the night sky company until the blue sky can return.

It's strange for me to think about gentry in that way, as people who had mothers who gave them names. People who wanted things they couldn't have, who were ordered to marry men they feared. Though I clean her plate and wash her unders, I guess until today, I never truly thought of my lady as a real person.

Later

I showed my lady the drawing I did of her smiling, and she said that I'm her best friend. I thought I should write that down.

Day 298

Daily I sing to my lady. Sometimes it's to help ease a headache or bellyache, and sometimes it's my continued attempt to cure whatever troubles her inside. Yesterday I tried a new song, one I'd nearly forgotten.

The song for unknown ailments is a wail. High the notes stretch, my throat stretching with them, the tune reaching up and up like a wounded bird's call, "Rain rips as it falls, it tears as it falls!" Just the sound of it echoing in our tower made my chest feel tight. My lady sighed and curled up against me, not crying but breathing as if she would. After she had a good rest, she seemed lighter. She even chatted with me over supper and joined me in a game of pea toss.

So I went to bed content last night, thinking I'd made some progress with her healing. But this morning she's the same again. If only she'd tell me why she's so sad and crooked-brained and lonely and often acts as if she's only half her age. Does *she* even know why? Maybe it's just how she is, maybe there's nothing in her to fix.

I'll keep trying.

Day 312

It's summer, and thank Evela, goddess of sunlight, that it's a gentle one this year or we'd roast in our brick oven. There were children running around our tower this morning. I think they've been here before, but I could hear them more clearly today. They were closer to the tower, perhaps daring one another to draw near, and their voices ghosted up the uncovered hole. As they ran around and around, I could hear broken bits of the song they sang. I believe it went like this:

Two dead ladies in a tower
Counting peas for every hour
In seven years

With all their tears
They drown in pea soup sour

I didn't care for their song much, but I sat near the hole all the same and listened, listened, listened. New sounds are like lost sugar.

Day 339

Most of the time, my lady sits alone and stares at things — her fingers, the floor, a single hair. I wonder how a person can sit so much without work in her hands. Are muckers born to work and gentry born to sit? This darkness makes me ask questions that never occurred to me under the Eternal Blue Sky.

But it doesn't seem fair, does it? Why can't my lady dip her hands into the wash water and give the clothes a good scrubbing or mend a rip or make a pot of something worth eating? I'd be pleased as anything if I never had to haul a bucket of water up the cellar ladder again, but some work isn't so bad, not when you have naught else to do but stare at a candle flame or into the shivering dark.

Later

Ancestors forgive me, but I offered to teach my lady how to cook dung cakes.

She said, "I don't know how, Dashti."

"That's why I'll teach you."

"I'll do it wrong."

"Of course you will, everyone does wrong when learning something new."

Then she started to cry. "But I'll do it *wrong.*"

I wish I understood my lady and her crying and her shaking. She looks at the whole world as though it crouches over, ready to pounce.

Day 457

Weeks and weeks go by, months and months. I wash, I cook. My lady is more shadow than girl. Once I tried to teach her to read. Her eyes wandered.

Some days I hate candlelight. Sometimes I think we'd be better in all darkness, then we'd just hold still until everything went away. But I keep cooking.

I keep washing. I keep singing. And I keep the fire and candles lit.

Day 528

Today I thought I would like to die, so I went into the cellar and smacked a few rats with the broom. It helped some.

Day 640

This summer is worse than last. The heat, heat, heat pushes against the walls of the tower, forces its way inside, and yells silently in our faces. We sit in the cellar, underground where it's a little cooler, and keep the rats company. Or we sit upstairs, where the barest slip of breeze comes through the crack between bricks. I can't light fires, lest we die of the heat. We eat cold food. We pour water over our heads and shiver.

The hearth is left bare for summer, and I feel as though we're living with eyes shut. Day and night we keep a candle burning, and that tiny fingertip of light wobbles before me, as if too weak to live on, gasping its last breath. It creates more shadows than light, filling the tower with corners. When my lady sits against a far wall, she disappears.

I don't dare light more than one candle. The rats have eaten many. A dying wasp of candlelight is so much better than none.

Some days I look at the bricks in the door and wonder how hard I'd have to hit them to knock one loose. If I managed to break us out, would the guards shoot me with their arrows? Are they even there anymore? Would her honored father know of our escape and stuff us back in for another seven years? Would Lord Khasar hunt us down?

This is more thinking than I've done in months, and I'm tired now. The heat is so huge, I have no space left for thoughts.

Day 684

Here's something true about darkness—after enough time, you begin to see things that aren't there. Faces look at me, and when I turn my head, they disappear. Colors wash themselves before my eyes, then fade away. Shiny gray dream rats dart between my feet but don't make a sound. I wanted to write this down so I can remember that those things aren't real.

My lady sees more than I do. Sometimes what she sees makes her cry.

Day 723

I think my . . . I think I . . .

What was I going to write? I can't think of words. The candle flame is glaring at me. My lady moans. I'm going to go to bed now.

Day 780

It's winter again. Over two years behind bricks. For weeks and weeks, my brain felt slow as ice pouring, but the past days, thoughts and questions and memories have started to roil in my head again. Is it a sign that something's going to happen soon? The longer I'm in the dark, the more memories are brighter in my eyes than the bricks in the wall. I begin to feel surrounded by ghosts, people long gone pressing around me.

My father died before I was old enough to call him Papa. It should've been all right for us because

Mama had three sons before me. The oldest was fourteen, of an age to hunt for food and protect us, as sons are supposed to do. And he did, for five years. But then we had a standing-death winter, when the night gets cold sudden fast, the air freezes like ice, and in the morning you find the horses and yaks and sheep dead on their feet.

Our family hadn't belonged to a clan for years, so we were on our own.

Three days after the animals died, my mama and I woke to discover my brothers gone. Their boots gone. Their bedrolls and knives and belts. Gone. I understand why they left us. With a mother and a young girl, they'd have little chance to earn enough to trade for new animals. Alone, they could pledge themselves to another clan, work for seven years, then find a bride in that clan and build up their own herd. But with father and animals dead, our family was a grave.

Mama and I were hungry lots after that, but we had our gher and one animal left, a mare named Weedflower who still gave milk.

We didn't dare go to the main pasturing places. Any mucker out of luck would see a woman and a girl with no men to protect them as an invitation to plunder. And besides, with only one animal, we couldn't live the life of a herder. So we camped near forests where we could hunt for small animals and gather what the trees would give us. We hunched up in the coldest places, the driest, the least inviting, where no one else wanted to be. And times when we had to go near the city to do piecework to trade for cloth or tools, we smeared Weedflower's dung in our hair and wore our rags, so no man would be tempted to carry one of us off.

We survived. And with Mama's singing, we stayed healthy enough. We may've eaten mudfish more than rabbit and stick birds more than antelope, we may've watered the milk gray and slept with our mare inside the gher for warmth, but times there were when we laughed enough to shake the forest and ripple the rivers. Times I thought, good riddance to my brothers. They don't know what they missed.

Here's a memory of my mama and home that my fingers long to draw:

And then I get to remembering when she died. I was fourteen. I'd been crying too much and was weak as wet laundry. But I laid her out on the open steppes under the Eternal Blue Sky, with her feet pointed at the Sacred Mountain so her soul would know which way to walk. I sat with her another day and night. I told her stories about our life together so her soul could remember who she was, then I sang her the parting songs. The songs that tell her spirit that she's ready to go, that it's all right, that she can leave me now and walk up the Sacred Mountain and back down again into the Ancestors' Realm. In cities, singing the soul out of the body is a shaman's work, but we muckers had to learn those songs ourselves, with no shaman around for miles.

I guess singing the parting songs to my mama was the hardest thing I've ever done. I would've rather had her ghost haunting my every footstep than be alone. But I felt proud after I did it. And now she'll be waiting in the Ancestors' Realm, ready to sing me in.

We were camped a long way from the city that summer, so far it made my legs hurt just to think of the distance. I took apart the gher and loaded as much as I could on Weedflower's back and the rest on my own. I had to leave the gher's heavy winter coverings behind, cast off to rot on the ground. It wasn't easy to do. Mama and I had pressed the wool ourselves to make the felt—aching work, longtime work. But what could I do? The load was already heavy enough to make me stagger.

As I walked toward the summer pastures, I offered Weedflower as a gift to everyone I met. None robbed me, thank the Ancestors, but none accepted my gift. If they had, it'd be the same as consenting to make me a member of their family and agreeing to one day find me a husband. It'd been a hard winter. None wanted another mouth to feed. Maybe if I were prettier. Maybe if I didn't have the red blotches on my face and arm, the sign of an ill-fated life.

I always thought I'd be a mucker bride, become a mama like my own one day. It's only now, as my brush touches this page, that I'm realizing I never will. I wish My Lord the cat were curled up in my lap and purring.

Eventually I found a clan headed toward the city, and I exchanged my gher for a place in their Long Walk. It was summer, so I could sleep on the ground. I had Weedflower's milk to drink, and I hunted for roots and birds and rodents when I could, and traded milk for a bowl of food from other people's pots. I'd never been around so many folk before, and yet it was the loneliest I ever felt. Is that strange? Well, the loneliest except for now in this tower.

I miss Weedflower, whom I had to sell in order to buy myself employment and lodging at the house of chiefs. I miss myself, how I used to be. How I used to feel under the sky. I miss the time when I could believe I'd die old with my own husband beside me, one who wouldn't think of me as a mouth to feed or leave after a standing-death winter.

I just looked at the dump hole and saw light outside. Morning? Did I write all night? Time is a wind that keeps blowing in my face and mumbling words that don't make sense.

My lady's calling. She says she's hungry.

She's always hungry.

Day 795

There's an odor about my lady, like a dung heap on a hot day. If my script looks ill, it's because I closed my eyes as I wrote that. I shouldn't even think it. But she does—my lady does smell like hot dung.

Day 812

It's my honor to serve. It's my honor, I know it is, and yet . . . Ancestors, don't read this, but I begin to wonder, is it right? The lady is jailed for neglecting her duty, but I'm jailed for fulfilling mine.

I miss My Lord. The cat.

Day 834

Under, god of tricks, keeps thinking of new ways to bully us. I cooked our meal from a new sack of grain, one that was buried under crates and the rats hadn't yet touched. My stomach wasn't feeling round and open, so I only nibbled, but my lady ate any quantity of flat bread. She grumbles as she eats, like a beast feeding on short grass. Ancestors bless her.

After dinner, I noticed how colors seemed to wave around me, so intense I thought it was real. The bricks were orange and moved like fire, though there was no heat. Strangely, I didn't feel worried till my lady screamed and pointed up, where I only saw the wooden ceiling and darkness.

"It's coming down," she screamed. "It's falling in!"

"What is? What?"

Then she turned to the hole in the wall, scream-ing anew. "A wolf! A wolf eats through our wall!"

There was nothing there.

I held her and sang to her while she screamed and vomited. By the time my eyes no longer saw or-ange fire rippling over the bricks, my lady had col-lapsed into a soggy, though quiet, mess.

Bad grain. My mama warned me once that if eat-ing stored grain makes you see things that aren't re-ally there, then it's gone bad, touched by Under, god of tricks.

I suppose I should be grateful the bread didn't kill us, though it near killed me to have to dump the entire bag of grain out our hole.

Day 852

Sometimes I spend several hours by our hole calling to the guards. There's been no answer since the night the wolf howled. If Lord Khasar did kill them, why didn't my lady's father send others?

Day 912

I can hear the rats squeaking madly down there. When I'm half asleep, it sounds as though they're holding a party just to laugh at me. I can't sleep in the cellar again tonight. Though the smells from outside speak of spring, it still gets mighty cold, and my limbs are frozen by half, my jaw sore from chattering.

There are so many rats, I can't think what to do. I can't think much. I'm so cold from sleeping in the cellar, my head feels like ice, and I imagine that all the worry is cracking it. It's only been two years and a half. I call outside, shouting of how we've not much time and to send more food or please break us free. I have to think that no one's there. Maybe my lady's family doesn't care if we die, or even remember us at all.

Later

I've moved most of the remaining food up to our ground floor. It'll spoil faster out of the cold cellar, but at least the rats won't get it as easily. I've counted and measured, and we can't live four years on what the rats left behind. If I'm not too cold and tower-addled to do my figures, then we don't have enough to last a month.

I won't tell my lady. I don't think she'd understand. She barely speaks of late, barely notices me at all, even when I'm singing to her unknown ailment. Besides, I don't have the patience to hear her cry again.

Day 918

I've decided. We're going to live. It's such a relief! I begin to feel more my mucker self just to settle my mind on it. A mucker survives. No matter that we've not enough food. We'll find a way.

Day 920

Yesterday morning, I sat scraping at the mortar between two bricks. I didn't make breakfast. I didn't do the washing. I just scraped, scraped, scraped. I broke our kitchen knife. It never was a good knife, but now we've got none at all. Today I tried a wooden spoon and grated the handle down to its bowl. I'll keep trying everything till the wall breaks or my fingers do. So what if the guards are ordered to kill us on sight? They may not even be out there, and that death isn't as sure as the starving death awaiting us.

Just now, rat meat sounds as tasty as winter antelope.

Day 921

Rat meat is *not* tasty.

I managed to beat one senseless with my broom. I cut it up and served the stringy meat boiled. It's all right for a mucker to hunt rats when the yak stops giving milk enough for cheese, but no gentry should, Ancestors forgive me. The rat tasted dull and bitter, as if it had been eating mud, but my lady just chewed and chewed and swallowed. How could she not ask where the fresh meat came from? Sometimes I wonder if her brain was set upside down.

Day 925

Under, god of tricks, must love rats. They remember me and won't let my broom near. Over the past two days, I've hit myself more times than I've come close to a rat. I wish I had a bow and arrow to hunt with, but I left all those mucker tools behind.

You know something odd? Even though their appetites are killing us, I actually like those rats. It makes me smile to think of how brilliant they are at surviving. I think her khan would laugh with me about this.

Day 928

If my script wiggles, it's because my hand won't be steady. This is what I've been hearing, echoing into our tower through the broken hole.

"It was a lookout tower that doesn't look out anymore." A man's voice. "See here? Steps lead to nothing, and these bricks aren't as old as the rest. The door's been bricked up just like the windows."

"And who told you there's a lady inside?"

"Who didn't tell me? That's been the rumor for years."

Some laughter. "Then she's waiting for us, isn't she? Just ripe for the picking."

"I get first go."

A muffled thump.

"Don't use your shoulder, you yak head. That's solid bricking. Here, help me with that log. Mongke, Delger, come lend a hand!"

Later

It's been an hour I suppose, though it feels like days. The horrible knocking goes on, and I feel bruised just for hearing it. They move around the tower, testing the bricks, banging, trying to find a weak spot. Ancestors, after all my calling and praying, these are the men you send to break us out? Perhaps only Under heard me.

Forgive the wet marks here. I don't know if it comes from sweat or tears. My lady heard the banging and came to see what's happening. I didn't tell her what I heard the men say, but she guesses it's not her father come to beg pardon, guesses it's not her khan at rescue. I've set her in the cellar. She's a ball of trembling, the rats chittering around her. I told her to put her face in her knees when she cries so the men won't hear.

If they've come for a lady, they'll search the tower till she's found, I'd warrant. But maybe if they find me, they won't look too hard for another. Maybe they'll mistake me for the lady and leave when they're done. Carthen, goddess of strength, how I try to be brave! But I want to lock myself in the cellar, too. I want to run away. I don't want to see those men, I don't want what they'll do to me.

I make myself laugh, though silently, just thinking how I'll scratch them first. How I'll bite and tear at their eyes. I'll be more dangerous than a mad rat, and I'll fight just as hard to survive. I'm holding the shard of the kitchen knife in my left hand, a rag wrapped around one end so I can grip it fast. I will find their pig parts and cut them out before they touch me!

It was silent for minutes while I sketched. Now the battering again. I'm having trouble holding the brush.

Day 929

The wall still holds. How odd it is that, just now, that's a blessing.

Silence slumped against our door after the cold told us it was sundown. We slept with no fire, my lady and I tight together on the same mattress, too scared to climb back into the cellar because the ladder squeaks. In the tar black dark she begged me for a fire, but if the men see smoke in the chimney they'll know we're here, they won't give up then. I know why she begged, though it might've meant death. Even though we've spent three years in near dark, the total black scared me more than the thought of mud fever or even Lord Khasar. The total black filled my eyes and nostrils and throat and felt like forever.

Now, daylight noses through the broken hole, around the last bag of dried peas I jammed in front of it. I warmed ink and water in my hands enough to write. I have naught to say. I'm just looking for comfort in words.

I wish I had a cat curled up in my lap, his sleep purr singing that everything is all right.

Another thought spins and spins in my head. If those men couldn't break our wall, what chance have we?

Day 930

A silent day. No fire. We chewed dried peas and drank water. Every moment I expect to hear another knock. I wonder if those men are crouching nearby, waiting to pounce at our first sound.

Day 931

The men haven't returned, or else they're removed from our tower, waiting for us to appear. It doesn't matter. We have to get out.

I spent the day chipping at the mortar around the dump hole, hoping that area was weaker than others. I used our pot lid, as the knife is now useless. No more voices, except the squeak of rats and my own scrape, scrape, scrape. The barrels are nearly empty, the last of the salted meat is reeking with rot. Even without rats and my lady's appetite, we wouldn't have lasted seven years unless her honored father had brought us fresh food. Now, we have just days left.

I pray to Evela, goddess of sunshine, bring us into your light again. Ris, god of roads and towns, let us find home. Vera, goddess of food, give us enough to eat. Goda, goddess of sleep, use your skill on Under so his tricks won't touch us. And Carthen, goddess of strength, make me strong enough to break down the walls.

We're not going to die. I already decided.

Day 932

Just hours ago a wonder occurred.

I was lying on my straw mattress. I was asleep, mostly, though I was still aware of my lady snoring. Forgive me, Ancestors, but it's the truth — my lady snores like a ram with a cold. And that wasn't the wonder.

I was dreaming of the rats. These past months, I dream asleep and I dream awake. Often I'm not sure which is sleep and which is madness, just as I'm never certain when it's noonday or deep night.

In the dream, I could see through the floor into the cellar, down to the ragged, silvery shapes of the rats scurrying. I saw them nosing along the cellar floor, finding a fallen grain here, a bit of wax from a cheese wheel there. Then I saw them climb some empty crates and leave the tower.

The dream shocked me awake, and I sat up.

"The rats got into the tower," I said, right to the darkness. "That means the rats can get out."

I lit a candle in the fire and crept down the cellar ladder. Little eyes looked back at me in the dark. One scuttled away, and I followed. It disappeared behind some crates, but I heard the sound of its claws as it climbed. I stepped onto an empty barrel and held my candle up close to the place where the wall and ceiling meet. This is what I saw.

I gave the area a hearty shove. The wall moaned. I hit it again. I tore a slat of wood from a barrel and wedged out a brick, then attacked it with my fists. I started to feel good striking the wall, and I got a little angry, too. The anger felt like a stinging breath of late autumn air after sitting by a hot fire.

I don't know how long I fought with the bricks, but my hands were bruised and my shoulders ached something powerful. The rats got out of my way. I guess they knew I wasn't fooling around.

Now there was a hole big enough for a girl. For me. Night air whooshed down into the cellar and tasted like grass. I stood there and just breathed. I guess I should admit, I was a little scared to leave.

But eventually I did put my hands through the hole and feel level earth, I did crawl up onto hard ground and fight my way out of some nasty shrubs, and I did stand on real dirt and look up.

I was outside. I was under the stars.

I breathed in as if it were the first time I'd breathed in years. My body felt stripped naked, washed hard in cold water, dried, and dressed again.

I was under the stars, like a fish is under water.

Tomorrow we'll leave the tower. If the guards are out there, ready to shoot an arrow at the mucker

maid escaping, or the knocking men wait to do terrible things, then know, Ancestors, that I did my best.
I tried to do my duty.

And save my lady, who once said that her mucker
maid was her best friend.

PART 2

The Adventure Thereafter

Day 1

I decided to start numbering the days at one again to mark the time when we began anew.

I was up all last night. Who can sleep when there's real air to breathe? Who can sleep when there's a sky? Still, I thought it wise to let my lady rest as long as she could, so for hours I kept company with the stars. When I couldn't stand to wait another moment, I clambered back inside, wrote in this book, and then woke her with the news.

She seemed happy. She seemed relieved. But at the hole in the cellar, she waffled. She said she couldn't climb up it, she said her ankle hurt, she said the hole was too small, she said anything to stay inside. After some time of this, I guess I got a bit tetchy and, Ancestors forgive me, I ordered her like I would a sulky sheep, pushing her from behind. I thought all she needed was to feel that glorious night air, but when I scrambled out behind her, I found her clinging to the side of the tower and shaking like a cornered rabbit.

I put my arms around her to make her feel tight and safe. I said, "Breathe the air, my lady! Look at the stars!" But she just shook.

Thinking it was the darkness of night that haunted her, I waited for the sun to come up. It was nearly dawn. The sky brightened in the east, turning white, yellow, then blue. It was perfect. I hadn't realized that by firelight, nothing in the tower had shown true colors. All we saw for years was black, gray, and orange.

My lady kept her eyes squeezed shut.

"Look, my lady. Open your eyes and see the colors."

It was the wrong moment, for just as she peeked, the first edge of sun rose over the horizon to peek back at her.

My lady screamed and fell to the earth. "The sun burst! We're going to burn up!"

"It's just so bright, I think, because we're used to darkness. We'll grow accustomed to it in time."

But she insisted that she was burning and rolled around, screaming and thrashing at nothing.

I dragged her inside.

We'll try again tomorrow.

Day 3

We've spent the past two days taking little steps out of the tower, shielding our eyes and looking around, then crawling back in. My lady tries to be brave, and she bites her lip and cries silently, sure she's on fire, but I tell her it's just the normal sun, that Evela, goddess of sunlight, will protect us. I've sung the song for good courage and the song for clear thought so many times, I feel hoarse and drained, as though the words plucked out my own courage and thoughts and tossed the rest of me aside like grain husks.

There are no guards with strung bows aimed at the escaping maid—at least I think there aren't since I'm still alive, but I can't yet see past my outstretched hand, not with the sun shooting bright arrows into my eyes.

Last night we sat under the moon for a long while, and my lady finally breathed in and sighed and seemed happy to be in the air again. She never once let go of my arm.

I spent this afternoon in the tower washing, making bundles of our blankets to carry spare clothing, and baking barley bread stuck with peas from the barrel scrapings. We'll leave tomorrow. I've packed brushes and ink enough, so I can keep writing of how we fare. I hope there will be much to tell.

Day 5

Oh, I feel so low, I want to curl up in the dirt and just moan, moan, moan. Everyone's gone. Everything's burned.

We knew from afar that something wasn't right. There should've been people passing us on the road to her father's city. The sun was so piercing I couldn't see much, but all the world felt wrong, as if the road appeared flat but was actually as steep as a mountain, as if we'd died in the tower and were just ghosts wandering a shadow world.

My lady wouldn't look up. I draped a blanket over her head and she stumbled along, her eyes on her feet.

"Would you like to go back to your father?" I asked.

"He won't have me. And even if he would, I won't have him." She gripped my arm as if without me she'd drown dead in the sunlight.

"We can't live out in the open like this," I said, "not for long, not without a gher. We need to—"

"It doesn't matter where we go. Lord Khasar will find me and wed me and then kill me."

"It won't come to that, my lady. If you won't go home, I'll take you to Song for Evela and reunite you with your khan."

"No! I won't see him."

"But he's your love," I said. "He'll take right care of you."

My lady had stopped walking and stood in the center of the road, hunched and shivering.

"He won't." Her voice went raspy soft and strange as she said, "He wants to kill me with arrows and knives."

Well, those words nearly knocked my feet out from under me. "Khan Tegus wants to kill you? Why would you think that?"

"I heard the whispers."

I nearly laughed as I asked, "Voices whispered to you that Khan Tegus wants to murder you with arrows and knives?"

She looked at me then, her eyes clearing a bit, and said, "No, I didn't hear anything. I just don't want to see Khan Tegus anymore. That's all."

My guess is that she's tower-addled something fierce, her brain awry in her head and her understanding tilted steep. But it's not proper for me to make decisions for her. So what's a mucker maid to do?

We slept the night under a tree, my lady's back

pressed to the trunk. I lay awake for hours, playing a game, trying to keep my gaze on the black parts of the sky, but my focus couldn't help but slide back to those bright stars. My eyes wanted the light. I breathed in as though I'd drink the sky cold. It was a good night.

Then this morning we approached her honored father's city. I saw a gray smudge that must've been the wall, but there was a dark spot that didn't seem right. As soon as we were close enough to make out details, I gasped right out loud. My lady looked up then and saw it, too.

"There's a hole in the wall," she said. "Someone broke the wall."

We kept approaching but stayed in the shadows of the trees that line the road, though they didn't feel any safer. The city gate was gone. Torn out? Burned?

"I don't understand," she said in her little-girl tone. "If something happened to the gate, shouldn't there be workers to fix it? And there used to be gate guards. Didn't there?"

She started to cry, and we had to stop. I held her head to my shoulder, rocking her, rubbing her back. Poor thing, I don't think she knows where to put the whole world.

We lay down under a tree and I sang a soothing song, one for deep sleep that goes, "Trout in the water, deep underwater, swimming so silver." She succumbed to sleep, and I left her in the shade and crept toward the city. Not only was there a hole in the wall, but the entire length was marred with black marks. Arrow shafts stuck between stones.

As I climbed atop the heaping rubble, a striped snake startled beneath my foot. It didn't attack, just swam deeper into the stones. The snake was surely a sign of something, though I'm not sure what. All creatures belong to Titor, god of animals, but the snake is the favorite beast of Under, god of tricks.

When I'd climbed high enough on the wall, I finally witnessed the whole truth of it. Her honored father's city is no more. It's razed, gutted, gone. No sounds. Even the smoke from the burning has blown away. I could see heaps of stone, charred wood, broken wagons. No people.

Qadan and Mistress. All the folk in my lady's house, her father, sister, brother. That city that teemed with people, all gone. All dead?

A cat passed me and meowed as though nothing were wrong in the world. My heart tipped up in hope that it was My Lord, but this cat's fur was brown and white. She didn't come when I sang. I guess she'd been a wild cat for too long and no longer craved the company of people.

I've had time to write, as my lady has slept all of the night and most of the day. We have just a day's worth of the flat bread left, so I need to scavenge more food, but if I'm not by my lady's side when she wakes, she screams. I braid her hair as tightly as I can without pulling loose her scalp, making sure every hair crisscrosses another. I sing, sing, sing every song I know and I even make up a few. But my lady's not well. She is not well.

Day 6

Is her khan's land burned down as well? Is everyone gone? Maybe we're the last living souls in the world and we'll drift from tree shade to tree shade, eating grass and speaking with snakes and cats until we're stooped from age and crumble into the dust. Today I keep thinking of all the people who have left and never returned—my brothers, Khan Tegus, our guards, this entire city. What a strange, dark world that swallows people whole.

I need to know if anyone still lives. The not knowing makes me queasy. My lady said she won't go to Song for Evela, but Ancestors forgive me, I'm going to take her anyway. She won't ask where we're going, and once she arrives and sees her khan, she'll heal and forget the whispers.

Before we journey, I should go into the city. We need food, and we need vessels to carry water in case we can't follow a stream. My lady fares a bit better today after many songs of healing. If I can coax her, she'll come with me. She knows her home and may find stashes of food that pillagers would leave behind. I'll admit, I'm afraid to go in to the city. If an army did this, then warriors may still lurk there.

And if the Ancestors did this, if in anger they wiped the land clean, then why did they let my lady and me live? Did they forget about us, locked away, hidden from the gaze of the Eternal Blue Sky?

I just looked back at the beginning of my writings and the title I gave this book of thoughts. It's all wrong now. I named it so, thinking that we would be seven years in the tower, and the idea of having an adventure thereafter gave me hope. I'm a stubborn mare sometimes and must dangle my own carrot. Here we are two and a half years later, saved from one coffin only to find my lady's city is but a second. My title is no longer correct. Two and a half years is not seven, but I'll leave it. I don't like the look of scratched-out letters.

Day 7

My lady came with me into the city, Ancestors bless her. She shook like a thin tree caught in a wind, but she came.

I don't fault her—there was much to shake at. Not a roof left intact, not a soul alive. And many a body, burned bones, some still stuck with arrows, some missing skulls. I won't describe any more because, truth be told, I don't want to frighten my own self.

The whole place was so still, I longed to find living people. But at the same time, every moment I feared running into another soul. There could be warriors or the knocking men, and I have nothing to defend us with but my own fingernails. Every shadow, every corner seemed dangerous. The dread was so powerful, I felt like I was walking on my own studded rat traps. Even the breeze hurt against my skin.

I can't say which is more terrible, to be locked

away from everyone or to be free in a world where all are dead. Both are different shades of darkness.

When we came at last to my lady's house, we stood and just stared. How grand it had been! So lovely and large my mama wouldn't have believed the tale. Now it was a heap of stones, green roof tiles, and cinder. My lady didn't cry. She didn't even shake. I think she hadn't had much happiness in that house.

My lady was able to point me to the spots where the kitchen had stood and the likely location of the food cellars. While I sorted through the rubble, she stared.

"Maybe it never really existed. Maybe this is all it ever was."

"No, my lady. It was real."

"I can't remember. . . ." Her gaze didn't stray from the heap of rubble. "I can't remember, Dashti. Are you sure?"

Sometimes my lady asks me questions that I can't answer with any degree of patience.

From under the lighter rubble, I pulled out a sack half full of barley meal, some rope, a large ceramic pot with just the spout broken, a wheel of cheese still covered in wax, a jar of oil with its cork intact, and three boots. By then my arms were too tired to lift a pebble, so I wandered around the ruins, scanning for a gleam of anything useful. By the Ancestors' luck, eventually I did find a knife. With that tool I can sharpen sticks to dig roots, spear fish and rodents, and gut them for the eating. It gave me a bit of hope.

I hadn't realized how silent all the world was until I heard a cry that made my stomach jump up into my throat. I thought warriors had found us, that we were dog's meat for sure. But then I saw.

Titor, god of animals, must've taken pity on us and sent a gift for the last lady of Titor's Garden.

At first the animal looked ready to bolt, but I sang the yak song, the one that bubbles up your chest and says, "He laughs, he laughs, he moans and laughs." I've never seen any creature respond so quickly to an animal song. He came to me at a near trot and stuck his muzzle right in my palm. This one's made of the friendly stuff.

I named him Mucker, and he's the handsomest yak I ever saw, with his coat a glossy brownish black, horns so long and proud as to make any she-yak blush, and grand teeth all still intact. He's so strong, carrying our few possessions must feel like a fly landed on his back. Yaks are the best animals for travel and will eat whatever stubby greens the road will produce. Give me one good yak over a herd of horses any day.

And what fine company he is! He nuzzles my hands and lips my ears, he stands close to me as we walk, sometimes pressing his broad head against my side, his horn wrapped around my back like an arm. I think he has a wonderful sense of humor, too. I told him a few stories and he turned his ears, listening heartily. Just writing about him lifts my mouth into a smile. Mucker and I will get along fine.

Day 8

This landscape is as familiar to me as the inside of my eyelids. West of the city, the terrain eases back into the steppes — stretches of grass growing as tall as my knees, low, rounded hills, stripes of streams carrying away the mountains' snow, and the occasional knotty tree, wind-whipped and bending.

I'd forgotten how the wind never sleeps out here. The clean air moving against my skin was more delicious than spiced food — at first. But when we stopped for the night, I couldn't fall asleep for all the memories of mucker life the smell of the wind thrust into my mind.

When I did finally sleep, I dreamed I'd been running through the ruined city, trying to find a way out. When I went into a house, I found it full of bodies, and before I could turn away, the walls sealed up around me. Goda, goddess of sleep, save me from such visions. Even after I woke, the dream still felt sticky, clinging to me as if I'd walked through a spider's web. I'm lying against Mucker now and feeling a bit easier for his warmth and sleepy grunts.

Stars light my page. We'll be starting our journey in earnest come dawn and I suppose I won't have a chance to write again for some time. Song for Evela is west of Titor's Garden, so we'll follow the road that stretches toward the setting sun. If it would take two weeks for the khan's party with their horses and decent supplies, for us, I guess it'll be more than twice that. We don't have food enough, but it's spring and there are trout in the stream. If there's something a mucker knows, it's how to eat from nothing. No walls trap us now!

The smell of grass and yak is making me drunk with wishes that I'd never left the steppes—but after Mama died, I didn't know how to survive alone. Did I give up everything to learn to make letters and words on paper?

No. I'm a lady's maid. She would've died in that tower without me, I know that. My worth lies in keeping my lady alive for her khan. The Ancestors will honor such a life as mine. I hope.

Day 33

Three weeks we've been walking and still not another soul. We spotted the remains of some villages, but whether the folk there fled when the city was destroyed or whether they were all killed, too, I don't know.

A few days ago we forded a wide river, and I believe it must be the one that marks the border of Titor's Garden and Song for Evela. If so, then we've crossed into her khan's realm. Will we find the city gutted and full of the dead unburied? Never mind, I'd rather not think on that question.

My lady's clothes begin to hang on her again. I get her off Mucker's back and walking as often as she'll allow, so her blood is moving and her breath is exhaling the tower poison from her body. But oft times she must ride, for she's so beset by darkness as to not see the road.

This morning she began to scream, "I'm drowning, I can't breathe. The air's not right, I can't breathe." She clawed at the air and grabbed her throat, and when my songs of healing did her little good, I found a hollowed overhang by the stream and stuck her inside. She calmed at once.

I'm sitting outside the little cave, where I can still see the sky, where the sunlight moves on my arms. Being inside that tiny space, even for a moment, that's what made me want to scream.

While she's been napping, I've combed Mucker's shedding hair with my fingers, sharpened a new stick, boiled the sting out of some nettle leaves, then speared a fish in the stream, wrapped it in leaves, stuffed it with nettles, and cooked it in coals. The smell of fish cooking is rich enough to wake up the trees, but still my lady sleeps.

So I ate my portion and then lay on my back, watching the clouds. Seven years of food isn't worth trading for the sky.

Day 41

Others live!

Since fording the river, the steppes have faded away, trees and then great woods taking over. Today we reached a crossroads and saw a group of traders traveling the north-south road. They were whole and living and speaking—real people, not ghosts. What a heavenly sight.

"How far is the city?" I asked when we were upon them. I didn't say Song for Evela, for my lady still doesn't know where we're going.

"Four days, if you walk straight. You weren't coming from the east just now, were you?"

"Sure enough, they're coming in from Titor's Garden," said another trader, then he leaned over and laughed hard.

The first rolled his eyes. "Hmph, very funny. As though anything comes from Titor's Garden."

"What happened there?" I asked.

"Lord Khasar happened. Wiped it out entirely almost a year ago. Now he's off making war with Goda's Second Gift. We're hoping he burns them down, too."

"Hoping?"

"As should you. If he just conquers, if he adds their armies to his, all the warriors of our realm will have little chance against him. He's bound to come our way next. Tales be true, there's nowhere in all the Eight Realms where Lord Khasar's shadow won't cross."

My lady's hands covered her face, her shoulders trembling.

Day 44

Our grain meal is long gone, as is the cheese and oil, and after days on nothing but nettles, I think we were both feeling twig-thin and cranky. This morning I killed a marmot with my stick. I stuffed its belly full of hot coals and let it cook from the inside out. We had no salt or spice, and the meat was so tough it took fifty chews each bite, but even so I guess I never ate a meal so delicious. Even my lady didn't complain.

Very soon, I'll reunite her with her khan. And then? If she wishes, I'll stay with her and be nursemaid to her babies. If not, I'll find work in the city, or perhaps I will return to the steppes and find a mucker clan, take a seven-year oath, and work in their herds in exchange for eating their meals and sleeping on the floors of their ghers. But I'd be twenty-five by the time I was eligible to marry, and that's old for a mucker bride, even if anyone would take me without a dowry.

I'll worry about it after I see my lady settled in her happiness.

The sky no longer seems breathlessly huge, but feels to press down on me. Perhaps I'm just afraid of the uncertainty to come. When I'm moving on a journey, the ending is still unknown and possibly wonderful. But once I arrive, it's hard to keep imagining.

Day 46

Ris, god of roads and towns, has guided our feet, for we are here at last! The city of Song for Evela is greater than Titor's Garden, with a wall three-men high and a small army on horseback beside each gate. They fear Lord Khasar, I think.

A caravan from the south entered the gate ahead of us. I'd seen caravans arrive in Titor's Garden when I ran errands for Qadan, and I knew that they offer their goods to the lord or lady of the city before setting up in the market. Following behind seemed the fastest path to finding the house of my lady's khan.

It was a bold sight, camels and wagons and dozens of traders swathed in the brilliant white cloth of the desert lands. They uncovered their cargo to excite interest in buyers, and I caught glimpses of dye pots, porcelain bowls, bolts of silk, casks of honey, bags of sugar, skins of wine, and bricks of incense. The incense and the scented woods wafted a heavenly scent over us, and I walked as though in a dream. Performers rode atop the cargo, their heads bare and painted faces smiling. Later they'll show off their talents in the market to attract buyers to the goods. Acrobats, contortionists, storytellers with wild, strange accents—I wish I could see them perform.

We followed the caravan up the streets, past the wooden houses, merchant stalls, and animal pens, toward the city center where the buildings are made of stone. It wasn't long before my heart was going as fast as a rabbit's stomp. I was wondering if her khan would be in his house, if we'd see him that very hour. If he'd welcome her back, if he'd take her in and marry her at once. And what would happen to me then?

The streets were clean and straight, as different from the crooked, narrow lanes of Titor's Garden as my lady's face is from my own. And as I ached for a way to tell her where we really were, she said, "This is Song for Evela, isn't it?"

"Yes, my lady."

Her face wrinkled as though she were pained.

"Khan Tegus isn't plotting to kill you," I said. "I spoke with him in the tower, remember? He is goodness from boots to eyebrows, my lady, I could tell that, plain as plain. The tower sits heavily on you still, that's all. And the whispers—"

"I don't hear any whispers," she snapped. "I'm fine. I'm not afraid."

She walked tall, her hand on Mucker's back, her other arm in mine. She was trying to be brave, I could see. And it twisted my heart.

She didn't say another word for all those long, straight streets. Perhaps she felt buried in all that life. I certainly did. There were people everywhere—cooking in the street, shouting and chasing, throwing wash water out the window, fighting and kissing and eating and just talk, talk, talking. The smells! And the noise, like having your head stuck inside a wasp's nest. I'd forgotten that people were so loud, that they move around so much. They were beautiful, their eyes, their hands, their voices and laughs. It was many blocks through the city before I realized I'd been crying and I didn't even know why. Is that strange? I think Mama would understand. And maybe Khan Tegus.

Her khan's house was fat and square, with a roof five tiers high made of yellow and blue enamel tiles, grander even than my lady's house had been. How can anyone believe such a claim? And yet it's true. A throng of guards stood at posts all around, and more clustered about the gate. We tried to enter, but they stopped us and a little man in a deel too long for his feet asked us our business.

"Tell them who you are," I said.

"No," said my lady.

I spoke in her ear so the little man wouldn't overhear.

"Please, my lady. Tell them you are Lady Saren of Titor's Garden, betrothed of Khan Tegus. Tell them so you can be fit up like gentry and live as you should."

"No. And I forbid you to tell anyone who I am." She was looking around now like a hunted thing. "Lord Khasar would find me, or Khan Tegus would—"

"He won't hurt you, my lady! He'll protect you."

Her eyes were wet, her chin quivered. "What if he's not safe, as I once thought? No one is, but you." She gripped both my arms with her hands, like a bird clutches a branch.

"I can't look after you forever," I whispered. "I don't have money or work, and I don't have status or clan. We're barely surviving, my lady. And come winter, we'll freeze and die without a gher. You're an honored lady. You need more than a mucker maid can give you. Please, tell them who you are."

My lady took a breath, turned to the little man, and said, "I'm a mucker."

Ancestors forgive me, but I think I cracked in half then. I turned my face into Mucker's neck and I cried and cried like a roof in the rain. I was so tired. Not just of walking or feeling hungry, or washing and keeping my lady. I was just tired of being Dashti, of breathing, of being alive. *Forgive me, Mama.*

"What's going on here?" A white-haired woman approached the little man. I found out later that her name is Shria. "Who are these girls blocking the way?"

The little man cleared his throat as if to signal us to leave. I took a deep breath and felt my heart stutter and my sobbing dry up, and I knew I couldn't be broken any more than I was. There's some comfort in that. Mucker was lipping the laces on my boot, and I thought, I can get by, and I can find a way to keep my lady alive, but I promised poor Mucker he'd have a stable and a brush down at the end of our journey.

So I wiped my cheeks and told Shria, "I bring a

gift for Khan Tegus. This is the best yak I've ever known. His name's Mucker."

The little man started to protest. "We don't buy animals from—"

"No, not buy. I want the khan to have him. It's an honest gift from a mucker girl."

It was a right stupid thing to do, I know, and as I sit here writing, I can't believe I was so thick-skulled as to give away our only possession. With no animal or tent, in a few months' time winter would whack us dead like a yak's tail slaps a fly. I might've traded him for employment at the least. But in that moment I only thought how much I loved that yak, what warm and happy company he had been for me when I thought all the world was dead, and how he deserved a stall like the kind her khan's house was sure to have. And a little I thought of her khan. He gave us My Lord the cat, who was the best cat who ever breathed. And though Khan Tegus never came back for us, I'd heard the sound of his soul through his voice, and I believe he's the kind of person who deserves the best yak in all the realms.

I kissed Mucker's nose and sang into his huge ear the song to ease parting, the one that goes, "Roads go straight and roads go on, my heart moves like the sun." A boy came to lead him away to promises of oats and that quickly Mucker was gone. I hadn't realized it would hurt to lose that yak, but I nearly gasped at the pain in my heart. Thank the Ancestors, Shria didn't give me the chance to think and mourn because she asked right quick, "Do you girls know kitchen work?"

I showed her my hands. She turned them over, felt for calluses.

"She's a good girl," she said to the little man. "Her face has the mark of bad luck, doesn't it? Even so, I'd bet my shoes she's a good girl."

"What about the other one?" The little man squinted at my lady.

I smelled hope in the air, and I snatched at it. "She's my clan sister, and we've survived in harsher living than most girls could imagine. Why, she's worth two of any city girl you can find."

I guess they believed me because here we are in her khan's house. Instead of placing my lady in a chamber of silk and pillows, as I'd hoped to do, she's sharing my blanket on the kitchen floor by the washing hearth.

Ancestors but I'm tired and kitchen work starts at dawn. I'll pay for this writing time tomorrow.

Day 54

Though it's middle night, I'll write now because I never have other time. I'm used to recording my thoughts by the ghost light of fire, anyhow.

This kitchen is like a herd of wild horses for how it runs and runs and never stops but to sleep. My lady and I tend the wash fire, boil water, scrub pots, and wash aprons and rags. There are two other scrubber girls that share our fire, and we all sleep together before it, using the dirty rags for pillows, or one another's legs and bellies. I'll tell you somewhat of the other girls.

Gal is thirteen and our youngest. Her eyes are pale brown and so sad. She's from Goda's Second

Gift, and her mother made her flee before Lord Khasar's armies arrived. Because of the mountain range to the west, she had to sneak southeast through Thoughts of Under and the ruins of Titor's Garden before finding safety here. She doesn't know where her family is or if they still live. At night, I hear her cry, but she's camel stubborn and won't let us comfort her. When she doesn't suspect what I'm about, I work close to her and sing the song for heartache. She's got a wicked tongue and quick temper and saves it all for my lady, who is a slow worker.

Qacha is eighteen like me, and what's more, she's a mucker! Her mama was in the city of Titor's Garden when Khasar attacked, but her papa survived, and he works in the stables. They have the same half day free each week and spend it outside the city walls, talking and hunting for roots and berries. We teach each other new songs and talk about the steppes. How she laughs! She laughs when she wakes, and laughs when they dump another load of washing before us, and laughs when Cook knocks her head with a spoon for spilling water.

I love Qacha like I love sunshine, but I don't seek her company more often than I must. When we laugh together, I see how my lady looks, her eyes cast down, as though she wishes she could curl up and cry.

I don't call her my lady in front of others, of course. Her name here is Sar, and she wears her braid down like all the scrubber girls. We say that she's my clan sister, since we don't look enough alike to claim the same mother. Clan sisters. Ancestors forgive me.

Day 60

This lie is making me feel heavy, as though all the world is under water and I can't run for its weight. I can't be a good scrubber because I'm looking after my lady. I can't be a good lady's maid because I'm scrubbing pots and rags. I'm failing at both and I hate it like I've never hated a thing in my life.

And my lady isn't well. She doesn't cry so often as

she did on our journey, but she still hangs like a willow in leaf. Always she stays near me, seizing my arm or standing so close our sides touch. She looks about as if everything in the world had teeth and was planning to bite her. She weeps at night more than Gal.

"Is it the work, my lady?" I asked her tonight, when we were cracking soap from the block in the cellar.

"I'm tired," she said. "I don't like Cook. I want to go to sleep."

"You don't have to be a scrubber anymore, my lady. Your khan is the master here. Go to him and remind him of your powerful love."

She turned white and shook like a hare facing a hunter. I patted her face and shook her and prodded her with my toes, but she wouldn't agree, she just stood there, dumb and shaking. Ancestors pardon me, but I dumped wash water over her head.

My lady was angry. "Why did you do that?"

"To wake you up! To make you make sense. Tell me, my lady. Why won't you go to him? Why?"

"I don't want to say. You won't believe me. But I know it, I know they all want me dead. And if one doesn't kill me, the other will. Lord Khasar will come after me. He's a beast and he tears out the throats of goats with his teeth. I saw him."

"Oh, my lady," I said, and turned my back so she couldn't see my expression. First she claimed Khan Tegus is plotting to kill her with arrows and knives and now Lord Khasar bites goats. In her mind, I don't think she's ever left the tower. She's still seeing things that aren't there.

Day 62

The girls at the next fire wash plates and platters and occasionally help Cook with the stirring. Sometimes they say things about us pot scrubbers, or about my mottled face and my lady's slowness. It makes Gal glare and Qacha hold her laughter. Maybe before the tower, such talk would have made me feel low, but I have no patience for it now. The world is far too beautiful to waste a moment on such nonsense. Even so, we four scrubber girls keep to ourselves.

Except there is one boy who's a cutter—that is, he cuts up vegetables, prepares meat, that sort of kitchen work. Well, he had some free time and he came and helped me scrub pots. *In his free time.* Then today we caught eyes as we worked and he winked. I giggled about it with Qacha, but I don't know what to think. His name's Osol and he has loads of hair and a fine jaw. Maybe he hasn't noticed my skin splotches? How could he not notice? All the same, I keep the left side of my face turned away from him whenever I can.

I haven't heard any gossip about Khan Tegus. Or Lord Khasar.

Day 64

Today was my free half day, but Saren had to work. I wasn't going to leave her, she's likely to fall apart without me nearby, but the girls insisted.

"Go have some freedom," said Qacha, walking me to the door. "You haven't taken a half day since you arrived."

"But Sar—"

Gal grumbled. "That girl works slower than a snail makes a trail. Let her get kicked out of the kitchens already."

"Never mind," said Qacha. "She'll be fine. I'll watch Sar. Go on!"

It felt so nice to have someone looking after me a bit, and I believed Saren would be just fine with a solid mucker girl like Qacha watching out for her. So I left.

It was strange walking about without my lady

hanging on my side. Ancestors forgive me, but I felt as though someone cut me loose from heavy chains. First I went to the market. A caravan visited the khan's house two days ago, and I hoped to view some splendid performers.

Sadly, this caravan had only one contortionist and all he did was stand on his head and occasionally wiggle his legs, so I moved on, gliding my hand over the finery for sale—bundles of cinnabar, camphor, and sandalwood, bags of brown and white sugar, pearls and purple gems safe under glass, fragrant waxes in square bundles, turquoise, pink coral, and my favorite—blue nuggets of lapis lazuli.

I was gazing at the blue stones when I heard the caravan storyteller's magnificent voice. She boomed during the dramatic bits and then went low and eerie to make your hairs rise. The desert folk don't know the Ancestors and their tales, so the stories she told were foreign to me. Stories of night and fear, some so strange they left me feeling shrouded in ghosts.

One was like the story of the skinwalkers that I'd heard before—people who deal with the desert shamans to gain animal powers, but the storyteller added more details than I'd ever heard. First, a skinwalker offers his spirit as barter to a desert shaman, then he must kill a close relative — the more he loves the person he kills, the greater his power will be. Imagine such a thing! After that sacrifice, the desert shaman summons a predator spirit into the person, who then gains the added strength and cunning of that beast as well as the ability change into its shape. The storyteller told of man-leopards that prowl the desert night and with one bite turn a living person into a corpse.

My mouth went dry and I wanted to cover my ears, but I sat and listened anyway. Could it be true? Only the shamans should have power to change into animals, as foxes in service of the Ancestors. Shouldn't they?

It was a dark story and I needed lightening, so I headed back to the khan's house and visited Mucker in the stables. That magnificent yak grunted happily and snorted over my hands, leaving them warm and somewhat sticky. I sang to him and brushed him, and he looked shiny as polished wood when I left.

Here I am out in the sunshine, a full hour left for me to just sit and smile. Osol passed by, making a run to the dairy, and he dropped a wildflower on my book. I called out a greeting as he scurried away, and he looked back at me and winked. And smiled. He has a smile to be proud of.

The sky is a yawning blue, big and delicious, as though it wants me to be happy.

Later

Saren didn't do quite as well as I'd hoped. She panicked, there was some screaming, and they had to stuff her in a closet before Cook heard.

"She threw a tantrum like a waddling child," was how Qacha explained it. "I don't know how you put up with her."

"She's had a time of it," I said. "She lost her family."

"Who hasn't?"

I couldn't explain about the tower, and about Saren being gentry and made of softer stuff than muckers. But are they? I mean, her khan is gentry and it makes me smile to imagine him throwing a tantrum. Would Saren be like Tegus if I could heal whatever ails her? Then again, didn't the Ancestors make gentry perfect? And if they did, what about Lord Khasar?

I'm not sure about any of it anymore, and that's the truth.

Day 67

Today Qacha, Saren, and I were sitting on the floor scrubbing pots, and we mucker girls got to reminiscing about the steppes. Living every day under the Eternal Blue Sky, surrounded by animals, milking in the mornings, making cheese and yogurt, washing and cooking and cleaning, and then running free through the grass like antelope. I can still imagine myself in that life, as clearly as if I'm eight and in two braids, drinking milk fresh from the mare and twisting dry grass into play dolls.

"I never, ever imagined, not for a moment, that I wouldn't stay there forever," I said.

Qacha nodded. "We had a nice herd of sheep and my father would tell me, 'You see that lamb there? That one will be part of your dowry. And that one, too.' But then Khasar attacked, and we were camped too near the city, and his men stole animals and scattered the rest and killed . . . well, never mind. But before the attack, I thought I'd marry some mucker boy within the year." She laughed at that, all pleasantness again.

"And now here we are," I said, scraping some slop out of the pot and flinging it into the fire.

For a time we scrubbed in silence, then Qacha asked, "Would you go back right now if you could?"

I tried to see my lady without looking at her. She was elbow deep in her pot, but her face was earnest, as if she might be listening. I wished I could tell Qacha, *I'm trapped. I've taken an oath. Sar is actually an honored lady, the Ancestors made me from mud to serve her. I can't leave her. She's a bird with a broken wing. She needs me.*

But I said, "It's an odd thing to live all your life in one place and then lose it forever. It's a strange thing not to know if I'll ever be a mama like my own."

Qacha just nodded. She's a good one, that Qacha. She seems to sense when to keep talking and when to let the words drizzle into silence.

Day 69

I'm in the root cellar with a candle, and Cook doesn't know. I should be scrubbing, but I have to write now so I can stop shaking.

Earlier when we'd worked through all the dirty pots, Cook had us wash some deels for the serving girls. When the clothing was dried and folded, she sent me and Gal to deliver them to the other side of the house. We walked down those long corridors, all fit tight with stone floors, the walls snug with tapestries over carved wood, windows set with glass, porcelain bowls resting on lacquered tables, the most beautiful place I'd ever been. We hooked arms as we went, both afraid and elated to be walking freely through such grandeur. She can be a nice girl sometimes, that Gal, she's just sadder than the last lamb.

We passed by the doorway to the feast hall, and what a sight! Glass windows in all colors, a ceiling so high someone on horseback couldn't reach it when stretching.

Then up ahead three men were walking. Toward us. One was younger than the rest.

"I saw him my first day here," whispered Gal. "That's Khan Tegus."

Khan Tegus. That was his face! Those were the shoulders, the arms, the chest, the whole being of the man who once was no more than a boot, hands, and a voice. Thinking of our talks, of the laughing parts, of My Lord the cat and the pine bough, it was hard not to shout hello. I nearly rushed forward to greet him as family does, gripping forearms, touching cheeks, smelling his neck to invite in the breath of his soul.

And then I remembered how I gave him my own shirt. If he knew what I'd done, how I pretended to be my lady, he could hang me on the south wall.

His face seemed a kettle of worry, those men talking at him as they walked, and I wished I could hold his hand and sing him some ease. As he passed us, the corridor didn't feel so wide anymore. His sleeve brushed mine.

He looked at me, for barely a moment.

Only just now did I realize what I should've done—tell him at once that Lady Saren is here. Or *is* that what I should've done? Is it my duty to obey my lady or to do what's best for her? Nibus, god of order, direct my thoughts.

Day 70

Why didn't he come for us? For her? He said he'd return, but he left us in that tower, for Lord Khasar, for the knocking men, for the rats.

I must return to work. Tomorrow her khan is holding a feast for visiting gentry from Beloved of Ris, the realm to our northwest. We've been preparing for days and a mountain of pots teeter, waiting for the wash water.

I wonder, does he ever think of us? Does he remember? Has he snapped a pine needle just to smell it?

Day 71

It's past midnight and I've been just sitting here, staring at the fire. I don't want to write, but I may as well, since I can't sleep.

Tonight we scrubbed more pots than I thought existed in all the realms. As I was hauling water in from the well, Koke, one of the serving boys, brought us his apron and asked if we could wash a spill out of it. Qacha grabbed it. She thinks Koke's a sweet boy, and he thinks she's the prettiest thing since the first flower. I think he spilled brown sauce down his front as an excuse to approach her. Osol the cutter came over while we talked with Koke, and he smiled at me once. I smiled back. Why wouldn't I?

"You should see the lady," Koke said. "The clothes she's wearing have so much embroidery, there's not a lick of plain cloth left. Even so, she's not pretty, though she's not like —"

He glanced at me and I think he was sorry he'd said it. I didn't want him to feel sorry, he's a good boy mostly, so I asked, "Who is she?"

"Lady Vachir? She's the ruling lady from Beloved of Ris. It's for her Khan Tegus is having the feast, you know. What with Lord Khasar bringing war to his right and his left, Song for Evela needs all the other realms to be allies as close as family, and Beloved of Ris is our nearest neighbor, now that Titor's Garden is ashes. Everyone expected Khan Tegus and Lady Vachir would announce their betrothal tonight, and sure enough—"

I dropped the bucket. I splashed water over me, soaking my deel robe two hands up the hem and breaking the bucket's handle in the process. Qacha tried to fix it for me fast, before Cook noticed. Gal ran for another bucket to fetch more water. My lady and I just stood there.

They asked me what was wrong, if I felt faint, if I should sit down. Qacha sang me the song for sudden illness and stroked my hair. No one noticed my lady, how pale she looked, how her hand trembled. I noticed. I should have gone to her, I should have counseled with her, sung to her, combed her hair. But I couldn't move.

Later

I guess I thought we'd work in the kitchens until Saren came to her senses, until she shook off the terror, breathed free of the tower, and saw fit to be a lady again. I guess I thought he'd wait for her forever, never love another. What should I do? What can I?

Day 74

Lady Vachir is gone now. They'll be wed this winter.

Day 78

News has tumbled down into the kitchens. Lord Khasar overcame Goda's Second Gift. He did not raze it, as those traders had hoped. He killed all gentry and swore all the warriors who'd survived into his own army.

I watched Gal as she listened to news of her

homeland, but if her ears heard, her eyes didn't show it. I think she believes her family dead. I think she has less hope than a rock has sugar.

Koke said Khasar will most likely rest his warriors, train his new recruits, and then turn his eye to Song for Evela.

"Engaged to Lady Vachir in the nick of time," said Qacha. "Now the khan's warriors will unite with hers."

"Could Khasar come to Song for Evela?" I asked Koke.

"I'd bet a mare on it. He'll be here before winter, that's my guess."

I think about taking my lady away, but where would we run? Without a gher in winter, we'd die as fast as the honeybees. Cold is its own kind of tower.

Day 79

That boy Osol who winked at me, I saw him today winking at one of the cutter girls. I guess he's just a boy who winks. It doesn't matter, not in the least. And I'm not going to think about him anymore.

Day 80

It's not as though I would've married Osol.

Day 82

Last night I saw Qacha staring at her hands—split fingers, raw skin torn from washing. Scrubber work is hard on the hands.

"My mama was pretty at my age," she said.

Then this morning, Cook saw Qacha rubbing mare's milk butter all over her fingers. There was screaming and cursing, and when it all died down, Gal and I found Qacha sitting on the ground outside the kitchen, weeping and too afraid to enter. I'd never seen her cry before. Her face showed a welt the shape of a wooden spoon.

"Cook says she'll have my hair torn out if I come back in. But my papa can't keep me in the stables and I've nowhere to go. If I leave the city, I'd have to leave Papa, and Koke . . . how'll I ever see Koke again?"

I could've sung her a song of comfort, but that wouldn't cure the cause of the sobbing. I guessed she'd hoped the butter would keep her hands pretty. Someone once said I had beautiful hands.

"Gal, come with me a minute, will you?" I said. "Qacha, I'm going to go see if we can't get Cook in a good mood before you ask for your post back."

Cook was sweating over a pot, greasy black smoke rushing at her face.

I said, "We're caught up on all the pots and—oh, Cook, you look hot as a fire stone. Would you let Gal stir for you a moment while you sit a step back from the heat?"

"For a moment," Cook said, though she looked suspicious.

I sat her down, brought a stool for her feet, and begged a chance to rub her shoulders. While she rested, I hummed.

What ails Cook? I wondered, humming, touching her shoulders, trying to get a sense of her pain. Soon my hum turned into a song. I started out singing the song for body aches, for tiredness that runs over all of you like water over stones, the one that begins, "Tell me again, how does it go?" I could feel Cook want to get up and I thought I'd lost her, but then I guess she chose to let herself feel better for a time. Her shoulders relaxed beneath my hands.

Taking the tune for body aches, I wove in the words

for common pain, "Swan on her nest and the sunlight just so," while touching her shoulders, her back. I guessed her feet were sore, too, but I didn't dare touch them or she might figure out what I was up to. Her face was singed from smoke heat, her hands raw around calluses, and I closed my eyes and thought of the sound of the song going into those areas. She sighed, and I knew she was allowing the song to sink in. But there's usually something deeper than simple pain.

I tried weaving in a new song, the one for heartache that goes, "Tilly tilly, nar a black bird, nilly nilly, there a blue bird." I sang it softly, like you should when the hurt's buried deep and you want to ease it out slowly. It was just a guess, but who in all the realms doesn't have some heartache? Her shoulders tightened, then relaxed. I thought to go deeper.

"Prick, prick, blood on the cloth," I sang, now joining the song for body aches with the one for betrayal. No sooner had I begun than Cook lowered her head and sighed, long and sad as a wind stuck in a chimney. Suddenly, that large woman seemed as small and fragile as any tiny girl.

"Enough, I need to get back to work," said Cook, pushing me off and standing, but now her voice had lost its hard edge.

I rushed back to Qacha and told her now was

a good time to apologize. When she asked to be a scrubber again, Cook scolded her right proper, but there wasn't fire behind it. Within an hour, Qacha was scraping pots beside us.

"I've never seen Cook so calm," she said, already laughing again.

Gal asked, "Do you muckers have the changing powers like the desert shamans? Trick things into being what they're not?"

Qacha and I laughed. It was an absurd idea.

"Just the opposite," Qacha said. "The songs nudge things to be what they really are—a healthy body, a heart as calm as a baby's in the womb."

I agreed. "But there's no power in them, they're just songs."

"Well, I don't know about that, Dashti," said Qacha. "I could hear you singing back there, and I've never known someone to combine two songs together. That was clever. And choosing the right songs just for Cook—it's quite a feat to tame a beast like her."

"Cook did it, I just helped," I said.

My lady sidled up close to me, asking for a hand with a pot she couldn't get clean, and we all set in to work as hard as silence permits. A bit later, I noticed that Gal kept sneaking peeks at me, her face thoughtful.

Later that night in the dark by our hearth, I'd just dropped off to sleep, my head on Qacha's leg, when something poked me. When I opened my eyes to darkness, I gasped, for a moment terrified that the whole world was gone, that I was trapped in the tower again. But it was just night, just Gal prodding me awake. I eased away from Saren, lifting her arm from mine so she wouldn't wake, and sat up.

"I hear you humming at me sometimes," Gal said. "I run away from it because I haven't wanted to be anything but sad. But . . ." Gal's chin trembled, and she rubbed viciously at her face with the backs of her hands.

"Easy, Gal."

"I just don't know," her voice was a grating whisper, "don't know if my family's dead, don't know if they'll ever come for me. . . ."

"And you can't let yourself give up hoping," I said, "not until you're sure either way."

"But the hoping, that's what really hurts."

I reached for her and she shoved me off, then just as suddenly changed her mind and leaned into me, as if she'd never been hugged in her life and didn't know how to hug back.

I rocked her as we sat there, in the greasy dark of

the kitchen, snores bumping around us. I sang the song for bitter sorrow, "Darker river, blacker river, faster river, pulling me." She cried, softly at first, then harder, and then calmed, her head resting on my lap. She's sleeping like a newborn now.

It's funny, I don't feel tired at all. So I sit here and wish and wish that I could find the song that would heal my own lady.

Day 88

I'm hiding in the cheese closet and hating the close walls and dim light, and if Cook finds me I'll be out on my hide, but I must write this. Shria, the white-haired woman who first gave us work in the khan's house, came into the kitchens today. She said the khan had requested a mucker who knew the healing songs to attend to him, and Cook said, "Qacha, you're a mucker, aren't you?"

"Yes, but so's Dashti, and she's a better singer than I am, by leagues."

"Dashti would be best," said Gal, acting bold and pushing me right up to Shria. And she smiled like I didn't know she could. In the way that the sun's so bright in the city after the rain wipes the smoke from the air, that was Gal's face after crying all night. "Whatever ails the khan, Dashti will fix him right."

I stammered and looked at my lady, who offered no help.

And so Shria will come for me tomorrow. She'll take me to my lady's khan. I don't know what to think. I cannot think.

Day 89

All morning, my heart never let me forget what was to come. *Thump-thump, thump-thump,* it tapped at me. I didn't know when Shria would appear, so I stayed startled and alert all day. It reminded me of summers as a child before my brothers left, when our family set up our gher in the summer pastures and there were loads of children around. The Hunt, we'd play, some of us being animals hiding in the tall grass, the others searching us out with small bows and blunt arrows. How my heart would pound! I waited, crouched, prayed to Carthen, goddess of strength, and wanted to cry for the thrill and the terror. That's how I felt today.

I was up to my shoulders scrubbing a pot when white-haired Shria was suddenly before me.

"You're the mucker girl?"

Thank the Ancestors that I didn't actually scream, though the sound felt as real in my mouth as a bite of potato.

"Come with me, but wash first. You smell like grease and smoke."

She watched me as I scrubbed my arms and face, as if to make sure I did it properly. I asked to bring Saren with me. My thought was if her khan saw her, he'd sweep her back into his love and the life of gentry, and all would be put to right. But Shria didn't even bother to say no as she walked away. I pled with my lady not to scream and to let Qacha take care of her, then I ran after the woman.

Shria led me down a lush corridor, through two chambers, and into a small, dark room with a low ceiling like that in a gher. My lady's khan sat cross-legged on the floor, leaning forward to speak with two other men, and Shria and I stood quietly, waiting to be acknowledged. I was glad she was there. I've spent so long alone with Saren, I'd nearly forgotten that on entering the presence of gentry, I must keep quiet until he acknowledged me, or until I died, whichever came first. Just then, I was relieved to stand still. My feet were wood planks, my back a brick wall. My heart was so loud in

thumping I waited for Shria to scowl at me for being noisy.

You're a mucker, I reminded myself. You're not
pretending to be Lady Saren and you're not trapped
in a tower. You're just a mucker and a scrubber. You
can be who you are just fine.

After a time, I found it interesting to watch her
khan like that, my eyes free to rove over him. I could
understand why my lady chose him. He must've been
a fine boy, lean and strong, and now he had the bear-
ing of a warrior. He also looked intelligent. Or at least
there was humor in his eyes, which to my mind makes
a person wiser. And I already know he can laugh.

Finally her khan looked up. Right at me. I think
I might've gasped.

"Shria, is this the mucker girl? What's your name?"

"Dashti, my lord," I said, wondering if he'd ever
known the name of Lady Saren's maid, but his eyes
showed no recognition.

He dismissed Shria and sat on a low couch, continuing to address the two men. "Years ago, I met a
mucker from Titor's Garden. She sang to me a healing song, made this old pain in my leg dissolve."

"If I'm not mistaken, my khan," said one of the
men, "that's the injury I myself gave you."

"It was you, wasn't it, Batu?" Her khan's frown

twitched with humor. "I'd forgotten. You were teaching that slicing maneuver with your sword and I turned my horse the wrong way."

He straightened out on the couch, and I knelt beside him, placing my hands on his leg just below his knee where I thought I could feel the subtle heat that hovers around pain. He nodded at me once as if to say that I had my hands on the right spot, then continued to converse with the men.

I didn't dare sing for him the same songs I had in the tower. If he realized who I was, that I'd given him my shirt, I think I would just crumble like old bread underfoot. Instead I offered the song for new wounds. It's a battle song, urgent, fiery, "Hold, hold, strike and flee." Though he was absorbed in his conversation, I could tell it wasn't working. He seemed disappointed, the unease of his pain making him tired of the whole world.

So I took the risk and voiced the same songs from the tower, going up with "High, high, a bird on a cloud," and then down with, "Tell her a secret that makes her sigh." I watched his face—his eyes closed briefly, his forehead relaxed, his lips let out a long breath. But no remembrance of me.

I've spent these years wondering if he held my shirt to his face, if he knew my scent, if he'd recognize the smell of my skin like a mother cat knows her own kits. But not even the sound of my singing made him blink.

Day 91

It's been two days since I sat on her khan's floor, my hands on his leg. Shria said she'd come again if the khan requested me. I don't sleep well at night for wondering what I should do. I hear my lady snoring. She's sleeping on the kitchen floor, still in her dirty apron because she was too tired from scrubbing all day to take it off. I'm surely the worst lady's maid who ever lived under the Eternal Blue Sky.

Her khan is betrothed. There's a promise between him and Lady Vachir now. By rights, his betrothed can take the life of anyone who threatens her marriage. Even on the steppes, betrothal is sacred, and a man who carries off a betrothed girl is declared by all clans to be marked for slaying. I can't risk my lady's life by telling him she's here.

Then again, he and my lady were promised together first. Or were they? I mean, they promised their hearts to each other, but there couldn't have been a betrothal ceremony with ribbons of scarlet and brooms sweeping away the past. Her father never consented. If Lady Vachir asked for my lady's life, the chiefs of the city might find justice in her claim and grant it.

Besides, how would her khan be sure she really was his lady love? Will he remember her by sight? He hasn't seen her in at least four years. She must've been a girl when they met, and now she's a woman.

I'll have Qacha sing me the song for a clear head and think on this tomorrow.

Day 92

I've decided. I can't tell him yet. I need to be sure first that he'd welcome her, that there'd been a promise between them that would protect her from Lady Vachir.

"Was there a promise?" I asked my lady.

She was scrubbing a rag but going about it all wrong, just sort of massaging it with her fingers instead of rubbing it hard against itself. I took the rag from her and began to work at the stain until she snatched it back.

"I'll do it myself, Dashti. And I don't know what you mean about the promise. I don't remember."

Too often my lady talks this way. She says she

doesn't know anything and remembers less, and spends each hour in silence, scrubbing, scrubbing, scrubbing. I don't know why I bother to keep singing her the healing songs. Maybe there's nothing to heal.

Day 100

I've returned three times to her khan. Each time I sing to his pain and help his bones and muscles remember how they used to be whole. Sometimes the khan's chiefs sit in the room, talking low about war and Lord Khasar. Sometimes we're alone but for a guard outside the door, and the room is stuffed with silence. He hasn't spoken to me since the first day when he asked my name.

Day 103

Ancestors, I did speak when I should've been silent, I did forget who I was.

This afternoon, Shria returned me to the khan's low-ceilinged room and left me there. Khan Tegus was reading papers, and for many long minutes, perhaps an hour, I stood by the door. How my feet itched! But it felt like a solemn time, too, watching him read, seeing how he hunched his neck when the news was bad, how his cheek twitched with the idea of a smile when something amused him. He scratched his brow, his chin (and once, his rear end).

The looking reminded me of how I used to stare at the Sacred Mountain after Mama died. For hours I would gaze at the peak, imagining her soul making the journey up its slopes and back down to find the whole world transformed into the Ancestors' Realm, brimming with souls and dancing with light. I think sometimes just being silent and watching can change a person.

I draw this from memory, so it won't be right:

After some time he stretched, turned, and looked on me, looking for the time of a breath in and a breath out before his eyes focused and he realized he was staring at someone. He gasped.

"Lord Under but you startled me," he said. "I didn't realize anyone was here."

I laughed. I couldn't help it. He didn't seem to mind.

I set to work on his leg and I could sense the pain lifting from him fast. When I sang the pain out of his leg two weeks ago, it had taken much longer, finally easing in the time it takes water to boil over a fire. The more I work his leg, the better it remembers what it felt like to be whole and uninjured. In time, I guess his leg will heal itself entirely. And he won't need me.

Maybe that thought was what itched me to look deeper for another pain. I placed my hands on his belly, then his chest. His eyes opened. I could feel a heat inside him, a sharp heat, a yellow heat that comes from two broken bits of something rubbing against each other. Not an injury of flesh, but a hurt he refused to let go. This surprised me because in all my life, I've only been able to feel the heat pain like this with my own mama and with my lady, and once with a lamb I loved like a baby. And yet I could feel it so clearly in her khan.

"May I . . . may I sing to you again, my lord?" I asked.

"My leg feels fine. That will be all."

That will be all, he'd said, and that meant I should've left as quick as a fish. But how could I sense such a wound and not try to heal it? A bit of my mama awakened in me, a bit of the stubborn mucker soul, the stuff that keeps you alive when all the world is frozen and the food sacks empty. Any fool would be happy to die then and go to the Realm of the Ancestors, but only a mucker is stubborn enough to keep living.

"Sit down," I said.

I squeeze my eyes shut even as I write these words, though they're true. I did tell my lady's khan, the lord of Song for Evela, an honored gentry, to sit down. Forgive me, Nibus, god of order.

I kept my hands on his chest, and I could feel how strong he was. It reminded me of touching the neck of a horse as it runs, all those muscles under skin. Khan Tegus was a warrior, he could've knocked me to the roof and back down again. Instead he leaned back.

And I sang. "Berries in summer, red, purple, green." And I sang, "Digging and scratching, the earth bears a kin."

He leaned back more, he tensed and relaxed, the

muscles of his forehead tightened. Then all of a sudden he gasped, not in pain but surprise, and his arm flailed, scattering papers.

"Are you all right?" I asked. My hands took to shaking, and I patted him all over his chest and belly, making sure I hadn't hurt him.

His eyes were wide, but he nodded. "You pricked me just then. I can't explain it."

"Was it . . ." I hesitated. I didn't want to tell him his own feelings, but I thought I understood. "Was it as though you had a splinter inside, deep in your chest, that had been there so long you'd forgotten to notice the pain, and the song reminded you so you could pluck it out?"

I think he really saw me then for the first time, if that makes sense. He looked in my eyes, and he smiled and said, "Thank you, Dashti."

I hadn't known that he remembered my name. I can't say why, but his words made me want to cry, so I turned my head away and started gathering up the papers that had scattered. I felt him kneel beside me, heard the rustle of parchment as he picked up others.

"Where's that food storage account?" he mumbled after a time.

"Here, my lord," I said, handing him a paper.

169

"You read?"

"Yes, my lord, and write."

"And where do you work when you're not attending to me?"

"In the kitchens. I'm a scrubber."

"You read and write, you have the voice of the goddess Evela, and you scrub in the kitchens."

I laughed. "Evela's voice! I'm no pretty singer, no sit-and-listen singer. My mama used to say my singing voice is as rough as a cat's tongue and that's why my healing songs work. They dig at you, get inside, clean you up."

"Where's your mother now?"

"In the Realm of the Ancestors." And just like that I started to cry. Five years she's been gone. I should think I'd be used to it, but just saying those words to Khan Tegus was like being swatted in the face with the sadness all over again—maybe because for the first time I was telling him some of my own truth. I handed him the papers right quick and begged dismissal, walking out his door before he'd even given me leave.

When I think on all the times I sinned against her khan's nobility, I'm shocked I haven't been struck dead. Perhaps in the morning I'll wake as a pile of ash.

Day 104

Not ash yet.

Day 105

I'm writing this from a clean room with its own hearth, a horsehair blanket, and a wood table and chair. There's a window that looks over the dairy. The room's half the size of a gher and for now it's my own. How mama would laugh! Privacy's a strange notion to a mucker, where five in a tent is a roomy place.

Yesterday Shria told Cook, "Dashti will be living upstairs so she can copy notes for the chiefs and attend to Khan Tegus with the healing songs."

Saren didn't like it, but what could I do? I begged Qacha to look out for her and help her keep up with her scrubbing, said good-bye, and that quickly, here I am. Perhaps I should've found a way to stay with my lady, but she's improved very little since the tower, and my daily singing doesn't heal her a bit. Maybe it won't hurt either of us to be apart.

I've spent the past two days brushing ink on paper, making copies of lists about supplies and weapons, and looking out the window to ease the cramping in my eyeballs.

Windows are the eyes of the Ancestors. Windows are better than food!

I had a free hour this morning and went back to the kitchens to fetch this book from where I'd hidden it beneath some empty grain sacks. No one in the kitchens can read, so far as I know, but I'd rather not risk it being found. There are things written in here that could get me hanged on the south wall.

The girls cheered to see me and wanted all the details, so I washed pots and described my room and the window and the horsehair blanket. My lady didn't speak a word. She wouldn't even meet my eyes. Sometimes I have to snap a twig to keep from shouting, "Why don't you tell him who you are? Why don't you smile? Why don't you stop worrying about your father and Khasar and the tower and just decide to be Lady Saren?"

I should scratch out those words. Maybe later.

Day 109

Lately all I do is write. I copy pages of notes, lists of food supplies, numbers of weapons. As I fall asleep, the soft sound of a brush grazing parchment continues to murmur in my ear. Already my scrubber hands have begun to heal and my ink stains make me feel like a real scribe. I'm mostly alone, but white-haired Shria comes to take the papers to the khan's chiefs, and twice a day Qacha brings my meals from the kitchen.

Sometimes when I'm sitting on the floor eating with Qacha, I feel about as content as a bird with a good lifting wind. In greeting, we always clasp forearms, touch cheeks, and inhale through our noses so as to breathe in each other's scent. Smell is the voice of the soul, and this greeting is the most intimate. It's common among family and clan, of course, but I've been on my own for so long, I'd forgotten how warm and wonderful it is.

And whenever I can, I return to the kitchen to see my lady and the other girls or walk around the stables and dairy and soak in the cheery summer sun. The window is wonderful, but any walls remind me of the tower.

I haven't seen her khan since I came to this small, clean room.

Day 111

Shria called me to the khan's chamber today. I was startled to see it full, seven of the khan's chiefs present, several shamans, all arguing about Khasar and scouting reports and the state of the city with the refugees near bursting the walls. Three other scribes were there. I joined them by the wall, taking notes of the talk as quickly as I could.

Khan Tegus never looked at me. I'm a mucker maid. I guess I needed to be reminded of that. So, good. Fine. Sometimes my fancy gets to floating inside me, threatening to carry me away like a leaf on a wind. Better to be a stone.

Day 112

Shria came flustering for me this morning.

"Come! Quick!"

We raced down the corridors, up another flight of stairs, and into the last of the khan's chain of rooms.

The first thing I noticed was a man lying on the floor and bleeding, bleeding fast. Another man was in the corner, his ankles and wrists tied with sashes, animal scratches on his face. Three men with drawn swords were guarding the bound man, all tense as a gher roof, shaking slightly as if hoping for a reason to stab the bound man through. I stopped on the threshold. I wobbled.

"Here's the mucker girl, my lord," said Shria.

The khan pulled me toward the wounded man. "My friend is hurt. Sing for him."

"I . . . I can't, my lord. A healing song can't stop blood from flowing or close a wound."

"Help him, Dashti."

How I longed for the voice of Evela and the strength of Carthen, for powers as mighty as the desert shamans are rumored to possess, for a way to force that man's body to do my will and heal itself. But I felt as thin as grass. I sat by the man's head, I touched his face. My body shook so hard I thought I heard my bones rattle, and I wondered if my limbs would fall right off.

Sing to him, Dashti, I ordered myself, but before I could find a tune, I got to thinking of Mama with the fever, her skin as yellow as this paper I write on, her lips dry like a snake shedding its skin. For hours, for days I sang to her. I pushed my soul into the words till my voice rasped to ashes. But she fell asleep, deeper and deeper till her skin went cold.

A shaman knelt beside me, letting his hands hover over the bleeding man's chest. Until I recognized his face, I didn't realize he was a shaman because he was dressed only in a robe and for some reason had removed his tassled hat and belt with nine mirrors.

"I feel a pulsing heat," said the shaman, his eyes closed. "The life heat leaves his body even as his blood does. His soul is teetering on a threshold, undecided to live or die."

"Help him to live," said Khan Tegus. He was speaking to me and to the shaman and he seemed near crying. "Tell his soul to live!"

Who am I to tell a man to live? Who am I to claim the powers of the Ancestors? I moved aside so the shaman could have more room to do his holy work. He's climbed the Sacred Mountain and seen the faces of the Ancestors. I have no place beside him.

I sat quietly in a corner, though I was tempted to curse like the horse wranglers and kick a chair. I was so angry at myself for not being smart enough, for not being a true healer, but I just sing the easing songs, the slow and cheery songs, the animal songs.

Later

When Qacha brought dinner to my room, she whispered that the bleeding man is an important chief to the khan.

"And the man who stabbed him?" I asked.

"An assassin. Sent by Lord Khasar to kill Khan Tegus, or so Koke heard."

"What less should we expect from the lord of the realm named for Under, god of tricks?"

"True enough, but Under played a trick back on him today. A shaman was present, and when the assassin attacked, I hear the shaman took fox form and leaped between the khan and the assassin. It seems not even Lord Khasar's warrior would dare to harm a fox."

"Ah," I said, the animal scratches on the assassin's face making sense, and the shaman wearing just his robe. He must've lost his clothes when he changed. Would that I'd been there to see that!

So it seems Under played everyone today. The khan is unharmed, but the assassin's blade still found a true mark. He's a slippery one, that Under. I knelt to the north and prayed thanks that Khan Tegus was protected, but I don't much like depending on the god of tricks.

Day 113

Morning was still as dark as night when someone tapped at my door. I wrapped my wool robe over my sleep clothes, thinking it must be Shria with an errand. Instead I found my lady's khan.

He looked as tired as dawn, and he leaned against my door and just stared at me for a time, eyes half closed. I hadn't realized that I'd stopped breathing until I heard him breathe in deeply. He said, "I know you'll say it's hopeless, that you won't be able to help, but Dashti, will you come with me?"

I didn't ask what he meant as I followed him down the dark corridor. I'd been too startled to think of putting on shoes, and the floor was slippery with cold. The blind walls around us reminded me of the tower, and I spent the walk imagining what those three years would've been like if my companion in the dark had been someone else.

We entered his chambers and the air was thick with the sweet smoke of burning juniper. A shaman woman was doing her wild dance between the bed and the fire, beating a flat drum, the tassels on her hat flying.

"You may rest for a moment, holy one," said Khan Tegus, and the woman stopped spinning and sat in the corner. For a moment, I could see my own face reflected in one of the nine mirrors on her belt. I looked away.

The bleeding man was asleep on a low couch, his chest rising and falling too fast for sleep. Khan Tegus knelt by the bed. I knelt beside him.

"The shamans tell me they've done what they can, but there's no change," said Khan Tegus. "They tell me that when all that blood poured out of Batu, his soul flowed with it. Now it's dislodged from his breast and wavering on the edge of his body."

The man's face was pale. I touched his arm and found the skin was prickly hot. "His soul doesn't know whether to stay or go."

The khan met my eyes straight on. He didn't blink as he said, "Help it to stay."

I looked at the shaman, squatting by the fire and humming. I knew to complete her training, she must've climbed the Sacred Mountain, fasted from all food, and prayed for four days, naked under the sky. Bareness is the ultimate debasement, so that's why shamans do it, to submit themselves completely to the

Ancestors, and even more, to prostrate themselves under the Eternal Blue Sky, naked and new as a baby.

These shaman healers had their souls washed by the Eternal Blue Sky. Who was I to try where they had failed?

"My lord—," I started.

"Please." The khan rubbed his eyes so I couldn't see his face, but I could hear how his voice was worn to crumbling. "Batu is my friend, but he's also my chief of war. Khasar is on the move, set to tear out the throat of my army, and I can't lose anyone else. Please help him, Dashti."

Right then, I would've scaled the forbidden heights of the Sacred Mountain for him, but I didn't know how to do what he asked.

The healing songs help things be as they are at first, as they want to be again. I wondered, could I sing to the man's very soul? Help it return to his breast and sleep peacefully again? If there's a song for souls, my mama never taught it.

I wanted to run away, I felt so useless and ashamed! But I couldn't. Khan Tegus had given me a pine bough and My Lord the cat, he let me sing the pain out of him, he remembered my name. I had to try.

I took Batu's hand, closed my eyes so my whole world was touch and sound, said a silent prayer to

Evela, goddess of sunlight and songs, and began to sing. I didn't know what song would come out of my mouth until I heard it.

"Little bird, little bird, that twits and flits and flies. Little bird, little bird, unfold your feathered skies."

It's not a healing song, it's a play song, one the mucker children sing in the spring, racing in a circle, leaping over stones. I almost laughed to hear myself sing it. I don't know why that song felt right. Maybe because it makes such a happy noise; the tune likes to skip on my tongue and tickle my throat.

The shaman glared at me through the tassels on her hat, as though saying, *That's not a reverent song for the dying!* I glared back, as though saying, *The whole point is to stop the dying!* I think Khan Tegus must've noticed the abundance of glares, for after a minute he dismissed the shaman from the room. We were alone now. I kept singing.

Sing to his soul, I told myself. So I sang more happy songs, things to remind him of how rich is living, how blue is the Eternal Sky, how good roasted meat tastes with a sprinkling of salt, how the steppes fill with thousands of yellow heartsong flowers after the frost breaks. When I began the lighthearted song that goes, "Bread on the stones, Mama, and how the belly groans," her khan joined in, knowing that one from his own childhood, I guess. Beneath my own voice, his felt like a horsehair blanket, rough and warm.

After a time, I let her khan sing that one alone, while I wove in "the earth breathes, the earth sings, its soul moves in the rivers," and other healing songs for sickness and injury.

Batu's breathing slowed, his voice mumbled sleepily in his throat, and if I were smart enough to know such things, I'd say his soul slipped back inside, curled up like a cat in his chest, and purred to be home.

By then, her khan was sitting on the floor beside me. He leaned his back against the couch, stretching his legs out before him. I leaned back, too. We both knew Batu was better. We didn't have to say it.

"You may return to your room, if you wish," he said.

I shrugged. "I won't sleep any more tonight."

"Neither will I." He watched the flames in the hearth. "It's a wondrous gift you have. I can't help wonder how muckers know songs that shamans have never heard."

I sighed before I talked, just because it felt right. "The people of stone walls, the ones who live in cities, they have healers to call and shamans to bless them. But the people of the felt walls, alone with the wind and grass, would die if Evela, goddess of sunlight, hadn't taken pity on us. She gave muckers the healing songs to help us keep living beneath her sunshine. Or so my mama said. And I believe her. You'd be a fool to doubt her. The grasses themselves bowed down before her foot touched them."

He chuckled, and when I asked him why, he said he'd had such a mother, too. She'd gone to the Ancestors' Realm seven years ago, but was such a powerful presence he still thinks to check that his sash is tied straight each morning so she won't scold him.

"And she named you Tegus," I muttered.

"What was that?"

"I was just thinking," I said, "how you can tell something about a woman by what she names her children. Tegus means *perfect* in the naming language."

He made a face. "I haven't always relished that name. My cousins gave me much grief about it growing up."

"I think it's lovely. I mean . . ." I returned my gaze to the fire, because it was easier to talk to him that way. "What I mean to say is, it's lovely to think of your mother holding her first baby, and looking at your fingers and toes, your eyes, your lips, and saying, 'Perfect. He's perfect. My Tegus.'"

"I can imagine her saying those very words." He was quiet a moment. "Dashti. That means 'one who is good luck,' doesn't it?"

"Another name that caused teasing. It's not an easy thing to wear a mark of bad luck on my face and have a name that means good luck. The story goes that a clan sister helped with my birth, and when she saw me, she told my mother, 'She should be called Alagh,' meaning *mottled*, you know. My father saw me and said, 'You must call her Alagh so all know she is destined for bad luck.' So my mama said, 'Her name is Dashti.'"

He raised his bowl of milk tea. "Let's drink to stubborn mothers."

He took a long sip, then offered the bowl to me. The same that he had drunk from. He shared a drink with me, gentry with commoner. I took it with both my hands to show my reverence, and when I drank, the warmth seemed to fill not just my belly, but my entire body down to my toes.

We kept watching the fire and talking about mothers and other things. I tried to keep in mind his status, but I was drowsy, and the sight of a fire sings its own kind of healing song, one that seems to say, "Easy, slow and easy, all is well." It reminded me of his third visit to the tower, when he sat on the ground and leaned against the wall, and I leaned on the other side, and we just talked. And the Ancestors let us.

He looked at my feet and said suddenly, "You're not wearing shoes."

I wiggled my toes. "I guess I'm not. But at least my sash is tied straight."

"Hmph, no comparison. What would your right good mucker mother say to that, walking around in bare feet?"

I had a joke on my lips about skinny ankles and had to choke it back. So near I came to revealing myself!

"What's wrong?" he asked, sitting up at my silence. "Are you hungry? Should I send for something?"

"No, strangely. Usually I could eat a plate of anything and be ready for another, but right now I don't want to eat." And I didn't. But mostly I didn't want him to get up and call for someone who might stay. Food wasn't worth losing our bit of peace.

He mumbled agreement and relaxed again, his back against the couch. Our shoulders almost touched. The heat between us mingled.

"May I ask you something, honored khan?"

"If you call me Tegus," he said. "You helped save Batu. You earned the right to say my name."

"Tegus," I said, and the name in my mouth tasted wonderful, so in my heart I quickly asked forgiveness from Nibus, god of order. "A few weeks ago, when I sang to your deep pain, what was it? What old hurt were you carrying?"

"Nothing I didn't deserve." His eyelids half closed and I thought he wouldn't answer, and rightly he shouldn't have—it was an impertinent question. But soon he went on. "I was in love with a lady once. I thought I didn't have the power to save her, so I didn't even try. And she came to harm because of my reluctance, my stupidity."

I didn't argue with him about the stupidity part, Ancestors forgive me. I did wonder, *Why didn't you come back for us? Back for her?* But I didn't dare ask her khan that, and I couldn't ask Tegus. The song of the fire's snaps seemed a bit sadder now, as though it realized it was dying and was sorry to go.

Behind us, Batu stirred in his sleep, and at the same time Tegus and I both placed a hand on the war chief's arm. Tegus smiled at me when he saw that my instinct to comfort had been the same as his, and he didn't withdraw. The moment made me imagine how her khan will be as a father, how he'll sit up at night and hold his wife's hand and talk to her as she rocks the baby to sleep.

Saren could only be happy with such a man.

He said he was in love with her. I am her maid. I must do what I can.

Day 115

Today I managed to get my half day free during Saren's time off. We walked through the streets where folk who escaped from Titor's Garden and Goda's Second Gift pitch tents and sleep on doorsteps. Saren kept her arm in mine, leaning as if she needed the support, all that air and sky making her feel unsteady.

"I've spent some time with your khan, my lady, and I know he's a good man. He's safe." It was hard not to laugh outright as I added, "He's not plotting to kill you with arrows and knives."

She frowned but didn't argue, so I went on.

"I'm going to say something that you may not want to hear—being in the tower did you harm, made you believe things that just aren't real. I'm sorry it's so, but it's true."

"I know," she said, really quiet, but she still said it.

"So you need to trust me, my lady, when I tell you that Khan Tegus is safe. He'll take care of you.

He was very much in love with you, and still is, despite his engagement. Though it's been years, my lady, he remembers you with sighs."

"He does?" She breathed in as she asked it.

"Oh yes. He still remembers the words of your letters, and I think he holds the image of your face in his heart."

She seemed confused, or maybe she was just thinking. With my lady, both attitudes appear the same. But she wasn't arguing, which was more than I'd hoped for.

"He's engaged," I admitted, "and that's another matter. But if he still loves you, and he promised himself to you first, then Lady Vachir can have nothing to say. There is a risk, but how can we keep living in his very house and not let him know?"

She stopped walking. Her face was fully in the sun, and I noticed how pale she was, how little she must leave the kitchens, how she's still bricked up in the tower. Her eyes spoke it most of all—dull, never looking far ahead.

"But . . . but he didn't come back."

I had no answer for that. "I don't know why, but I do know his heart was broken, and you have the power to heal him. How can you not?"

"I can't just go to him, claiming to be Lady Saren."

"But you *are* Lady Saren."

She looked at her hands. The wash water had done its damage — fingertips splitting, palms callused and bruised, skin mottled red almost as dark as my own birthmarks. Didn't I once take an oath to keep her hands beautiful? My heart turned, and if we hadn't been standing in the street, I would've knelt before her and begged forgiveness. Instead, I took her worn hands and kissed each one.

"How I've failed you, my lady. I will help you. I'll do whatever you ask to set you back in your place again."

She wrinkled her brow, thinking hard for a few moments, then said, "Pretend to be me, Dashti. Say you're me. Find out what he'd do, how he'd react, and if it's favorable, then I'll tell all."

"My lady, it was one thing in the tower when he couldn't see my face —"

"He won't know me by sight."

"It's been years, I know, but still . . ." My face. My blotchy face and arm, my dull hair, my solid mucker body, my everything that isn't like my lady.

"You swore an oath," she said.

And so I had. Oath breakers will find no haven in the Ancestors' Realm where my mama waits. And besides, it's not fair to ask my lady to risk her life against Lady Vachir's wrath. I am her maid. It should be my duty to keep her from harm and face it myself. But to pretend to be Lady Saren again, and this time not hidden in a dark tower but out under the Eternal Blue Sky. . . .

My stomach's icy cold, and I don't feel like writing anymore. I'll sketch instead.

Day 119

I wasted three days worrying, praying for the lie I hadn't yet made, and imagining Tegus's face when I spoke the false words "I'm Lady Saren." Three days wasted, and my lady remains a scrubber indefinitely, because now her khan is gone.

His warriors marched today, sudden, like when the wind shifts from west to south. They left as soon as word came from Beloved of Ris—Khasar's armies are advancing on that realm.

Everyone thought Khasar would attack Song for Evela next because he proclaimed he'd have Tegus's title of khan for himself. It seems he isn't coming for it yet, instead striking at the weaker realm first.

We may not hear news for days and weeks. I feel set to cry and kick and curse.

There's not as much scribe work now while the khan is absent, so I volunteered to go back to the kitchens. I don't mind leaving my little room so much. Privacy begins to feel somewhat like loneliness.

Day 122

No news of her khan. It's getting cold at night. I wonder if he has enough blankets.

Day 125

Still no news. I feel dog-crazy, as if I'd like to bite someone. This kitchen smells.

Day 126

Mama would scold me. All I seem to do is mope, mope, mope. No one has enough news for me. Osol set to winking at me again, but I'm all worry with no space left to sigh for a cutter boy. I wash rags as if I held Lord Khasar's neck in my hands. I scrub pots as though the faster they're clean the sooner the war will be done. Cook declared at the rate I was going I'd soon have her position. Then she laughed. Scrubber is the lowest position in the kitchens, of course.

"I'm a scribe," I said.

She laughed again.

And while I mope, my lady scowls.

"You swore an oath," she whispered at me while we scrubbed. "And then you didn't do it."

I washed my next pot a little harder.

Day 127

I can't believe . . . the news is too big to write, I can't make my letters large enough to contain what I have to say. But I must say it somehow.

He's alive! He's here, he's strong and pretty as ever he was, and purring like to shake the house down.

My Lord the cat, my beautiful cat.

He must've escaped the wolf, must've scratched that demon's eyes and run straight home. In the way he used to know when it was morning though the tower was all darkness, he must've known how to find the land of her khan again. Cats are wise like that. They have a shaman's eyes.

Today was my half day free, and I went to visit Mucker in the stable, only he was out pulling a cart. So I just wandered, because the sun was pleasant and round above me and made my shadow look strong and straight. I was thinking how you can't tell if a person's beautiful or not by her shadow when I saw a gray tail disappear into the dairy.

He was gone so quickly I couldn't be sure, so I ran after him, slipped on some spilled milk, and slid under the dairyman's legs. He hollered at me and before he could kick me out, I blurted, "Excuse me, but my cat came in here."

My Lord the cat leaped up on a stall, balancing above our heads.

"And how am I to know that he's yours?" the dairyman asked.

Khan Tegus gave him to me, I wanted to say, but of

course I couldn't. If I'd thought of a good lie, I would've spoken it just then and let the Ancestors strike me dumb, so desperately I wanted to hold My Lord again.

I'd started to stutter something when My Lord leaped down onto my shoulder and wrapped his tail around my neck, just as he used to do in the tower. The dairyman laughed.

"Looks like he's yours, right enough. Get him out of here, then."

He remembers me. Don't these letters I'm writing fairly dance off the page? He's alive, and he remembers me!

These past days, it seemed I could scarcely draw breath for feeling so gray, and then today . . . well, the change makes me think about the sky over the steppes, cloudy one moment and Eternal Blue Sky the next. There's never a day that we don't see some blue sky. That's the way with a mucker's emotions, too. My mama used to say, "Are you sad? Then just wait a minute."

Day 128

My Lord the cat slept beside me last night. I didn't wake up once.

Day 129

All the girls are utterly smitten with My Lord, of course. He sits on my shoulders, and they gather around and coo. Qacha can't help petting him whenever she passes by, even when her hands are sudsy. A wet coat puts My Lord in grumpy spirits, but he never shirks the attention. Cook complained about him at first, but soon she was saying things like, "That cat's prettier than a man," and "I'd eat my own toenails before I'd cook that one up."

Day 131

I love My Lord the cat! I love him, I love him. He sleeps again in the curve of my belly, he purrs when I wake in the night for wondering about the war and her khan and the lie I must tell. His rumbling song soothes me back to sleep. He is even better than windows.

Day 133

Last night as I lay down by the kitchen hearth, My Lord loped in from somewhere and took his place against my side. Snores already surrounded us. As I settled in, I noticed that my lady was awake, watching me. Watching us.

She whispered, "Why is he your cat? Didn't Khan Tegus give him to me?"

"Well, he gave him to me—"

"After you told him you were Lady Saren."

I didn't answer. My heart felt like a furnace spitting fire.

"I think he should be mine." She reached out and grabbed him from my arms and pulled him to her own side. He writhed free and came back. Again she grabbed him, and this time in the struggle he clawed her arm and made an angry "rawr!" that provoked Gal to snort in her sleep.

"I'm sorry, my lady," I said, though I wasn't. I liked very much that My Lord preferred me. I rather felt like clawing her myself.

I hadn't even realized until that moment how over these past weeks, I'd begun to bubble with dark things, and my heart was boiled hard like tough mutton. I don't think I've ever truly hated a thing in my life like I hated Saren then. Hated everything about her—the whine her voice took as though she thought herself a child of six, her perfect face and shiny black hair, her honored father, her smell, her shaking hands when she stood under the sky. Her cowardice, her slowness. Her everything. I hated her.

I curled back up with My Lord alongside my body and pretended to be asleep. After a time, I heard sniffling. There's nothing more aggravating in the world than the midnight sniffling of the person you've decided to hate.

Finally I sat up, and My Lord the cat, annoyed with all the talking and wiggling, sprang away to the door and set to cleaning his paws.

"What's wrong now, my lady?" I asked, and not very nicely.

She started to cry. Of course. "I order you to do one more thing for me."

She wants the cat, I thought. Let her try and take him.

"I want," she said, sniffling and sobbing, "I want you to kill me."

My lady never plays games with words. She means everything fully, she drinks down the world whole and spits nothing out. I knew she meant what she said, and it set me spinning.

"No," I whispered, my throat dry as salt meat.

"I order you to —"

"Order until you're out of breath," I said, glancing at Gal and Qacha, who were still dead asleep. "If I did such a thing, there'd be no place for me in the Ancestors' Realm, nor for you either. We'd wander in the gray beyond the borders forever, with nowhere to sit and no milk to drink, and I'd never see my mama again. Punishment for disobeying your order can't be worse than that."

Saren turned on her side, her back to me, and set to sobbing so violently I thought she'd vomit.

"I don't want to live anymore," she said, the words almost lost with each wet sob. "Every night I think the sun's gone forever, but when it rises in the morning anyway I wish it wouldn't. Because then I spend all day scrubbing. And my chest hurts like it's stuffed with rocks. And everyone's dead in my father's city. Because of me. All those bodies, because of me. Because I wouldn't marry Khasar. It's my fault and it's too much and I can't carry it anymore. And Khasar's still coming for me anyway. He'll find the tower empty and come looking. And Khan Tegus will never love me because I'm not clever and I smell like dirty pots and I want to die, Dashti. Please, I can't do it myself, I've tried. I'm too afraid and I'll do it wrong. You have to do it for me. Please, Dashti."

I didn't move all the while she pleaded. I felt buried by her sobs and words.

I turned toward My Lord and very quietly sang the cat song, the slow, sliding song that goes, "Twitch and itch, the world is meat, the world is mine." He put his nose out as if he could smell the song, then he padded to me and pressed his head against mine. I felt a jab in my heart as though someone had just told me that he was dead after all and never coming home.

Then I sat behind my lady, sang the cat song, wrapped my arms around her shoulders, and placed the cat onto her lap.

"Now you sing," I said.

At first she was timid and still sobbing too hard for the cat to hear any tune, but she calmed and her voice found the song.

"Temple to tail, purr zipping through." Her voice was softer than mine, but sweeter too. Whereas my singing's a hot, hearty meal, hers is a drink of sugared milk.

I didn't know if My Lord would accept her song or if he'd scorn her still—it's always the hearer's choice to heed a calling song, and cats are more stubborn than most. But he is a friendly cat, a happy soul. He curled up inside her crossed legs. After a time, he purred. She's no mucker, but that song she sang as well as my own mama.

She kept on singing and stroked his fur, but she stayed rigidly still as if afraid to spook him.

"It's all right. You can lie down," I said. "I think he'll stay with you."

Very slowly, very carefully, she eased herself down on her side. My Lord curled up beside her with a pleased rumble.

It was a long time before I slept that night, and I slept fitfully. When I sat up again, the fire was lower, and everyone was still snoozing except for Saren, who kept whisper-singing all night long and stroking his fur. My Lord the cat lay asleep, nestled in the curve of her body.

Except for singing my mama into the Ancestors' Realm, giving My Lord to Saren was the hardest thing I've ever done. And I felt emptied, a well dug out of my chest, and as pathetic as a three-legged cricket. But, strangely, as I rolled over to find sleep again, I realized that I didn't hate her anymore.

Day 134

When My Lord the cat came in from his morning prowl, Saren sang the song for cats, and he jumped onto her shoulder, curling his tail around her neck.

Qacha touched my elbow. "Dashti, Sar is —"

"I know," I said. It's a gross sin among muckers to sing a calling song to another person's animal, so I explained, "I gave her permission. He's her cat now. He was all along, actually. I was the one who first took him from her."

Qacha shook her head as though she didn't believe me. She doesn't think so highly of Saren. Not knowing that she's an honored lady, how can she be expected to be patient with this girl who doesn't do her share of work, who won't talk to anyone but me, who fusses like a small child when I'm not around? I understand Qacha's glares, but then I see Saren smiling at the cat as he extends his nose to hers, and my heart does a little flip. A happy flip, I think.

Still no news from her khan's army.

Day 136

Something has happened, and I thought I needed to write it down so my nerves can quiet, but now I hesitate. There was a tribunal today and . . . Ancestors, how my stomach hurts! Let me distract myself with other thoughts first.

I never realized before that every city in the Eight Realms has eight chiefs as well as a lord or lady—nine rulers to mirror the sacred nine, the eight Ancestors plus the Eternal Blue Sky. Each chief serves one of the Ancestors and is always of the opposite gender. For instance, Batu, the war chief, serves Carthen, goddess of strength. I like to see things ordered, and right now I need a bit of calming, so I'll jot it down here:

Khan Tegus (lord of the city)—serves the Eternal Blue Sky, and so is over all.

Chief of war (commands the warriors)—serves Carthen, goddess of strength.

Chief of city (maintains walls, structures, and trade routes)—serves Ris, god of roads and towns.

Chief of animals (keeps livestock, dairies, monitors hunting in the woods)—serves Titor, god of animals.

Chief of food (supervises the farms that feed the city and the market, and keeps the town's food supply) — serves Vera, goddess of farms and food.

Chief of order (sits in judgment) — serves Nibus, god of order.

Chief of night (leads the night watch, keeps the peace) — serves Goda, goddess of sleep.

Chief of light (hosts festivals and directs the shamans) — serves Evela, goddess of sunlight.

Once I learned all this, I wanted to know, what about the eighth chief? The one who would serve Under, god of tricks? Koke explained that she's the invisible chief, and there's always an empty chair for her at counsels. That thought scattered skin prickles down my back.

So I'm going to record now what's happened, though my stomach squeezes just to think of it. But it pesters my mind, so I will. The tribunal today was for Osol, the boy who used to wink at me, who once gave me a wildflower. Word in the kitchens is that he and a girl were having loud words in the dairy, and the chief of animals was passing through. When she heard the ruckus, she commanded them to silence, but Osol was in a rage and pushed the chief, and when she fell, he kicked her.

For minor offenses, the chief of order would

decide punishment, but this is not minor. The chief of animals is one of the khan's cousins, so she's gentry. Without Khan Tegus and Batu, there are still six chiefs in the city (plus the empty chair), and it only takes. four of the nine to pass judgment. So they met together and they decided—Osol will hang tonight on the south wall.

I know this is the punishment for such an offense. I know I shouldn't be stunned, but I never knew a person who was hanged. I've glimpsed the bodies sometimes, hanging there, but I never knew. It changes it all. It makes me cry to miss seeing his smile, it makes me wince at the memory of his winking, it makes me shudder to imagine how he's feeling tonight. It makes me feel as if I'm the one who will hang.

He shouldn't have struck gentry, no, but Ancestors, does he really deserve death? Sometimes I wonder if that eighth chief, the absent one who serves Under, isn't getting more of a voice in things than we suspect.

Day 137

Osol died last night. I won't go see his body.

Day 140

I haven't had time to pick up the brush and ink these past days because I've been working my fingers to the marrow, but here's my news — so has my lady! She scrubs and mops and hauls water, and she hums all the while. And when Cook says, "Hurry with that pot, girl," my lady smiles, dimples and all. Under strike me silly if I lie.

She has her willow tree moments, she has her mopes, and she still startles at sudden sounds like a dropped pot or slammed door. But other times, in the in-between easy moments, she's calmer than pond water. Sometimes, she even seems happy.

I keep kissing her cheek and once I tickled her side, and hear this — she laughed! She says such things as, "Look at how clean that rag is," and "That's a pot I'd eat out of, sure enough." After she worked through her stack of pots today, Cook let her take over the stirring of the soup kettle, and I thought Saren would burst from joy. It's that cat's doing, no doubt in me. The creature loves her true as true, and she knows it. It's the knowing that's made the difference, I think. He wraps around her ankles or neck, even when she isn't singing to him. He finds her at night and purrs into her belly. A cat can make you feel well rested when you're tired or turn a rage into a calm just by sitting on your lap. His very nearness is a healing song.

We've all been worked to bruising lately because now we cook for Lady Vachir and a large entourage from Beloved of Ris. They fled the war and a feared winter siege. I wish they'd brought more news with them. So far, I've learned little about our khan's warriors and how they fare, but surely the Ancestors will protect them.

When her khan returns, I don't rightly know how I'll tell him I'm Lady Saren. Having his current betrothed sleeping in his house does add a complication to this already thorny situation. Thank the Ancestors I hadn't made the claim before. With Khan Tegus gone, there'd be no one to prevent Lady Vachir from deeming me a threat to her betrothal and taking my life. That's how the law's written, that's how Nibus, god of order, made the world. And Osol's death has reminded me that the chiefs wouldn't hesitate to carry out that law.

Day 145

Last week, Cook was so impressed with my lady's new devotion to working, she moved Saren out of the scrubbing kitchen and into the presenting kitchen, where she arranges food on the platters before they're taken up. It's one step below server and one of the highest duties any kitchen worker achieves. Saren fairly glowed at the news. My Lord entwines himself in her ankles, and she hums as she works, her cheeks bright and pink as though she were a healthy mucker girl living under the sun.

"Cook only chose her because she's pretty," said Gal, "in case she moves up to server. It's not fair. You're the fastest worker in the kitchens. It should've been you."

"It doesn't matter. I'm a scribe," I said, though I don't know if I'll ever be again.

Today was my free half day, and I sprang outdoors and into the city. I was anxious to see if I could find any news about the khan's army, but all the talk was the same — Khasar invincible, bloodshed imminent — enough dismay and fear to please Under, god of tricks, for years to come.

I passed the jobbers market where refugees stand in long rows hoping for employment, all holding the symbols of their trade: jewelers with magnifying glasses, goldsmiths with tiny mallets, teachers with books, merchants with scales, smiths with hammers, carpenters with saws, and scribes with brushes and ink. I felt kind of funny when I saw those scribes, wondering if I'd join them there after my lady marries.

Day 150

We've all been in such a flurry only now am I able to write. Khan Tegus is back, wounded, a tenth of his warriors dead. They rode hard into Song for Evela, bringing in villagers and shutting the city gates behind them.

I spent an entire helpless day scrubbing so hard I feared I'd make holes in the pots, until at last Shria came for me. Since then I haven't spent much time here in my quiet little room. I only came now to get some sleep because I was so tired I was beginning to see frogs leaping about in the corner of my eye. It'd make me laugh if times weren't so scary.

Three days I've spent with the shaman healers in Khan Tegus's room, singing until my throat's fair scalded with songs. He bears an arrow wound through his side and it's turned to fever. His breath wheezes while he sleeps, a sound that makes my own skin hurt as if a thousand red ants bit me at once.

The shamans change his bandages, give him drinks, dance with their drums, pray toward the Sacred Mountain, burn incense, and read the cracks in fire-heated sheep bones for any signs of hope. I hold Tegus's warm hand and sing and sing. My lord, my poor lord. It's too much like my mama's end. Times there are these past days when I lay my head on his couch and begin to dream as soon as my eyes shut, and my dreams are always the blackness of the tower falling over all the world, an endless city of corpses, and my lord's body there, too, cast on the ground.

I need to try and rest so I can return to him and sing some more.

Day 151

The shaman healers dismissed me. Tegus isn't improving. My singing does nothing. So they said. And I was lying here on my horsehair blanket and believing them. But then I remembered how Tegus asked me to help Batu, how he said please. Please, Dashti. And I did. And he got better.

Then I got to wake-dreaming about a time when I was ten and I fell into a thorn bush and scraped my arm, and it swelled and swelled, my arm on fire, my whole body trembling with heat. Mama and I were alone on the edge of a great forest, with no one around to help for miles, but I remember how calm she was, how cool her hands on my face. And while I thrashed and sweated on my bed, she never stopped singing. On the third night, I woke from death dreams and looked up into her eyes, and I remember how I could see her confidence. She knew I could heal. So I curled up on her lap and felt her song move inside me until my skin cooled and I could sleep a healing sleep.

I'm going to go back to the khan's chamber now. I'm going to keep singing.

Day 153

It's still dark, the autumn morning too tired to rise, and I'm writing by firelight. The shaman healers feared that the khan's fever was the kind that comes with an open wound and stays and stays until it takes a warrior down days after battle. But at midnight his fever broke. They said it was a miracle, mumbled prayers to the north, then left or curled up to sleep on pallets on the floor.

I stayed by my lord's couch. It was the same couch where Batu had lain ill, where Tegus and I had leaned back together and stared at the fire, touching Batu's arm. This time, I touched the khan's arm and watched his chest rise and fall.

Over the past six days, I'd sung all the healing songs I knew, I'd stitched each one with my memories of sunlight, I'd poured any blue sky from my soul into the sounds. Now I was a snail's shell. There was nothing left for me to give.

So I sang him the nonsense song he'd given me in the tower. My voice was a horse's bray, I'm sure, raw with little sleep and so much singing. But I didn't want him to feel alone without any music to keep him company. "The piglet rolled while squealing, moving by snout and by jaw, happily snuffling for treats without use of hoof or paw." I sang it wrong. It needs a happy voice, the words jigging and the tune lilting up. All I could manage was a slow whisper, but I think it served.

I kept one hand on his arm and smoothed the hair back from his brow with the other. I sang. His eyes opened, and I should've withdrawn my hands. Really, I should've scuttled under the couch and hidden for shame. But I kept singing. And I kept one hand on his arm and the other on his forehead. And I stroked his hair back.

He watched me while I sang. He looked at my eyes. My heart felt so big, it hurt against my ribs. At last I felt some shame and started to pull away, but he put his hand over mine on his chest to hold me there longer. He knew I was just the mucker girl, the scrubber, and still he wanted to keep me close. I don't think I breathed for a long, long while.

I remembered in the tower before he came to visit, wondering if he'd been formed by Evela, goddess of sunlight. I think it might be true after all, because I began to squint wretchedly and couldn't look at his face.

When he slept again, I left him with the healers. I think I'll curl up in my horsehair blanket until the shivering in my limbs stops.

Day 155

This morning when I entered her khan's chamber, he was sitting up, his face not so pale. The icy fear that had lodged in my belly this last week at last began to melt. He was speaking with one of his chiefs, his face troubled, but when he saw me, he broke out in a grin so wide I have to believe it came right from his soul. Then he held his arms out before him, palms down, inviting me to clasp forearms as though we were of a clan, meeting again after a long absence.

"A warm greeting, Dashti," he spoke in the formal manner, though the cheerfulness in his smile made me think he wanted to laugh.

"A warm greeting, my lord," I replied, kneeling beside his bed and grasping his forearms with my palms up.

Then he did what I didn't expect from gentry to commoner—as we gripped arms, he pulled me closer, resting his cheek against mine, and inhaled through his nose, taking in the breath of my soul. I was too terrified to breathe. I hope he didn't notice that I didn't sniff as well, because refusing would mean insult, but I couldn't help but think, *Did he keep my shirt from the tower? Does he remember the scent?*

When he released me, he said, "So, just come from milking the sheep, have you?" which made me snort in laughter. It's a common mucker tease after a cheek greeting and means, of course, that I smell like a ewe, which I know I don't because I've been indoors for two weeks and bathed two days ago. His sly half smile made me think he'd actually sought out some other mucker and asked for something right silly to say to me.

So I answered, "I have, in fact. They send greeting to their brother Tegus."

Day 156

This morning, Tegus welcomed me again with an arm clasp and cheek touch. I wasn't startled this time, and I breathed in at his neck. How can I describe the scent of his skin? He smells something like cinnamon—brown and dry and sweet and warm. Ancestors, is it wrong for me to know that? To write it? Is it wrong for me to imagine laying my head on his chest and closing my eyes and breathing in his smell?

Yes, it is wrong. I won't think it again.

He told me he likes me close by, says my singing eases the pain. Even though I don't always sing. Mostly we talk. Often we laugh, at least until his arrow wound pierces him and the shaman healers shoo me away. But I always return before long, and they always let me back in. And I sing and we laugh.

I haven't touched him again, as I did when he

first woke from the fever sleep. I wonder if he remembers or if he thinks it was a dream.

Day 157

I've seen Lady Vachir at last, and she dresses in all
the splendor I would imagine for a lady of a realm.
Indigo powder colors her eyelids, sandlewood per-
fume wafts from her skin, and when she moves, the
dangling pearls in her hair click against her tortoise-
shell combs. One would imagine such finery could

make a lady happy. Not so. I find it easier to imagine a snake smiling than our Lady Vachir. Her mouth is stern, her eyes are sad, her hands lie in her lap like frozen things. For the past two days, she's been attending Tegus in his resting chamber. They brought in a second couch for her and her three lady's maids, and they sit with their backs straight, look at us, and whisper. Khan Tegus and I don't laugh much anymore.

When he's awake, I rest my hands on his belly wound and sing to his bones and skin, his muscles and blood. When he sleeps, I sit in the corner and do scribe work. To tell the truth, the scribbling has become about as much fun as picking lice out of a goat's hair. While I write, I can feel Lady Vachir's gaze prickling me. I don't like it much.

Today when the khan was asleep, Lady Vachir said, "My back pains me. What is that girl's name, the commoner there?"

Batu the war chief was present, and he answered, "Dashti, my lady."

"I want her to use her healing songs on me. Tell her to come to my chamber."

She and her ladies rose and left, and I supposed she meant me to follow, so I did. Halfway there, she claimed that her own chamber was being cleaned and I should take her to mine. So I led her to my little room and lay her on my horsehair blanket. Her three lady's maids stood around me like so many vultures waiting for something meaty to die. I placed my hands on the lady's back and sang the tune with the lilting high parts that says, "Tell me again, how does it go?"

When I finished, she stood and said, "I don't know why they let you hang about. Your song didn't make a drop of difference."

Well, that put some fire in my lungs, sure enough, so I said, "A song can only work if the hearer wills it. Do you perhaps enjoy the back pain? Or maybe your back didn't pain you to begin with?"

She slapped my mouth. What is it about gentry that they're always slapping people? It made me giggle, which made her glare. What's come over me to speak casually and laugh at an honored lady? As she swept out of the room, I noticed her gaze fall on this book, lying in the corner.

From now on, I'll keep it with me. Lady Vachir is the last person in the Eight Realms I'd want to see these words.

I like that woman about as much as I like skin rot in the summer. Maybe she rankles me so because she's standing between my lady and her beloved. Or maybe the woman is just plain unpleasant. I shouldn't be so hard, but there it is. I look at Lady Vachir and I see someone who loves nothing much, who's seen a great deal of death in a short amount of time, and rather than feel sorrow, has decided to turn into stone.

Day 159

These past days in my lord's chamber, all the talk is on Khasar. I try to ignore it and focus on what I'm copying on parchment, because there's nothing more frustrating than hearing of a problem you can't do anything to fix. But I can't help hearing some, and my mind keeps working over the trouble, like chewing on tough meat till my jaw's sore.

I don't like Khasar. I guess I've never been so terrified in my life as the time he flicked burning wood chips into our tower. His voice, even in memory, makes my bones shiver. The sounds of the healing songs remind the body of how it should be, but the sound of his voice had the opposite effect on me. Whatever he uttered, his laugh, his snarl, his words, seemed a song of ill. Just the memory of that sound greases my dreams some nights like fatty pot scrapings smeared on my hands.

The news today was that Khasar's warriors have rested and regrouped from their assault on Lady Vachir's land and are on the march again.

"He'd been laying siege on Beloved of Ris, my lord," said Batu, the war chief, who was healed and standing, strong as a yak after a good summer. "We thought he'd continue his siege through the winter, but he's moving again. Coming this way."

Khan Tegus winced as he sat upright. "I'd hoped to lead our army against him before the bitter cold comes, drive him away from Beloved of Ris. We can't risk the defeat of that realm and the warriors Khasar would add to his own."

"Is he marching to attack Song for Evela?" asked the chief of night, an old man whose fading brown eyes always seemed kindly to me. "Or is he returning to Thoughts of Under for winter?"

"There is no more Thoughts of Under," said Batu. "He's changed the name of his realm to Carthen's Glory."

That silenced everyone. Changed the name of his realm! I'd never heard of, never imagined such a thing. He must mean the change as a mighty prayer to Carthen, goddess of strength.

"Ancestors spare us," someone whispered.

They kept talking about strategy, numbers versus numbers, tactics if he marches on our khan's city and such, but my thoughts were running through a different forest. And though now I should be curled up in my horsehair blanket and long ago asleep, I had to write these thoughts first. They gnaw at me, like to chew me to bits before morning.

Khasar has betrayed Under, god of tricks, by abandoning his name, and pledged himself to Carthen. That makes me think the means to defeat him will be through trickery, not strength. He destroyed the realm of Titor, god of animals, and overthrew the land named for Goda, goddess of sleep. Animals, sleep, and trickery will not be his friends.

These thoughts feel true, but they also seem like the bones of some animal all in a jumble, and I can't see how they fit together and what they form. Maybe the Ancestors are trying to help me, if I could only see.

Day 161

Khasar's warriors are coming closer. It doesn't seem they mean to pass us by. I spend all my time in my lord's chamber now with his chiefs, Lady Vachir, and her whispering maids. When Tegus hurts too much to continue, I'm there to sing. But I miss the laughing parts.

Outside, the world is starting to crack with cold.

Day 162

Many were gathered in the khan's chamber today, the mood stiffer than winter laundry.

"His army is setting up camp outside our walls," said Batu. "They're well equipped with ghers and supplies. They can hunt our woods all winter and get on well."

"But we won't," said the town chief. She has gray and black hair, thick and tangled in braids all over her head. To me, her eyes look as dark as deep wells.

"We were prepared for a siege before," said the food chief, "but now with all the people we've taken in from Titor's Garden, Beloved of Ris, and Goda's Second Gift, not to mention our own villagers who have sought refuge inside the city walls, our stored food won't last two months."

"Longer if we eat the livestock," said the chief of animals. "But that choice is death still, just a slower death, if we have no animals next year."

"And there's the matter of the terror Khasar inspires," said the chief of light. He was resting his forehead on his templed fingers and just then didn't look much as if he were filled with sunshine. "Your warriors brought back tales of Khasar in battle, his ferocity, his eerie strength. And other rumors fill the barracks—the midnight killings in Beloved of Ris, how sentries and warriors disappeared from their posts and their bodies were found with their throats and organs eaten away. These stories will spread throughout the city and cause panic when Khasar attacks. Panic can defeat us as surely as lack of food."

"Worse news," said Batu. "The strange killings have already begun here. This morning, two men were found outside the city gates, ravaged as if by a wild beast."

Did Khasar have some dark alliance with predatory animals? How could he make a wild wolf attack on his command? My thoughts took me back to the tower, and I was hearing in memory the screams that night when a wolf howled. The screams of our guards who never appeared again. It was not a comfortable memory and it made me want to curl up somewhere with a wall at my back.

The chiefs had gone quiet and Khan Tegus was staring at the fire. At length he said, "Batu, what do you recommend?"

"We must attack. Now, before full winter. There's no choice."

"Holy one?" Tegus spoke to a shaman crouched before the fire.

The shaman was removing sheep anklebones from the embers and spreading them out on the floor. He hopped around, squinting at the cracks in the bones, humming sometimes and moaning others. We all waited.

"Foretelling is never exact, my khan," said the shaman. He peered up through his hat tassels. "But your victory won't come from strength, so I see in the bones."

"But it's not exact," said the town chief, "and if we have no other way —"

"Strength can't be your friend," said the shaman, "not since Khasar pledged himself to the goddess Carthen."

"That's right!" I said. I did shout out those words just like that, with all those people present. The shaman spoke the thoughts I'd been thinking, and now in my mind the jumble of bones was beginning to click together. "He'll have Carthen on his side, but he betrayed Under, god of tricks. My lord, I think that might be the way to defeat him."

Some scowled at my outburst, but Tegus asked me, "What hope do you see, Dashti?"

"With no offense to the holy one or to Dashti,"

said Batu, "this isn't the time to bet our lives, our entire realm, on uncertain foretelling or mucker faith. We can't hesitate with this monster, my lord. His assault is terrible. His warriors attack night and day. All say it's as though he never sleeps. We must hit Khasar from the front with every warrior we have."

The khan nodded. "First, Dashti, tell me your thoughts."

I smiled at him. I couldn't help it. He makes me smile. "In battle, we'd have no chance. As the holy one said, with Carthen as his ally, no one can defeat him by means of arms. But Under is bound to be angered by the betrayal. With Under's blessing, I think you can trick Khasar."

"How do you propose we trick him?"

I didn't know, to be honest. I still don't. I just felt coolness and motion inside, like underground rivers running through me, and a sureness that it could be done. Something to do with Under, some trickery involving animals. Perhaps the very wolf Lord Khasar uses to kill warriors at night would turn on him. And somehow, we could make that happen. And then I remembered what Saren once said about Khasar, how he ripped out the throat of a goat. I'd thought she was just tower-addled at the time, but I begin to wonder what she may know.

"Well?" said the town chief. "We're waiting for your cunning plan."

I looked at the shaman for help, but he shrugged. Apparently the sheep bones didn't tell him anything more.

I cleared my throat. "Let me think about it. I—"

One of the chiefs laughed. The chief of animals, I think it was. The chief of camel dung and jackasses. I'm sitting in my room under the horsehair blanket, and I feel that laugh still crawling all over me.

Later

After last I wrote, I begged Cook for a moment with Saren. I took her into the sugar closet, where I feel suffocated but she seems to calm. Cook used to keep it locked, the sugar safe from prying fingers, but this one's empty now, what with traders from the south avoiding the Eight Realms since Khasar began his warring. I took Saren's hands. I met her eyes. She's more relaxed of late, but she set to blinking when she heard me mention Khasar's name.

"My lady, once you told me that Khasar is a beast, that you saw him tear a goat's throat with his teeth. I need to know what you meant. Please tell me."

Her eyes went so wide I thought she'd never blink again, and she shook her head.

"He's here, my lady. His armies are camped outside the wall. They'll do here what they did to Titor's Garden if we don't—"

That was stupidity on my part. I should've kept that news silent, because then she set to shaking and moaning. "He's here, he's coming in for me, I knew he would, he won't let me be, I'd rather be dead—"

"Please, my lady, help me stop him. You know something about Khasar that no one else knows, don't you? What is it?"

"I can't remember," she said.

I was cruel then. I should've spared her the memory, but I pressed. I reminded her of how I've cared for her, how I stayed with her when all others left. I took her shoulders and held her, and I demanded, I ordered her as she would order me.

"By the Ancestors, Saren, tell me!"

"I'm trying, Dashti! I am. I'm trying. I try to think but my thoughts slip out of my hands and everything's darkness and . . ."

She started to cry, which made me realize I hadn't seen her cry in weeks. My poor lady, who is just chaff in the breeze. I held her as I used to do when she was tower-addled; I rocked her and sang the calming song, "Oh, moth on a wind, oh, leaf on a stream." Patience, I told myself, though the knowledge of Khasar's nearness pressed on me, like being out in the heaviest of cold.

I placed my hand on her forehead, and I wove the calming song into the tune for Goda's prayer. The goddess of sleep knows the mind.

After a time, Saren shuddered but stopped crying. Her eyes closed, and she leaned against me as if too tired to sit. While I was singing, My Lord the cat nosed the door ajar and leaped onto her lap, purring under her hand.

She took a deep breath, leaned into me more fully, and told the story she'd been keeping for seven years. "I was twelve years old and was visiting Lord Khasar with my father. His house was vast and cold, like my father's but darker, heavier. We ate a huge feast. I knew my father had hopes of betrothing me to Khasar, but I didn't pay any mind. It seemed as though it had nothing really to do with me. They talked and I ate and played with a little dog that begged under the table. Sometimes I felt Khasar watching me.

"I had a room to myself while we stayed in his house. I thought it was such fun at first. I'd never been alone before, and I could run around the room and climb on the furniture and not worry about my maids and my father and what they thought of me. But at sundown, one of Khasar's men came to my door. His name was Chinua. He was Khasar's war chief and had constantly been at his side. He said my father and Khasar sent him to fetch me."

Her forehead furrowed, but she didn't open her eyes. "I was afraid," she stated simply. "I thought my father would have me do something humiliating before Khasar, like make me dance while they laughed. Or he might slap me, just for show. He never slapped me when we were alone, only in front of people. While I didn't dare refuse my father's call, I did wonder why Chinua seemed full of some secret joke.

"He took me to a courtyard outside Lord Khasar's house, hidden from the eyes of windows. My father wasn't there. Lord Khasar was. He called me Saren. He said, 'Fitting that a girl named for moonlight should see me as only the moon knows me. What do you say, Chinua, is it time to show myself to this moon?' He smiled as the sun finished setting, then he took off all his clothes until he was naked."

"Naked?" This part surprised me. To be naked outside is utter submission, and to be unclothed before anyone besides family is humiliation. "That doesn't sound like Khasar. Why would he willingly debase himself?"

Saren shook her head. "It was different with him. It was as though he was naked to embarrass *me*. It was so strange how Khasar just stood there and laughed at my discomfort. So strange, and I was too afraid to do anything, even to look away. Then the last of the sun-light faded, and I realized why he'd taken off his clothes. It was so they wouldn't rip." She shook. "In the darkness he changed, Dashti. Right in front of me, Khasar changed from a man into a beast. A wolf."

She was quiet for a time and I was glad she was. I had to make sense of this in my own head. In one way it seemed impossible, and in another I felt as if I'd known this all along.

"At first I thought he meant to kill me," Saren continued. "But then I noticed a goat on a tether, and so did Khasar the wolf. Chinua held my head and made me watch while the wolf devoured the animal. I was sure I'd be next, but after the goat was a wrecked carcass, Chinua moved us behind a fire. The wolf ig-nored us, sniffed the air, and ran off into the woods.

"Chinua laughed and laughed, and while he laughed he told me things. That his lord had gone off to hunt in the woods until sunup. That his lord had made quite a bargain with the desert shamans and now was the greatest hunter in all the realms. He said, weren't we lucky to be the only ones alive to know Lord Khasar's secret? Once his lord had allowed another girl to witness his transformation, but she'd told a boy. Afterward, both were found in a pile of their own innards, and if I ever told a soul, I'd be the next goat."

Saren's eyes fluttered, then she closed them again. "I saw Lord Khasar the next morning, and he smiled at me and touched my braids and told me I was beautiful. He'd eaten that goat and hunted other things in the woods as well, and yet when I looked in his eyes, I knew he's never full."

"He killed our tower guards," I said, realizing it as I spoke. "As a wolf, he attacked them, and all those guards with their weapons couldn't kill him. You knew all along and yet you didn't dare tell me."

She sat up and opened her eyes, speaking straight at me with no fear. "I'm telling you now. Khasar becomes a beast at night. In the dark, he's a wolf. I want you to know. I guess he'll kill me like the goat now that I've told, but I don't care anymore. Even if I have to die, I want it to be over. I'm tired of being afraid."

"I'll find a way to end it," I told her.

She rested her head on my shoulder again and didn't cry. I thanked her and I sang to her, and she sighed like a traveler who can rest at last. My poor lady. All she's been for years is a frightened little girl. I've promised her I'll make it better, and I will. I must.

So, how does one trick a wolf?

Day 163

I'm alone in a room, though not the small clean room, not the kitchen, and not my lord's resting chamber. There are windows, but these look out on the city, these are high up. It's not a tower, not quite, though it seems as much like a prison. Just now, I understand my lady's plea that she wanted to die. My stomach feels like the winter sky.

After Saren remembered Khasar's horror, I passed the night drowsing between ideas, then waking again with thoughts of what to do. What to do? Could I trick him into becoming a wolf by daylight? Is there a way to sing him into that shape? What would happen if he did become a wolf under the sun? And how could I get close enough to make it happen?

As soon as it was light enough, I went to Khan Tegus's chamber to share what I knew, but it was filled with chiefs and shamans, and of course Lady Vachir and her vulture maids sitting on their perch.

As I entered, the war chief was saying, "He's

declaring he won't attack Song for Evela if we give him Lady Saren."

I stood in the threshold, though I know it's bad luck. I couldn't move, not forward or back. My mama said I'm as brave as the lead gazelle with hunters on her tail, but I wasn't then. Since coming to Song for Evela, too many times I've put my mama to shame.

"Lady Saren?" The khan rubbed his forehead. "Is Khasar truly insane? He has Lady Saren already, if he hasn't killed her yet."

"What do you mean Khasar has Lady Saren?" I asked. I just couldn't keep quiet.

Some of the chiefs glared at me for interrupting, but her khan answered.

"Dashti, I didn't see you. Have you heard of the lady in the tower? I knew her." He glanced at Lady Vachir before continuing. "I visited her one autumn. When I returned to Titor's Garden in the spring, Khasar was at the tower before me, and two hundred of his men camped with him. I'd only thirty men and couldn't risk attacking."

He came back! I smiled at him. I wanted him to know how wonderful he was, but he was looking out the window.

"Surely Khasar was there to break her out," he said, "take her back to his own realm."

"But now he's asking for her," said the town chief.

"Maybe he didn't take her." Tegus drummed the pane with his fingers. "But if he didn't, where is she?"

There was silence for a few moments, and my soul rumbled inside of me, rolling around like a ball in a box, shaking my bones.

I'd sworn to protect my lady. I'd said I'd claim her name and title and see if the khan would welcome her. I knew I should speak up now, the Ancestors designed this very moment to allow me to do my duty. But instead, I quaked and stared at my feet. And the moment passed.

"He claims he has one hundred villagers on neck ropes," said Batu, "ones too slow to flee before his army's advance. He's shouting that he'll catapult them into our city if we don't turn over the lady. Scouts confirm the hostages."

"Ancestors," sighed an old chief, rubbing his back as if the news made him ache.

The khan stared hard at Batu and finally asked, "And what's the part that you aren't telling me?"

Batu sighed. "He said he wanted Lady Saren, but he'd accept you, my lord. He goaded, said a true khan would give his own life to protect his people."

"A true khan . . . ," said Tegus.

Silence. The fire in the hearth shivered.

"I don't advise believing anything Khasar says, my lord," said Batu. "He still believes if he kills you and conquers Song for Evela, he can take the title of khan, and after that I doubt he'd stop until he seizes all the Eight Realms and declares himself Great Khan. Even if we had Lady Saren to release to him, I can't believe he'd give up his war."

"But those hundred villagers . . ." Tegus covered his face with a hand, shaking his head. "And where is she? Where's Saren all this time?"

"Here." I couldn't believe I'd spoken it even as I did, and my stomach ached and my blood stopped running in my veins. "Here," I said again, just to make sure I really had. I swore an oath to my lady, and I have to believe that if I do the right thing, the Ancestors will take care of the rest.

Everyone was staring at me. At least, I felt like they were, but I was only watching Tegus. I'd grown used to his amused expression when he looked at me. Now the confusion on his face felt as unpleasant as a slap.

"Dashti?" he said. "What are—"

"I'm Lady Saren." I was amazed how sure I sounded as I spoke. "Dashti is my maid's name."

He took a step forward, stopped. Everyone still stared. I was waiting for laughter, or maybe to be tied up with their sashes like the assassin who'd stabbed Batu. Tegus took another step forward. I would've accused him of dancing if I hadn't been shaking with the fear that he'd frown at me and demand I be strung up on the south wall.

"Khasar didn't take us from the tower," I explained. "He just came to mock us. We wouldn't go with him willingly, so he left us to rot. When we ran out of food, we broke our way out. Titor's Garden was razed, so we came here, but I wasn't sure if . . . you were engaged to Lady Vachir, and I didn't know if . . ."

My throat burned with the lies. Tegus still just stared.

Lady Vachir stood up from her couch with a not very nice expression. I guess she wasn't feeling much fondness for me. I guess she was imagining me on a spit, slowly turning over a fire. Truth be told, that's pretty much how I felt.

"You broke out?" asked Tegus. He took another step closer.

Why wasn't he calling me a liar? I look nothing like Lady Saren, and surely at a glance anyone can see I'm not gentry.

"It was the rats, my lord," I said. "They ate our food, but they also dug a way through the bricks. Funny how the thing I thought would kill us actually saved us in the end, isn't it? The cat you gave me was a brilliant rat hunter! But he was chased off when Khasar came back, and in his absence the rats took over. I was sorry to leave the pine bough behind in the tower. I kept it those three years."

"The pine bough." He stepped even closer. He took my hands, lifted them to his face, and breathed in through his nose, the formal greeting between gentry. Despite it all, a thrill tickled me.

"Lady Saren? After all these years to see you for the first time with Lord Khasar at the city walls. . . ."

"My lord?"

"Hearing your voice in the tower, I'd imagined meeting you so many times. And now you're Dashti . . . I . . . my lady." He shook his head and winced and smiled all at once. "I'm not sure if I'm standing on my feet or on my head."

So. That jumble of animal bones was beginning to come together. He'd never seen Lady Saren before. He'd never seen her! They'd never met when they began to communicate through letters. The only time he'd spoken with Lady Saren was in the tower. But it had been me. Ancestors, what a thought.

"I should've come forward before," I said, "but I was afraid. I'm sorry, my lord. Please forgive—"

"Don't you dare ask my forgiveness! After abandoning you, leaving you to Khasar and rats and darkness and starvation, all because I was too afraid. I'm unforgivable, Dashti . . . my lady. But will *you*?" He knelt at my feet, he held my hands against his face as he bowed before me. His voice broke. "Can you forgive me?"

Everyone began talking at once, which was just as well, since my breath had frozen solid inside me and I couldn't make a sound above a croak. Lady Vachir wanted to know who I was to threaten her betrothal, and Batu proposed that all questions of betrothal be set aside until Khasar was vanquished, and all the chiefs who didn't know the story of Lady Saren were clamoring for explanations, so others began to explain.

And all the while, Tegus held my hands to his face. I didn't mean to stroke his cheek—my thumb moved of its own accord, I swear. He smiled up at me, and my face felt hot.

I tugged him to his feet, saying, "Please, my lord, please don't kneel to me."

He arose and clasped my hands inside his. We were standing so close.

"I'm sorry," he whispered beneath the clamor around us. "My lady, I am so sorry." Then he grinned. "But even more, I'm happy. You're Lady Saren. And you're alive and well and here. Thank the Ancestors, you're here."

I felt ready to fall apart with all the elation and frustration and fear. The lie was heaps of cold mud on top of me, fit to suffocate me dead. Shria began talking about getting me into garments befitting my position and letting me rest in a proper chamber and chiefs were begging they return to the matter of war when I remembered my purpose.

"He's a wolf." I spoke quickly before they could interrupt, my voice tumbling over the noise. "Khasar never sleeps, he fights by day and hunts by night. He's a skinwalker, empowered by a desert shaman ritual to add the strength of a wolf to his own. That's why he's so fierce in battle. And at night, he takes wolf form, killing by stealth and spreading fear. But this might be the means to trick him. Send me down to him, send him Lady Saren, and let me—"

It was as much as I could explain before Tegus refused to let me anywhere near that butcher and Lady Vachir objected to my presence and the chiefs were in an uproar about the battle plan, that they must attack Khasar, that his deadline was for tomorrow noon and the warriors were preparing and needed the khan's attention now.

Sometimes I think they're all ridiculous. There I was, a sensible person with thoughts in my head, offering a solution. And they wouldn't listen. What aggravation, to believe I can help and yet not be allowed.

Shria took me by the shoulders and rushed me away, saying, "We'd no idea, my lady, if we'd known, my lady . . ." As I left, I caught sight of Batu, who seemed to be considering me seriously.

And here I am, in a different room, this one with a low couch and a silk coverlet, a lacquered table and a porcelain bowl filled with nuts for cracking. It's higher up in the khan's house, its window larger. At my request, Shria brought me my things—the horsehair blanket, my wool cloak and my boots, and my ink and brushes.

"Here's Sar, my lady, who I realize now must be your maid," and Shria ushered Saren into the room, still wearing her apron and smelling of kitchen smoke.

It was rather awkward while Shria remained with Saren pretending to be a lady's maid but mostly standing there staring at me like some baby animal. When the white-haired woman finally left, Saren collapsed on my pallet.

"I did it, my lady," I said.

She stared at the ceiling. "Thank you."

We were quiet.

"Would you like some nuts?"

"No," she said. Then, "Cook was having me decorate a serving platter for dinner. I'd like to go back to it. And make sure My Lord the cat gets his meat shavings."

"Of course."

So she left. And I'm relieved because I have enough thoughts and fear quakings to make me happy to be alone. It's night now, and even from here I can detect the bleary lights beyond the city walls. Khasar's men and their fires, their numbers rivaling the stars, laughing back at the eternal blackness of the night sky.

I'm afraid to put down my brush and ink. I'm afraid I'll be chilled by the quiet that comes after my brush ceases stroking parchment, that the silence will lower me into the night like into a grave. Now I'm being dramatic, I guess. I should say that I'm just plain afraid. I've got to do something and I don't know if I can.

Day 164

Or is it still yesterday? I write by firelight. I write because I want these ink strokes to give me courage, as I seem to be lacking it. My veins feel dry and dusty of blood. Not much of a mucker, am I, to be so terrified? I've tried laughing at myself, but it hasn't helped yet.

An hour ago, I went in search of Batu, the war chief. I woke Shria, and she told me where to find his room. She thinks me gentry, she'll do what I ask. What an unhappy laugh that gives me.

Batu didn't seem surprised to see me at his door in the middle of the night. He stepped into the hall so neither of us would invoke the bad luck of the threshold.

"Did you promise the khan anything regarding me?" I asked before revealing my plan.

"No, I didn't."

"Then I'll tell you that I'm going down to Lord Khasar. I've been praying to Under all night. He hasn't answered me, but when does the god of tricks offer signs to his petitioners?"

"Indeed."

I cleared my throat. My voice was sounding an awful lot like a rat's squeak, and I've had enough of that noise for a lifetime. "I'm going of my own will, as Lady Saren. Would it be against your oath to Khan Tegus to help me?"

Batu frowned at me a good long while. Then he

shook his head. "No, it would not. But what do you plan to do?"

"Get close enough to Khasar to sing. A song can't force Khasar to do anything, but if I sing to the wolf inside him, maybe the wolf will choose to come out."

"And then what will happen?"

"Something," I said with much conviction to hide the feeble answer. "None of his men know he's a skinwalker, except his war chief. At least, that was true a few years ago, and I think it must still be so. And if they find out—"

"Who knows," said Batu, "it might cause them to revere Khasar all the more."

"Would your warriors follow you if they believed you'd traded the life of your soul to desert shamans?"

Batu considered. "Their loyalty would be dented, no question, and after a time I believe they would abandon me. But in the midst of a war, they might follow me into battle all the same."

"Yes, but . . ." I didn't know how to form my impressions into words. "But if they actually saw him. I mean, how would you react if you saw someone change into a wolf? He's never a wolf by day, so he'd be confused and they'd be confused and . . . and . . ."

What would happen then? Would he attack his own men? Would they fight back? I don't know. But

I have these ideas, and I have a strong body to carry them out, and a reason to do it. How can I not?

"My lady, I don't think you should throw away your life, and I don't think I should take your hand and lead you to your end."

He put a hand on my shoulder as if to usher me back to my room, but I grabbed the doorpost.

"Did you see Khan Tegus today, when you told him Khasar would take his life instead of Saren's? Is there any chance that Tegus will offer himself to save those hundred villagers? For the war, for this realm, isn't Tegus more important than any risk I might take?"

Batu shut his eyes. He was tired, I could see that now. We all are lately, I guess. At least he didn't argue with me again.

We agreed to meet at the kitchen door at dawn. He'll lead me to the east city gate and tell the guards to let me pass. From there, I'll go alone. I'll walk toward Khasar's camp from the east, so the sun will rise behind me, granting me a shadow on my face. I'll wear my hair down and loose, so he won't see me well enough to know the lie. Unlike Tegus, Khasar has seen Saren. I'll go barefoot so he'll see my naked ankles beneath my cloak and know I am a girl and not a warrior, and so perhaps let me get close enough to sing. I'll go alone.

Carthen, goddess of strength, I need your smile more than Khasar does. Evela, give me a bright sun and a dark shadow, and grant me a powerful song. Under, I plead the honor of being the dagger of your revenge.

Later

Is it still the same day? It feels years later. I can't sleep tonight in this strange place, in yet another new room. I managed to keep my book, and I have a new brush and ink and nothing to do but fret and write, so I'll tell you all that's happened. Ancestors have mercy.

When I met Batu at the kitchen door, I brought Mucker with me. His exhales were billows of white, and he leaned his head against me like an enormous cat. Titor, but I love that beast.

"I'll ride the yak to the gate," I said.

I didn't say that I hoped riding a yak, Titor's favorite animal, might grant me a kind glance from him, because Batu didn't seem to believe in "mucker faith."

And I didn't say that I wanted to put my fingers on an animal's neck to feel some steady comfort or I was likely to break down and sob like a newborn. I certainly didn't say that.

Batu led the yak through the streets. The ways were narrow, clogged with the ghers of refugees, and by the time we reached the east city gate, the sun had cleared the horizon. I couldn't feel its heat. The air was ice that seemed ready to break under my fist. My hands were shaking like to come off my arms, though I don't think I can blame the shaking on just the cold.

Batu spoke to the gate guards, and they inched the gates open. Two arrow shots away, Khasar's warriors camped. They resembled ants in an anthill, for all that I could ever hope to count their number.

Batu put his hand on Mucker's neck. "Are you certain, my lady? There's little chance Khasar will keep his word once he has you."

"I'm wagering on the god of tricks today," I said.

"That's a poor wager," one of the gate guards muttered.

I slipped off my boots then slid off Mucker's back, and the moment my bare feet touched earth, they went numb with cold. I patted Mucker's nose once before beginning the walk across the empty field toward Khasar.

How can I say what it was like? Cold. Long. Lonely as ghosts. I guess it was about the worst moment of my life, almost as hard as singing my mama into the next Realm—and much colder. Khasar and his men were so far off it felt like forever to get there, and even though I wasn't eager to arrive, the journey itself was misery. Does fright hurt? It did then, it did for me, in my stomach and in my limbs. And it didn't help that my feet were so frozen I couldn't sense where they ended and the ground began, twice causing me to trip. I'd really rather not have fallen on my face in front of thousands of warriors who were waiting to kill me. Under seemed to be playing tricks on me, and I began to doubt that I'd any hope. But by then I was already there.

"Lord Khasar!" I shouted. At least that part of my plan worked. I'd intended to shout his name and it actually came right out.

"Khan Khasar, you meant to say." He stepped out of his gher but stayed so far back, I couldn't make out his face. I knew his voice, of course. It was turning my bones to soup. "I'm letting you live for the moment because I'm curious about this girl who crosses my battlefield. Just what are you offering? I won't pay."

His men laughed roughly. Khasar lifted his sword, making some call I didn't understand, and two dozen of his men moved into a half circle between me and Khasar, fully armored, bows pulled back, swords bare.

"Take another step and I'll show the Eternal Blue Sky the color of your liver. If Tegus thinks to use an assassin, he'll not fool me by sending a woman with a poisoned dagger."

I stopped walking, gripping my cloak tighter. The cold was slithering up my bare legs.

"Chinua, check her," said Khasar.

"Show me your hands," said a man to Khasar's right, a tall, thin man. I figured this was Khasar's war chief, the one who'd taken Saren to watch Khasar become a wolf.

I raised my hands and for some wild reason, I

found myself remembering how Tegus had once called them beautiful. Spared from the scrubbing waters of late, they've softened, though if Khasar looked too closely, he'd see the scars and calluses.

"Now deliver your message before I gut—"

"My lord, it's me, Lady Saren." My voice went soft. I was ashamed to tell a lie right beneath the Eternal Blue Sky. Lies are for dark holes and rooms without candles.

"Speak up!"

"I'm Lady Saren," I said, louder.

"Lady Saren." He snarled a laugh. "I knew that khan wouldn't be able to resist breaking you out. Take off your hood, I want to see your scared cow eyes."

I pulled my hood back. My hair hung down, the sun was behind me, and I hoped he was still too far back to see. I thought I should say something quickly to prove I was Lady Saren, something true, before he could see in my face who I was not.

"The day you threw flames into the tower," I said, "the day you tried to smoke me like winter meat, I guess I've never been so scared in my life."

He laughed. I hate his laugh.

"All you are is fear," he said.

"I believe that was also the day you bathed in my waste," I couldn't help adding.

249

I was happy to see him flinch. I guess he didn't much like my mentioning that in front of his men.

"You told me you'd only take me if I came willingly," I said. "And here I am."

I started toward him, but three of his men moved to block my way.

Though he thought me the frail Lady Saren, he still wouldn't let me near. He was too clever to risk the chance I might have a hidden weapon. This morning before going out, that possibility had haunted me, so I'd disrobed completely under my cloak. I'd been praying since that I wouldn't have to take it off, but that ultimate submission seemed to be the only way he'd think me harmless, the only way to get near enough to sing.

I shut my eyes as I unhooked the neck clasp and let the warmth fall to the ground. Winter blasted my skin, and the cold shot up from my feet through my entire body.

Khasar stared, suddenly with nothing to say.

"You see I'm hiding no weapons, my lord." I tried to sound brave as gentry, but I was shivering so hard, my voice warbled like a bird's, my words knocking against each other. I had to bite my tongue to bleeding to keep from picking my cloak back up, wrapping it around myself, curling up to hide. "You see I submit to you. I'm here of my own will, as you wanted. I'm sacrificing myself for this realm. If you are a man of honor, before the Ancestors, under the Eternal Blue Sky, you'll keep your word. Take me and leave this realm in peace."

He didn't say anything. He stared at me. His men looked away, at the ground, at the clouds. Though hard warriors, I think they couldn't help being embarrassed for the poor naked girl. There was some revenge in this, I realized, remembering how Lord Khasar had stood naked before my lady. But I couldn't glory in it. The shame hurt me like the cold, and I trembled inside and out and winced when tears burned my eyes.

"Please don't make me stand here like this," I said, my words shaking. I didn't mean to beg, but there it came. "Please say you accept my sacrifice and let me put my cloak back on. Please."

He started walking toward me now. Slowly. His men stepped aside.

"You surprise me, Lady Saren."

He kept coming nearer.

"I never expected you to do anything but tremble and cry. Though I see you're trembling, where are the tears? Ah, I think I see one. That's better."

And nearer. My stomach quivered, my blood was hot. This was the moment. I bowed my head, as if meekly. The sunlight was strong behind me, Evela was smiling on my hope, but I knew the moment he saw my face, he'd kill me. He was near enough now that through my hair I could make out his own features. I can't say if he was handsome or ugly. He looked like pain to me. Then I noticed one detail—he had three thin white scars down his cheek, like the marks a cat might leave. It seems My Lord had drawn some blood that night he escaped the wolf's jaws. The thought gave me a gust of warm courage.

Before Khasar's hands reached me, I had to act.

"Witness all!" I lifted my arms and knelt, the frosty grass snapped like glass under my knees. "See Lady Saren surrender to Khan Khasar. I sing the song of submission."

Here was the trick. I don't know a song of submission. Instead, I began to sing the song of the wolf.

"Yellow eyes, blink the night," I sang. "Two paws in, two paws gone," while praying that there were no muckers among his warriors, that they wouldn't know what it was I sang. I remembered the voices of my brothers chanting those words, yelling them at the night to save the sheep, felt that childhood tune hum inside me now as if in harmony. I reached forward, I touched Khasar's boots, hoping the contact would make the song stronger.

Khasar stared down at me and did nothing, his face puzzled, his body rigid. I think I understood him then—I think he felt that something was wrong but he couldn't allow himself to be afraid, not of me, not of a naked girl singing. And because he did nothing to stop me, neither did his men. I kept singing, calling the wolf out of the man.

Too late Khasar asked, "What are you—"

He didn't finish his question, because his head was thrown back, and he stared up, in pain or thrill I don't know. I almost stopped singing then, my limbs shook so that the ache was nearly unbearable. I didn't know what would happen. Would the wolf in Khasar hear my song and flee its daylight form? Would it come out under the sun?

With my voice I sang, and with my heart I prayed. Titor, god of animals, whose realm this man destroyed. Under, god of tricks, whose name this man cast off. Goda, goddess of sleep, I gave you a sleepless night in prayer. Evela, my lady, goddess of sunlight and songs, give me voice. Ancestors, let me sing this man into his animal form, his sleepless form of night, trick him into it under this sunlight.

I sang to him the song of the wolf.

He stumbled back a step, but it was the most he

could manage. All his force seemed focused on trying to hold his shape. His men were still looking away, ashamed of my shame, unaware of their lord's danger. Then Khasar groaned.

"My lord? Khan Khasar?" Chinua asked, as if beginning to wonder if something was wrong. The rest didn't suspect me still, I think. I'd completely debased myself, I'd become a thing too low to contemplate. Still, I guessed I wouldn't have long. The moment they thought me dangerous, they'd let their arrows fly.

Louder I sang. I stood, trembling for cold and fear, and I put my hands on his chest. So close I was, he could've snapped my neck by accident. If he'd looked, he'd have seen the lie in my face. But his neck arched and his glance flung up toward the sky. My voice quavered so that on the low notes it was nothing but a rasp, two stones grating together.

Please, I prayed. *Please change. Hurry. Become that wolf. Now, now.*

"My lord? Are you all right?" asked Chinua. He stepped forward two paces and pulled his bow back tighter. "I think you'd better stand back now, girl."

But I couldn't stand back until Khasar was gone where he couldn't hurt Tegus or make my lady quake or sneak into my nightmares. I clung to Khasar, so the warriors couldn't shoot at me without risking their lord.

"The night, the night!" I sang, and my voice was getting more desperate. I knew I didn't sound very meek anymore, but the wolf in Khasar wasn't coming out. "The night drips from your teeth. The night melts from your eyes. Yellow eyes!"

"Stand back," said Chinua, "or your eyes will be strung together on my arrow!"

He aimed at my head, I screamed my song, and Khasar thrust back his head and howled. Not at the moon, not at the shifting stars, but howled right at the Eternal Blue Sky.

That, I thought *should get the Ancestors' attention.*

Khasar pulled out of my grip, and I dropped flat to the ground just as an arrow whisked over me. I kept singing. And Khasar kept thrashing. His men were advancing, but for the moment they forgot me in favor of their lord, who had begun to screech and howl, his hands clawing the air. I held no weapon; they must not have understood that I could harm him. So I sang on, though I don't know how I found any voice with all the shaking and barely a breath trickling into my lungs.

Then the change happened. It really did. I'd believed Saren when she'd told me what she'd seen, or I'd thought I had, but until I saw the change myself,

I guess I hadn't truly understood. Just the sight of its wrongness made my stomach seize up, and I would've lost my breakfast if I'd had any.

I don't think I can describe the sound of flesh bulging and ripping, or the smell that clouded around Khasar, strange and rancid. I can say that his face thrust out, his back hunched with fur, his clothing tore, his armor bent and groaned before popping off. He dropped down on all fours and where Khasar had stood, a wolf now growled.

Khasar the wolf was enormous, as tall as an antelope, as fat as a mare, with jaws that could take down the largest yak. The size, the sheer menace of the thing made me quake, and the song choked in my throat. His men hollered and jumped back from the snarls, the teeth, the daggered paws.

"It's our lord!" shouted Chinua. "Do not harm him!"

Here's where my plan took the greatest risk. What would the wolf do? I was bargaining that the wolf who had snarled at me in the tower was more instinct than thought, that he loses his humanness when he's a wolf. Saren's story suggested such, when Chinua moved them behind a fire to protect them from his lord. Here was my hope—that Khasar the wolf would now attack his own men.

"It is our lord," Chinua was shouting. "Do not harm him!"

Chinua ran about, bellowing, trying to get warriors to move so the wolf would have an escape, but the camp completely ringed the woods. With city wall before us and forty thousand warriors and their ghers and animals all around, there was nowhere for the beast to flee. He paced and growled and wiped his face against his legs as if the sunlight were painful.

My plan was failing. The warriors kept their swords and arrows pointed at the wolf but didn't strike, and the wolf just snarled and snapped at nothing.

"Change back, Lord Khasar," Chinua said. "It's day! Change, my lord, change."

He's going to turn back, I thought. And then he'll kill me or worse.

His men now knew that he was a wolf skin-walker, but the warriors weren't fleeing their posts. As Batu said, there was the possibility that they'd revere him even more. I'd lost, I'd lost.

The failure was painful and I was so cold, I moved to crawl back into my cloak. That was a stupid thing to do. Stupid. Because then the wolf noticed me.

His eyes were on me, and he crouched and snarled.

Sing, Dashti, I told myself. *Push him back with your song. Sing!*

But I was so cold, so terrified, my voice iced in my throat. I couldn't squeak even a word. So I tried to run. I didn't make it three steps.

He pounced, landing on my leg, and I heard a crunch before I felt pain. His foul breath filled my mouth as he snapped in my face, and my stomach tried to vomit. I turned my head as he lunged. The sides of our skulls collided. I could taste blood.

Then, the eerie whistle of an arrow scratched the air. The arrow nipped the beast in the rear and he yelped and turned. His warriors stared back, shaking. One warrior held a bow with no arrow. Maybe it had been a mistake and the bowstring had slipped in his fingers. Maybe he had a sister or daughter my age and thought of her when the wolf leaped on me. Or maybe it had been Under's doing. However it was, Ancestors, please bless that man.

The wolf made a new noise in his throat now, one of hunger and rage. He turned his jaws toward the warriors, and he lunged.

"Don't shoot him," Chinua yelled, but three men, their eyes wide with terror, began emptying their quivers. It didn't matter—the wolf leaped and rolled at incredible speed, and nothing could touch him. When one arrow grazed his leg, the wolf wailed in rage. He sprang, his jaws tearing out the throats of two men.

More arrows cut the air, and the wolf's attack became so swift and deadly, several warriors lay bleeding before I could even comprehend what was happening.

The wolf was smearing his muzzle in the blood of another soldier when at last one of the arrows struck him hard, then another and another. He roared and clawed at the warriors, killing two more. The men were running back, letting arrows fly as they tried to get out of his reach. Chinua was yelling something, but so was everyone else. Another arrow struck the wolf, another, and another. He howled and snarled, running a circle in mad fury.

He was too wounded to make chase, and all the warriors had retreated beyond his reach. That's when his horrible eyes found me again. I'd managed to pull my cloak on and was trying to drag myself away, but I couldn't stand, I couldn't run. How I prayed to Carthen, goddess of strength! I wept so hard my throat ached, though I was too cold to make tears.

The wolf padded toward me, stuck with arrows, his head low to the ground. He was still tense, growling as if he would attack. I pressed my hands against the crackling grass and pushed myself back, back, as hard and fast as I could, my wounded leg dragging on the ground. But he was faster.

He pounced, and I screamed my song again, just

one line, one rattled tune. His jaws snapped a handsbreadth from my face, his spittle flying against my lips. His breath stank of blood, and I couldn't seize enough breath to sing again. His maw opened toward my throat, but before he could clamp down, his body slumped. At last the weight of those arrows in him was too great. The full force of his body collapsed on me. He didn't move again.

I thought I was dead too. A hot pain pierced my ankle, a dull pain throbbed in my head. I was pinned to the ground by the wolf's corpse and surrounded by an angry anthill of soldiers. Chinua, his face full of rage and grief, ran forward and prodded his wolf lord to see if he was dead. I pushed against the hairy body with all my strength. The corpse rolled a little to the right, but it was so heavy, I couldn't budge it from my leg.

Then for whole moments, I heard no sound but my own heartbeat.

I let my head fall back, and I gazed into the Eternal Blue Sky. It was morning. Some of the sky was yellow, some the softest blue. One small cloud scuttled along. Strange how everything below can be such death and chaos and pain while above the sky is peace, sweet blue gentleness. I heard a shaman say once, the Ancestors want our souls to be like the blue sky.

I prayed to the sky—*Here I am. I took what the*

Ancestors gave me and I avenged their names. You saw it. You're above all, even the sun, even the Sacred Mountain, even the Ancestors. I submit to you, and if you're sending me on to see my mama again, I'm ready to go. Just take care of my lady, please, and Tegus, too.

And I closed my eyes to die. But you see that I'm not dead, as I'm still writing. Under heeded my pleas today, though he still tricked me in my turn.

The drums rapped and the horns called. I turned my head and saw five hundred warriors coming from the west gate of the city, Batu at their lead. They halted a safe distance from Khasar's men.

"My lady, are you all right?" Batu shouted to me.

"Yes," I said, because it seemed what he expected to hear. And I was alive still, which I guess was all right.

He gestured with his chin to the dead creature pinning me. "Is that Khasar?"

"It was."

"In wolf form, just as you said. Beware a lady's faith, you warriors of Under's Scorn."

Chinua looked made of wrath. A company of warriors had come forward, standing behind him with weapons in hand. "You should beware us, Evela's peasants! Carthen's Glory is not defeated by the slaying of one wolf."

Batu shrugged. "I have nearly thirty thousand

warriors ready at the gates, men fighting for their homes. Your numbers are larger, true, but with your wolf lord dead, how many will fight? He was your real strength. If you leave now, you'll make it home before true winter falls. Don't waste the time. Throw down your weapons, let us take Lady Saren safely away, and we won't pursue."

There was more talk, I think, but I didn't catch it. It took so much effort to try and listen. My ears were so frozen I wouldn't have been surprised to see them break right off my head. My feet seemed to have never existed at all, and my throat screamed with every inhale. Pressed against the ground like that, I was so cold, the only parts of me I could feel were throbbing something vicious, and I wanted to howl and cry with the pain, but I couldn't move enough to do that much.

Suddenly the ache in my ankle pierced me like a new wound, and I screamed before I realized what had happened. Chinua and two other warriors had rolled the wolf off me. They began to tow the carcass toward their camp, and behind them, Khasar's warriors retreated. I guess Batu had been pretty convincing.

I sat up and almost fainted from pain. I paused, waiting for the blackness in my vision to go away so I could stand, and I found myself looking into the eyes of the wolf. They were dragging him by his hind legs, and his dead eyes stared back at me. In death, his eyes lost their wildness. They calmed and saddened some, and I realized that his wolf eyes were as blue as the Eternal Sky. I wonder if right at the moment of his death, Khasar remembered the price his wolf strength cost. He offered his soul to the desert shamans. Now it can never climb the Sacred Mountain, never enter the Realm of the Ancestors. I suppose it's the path he chose. I suppose it's what he deserves.

"My lady," said Batu, "can you come to me?"

Chinua and his warriors had withdrawn, but I understood that Batu didn't dare turn his back on them, nor could he risk riding to me and putting any more distance between him and the path of retreat.

I nodded and stood on my left leg, making sure my cloak was tight around me. I couldn't feel its warmth.

I didn't know how I would walk. I hopped a few steps and felt ridiculous, a just-hatched bird, hobbling and unsure, while thousands of warriors watched me. So I thought I'd risk one step on my right foot. That was a mistake, I thought, as I yelped in pain and fell forward.

Suddenly one of Batu's soldiers was dismounting, running to my side. He lifted me under my knees and carried me back to his horse, boosting me up onto his saddle as if I weighed no more than a cat. His face was buried in a deep, fur-lined hood, and he rested a moment against his mare, bent forward as if he'd a pain in his middle. He groaned as he pulled himself into the saddle behind me, but he held me on his lap, one arm under my knees to keep my legs from bouncing against the horse. He wrapped his other arm around my waist as if to warm me as well as keep me on the saddle.

"My lord," I said as we rode back toward the city.

The horse's canter jostled my ankle and I couldn't help whimpering. The pain was like being stuck with a knife again, again, again.

Tegus held me tighter. "We've got to get you

inside city walls and out of bowshot, and then I'll ask Bloodnose here to give us a nice, smooth walk. Just a little farther, just hang on."

"I'm all right," I said, pretending I didn't have pain tears streaking down my face. And I was so cold, my teeth had begun to chatter like a hammer against my jaw. "I could keep riding . . . all day. Why don't we . . . go mushroom hunting?"

"Now that's a fine idea and I would agree, but I must admit I'm embarrassed to be out with such a scatterbrain. It seems, my lady, you forgot yet again to put on shoes this morning. What would your mother say?"

"I just wanted Khasar's opinion . . . on whether my ankles are . . . sturdier than yours."

"And what did he say?"

"I don't think he . . . liked my ankles so well. He fell on me . . . and broke one."

"That wasn't very kind," he agreed, talking lightly as if to distract me from the pain. "I think there are better ways to tell a person you don't approve of their ankles than to break them."

"That's what . . . I thought, too. His manners always were . . . la—lacking."

His arm held me tighter to him. "You're going to have to marry me now."

"But . . . I . . ."

"You slew Khasar, you healed me, and you have perfect ankles. I really don't think this is a question we need to debate."

"As always . . . my lord, you make perfect sense."

His cheek was next to mine. He pulled me closer, his warmth so wonderful, my skin stung against his touch. And he kissed my neck, behind my ear. Kissed me once, quietly.

So you see, I agreed. To marry Khan Tegus. As Lady Saren. Ancestors, my thoughts must've been as numb as my feet.

And now here I am in a chamber stacked with furs and silks, with a fire at both ends of the room and three large windows, ice covered in a soft cloth pressed to my swollen jaw, my broken ankle wrapped and resting on pillows. And everyone calling me Lady Saren.

The sticking-needle pain of my warming feet has passed. I should go to the kitchens and tell my lady. Tell her that her khan wants to wed her. And it's time for her to say who she is. And who I'm not.

I'll go tomorrow.

Day 165

Shria visited me this morning, smiling. She said the chiefs voted that although Lady Saren's betrothal to Khan Tegus wasn't sanctioned by her father, he's dead now so that matter is meaningless, and since our (their) betrothal came first, he'll marry me (Lady Saren) and not Lady Vachir.

Shria said, "It's complicated for a ruling lady of one realm to marry a ruling lord of another— usually that lot is left to younger siblings. And now that Khasar's war isn't an issue, Lady Vachir's advisers seemed relieved that the betrothal ties were released."

She seemed to be holding something back, so I asked, "How did Lady Vachir take it?"

Shria frowned, then patted my cheek. "Don't worry about that. Even if her pride is hurt, Lady Vachir can't cause you any trouble now that the chiefs have decided. You'll have your wedding day."

She handed me a note from Khan Tegus and left me to read it.

We've been betrothed for five years so it doesn't make sense to wait longer. We'll have the wedding in nine days. Now that the date's set, I won't come see you until our wedding day—because it's bad luck and because you might protest the haste. If you try to put it off, I'll have Batu argue with you, and he's very good at it. Rest your ankle. There will be dancing.

— Tegus

So it's real. It's happening. And I'm lost.

I went to look for Saren, hobbling out of my room with the help of two canes, when Tegus came down the hallway. When he saw me, he skipped a step. He looked to see if we were alone, picked me up, hurried around a corner, and kissed me. Kissed me long. My canes clattered to the floor, my arms fit around his neck. I felt as though my whole body only now was thawing. While he was holding me I forgot that I'm not who I say I am, that he doesn't know that I'm just Dashti. How can anyone forget? But I did. And I wish I hadn't remembered again.

When we stopped to breathe, he said, "I wanted to show you something," and pulled from his belt a blue shirt I remembered well.

"The one I gave you," I said.

"I kept it with me until your scent faded from the

fabric. I should have known you when you first came to sing for my leg, I should have remembered. . . ."

He pressed his cheek against mine. He breathed in against my neck and sighed deep inside. I closed my eyes. I tried to memorize the warm, brown, cinnamon smell of his skin. In case I never smell it again.

"Will you take your shirt?" he asked. "Will you wear it for me? Against your skin, so it carries your scent again."

"Yes, my lord," I whispered. "Yes, Tegus."

"Do you have a lady's maid with you? Would you like me to find you one?"

"No, I'd rather not have a maid. I'm fine."

"Are you? Have you warmed back up again?" He rubbed my arms.

"Yes, I have. I'm fine, really. Actually, I'm wonderful." Just then, I felt it.

"You are," he agreed. Then he kissed me again, saying, "Mmm," as though my lips tasted better than candied fruit. "Don't tell. The chiefs believe I won't see you until the wedding, and you know how rigorous those chiefs can be about tradition."

He set me gently down, fetched me my canes, then ran off.

I came back to my room and sat alone. I can't go see my lady right now, not until I can stop crying.

Later

When I made my way to the kitchens, I passed by Lady Vachir's open door. Since travel in the winter is uncomfortable, even deadly, she's staying in the khan's house until spring, the thought of which makes me want to scratch the spider tickles off my back. She and all her maids stared at me as I passed by. I'm feeling like an antelope without a herd, with hunters riding down the hill.

Cook let me talk to Saren, saying, "Yes, my lady," and "Certainly, my lady," eyeing my new clothes as though the yellow brocade was fresh meat and she was starving. Saren and I sat in the empty sugar closet and I explained it all to her, as simply as I could.

"I did what you asked, I did my duty, and he's proved himself true to you. The chiefs ruled in your favor, Lady Vachir's betrothal is no more, and your wedding date is set. Now is the time to tell him who you are."

She shook her head. "You marry him as me first, then he won't be able to change his mind. Once he takes the vows for Lady Saren—"

"But I'm not Lady Saren!"

"You'll be acting as me. They'll understand."

Ancestors, what have I done? I think I'd rather face Khasar again, naked on a winter battlefield, than marry Tegus as Lady Saren. Won't he feel betrayed? I wish I had someone to plead for advice, but I've sworn secrecy. Besides, if any discover I've claimed nobility, they could hang me just like Osol. I think I know what Lady Vachir would do—something involving removing my intestines while I still breathed. I've seen her eyes. I think she'd take pleasure in it.

Here in my room, I fold myself toward the Sacred Mountain for hours, praying, praying. Meanwhile, her lord's house is aflutter with wedding preparations. The poor girls in the kitchen must be drowning in dirty pots.

Day 167

The answer occurred to me early in the morning. I have to leave. My lady doesn't know what it is she's asking me to do, and I can't make her understand. Ancestors forgive me, but I can't dress in a marriage deel and pretend to be Lady Saren, take the vows to love her khan, and then step back for my lady. I can't make that lie, and I can't watch what will happen next.

Tegus, I'm leaving this book behind for you, so you will know the why of it all, and maybe you'll forgive me, or maybe you'll think me false and reprehensible. You'd be justified. I couldn't stand the thought of your reading all my words unless I knew for certain that I'd never have to face you again, so please don't look for me. If you read the book in its entirety, you'll know for truth who is Lady Saren. And I guess you'll also know that I'm a silly girl who writes down every word you said to me.

Please, Tegus, dress Saren in blue silk and let her hands be beautiful again. I think you'll worry for me because it's winter and I don't have a gher, but I'm a mucker and I'll find a way. Thank you. Forgive me. Don't worry.

I'll leave tomorrow.

Day 169

I thought I'd never write in this book again. I'm in yet another new room, though this one has no window, this one has a door that locks. It's underground, but it smells like the tower, and that smell makes my stomach spin and my vision dim and my skin itch as if ghost spiders cover me, and I scratch and scratch here in the dark. I'll be hanging before the week is out. But I'm trying not to think about that.

Yesterday I was too slow leaving, and I can't blame it all on my ankle. Why didn't I just get out into the city as quickly as I could hobble? I'm such a fool. And yet mostly what I feel right now is sad, all-out-of-food sad, lonely sad, sorry sad. Shamed sad, and hoping never to have to look Khan Tegus in the face again. And yet every moment hoping that he'll open that door. Why is that?

Yesterday I crept from my room early in the morning. I put on the blue shirt Tegus returned to me, my old wool deel, sheepskin cloak, and boots, forgetting my gloves in my hurry. I left this book behind for Tegus. When I passed Lady Vachir's room, her door was open and she watched me walk by.

My thought was to join the refugees in the streets. If I took the seven years' vow of servitude, maybe someone would take me in. I hoped to find a family who planned to leave Song for Evela come spring so I could disappear from the city as soon as I might.

My mistake was stopping in the kitchen. I'd thought it too cruel not to explain things to Saren and say good-bye to Qacha and Gal. I found the two girls scrubbing pots, and I sneaked in to work beside them a last time, whispering as we washed.

"I can't tell you why I lied, but I think rumors will bring it to your ears soon enough."

They didn't press, though they seemed sorry to have me go. I thought Qacha would miss me as much as I'd miss her, and poor Gal had heartbreak in her eyes.

"I liked thinking that you'd been gentry all along," Gal said, "that you were going to be the khan's bride. And if your story isn't true, then what about . . . well, how can anything impossible actually happen?"

I knew she was thinking of her family, if they were alive, if they would find their way to Song for Evela. I said, "If they come for you, it'll most likely be in the spring." I didn't have a better answer.

My lady didn't take the news as kindly. We sat in the empty sugar closet. I closed the door when she began to yell.

"I order you to stay! I order you to marry him in my name. By the sacred nine, Dashti, you'll do what I say."

Strangely, her words held no sway over me. Maybe it's wrong, but I don't think I have to do what she says just because I'm a mucker and she's an honored lady. I smiled to myself then, thinking that if I were in a tower now and a black-gauntleted Khasar told me to put my hand back down so he could slap it, I'd tell him to go slap himself.

"No, my lady," I said as gently as I could. "I've tried to do my duty by you, but I won't do this."

Then she struck my face, just like her father and Lady Vachir, too. This time I didn't laugh. I just stood up slowly. Her eyes went wide, and I think she was afraid I'd hit her back. Not to say that I wasn't tempted.

"I'm sorry, my lady," I said. "My Lord the cat is a better companion for you than I am anyway."

My lady didn't cry, though her chin set to quivering. "Don't abandon me, Dashti. Everyone does, but you don't, you never do."

Those words pinched my heart. Poor little lost lamb, poor thin and wind-tossed thing.

"Oh Saren." I sat beside her and she put her head on my shoulder and lost every inch of the slapping, commanding gentry. "I could take you with me, but you really are better off here than living like a mucker. Khan Tegus is a good man, the best of men, the very best. He'll take care of you." I held her hands, I smiled to show her my confidence, and I felt as much like a good mucker mama as I ever hope to. "You've done so well these past weeks. I think you can be strong without me. This is your time, Saren. This is your chance to be brave. Stand up. Declare who you are. Will you do it?"

She hesitated. "I'll try. I'll think about it."

I left then. I should've gone straight out, hidden my mottled face beneath my hood, and lost myself in the city, but I slowed to say good-bye to Mucker. Fool, fool, fool. The yak would've been fine without a farewell, but now I am not.

When I emerged from the stable, Lady Vachir was in the kitchen yard, and with her the three vulture maids and a dozen warriors from Beloved of Ris. In her right hand, she was clutching this book.

I turned and fled. The ground was thick with ice. I could hear them shouting. I didn't look, I just hobbled toward the gate. I was nearly there when my canes slipped and my feet flew out from under me. I was on the ground, and when I looked up, warriors from Beloved of Ris surrounded me.

I screamed, I couldn't help it. Hands were on my arms and legs, pulling me to a chopping block in the center of the yard, and they were none too gentle with my broken ankle. One stood by, ready with a sword. I screamed louder and thrashed and kicked with my good leg. Everyone working in the yard stared, but no one moved to interfere with Lady Vachir's business.

The girls emerged from the kitchens, shivering without cloaks but too curious about the commotion not to peek. When they recognized me in the hands of the warriors, they ran forward. All except Saren, who went back inside.

"What are you doing?" Cook hollered, running at them with a kitchen knife. "Put Lady Saren down, you mangy villains!"

"This isn't Lady Saren." Lady Vachir spoke loudly enough for any bystander to hear. "This is Dashti the mucker maid. Isn't that right?"

If ever there was a good time to lie, that would've been it. But there we were, under the Eternal Blue Sky, and I just couldn't do it. Cook frowned at my silence and took a step back.

"By the ancient law of the Ancestors," said Lady Vachir, "it's my right to take the life of anyone who interferes with my lawful betrothal. This girl isn't Lady Saren, she isn't a lady at all. She's a commoner, a mucker from Titor's Garden, and confessed the truth herself in this book."

Gal and Qacha were beside us now, tugging on the warriors' sleeves, pushing their way to me. The warriors didn't strike the girls, just shoved and wriggled them off their arms. My head lay on the chunk of wood where fowl get their necks chopped. It was stained muddy red and colder than ice, and with my last thought I felt some real sympathy for those poor chickens.

The warriors had dragged Gal out of the way. Now only Qacha stood between me and the sword.

"You can't just kill her!" said Qacha. "Can they?"

"No, not until the khan's chiefs rule it so!" Gal shouted.

The warriors hesitated. Lady Vachir scowled. Apparently she knew that Gal was right.

"Then cut off one of her feet," said the lady, "so she can't run away again."

At those words, my ankles flamed with pain.

The warriors rolled me around until my broken and wrapped ankle lay on the chopping block. Maybe they figured it was already damaged and so not such a tragedy. I tried to kick with my left leg until someone pinned it to the ground. I screamed and fought, but I couldn't move.

The sword rose above me. I looked up at it, silver against blue sky, and I was a fool enough to think, *Isn't that pretty? Silver on blue.* I held my breath while I waited for the blade to drop. I didn't look down, I didn't want to see blood, see my leg end at my ankle. I just kept staring up and thinking, *silver on blue, silver on blue.*

I hadn't realized that the girls had been screaming until they stopped. The sword quivered and didn't fall.

The hands holding me let go, and I thumped onto the ground. I wiggled my toes. All ten were still there.

Khan Tegus was crouching beside me, short of breath. I could see Saren standing behind him, her cheeks pink from running.

"I got him," she said, proud as a rooster. "I found him, Dashti. I was brave."

Tegus scooped my hands into his. The mist of his breath wrapped around my face, and he spoke to me as though we were all alone. "Ancestors, your hands are cold. First I find you bootless on a battlefield, now with your feet on a chopping block. And with bare hands, no less."

"Hello," was all I could manage back.

"Are you hurt?" he asked, and though his voice was gentle toward me, I sensed anger in it. He wasn't angry at me then, but I knew he would be soon.

"Alive still," I said, "and with both my feet intact even."

There's something about being with Tegus that feels like privacy. The way he looks at me or touches me, we can be in a room full of people but I always feel as though we're alone, no one else in the world. I felt that way then, his white breath and mine mingling, his large hands trying to warm my own.

But then Lady Vachir spoke up. Of course she would.

"My lord, that girl is not Lady Saren."

He helped me to my feet, and I wobbled on one leg, so he put an arm around my waist to hold me steady. The shouting and explaining and accusing had started again, but I didn't hear much of it. My head felt as though it were still pressed to the block, and everyone was talking at once, and I was watching Tegus, the anger in his eyes, the doubt creasing his forehead. All I could think was, *When will he let go of me?* That wondering was bigger than my head.

"Enough!" Tegus shouted. He turned to me. "Is it true, what she says she read?"

"My name's Dashti," I said, as simply as I could. I knew it was all about to end and I didn't want to lie anymore. "I'm not Lady Saren. I'm a mucker maid, no more." I wouldn't point out the real Saren now, not with Lady Vachir there hoping for someone to chop up.

He asked Lady Vachir for my book. She gripped it.

"Lady Vachir," he said quietly, "stealing is also a crime."

She placed it in his hands, her expression carefully casual. He pressed it back into mine.

"Keep this close to you," he whispered.

280

Then, at last, came the moment when his arm fell away from my waist. I shivered as he took a step back, suddenly as frozen inside as out. Perhaps it's irony that I'd met Khasar naked on the battlefield, but I felt colder now.

After he let me go, warriors carried me here, locked me in. I stared at my one candle for hours. I couldn't bear to look away.

This evening Shria brought some supper, and with it my horsehair blanket, some ink, and a brush. She didn't speak to me, but she touched my cheek before she left. I tore a blank page out of this book and thought to write Tegus an explanation. I crossed out the words again and again before I gave up. Every word I write to him sounds false. I can't speak the whole truth—that I wasn't only acting out of duty for my lady, how it was my own shirt I gave him. How parts of me wanted to be his lady, just for a moment even.

Stop it, Dashti. None of that matters now. My whole, heavy world hangs by a thin rope. I remember a time when I comprehended Saren's plea to die, but not now. Now I want to live. Ancestors, please, I want to keep on living.

It's cold down here.

Day 170

Khan Tegus came this morning. He asked me again if it was all true.

"Yes," I said.

He groaned and paced. I didn't explain. I guess I always knew it would come to this, and trying to change it now seemed like trying to stop the wind from blowing across the steppes. Besides, the excuse "my lady ordered me to" sounded so feeble in my head. She ordered me, but I chose to obey.

"Lady Vachir is claiming blood rights," he said. "Protection of binding betrothals is as old as cities, since the days men would get brides by kidnapping. The law is severe on that point, and my chiefs say she's within the law, and . . . Dashti, I don't know what to do."

"Have you spoken with Lady Saren?"

He looked sharply at me. "Is she Lady Saren? She's been claiming such, and I told her to be quiet about it and stay hidden in the kitchens. No need to give Vachir another target."

"If it comes to dying"—I sat on my hands so he couldn't see them shake—"if it comes to that, don't be anxious for me. I have a mama in the Ancestors' Realm. She'll sing me in. I'll be all right."

I didn't want to say that. I wanted to throw myself on my knees and beg to keep breathing, but I can't have him breaking his heart for worrying about me. Even so, my words didn't seem to relieve him any. He put his face in his hands and breathed slowly for a long while. I think he might've cried, if he'd let himself. He might've cried for me. What a powerful thought.

"You're our champion." He let his hands drop. "You went out alone, you took down Khasar. But now Lady Vachir has made certain there's not a soul in this city who doesn't also know that you lied, you claimed to be gentry, you . . ." He sat beside me and was quiet for a while. I kept my eyes on his hands until he spoke again.

"Lady Saren's father visited Song for Evela when I was eight. I remember at a banquet, my father pulling me in close and saying, in almost a teasing way, 'He has a daughter named Saren. You might marry her one day, you know. What do you think about that?' When I was fourteen and received her first letter, it didn't seem strange because I'd had her in my mind all those years."

"You were meant to marry her," I said.

He shrugged. "The letters were a game. I was

young, I felt as though I were playing at being in love. I read poetry to try to learn how one courts with words, and I failed at it miserably. But it was fun, anticipating a new letter, hiding it from my father and hers, and we kept it up for a few years. When my father died before declaring who he wanted me to marry, I realized I might actually wed Lady Saren. I looked over her letters again, and I saw them anew—they were simple, little humor or life. To tell the truth, I was apprehensive at best. And then came news of the tower.

"I felt responsible, but I was dreading the meeting, too. It was you, wasn't it, Dashti? You were the one who spoke to me."

I nodded. I was wrapped up in the weave of his story and didn't want to speak.

"Of course it was you. I never should've left you in there. I should've risked war with Titor's Garden and Thoughts of Under. We met war anyway. When I spoke with Lady Saren in the tower, with you, it was a wonder. It felt right." He smiled. "Then I met you as Dashti, but when you told me you were Lady Saren, that felt right, too. And all has seemed right until . . . Ancestors, it's all wrong. You weren't Lady Saren in the tower, you weren't when you faced Khasar, you're not now and you won't ever be, and for that the chief of order says you must hang."

I thought I'd prepared myself for that end, but hearing him say it made my heart sting.

He rubbed his face again. "Dashti, I don't know what to do. I don't know. Can you, will you sing for me?"

So I sang him the song for clear thoughts, and after a time he leaned back against the wall with me and rested his head against mine, humming along. It was strange, as I think back on it now, that I'm the one scheduled to die but I was comforting him. At the time, it felt just right. It was a moment of peace, and it gave me space to think. We were betrothed once. I always knew it was ill-fated, but he truly believed I would be his bride. I guess I'd never realized that before. He had taken my mucker hand and looked at my mottled face and believed we would wed. And he hadn't seemed sorry. In fact, he'd swooped me up in the corridor and kissed me.

That set me to crying. He sat up and took my hand, the one mottled, holding it to his lips.

"Dashti, oh Dashti, I'm sorry." He smoothed my hair against the back of my head, he held my forehead to his. "Please, I'm so sorry. Listen, nothing's settled yet. The chiefs may vote to preserve your life.

A lesser sentence might be banishment from Song for Evela."

Ancestors know that I never would've said aloud what I thought then—that living didn't matter to me if it meant I'd be alone, that I'd have to leave Tegus behind. Is that silly? And yet I really feel it. Here's what I wished I could say—*Tegus, I'll not find a better man than you, not on the steppes, not in any city or in all the wilds of the Eight Realms. You're better than seven years of food. You're better than windows. You're even better than the sky.*

But I couldn't tell him that, and since I had to hold back words, I wanted to give him something. "Take my book of thought keeping," I said. "It's all I have that I care about."

"Haven't you destroyed it yet? I gave it back to you so you could. It's the best evidence against you." He put it back in my hands and stood at once. Before he passed through my door, he turned and said, "I'm sorry, Dashti."

And I guess that's the last time I'll ever see him.

After he left, I sat on the ground and stared at the door for a long time. A very long time. I didn't want to move ever again. Eventually I got myself up so I could write what Tegus said. To keep telling my story seems like the last bit of living I can still do. I feel like a dragonfly clinging to a grass blade in a windstorm, but I can't just let go. I can't. I stare at the candle, how the flame shivers and bends when the wick is too long. The light is small and unsteady, but unless it's snuffed out, it'll keep burning for as long as the wick runs.

There's a stinging, cold sensation that shivers through my blood. I look at my hands, stare at how they're shaking, and wonder if this is how Osol felt the night before he died. I wonder if everyone who faces death hurts like this. It's as though for the first time I realize how much just being alive makes my body ache. But I don't want that ache to stop.

Day 171

What a long, cold night it was. I guess I can admit that I wept instead of sleeping. Odd how much that made my throat hurt. With no window, no way to track the time, I felt as though I spent days here alone. When Shria came with breakfast, she assured me that it was just barely morning out in the world. Along with cheese and bread, she brought news.

"There's quite a tumult in your kitchens," she said. "The family of one of the girls made it out of Goda's Second Gift and came here. Seems it was pretty rough going, traveling into winter, but they didn't stop until they found their daughter."

"Gal," I said. A grin took over my face and felt like an old friend come home.

The news changed me, and I've been thinking and buzzing for hours. Though the only light I have is a candle and even wrapped up in my blanket my bones are cold like stones, I'm filled with a kind of wonder, I guess. A wonder that burns. If Gal's family is alive and found her, if her impossible wish came true, what else can happen? It makes me almost believe that everything works out somehow, and even if the best possible ending for all this is for me to speedily join my mama in the Realm of the Ancestors, then so be it. That is an ending to be proud of.

And I've decided a second thing—I don't care if this book is evidence against me. I've thought and thought and folded myself toward the Sacred Mountain and prayed to all the Ancestors, and what I know is that I'm tired of deception and lies. I want Tegus to know all. Even if it be my end. Endings aren't so bad. After the night I endured, any ending sounds like peace.

When Shria returns, I'll send this book with her to the khan. The thought of him reading these silly thoughts of mine makes me want to pull the horsehair blanket over my head. But so be it. I am done. Besides, if I'm being truly honest, I must admit that ever since I first heard his voice outside the tower, I've been writing this book for him. To him. It's his more than mine.

And whoever reads this, be it Tegus or Shria or anyone, I've kept my wages in the far left corner of the sugar closet beneath the pile of empty sacks. I wish you'd give them to Gal's family to get them started. I hate to think of those coins lying idle and doing no good.

Day 174

This book of thought keeping must have the soul of a good mare who always returns to her master, for here it is, in my hands again. I have much to tell and little time, so here I go.

After I last wrote, Shria came again to my locked room, bringing supper, and I sent her away with this book in hand and a request to give it to Khan Tegus. I waited two more days, knowing nothing. No one came but a kitchen boy whose name I never learned, bringing raisin rice, carrot salad, and milk to drink. No meat for prisoners. That's the law.

Those two days felt as long as a tower year. I've grown accustomed to easing loneliness and worry by writing my thoughts here or making a sketch of what I see. Being alone, without even this book to write in—well, I guess that's about as lonely as I've ever felt. I began to imagine that the world had swallowed me and I was lost and trapped deep in its belly with . . . never mind, I don't want to think about it anymore.

After two days Shria returned. Her mouth was wrinkled like a winter carrot as she frowned at me— she wasn't angry, more sorry.

"Say prayers if you wish, Dashti," she said. "You won't be coming back here. Whatever fate they decide for you, they'll enact it today."

I said prayers. I didn't know what to pray for, so instead I just folded myself toward the north and, closing my eyes, tried to fill myself with memories of the Eternal Blue Sky. How can a body be too sad or frightened or lonely when she's filled up her soul with the highest sky blue? I left my horsehair blanket behind but told Shria that if they were to hang me, I wouldn't mind my body being covered in that brown blanket. It's been a good comfort to me. She nodded. I think she was too teary to speak. Ancestors bless her.

Then upstairs to the large feasting hall. Lady Vachir was there, the seven chiefs of Song for Evela and one empty chair, four shaman, my lady, and Khan Tegus. I hadn't realized that he'd be there. Everyone was frowning at me.

The city chief, a squat woman with black eyes, led the tribunal. "We're here to decide the fate of Dashti, a lady's maid, who claimed nobility and betrothal to our khan."

It was the chief of order's responsibility to lay out my crimes, and she did a very good job. While she spoke, she held this book in her hand, and I guessed that before Shria was able to deliver it to the khan, the chief of order had taken a look.

"Dashti," she said. She had a very tiny mouth. It unnerved me. "Dashti, why did you claim to be Lady Saren?"

"My lady asked me to," I said. "She ordered me on the sacred nine, and I had sworn to obey her."

"Hmm," said the chief. Then she opened this book and began to read parts aloud, parts that made me wish I could bury myself alive. How I gave Tegus my own shirt, when I said my lady smelled like hot dung, when I said I hated her, when I described the smell of Tegus's neck . . . Ancestors, it was horrible to hear. Every word made me hate myself more, and I decided that they'd be right to hang me.

"Do you have any defense for yourself, Dashti?" asked the chief of order.

I didn't. I couldn't think of anything, and I couldn't bear to look at Tegus. At that moment, my one wish was for a rope around my neck as fast as possible.

"Then I demand her blood!" Lady Vachir arose and began to shout for my death, and not by hanging but my head on the chopping block so my blood would be spilled. That bit seemed to go on forever, and I thought, *I really am going to die today. And the end is just and everything will be fine.*

While they shouted, I concentrated on sitting up straight. My thoughts kept returning to the idea of silver on blue, silver on blue. Oddly enough, that image of the sword against the sky was comforting to me. Maybe because the sword never fell?

And then the khan stood, calming Lady Vachir back into her seat.

"Since Dashti doesn't give her own defense, chiefs, I ask for the right to do so for her."

The chiefs nodded. The khan approached my chair, and I kept my eyes on his boots.

"First, allow me to examine other entries." He opened the book and read some from times in the tower, when I didn't want to speak for Saren, when I worried and prayed, when I begged her not to order me to. He read the entire entry from the day I gave My Lord the cat to Saren. He read my encounter with Khasar. There were murmurs of approval from some of the chiefs then.

"There was another part that caught my interest as well," said the khan. "The day you arrived in Song for Evela. First, Dashti, you are a mucker, is that correct?"

"Yes, my lord."

"Forgive our ignorance of mucker ways, but as more folk from the steppes come here, we're beginning to learn. I understand that, according to the law of the steppes, if a mucker offers her last animal to another family or clan, accepting that gift means recognizing the mucker as a member of the family. Is that so?"

I guess I just gaped at him then, I was so confused. What in all the realms was he saying? And when was he going to condemn me to death?

"Shria, please relate your first encounter with Dashti."

The white-haired woman stood. "She arrived at the gates with Lady Saren and a brown yak. She said she wanted to give the yak to Khan Tegus, that it was a gift for him."

"Did she ask payment?"

"No, in fact the gatekeeper stated no payment would be given, and she offered it anyway."

"Did she trade the animal in return for employment?"

"No, she gave the animal freely. I offered her scrubber work after the gift had been given."

The khan nodded, satisfied. "I submit to you, chiefs, that Dashti presented me with her last animal, her only means of livelihood, and as such has the right to expect family status. I formally accept her gift of . . . ," he turned to me, "a yak, was it?"

"Yes, a very fine yak," I said. For he is—the finest yak I've ever known.

The khan nodded. "Of a very fine yak. Here's where two laws collide, chiefs. Do we honor Lady Vachir's claim of blood against any who threaten her betrothal? Or do we protect Dashti as a member of my own family?"

Lady Vachir stood. "Chiefs, I demand—"

"Wait, please, my lady, wait a little longer before getting back to the demands. I recognize that this argument isn't enough to stay your claim to blood right, but there is more. Lady Saren?"

He took Saren's hand to help her rise from her seat, and I thought, *That's how they'll hold hands when they're wed.*

"This is the true Lady Saren of Titor's Garden. I have her letters here," he placed parchments on the table before the chiefs, "accepting my offer of betrothal."

"My lord," said the chief of order, "we've already ruled that your betrothal to Lady Saren precedes that to Lady Vachir. You have every right to marry the true Lady Saren, but this doesn't excuse Dashti's crimes."

"Lady Saren," asked the khan, all business. "Why did Dashti claim she was you?"

"I ordered her to. I told her to act in my name." She turned to Lady Vachir and said, "It was my right," offering along with the words a very convincing glare.

The chief of animals shook her head. "Acting for her lady is the duty of a lady's maid, but professing to be her? Claiming her name? No. We're hearing reasons for the behavior but nothing that pardons the maid. Pretending nobility is the grossest crime imaginable."

"Grosser than trading the soul's freedom to the desert shamans?" Batu said in a grumble that didn't carry far beyond the chief's table. "Grosser than razing Titor's Garden?"

All were quiet for a moment. Then the chief of animals spoke again.

"Nevertheless, the law is paramount. If we don't obey the law, then we create as much chaos as Khasar and his army. If I had to vote now —"

"A moment, chief, please, I beg you. Don't cast your vote just yet." Khan Tegus turned back to Saren. "My lady, tell me what you told me this morning."

Saren smiled, dimples and all, and didn't even clutch her own hands as she said, "Dashti is my sister."

I started to gasp but choked on it.

"Now let's be clear," said Tegus. "Has she always been your sister?"

"No." Saren was smiling fit to split her face in half. Her voice clipped in such a way that I guessed she'd rehearsed this answer and was proud to be getting it right. "But she stayed with me when everyone else left. And . . . and we spent nearly three years locked in a tower, and when we came out, it was as though we were birth . . . uh, being born anew. All my real family was dead."

"How did they die?"

"Killed by Lord Khasar. And then Dashti faced him and helped av — aveg . . ."

"Avenge," said the khan.

"Avenge my family and defend my honor." She looked at me, hard, and then she straightened up, turned herself toward the chiefs, and said in as bold a voice as I've ever heard, "Hear me, chiefs, the last lady of Titor's Garden. Dashti never betrayed me, never abandoned me. She was as true a lady's maid as the Ancestors ever created."

There was power in her voice, and the chiefs took notice. How could they not? I've seen my lady begin to change since the cat purred in her lap, since she found use for her hands in the kitchen, since Khasar died, but never until that moment had she looked like I thought gentry should. Like anyone should. More than a thousand days we've been together, more than a thousand songs I've sung for her, and only now, I think, do I see Saren truly begin to heal.

"And since I have no more family," Saren said, "it's my right under the Ancestors to declare Dashti my sister and an honored daughter of Titor's Garden."

I think that's the part where I did gasp and gulp at the same time, which set me coughing.

"Oh, one more question for Shria," said the khan. "Please tell the chiefs what you told me before, what you found in Dashti's room after she fled this house, the day Lady Vachir's warriors tried to cut off her foot."

Shria cleared her throat. "Nothing, my lord. I mean, everything. That room was filled with silk and brocade deels, silver and porcelain bowls and cups, hair combs decorated with pearls. She left them all behind, only took her old clothing, the very rags she'd been wearing when she arrived." She looked at the chiefs. "Seemed to me that if she were lying about who she was for selfish reasons, she would've taken some of those nice things to sell out in the city."

"Thank you, Shria." He turned to the chiefs. "I submit to you Dashti, a mucker maid. She said she was gentry, but is that a crime for one who was named as a sister by the lady of Titor's Garden, or for one who earned the right to be considered a member of my own honored family? She proved herself loyal to her lady even unto risking her own life, an act that should far outweigh any impropriety. As well, she faced Khasar alone on the battlefield and, blessed by the Ancestors themselves, walked away from it, victorious. For my vote, one in the nine, I find her actions justified, and what some would call a crime, I declare a noble act of loyalty. How find you?"

There was a horrible silence as the chiefs thought, some whispering to one another, some shaking their heads. Khan Tegus clenched his jaw and his eyes were fearful. I knew it would take just four chiefs to find me guilty. It is assumed that the chief in the empty chair will always vote for death.

The oldest chief, the one who serves Evela, goddess of sunlight, turned to the four shamans and asked, "What say you, holy ones?"

The shaman who'd read the sheep bones and declared Khasar couldn't be defeated by strength looked at me when he spoke. "I haven't read the signs or submitted to a trance, but my instinct says the Ancestors love this girl."

"Hmm," said the chief. And again, the horrible silence, which was finally broken by Batu, who hit his palm against the table, making everyone jump.

"Come now, my friends. This isn't so difficult. Our khan has done a mightier job here than even we dull-brained lot needed. Who among you really thinks this girl committed a crime?"

Several chiefs shook their heads, a couple squirmed, but not one raised a fist to vote. The mood exhaled. I think I might've cried.

"Disgraceful," said Lady Vachir, as she and all her vulture maids marched out of the room. Winter or not, I doubt Lady Vachir will be staying long in Song for Evela.

As soon as she was gone, Khan Tegus leaned against the table and sighed for relief so loudly, several people laughed. I didn't. I still couldn't breathe right.

"Thank the Ancestors," he said. "And you as well, honored chiefs. Thank you."

Saren embraced me. She did it clumsily, placing one arm around my neck and resting her head on my shoulder. She whispered, "I was scared, Dashti. I was really scared. I thought you might die and I really, really didn't want you to."

"You did well," I whispered back. "You spoke up like a lady. You were so brave." It made my eyes sting to say it, I really did feel as proud as any mucker mama. "Thank you, my lady."

She looked at me now and said, "No more 'my lady,' Dashti. No more of that."

I couldn't respond. I didn't know what to say. No

chance my mouth was going to let me call her sister. Not yet.

Batu was slapping Tegus on the back and laughing with relief. All the chiefs were standing, talking. A few were a bit disgruntled, but most seemed happy, excited even.

"And now at last," said the chief of light, "we'll have our khan's wedding. Lady Saren, may I be the first to congratulate you."

Tegus and Saren looked at each other. The whole room quieted. And I found reason to be glad I was still sitting.

Of course this is how it'll end, I told myself. This is how it should end. She's an honored lady. Isn't this what I've wanted for her? And I'll stay with her still and be her friend and coddle her babies, their babies, and keep my thoughts to myself and the pages of my book. It'll be all right. Saren will be the lady of Song for Evela and maybe I can write letters for her, advise her on things, be useful. It won't be so bad. It's an ending.

And though I reminded myself that I was just happy to be alive, some part of me wanted to shrink and die.

Tegus glanced at me once before saying, "Lady Saren, we *are* betrothed. Do you wish to wed me?"

Saren was watching me, and her eyes seemed troubled, but I can't be sure about that, because I felt like I was falling through the floor and seeing her from so far away.

"I'm not sure —," she started before the chief of order rushed forward and shushed everyone.

"My lord, may I hastily remind you that if you and Lady Saren break your betrothal, Lady Vachir will have full claim on your hand."

"Thank you, honored chief," said Tegus. "But Saren and I spoke this morning, and we both felt —"

"Careful," said the town chief, her eyes on the door. "I wouldn't advise you to say anything."

Saren was still looking at me when she said, "Then I will say." She drew herself up tall. "Khan Tegus, I would rather not marry you. However . . . ," she said loudly, cutting through the outcries from the chiefs, "however, I retain my right to our betrothal, and I exact it for my sister, Dashti."

Batu chuckled. Why was he laughing? Was it a joke on me?

Tegus didn't seem surprised. He offered Saren his hands, palms down. She took them, and he kissed her forehead as he would a younger sister.

Then he smiled at me, and I knew it wasn't a joke. Tegus would never play a cruel trick on me, and he never smiles by accident. He means each one. Then he was beside me. Then he was on one knee and taking my hand. And it felt like the tower, after he'd given me My Lord the cat when he held my hand, and everything in the world was inside that touch. And only the Ancestors know why, but I stopped feeling dizzy and confused, and all I wanted to do was laugh. So I did. Tegus did too, a surprised laugh.

"All right, all right," he said, forcing a straight face. "Here I go." He took a deep breath. "Dashti of Titor's Garden, Dashti of the steppes, will you please be my betrothed and my bride and my wife in this realm and the next?"

At those words, all laughter left me. Now, I've trembled before in steppes cold that's fit to freeze a yak. But when Tegus spoke those words, my arms took to shaking like I've never seen, and my legs knocking, my knees chattering, my whole body consumed to shivering so that I was afraid I couldn't keep my seat. I think I was crying too, and I wished I could leap up and dance, but it was all so much, my body couldn't hold it in. I shook and shook, my voice lost in the shudders.

So I looked to my lady. After all, I figured it was her turn to speak for me.

And Saren, understanding precisely what I wanted of her, faced Tegus and said, "Yes. She will."

Day 178

Today Tegus and I were wed, and Ancestors, but there was so much food! I wore a deel dyed as blue as the Eternal Sky, embroidered with yellow and gold thread, sunrise and sunset running up and down my sleeves. Qacha and Gal helped me dress and cooed over me as if I were the prettiest bride anyone had ever seen. Truth is, I felt it. I tried to wear a veil, but Tegus wouldn't have it.

"I want to see you as we take the vows. I want everyone to see you. My Dashti."

Then he kissed me on the mouth, though there were five chiefs in the room. Kissing like that in front of others may not be proper, but I felt certain that even the Ancestors didn't mind. I put my arms around his neck and kissed him back. Can a person actually float away from happiness?

A thing of wonder happened as Tegus and I took the vows. It was as though I'd been standing on one side of the room and suddenly everything swooped around and changed places, though nothing actually moved. It sounds strange, I know, but I felt the whooshing feeling in my belly, as if I were riding a mare that leaped from standing right into a gallop. And what caused that feeling inside me was this thought—I'm not a mucker marrying a khan. I'm Dashti marrying Tegus. And that feels just right. How Mama would laugh.

At the feast, Saren showed me all the trays of food she helped prepare. She doesn't have to work in the kitchens anymore, she has her own room and two sweet-voiced maids to call on for anything. But she likes to work with food, she says, and she likes to arrange things and make them look pretty. She looked more than pretty in a peach silk deel tonight, her hair in eight braids twisted up. Two of Tegus's cousins held a mock sword battle with tiny fish bones to see who got to sit beside her. I guess I've never heard her giggle so much. It *was* pretty funny, actually, and they do seem like decent boys, but I told Tegus no one has permission to court her until I know every detail of his life and personality. Saren deserves a gentle man, someone sweet who makes her laugh, who doesn't make her feel dull-witted, and when his arms are around her, she knows she's in the safest place in all the realms. We'll find the right one. Tegus has thirty-seven cousins.

There's still more feasting to be done and dancing

until the sun sets, and Tegus swore he could hold me as we danced so my injured leg would never touch the floor. I can hear the music just starting, but I hopped back here to our rooms so I could change my clothes.

During the tediously long ceremony, I was re-membering when Tegus and I spoke through the tower and he'd said, "Would that I could take you out of here, and hold a feast and a dance, and see you be-decked in a silver deel." And there just happens to be a deel in the wardrobe made of silver silk. I can't wait to see his face when he sees me in it. I plan to laugh and laugh and dance and maybe I'll kiss him again, kiss my khan, right in front of the whole world.

ACKNOWLEDGMENTS

This book is based on the fairy tale "Maid Maleen," as recorded by the Grimm brothers, though I took many liberties with the original in my quest to find Dashti's story. Although I invented the Eight Realms, the setting was inspired in part by medieval Mongolia. Jack Weatherford's *Genghis Khan and the Making of the Modern World* was a fascinating read and huge help. Special thanks to Burd Jadamba, Sarantuya Batbold, Ariunaa Buyantogtokh, and Bonnie Bryner for the many stories and facts about Mongolia.

In researching and writing this story, I was impressed by the lifesaving difference one animal can make in a family's survival. We've been able to donate some of the proceeds of this book to Heifer International, an organization that gives important domestic animals to families in third world countries. Check out www.heifer.org, where you can donate a goat or water buffalo or flock of geese to a family in need.

As always, much credit goes to Victoria Wells Arms and Dean "The Family Yak" Hale for being inspired editors and readers, and to Max, for making the whole world new.

Six Years

"With *Six Years*, the author shows once more how it's done. . . . The beauty of Coben's craftsmanship here is how often he can lure us into not perceiving what's right in front of our eyes. . . . Furious plot twists." —*The Washington Post*

Stay Close

"Funnier and darker than many Coben thrillers and packs a lot of surprises. It's the beach read of the pre–beach season." —*People* (4 stars)

Live Wire

"Mr. Coben's unique imagination has made him a past master of fast and witty dialogue and architect of memorable characters. *Live Wire* follows that tradition with a meticulously plotted storyline. Gripping and full of genuine page-turning surprises." —*The New York Journal of Books*

Caught

"The thrill-a-minute action zooms on sharp, slippery twists and turns in a white-knuckle race from start to finish." —#1 *New York Times* bestselling author Nora Roberts

Long Lost

"The action unfolds with the intensity of TV's 24. . . . Nobody writes them better than Coben." —Associated Press

Hold Tight

"A thriller for the Google era." —*The New York Times*

The Woods

"A lively, fast-moving entertainment, jam-packed with the bizarre plot twists that are his stock-in-trade." —*The Washington Post*

Promise Me

"Truly surprising." —*Entertainment Weekly*

The Innocent

"Another twist-filled triumph." —*Life*

Just One Look

"The only plausible reason for setting down this book is to make sure your front door is locked and double-bolted." —*People*

No Second Chance

THE FIRST INTERNATIONAL BOOK-OF-THE-MONTH CLUB® SELECTION

"Every time you think Harlan Coben couldn't get any better at uncoiling a whip snake of a page-turner, he comes along with a new novel that somehow surpasses its predecessor."
—*San Francisco Chronicle*

Gone for Good

"This killer thriller has more twists and turns than an amusement park ride. . . . *Gone for Good* is great." —*USA Today*

Tell No One

"Pulse-pounding. . . . Coben layers secret upon secret, crisscrossing years and crime scenes." —*People*

SIX YEARS

HARLAN COBEN

SIX YEARS

DUTTON

DUTTON

An imprint of Penguin Random House LLC
375 Hudson Street
New York, New York 10014

Previously published as a Dutton hardcover and a Signet and Dutton mass market paperback
First Dutton trade paperback printing, August 2018

ISBN 9781524744335

Printed in the United States of America
10   9   8   7

To Brad Bradbeer
Without you, dear friend, there'd be no Win

Chapter 1

I sat in the back pew and watched the only woman I would ever love marry another man.

Natalie wore white, of course, looking extra mock-me-forever gorgeous. There had always been both a fragility and quiet strength to her beauty, and up there, Natalie looked ethereal, almost otherworldly.

She bit down on her lower lip. I flashed back to those lazy mornings when we would make love and then she'd throw on my blue dress shirt and we'd head downstairs. We would sit in the breakfast nook and read the paper and eventually she'd take out her pad and start sketching. As she drew me, she would bite down on her lip just like this.

Two hands reached into my chest, grabbed my brittle heart on either side, and snapped it in two.

Why had I come?

Do you believe in love at first sight? Neither do I. I do, however, believe in major, more-than-just-physical attraction at first sight. I believe that every once in a while—once, maybe twice in a lifetime—you are drawn to someone so deeply, so primordially, so immediately—a stronger-than-magnetic pull. That was how it was with Natalie. Sometimes that is all there is. Sometimes it grows and gathers heat and turns into a glorious inferno that you know is real and meant to last forever.

And sometimes you just get fooled into thinking the first is the second.

I had naively thought that we were forever. I, who had never really believed in commitment and had done all I could to escape its shackles, knew right away—well, within a week anyway—that this was the woman I was going to wake up next to every single day. This was the woman I'd lay my life down to protect. This was the woman—yes, I know how corny this sounds—whom I could do nothing without, who would make even the mundane something poignant.

Gag me with a spoon, right?

A minister with a cleanly shaven head was talking, but the rush of blood in my ears made it impossible to make out his words. I stared at Natalie. I wanted her to be happy. That wasn't just lip service, the lie we often tell ourselves because, in truth, if our lover doesn't want us, then we want her miserable, don't we? But here I really meant it. If I truly believed that Natalie would be happier without me, then I would let her go, no matter how crushing. But I didn't believe that she would be happier, despite what she had said or done. Or maybe that is yet another self-rationalization, another lie, we tell ourselves.

Natalie did not so much as glance at me, but I could see something tighten around her mouth. She knew that I was in the room. She kept her eyes on her husband-to-be. His name, I had recently found out, was Todd. I hate the name Todd. Todd. They probably called him Toddy or the Todd-Man or the Toddster.

Todd's hair was too long, and he sported that four-day-stubble beard some people found hip and others, like me, found punchworthy. His eyes smoothly and smugly skimmed the guests before getting snagged on, well, me. They stayed there a second, sizing me up before deciding that I wasn't worth the time.

Why had Natalie gone back to him?

The maid of honor was Natalie's sister, Julie. She stood on the dais with a bouquet in both hands and a lifeless, robotic smile on her lips. We'd never met, but I'd seen pictures and heard them talk on the phone. Julie, too, looked stunned by this development. I tried to meet her eye, but she was working that thousand-yard stare.

I looked back at Natalie's face, and it was as if small explosives detonated in my chest. Just boom, boom, boom. Man, this had been a bad idea. When the best man brought out the rings, my lungs started shutting down. It was hard to breathe.

Enough.

I had come here to see it for myself, I guess. I had learned the hard way that I needed that. My father died of a massive coronary five months ago. He had never had a heart problem before and was by all accounts in good shape. I remembered sitting in that waiting room, being called into the doctor's office, being told the devastating news—and then being asked, both there and at the funeral home, if I wanted to see his body. I passed. I figured that I didn't want to remember him lying on a gurney or in a casket. I would remember him as he was.

But as time went on, I started having trouble accepting his death. He had been so vibrant, so alive. Two days before his death, we had gone to a New York Rangers hockey game—Dad had season tickets—and the game had gone into overtime and we screamed and cheered and, well, how could he be dead? Part of me started wondering if somehow there had been a mistake made or if it was all a great big con and that my dad was maybe somehow still alive. I know that makes no sense, but desperation can toy with you and if you give desperation any wiggle room, it will find alternative answers.

Part of me was haunted by the fact that I never saw my father's body. I didn't want to make the same mistake here. But, to keep within this lame metaphor, I had now seen the dead body. There was no reason to check the pulse or poke at it or hang around it longer than necessary.

I tried to make my departure as inconspicuous as I could. This is no easy feat when you're six-five and are built, to use Natalie's phrase, "like a lumberjack." I have big hands. Natalie had loved them. She would hold them in her own and trace the lines on my palm. She said they were real hands, a man's hands. She had drawn them too because, she said, they told my story—my blue-collar upbringing, my working my way through Lanford College as a bouncer at a local nightclub, and also, somehow, the fact that I was now the youngest professor in their political science department.

I stumbled out of the small white chapel and into the warm summer air. Summer. Was that all this had been in the end? A summer fling? Instead of two randy kids seeking activity at camp, we were two adults seeking solitude on retreat—she to do her art, me to write my poly-sci dissertation—who met and fell hard and now that it was nearing September, well, all good things come to an end. Our whole relationship did have that unreal quality to it, both of us away from our regular lives and all the mundanity that goes along with that. Maybe that was what made it so awesome. Maybe the fact that we only spent time in this reality-free bubble made our relationship better and more intense. Maybe I was full of crap.

From behind the church door I heard cheers, applause. That snapped me out of my stupor. The service was over. Todd and Natalie were now Mr. and Mrs. Stubble Face. They'd be coming down the aisle soon. I wondered whether they'd get rice thrown at them. Todd probably wouldn't like that. It'd mess up his hair and get stuck in the stubble.

Again I didn't need to see more.

I headed behind the white chapel, getting out of sight just as the chapel doors flew open. I stared out at the clearing. Nothing there, just, well, clearing. There were trees in the distance. The cabins were on the other side of the hill. The chapel was part of the artist retreat where Natalie was staying. Mine was down the road at a retreat for writers. Both retreats were old Vermont farms that still grew a bit of the organic.

"Hello, Jake."

I turned toward the familiar voice. There, standing no more than ten yards away from me, was Natalie. I quickly looked toward her left ring finger. As if reading my thoughts, she raised the hand to show me the new wedding band.

"Congratulations," I said. "I'm very happy for you."

She ignored that comment. "I can't believe you're here."

I spread my arms. "I heard there would be great passed hors d'oeuvres. It's hard to keep me away from those."

"Funny."

I shrugged while my heart turned into dust and blew away.

"Everyone said you'd never show," Natalie said. "But I knew you would."

"I still love you," I said.

"I know."

"And you still love me."

"I don't, Jake. See?"

She waved the ring in my face.

"Honey?" Todd and his facial hair came around the corner. He spotted me and frowned. "Who is this?"

But it was clear that he knew.

"Jake Fisher," I said. "Congratulations on the nuptials."

"Where have I seen you before?"

I let Natalie handle that one. She put a comforting hand on his shoulder and said, "Jake has been modeling for a lot of us. You probably recognize him from some of our pieces."

He still frowned. Natalie got in front of him and said, "If you could just give us a second, okay? I'll be right there."

Todd glanced over at me. I didn't move. I didn't back up. I didn't look away.

Grudgingly he said, "Okay. But don't be long."

He gave me one more hard look and started back around the chapel. Natalie looked over at me. I pointed toward where Todd had vanished.

"He seems fun," I said.

"Why are you here?"

"I needed to tell you that I love you," I said. "I needed to tell you that I always will."

"It's over, Jake. You'll move on. You'll be fine."

I said nothing.

"Jake?"

"What?"

She tilted her head a little. She knew what that head tilt did to me. "Promise me you'll leave us alone."

I just stood there.

"Promise me you won't follow us or call or even e-mail."

The pain in my chest grew. It became something sharp and heavy.

"Promise me, Jake. Promise me you'll leave us alone."

Her eyes locked on to mine.

"Okay," I said. "I promise."

Without another word, Natalie walked away, back to the front of that chapel toward the man she had just married. I stood there a moment, trying to catch my breath. I tried to get angry, tried to make light of it, tried to shrug it off and tell her it was her loss. I tried all that, and then I even tried to be mature about it, but I still knew that this was all a stall technique, so I wouldn't have to face the fact that I would be forever brokenhearted.

I stayed there behind the chapel until I figured everyone was gone. Then I came back around. The minister with the cleanly shaven head was outside on the steps. So was Natalie's sister, Julie. She put a hand on my arm. "Are you okay?"

"I'm super," I said to her.

The minister smiled at me. "A lovely day for a wedding, don't you think?"

I blinked into the sunlight. "I guess it is," I said, and then I walked away.

I would do as Natalie asked. I would leave her alone. I would think about her every day, but I'd never call or reach out or even look her up online. I would keep my promise.

For six years.

Chapter 2

The biggest change in my life, though I couldn't know it at the time, would arrive sometime between 3:29 P.M. and 3:30 P.M.

My freshman class on the politics of moral reasoning had just ended. I was heading out of Bard Hall. The day was campus-ready. The sun shone brightly on this crisp Massachusetts afternoon. There was an Ultimate Frisbee game on the quad. Students lay strewn all over the place, as though scattered by some giant hand. Music blasted. It was as if the dream campus brochure had come to life.

I love days like this, but then again, who doesn't?

"Professor Fisher?"

I turned to the voice. Seven students were sitting in a semicircle in the grass. The girl who spoke was in the middle.

"Would you like to join us?" she asked.

I waved them off with a smile. "Thanks, but I have office hours."

I kept walking. I wouldn't have stayed anyway, though I would have loved to sit with them on such a glorious day—who wouldn't? There were fine lines between teacher and student, and, sorry, uncharitable as this might sound, I didn't want to be *that* teacher, if you know what I mean, the teacher who hangs out a little too much with the student body and attends the occasional frat party and maybe offers up a beer at the football game tailgate. A professor should be supportive and approachable, but a professor should be neither buddy nor parent.

When I got to Clark House, Mrs. Dinsmore greeted me with a familiar scowl. Mrs. Dinsmore, a classic battle-axe, had been the political science department receptionist here since, I believe, the Hoover administration. She was at least two hundred years old but was only as impatient and nasty as someone half that age.

"Good afternoon, sexy," I said to her. "Any messages?"

"On your desk," Mrs. Dinsmore said. Even her voice scowled. "And there's the usual line of coeds outside your door."

"Okay, thanks."

"Looks like a Rockettes audition back there."

"Got it."

"Your predecessor was never this accessible."

"Oh, come now, Mrs. Dinsmore. I visited him here all the time when I was a student."

"Yeah, but at least your shorts were an appropriate length."

"And that disappointed you a little, didn't it?"

Mrs. Dinsmore did her best not to smile at me. "Just get out of my face, will you?"

"Just admit it."

"You want a kick in the pants? Get out of here."

I blew her a kiss and took the back entrance so as to avoid the line of students who signed up for Friday office hours. I have two hours of "unscheduled" office time every Friday from 3:00 to 5:00 P.M. It was open time, nine minutes per student, no schedule, no early sign-up. You just show up—first come, first served. We keep strictly on the clock. You have nine minutes. No more, no less, and then one minute to leave and let the next student settle in and have their turn. If you need more time or if I'm your thesis adviser or what have you, Mrs. Dinsmore will schedule you for a longer appointment.

At exactly 3:00 P.M., I let in the first student. She wanted to discuss theories on Locke and Rousseau, two political scientists better known now by their *Lost* TV show reincarnations than their philosophical theories. The second student had no real reason to be here other than to—and I am being blunt here—suck up. Sometimes I wanted to hold up a hand and say, "Bake me some cookies instead," but I get it. The third student was into grade groveling; that is, she thought that her B+ paper should have been an A-, when in fact it probably should have been a B.

This was how it was. Some came to my office to learn, some came to impress, some came to grovel, some came to chat—that was all okay. I don't make judgments based on these visits. That would be wrong. I treat every student who walks through those doors the same because we are here to *teach*, if not political science, maybe a little something about critical thinking or even—gasp!—life. If students came to us fully formed and without insecurities, what would be the point?

"It stays a B plus," I said when she finished her pitch. "But I bet you'll be able to get the grade up with the next essay."

The buzzer on the clock sounded. Yes, as I said, I keep the times in here strict. It was now exactly 3:29. That was how, when I looked back at all that would happen, I knew exactly when it all first began—between 3:29 P.M. and 3:30 P.M.

"Thank you, Professor," she said, standing to leave. I stood with her.

My office hadn't been changed one iota since I became department head four years ago, taking over this room from my predecessor and mentor, Professor Malcolm Hume, secretary of state for one administration, chief of staff for another. There was still the wonderful nostalgic essence of academic disarray—antique globes, oversize books, yellowing manuscripts, posters peeling off the wall, framed portraits of men with beards. There was no desk in the room, just a big oak table that could seat twelve, the exact number in my senior thesis class.

There was clutter everywhere. I hadn't bothered redecorating, not so much because I wanted to honor my mentor as most believed but because, one, I was lazy and really couldn't be bothered; two, I didn't really have a personal style or family photographs to put up and didn't really care for that "the office is a reflection of the man" nonsense or if I did, then this indeed was the man; and three, I always found clutter to be conducive to individual expression. There is something about sterility and organization that inhibits spontaneity in a student. Clutter seems to welcome free expression from my students—the environment is already muddled and messed, they seem to think, so what further harm could my ridiculous ideas do to it?

But mostly it was because I was lazy and couldn't be bothered.

We both stood from the big oak table and shook hands. She held mine a second longer than she had to so I disengaged intentionally fast. No, this doesn't happen all the time. But it does happen. I'm thirty-five now, but when I first started here—the young professor in his twenties—it happened more often. Do you remember that scene in *Raiders of the Lost Ark* where one student wrote "LOVE YOU" on her eyelids? Something like that happened to me in my first semester. Except the first word wasn't "LOVE" and the second word had been switched from "YOU" to "ME." I don't flatter myself about it. We professors are in a position of fairly immense power. The men who fall for this or believe that they are somehow worthy of such attention (not to be sexist, but it was almost always men) are usually more insecure and needy than any daddy-issued coed one might happen upon.

As I sat down and waited for the next student to arrive, I glanced at the computer on the right side of the table. The college's home screen was up. The page was typically collegiate, I guess. On the left, there was a slideshow of college life, students of all races, creeds, religions, and genders having a studiously good time, interacting with one another, with professors, extracurricular activities, you get the idea. The banner on the top featured the school's logo and most recognizable buildings, including prestigious Johnson Chapel, a large-scale version of the chapel where I had watched Natalie get married.

On the right part of the screen, there was a college newsfeed and now, as Barry Watkins, the next student on the sign-up sheet, entered the room and said, "Yo, Prof, how's it hanging?" I spotted an obituary in the feed that made me pause.

"Hey, Barry," I said, eyes still on the screen. "Take a seat."

He did so, throwing his feet up on the table. He knew that I didn't care. Barry came every week. We talked about everything and nothing. His visits were more watered-down therapy than anything in the realm of academia, but again that was perfectly okay with me.

I took a closer look at the monitor. What had made me pause was the stamp-size photograph of the deceased. I didn't recognize him—not at that distance—but he looked young. In a way, that was not unusual for the obituaries. Many times the college, rather than securing a more recent photograph, would scan in the deceased's yearbook photograph, but here, even at a quick glance, I could see that this was not the case. The hairstyle wasn't something from, say, the sixties or seventies. The photograph wasn't in black-and-white either, something the yearbook had been up until 1989.

Still we are a small college, four hundred or so students per class. Death was not uncommon, but maybe because of the size of the school or my close affiliation as both a student and member of the faculty I always felt somewhat personally involved when someone from here died.

"Yo, Teach?"

"One second, Barry."

I was now infringing on his clock time. I use a portable scoreboard timer, the kind you see in basketball gyms all over this country, with giant red digital numbers. A friend had given it to me as a gift, assuming because of my size that I must have played hoops. I hadn't, but I loved the clock. Since it was set to automatically count down from nine minutes, I could see now that we were on 8:49.

I clicked on the small photograph. When the larger one came up, I managed to hold back the gasp.

The name of the deceased was Todd Sanderson.

I had blocked Todd's last name from my memory—the wedding invite had just said "Todd and Natalie's Nuptials!"—but, man, I knew the face. Gone was the hip stubble. He was clean-shaven here, his hair closer to a buzz cut. I wondered whether that was Natalie's influence—she had always complained that my stubble irritated her skin—and then I wondered why I would be thinking about something so asinine.

"The clock is ticking, Teach."

"One second, Barry. And don't call me Teach."

Todd's age was listed as forty-two. That was a little older than I expected. Natalie was thirty-four, just a year younger than me. I had figured that Todd would be closer to our age. According to the obituary, Todd had been an all-league tight end on the football team and a Rhodes Scholar finalist. Impressive. He had graduated summa cum laude from the history department, had founded a charity called Fresh Start, and during his senior year, he had been president of Psi U, my fraternity.

Todd was not only an alumnus of my school but we had both pledged the same fraternity. How had I not known any of that?

There was more, a lot more, but I skipped down to the last line:

Funeral services are Sunday in Palmetto Bluff, South Carolina, near Savannah, Georgia. Mr. Sanderson is survived by his wife and two children.

Two children?

"Professor Fisher?"

There was something funny in Barry's voice. "Sorry, I was just—"

"No, man, don't be. You okay though?"

"Yes, I'm fine."

"You sure? You look pale, man." Barry dropped his sneakers to the floor and put his hands on the desk. "Look, I can come back another time."

"No," I said.

I turned away from the monitor. It would have to wait. Natalie's husband had died young. That was sad, yes, tragic even, but it had nothing to do with me. It was not a reason to cancel work or inconvenience my students. It had thrown me for a loop, of course—not only Todd dying but the fact that he had gone to my alma mater. That was a somewhat bizarre coincidence, I guess, but not exactly an earth-shattering revelation.

Maybe Natalie simply liked Lanford men.

"So what's up?" I asked Barry.

"Do you know Professor Byrner?"

"Sure."

"He's a total tool."

He was, but I wouldn't say that. "What seems to be the issue?"

I hadn't seen a cause of death in the obituary. The campus ones often didn't have one. I would look again later. If it wasn't in there, maybe I could find a more complete obituary online.

Then again, why would I want to learn more? What difference did it make?

Best to stay away from this.

Either way it would have to wait for office hours to end. I finished up with Barry and kept going. I tried to push thoughts of the obituary aside and focus on my remaining students. I was off my game, but the students were oblivious. Students cannot imagine that professors have real lives in the same way they can't imagine their parents having sex. On one level, that was fine. On another, I constantly remind them to look past themselves. Part of the human condition is that we all think that we are uniquely complex while everyone else is somewhat simpler to read. That is not true, of course. We all have our own dreams and hopes and wants and lust and heartaches. We all have our own brand of crazy.

My mind drifted. I watched the clock trudge slowly forward as if I were the most bored student in the most boring class. When five o'clock came I headed back to the computer monitor. I brought up Todd Sanderson's obituary in full.

Nope, no cause of death was given.

Curious. Sometimes there was a hint in the suggested donation area. It will say in lieu of flowers please make a donation to the American Cancer Society or something like that. But nothing was listed. There was also no mention of Todd's occupation, but again, so what?

My office door flew open, and Benedict Edwards, a professor in the humanities department and my closest friend, entered. He didn't bother knocking, but he never had or felt the need to. We often met on Fridays at five o'clock and visited a bar where as a student I worked as a bouncer. Back then it was new and shiny and hip and trendy. Now it was old and broken-down and about as hip and trendy as Betamax.

Benedict was pretty much my physical opposite—tiny, small-boned, and African American. His eyes were magnified by giant

Ant-Man glasses that looked like the safety goggles in the chemis-
try department. Apollo Creed had to be the inspiration behind his
too big mustache and too poufy Afro. He had the slender fingers of
a female pianist, feet that a ballerina would envy, and he wouldn't
be mistaken for a lumberjack by a blind man.

Despite this—or maybe because of it—Benedict was also a total
"playah" and picked up more women than a rapper with a radio hit.

"What's wrong?" Benedict asked.

I skipped the "Nothing" or "How do you know something's
wrong?" and went straight to it: "Have you ever heard of a guy
named Todd Sanderson?"

"Don't think so. Who is he?"

"An alum. His obituary is online."

I turned the screen toward him. Benedict adjusted the goggle-
glasses. "Don't recognize him. Why?"

"Remember Natalie?"

A shadow crossed his face. "I haven't heard you say her name
in—"

"Yeah, yeah. Anyway, this is—or was—her husband."

"The guy she dumped you for?"

"Yes."

"And now he's dead."

"Apparently."

"So," Benedict said, arching an eyebrow, "she's single again."

"Sensitive."

"I'm worried. You're my best wingman. I have the rap the ladies
love, sure, but you have the good looks. I don't want to lose you."

"Sensitive," I said again.

"You going to call her?"

"Who?" I asked.

"Condoleezza Rice. Who do you think I mean? Natalie."

"Yeah, sure. Say something like 'Hey, the guy you dumped me for is dead. Want to catch a movie?'"

Benedict was reading the obituary. "Wait."

"What?"

"Says here she has two kids."

"So?"

"That makes it more complicated."

"Will you stop?"

"I mean two kids. She could be fat now." Benedict looked over at me with his magnified eyes. "So what does Natalie look like now? I mean, two kids. She's probably chunky, right?"

"How would I know?"

"Uh, the same way everyone would—Google, Facebook, that kinda thing."

I shook my head. "Haven't done that."

"What? Everyone does that. Heck, I do that with all my former loves."

"And the Internet can handle that kind of traffic?"

Benedict grinned. "I do need my own server."

"Man, I hope that's not a euphemism."

But I saw something sad behind his grin. I remembered one time at a bar when Benedict had gotten particularly wasted, I caught him staring at a well-worn photograph he kept hidden in his wallet. I asked him who it was. "The only girl I'll ever love," he told me in a slurry voice. Then Benedict tucked the photograph back behind his credit card and despite hints from me, he has never said another word about it.

He'd had that same sad grin on then.

"I promised Natalie," I said.

"Promised her what?"

"That I'd leave them alone. That I'd never look them up or bother them."

Benedict considered that. "It seems you kept that promise, Jake."

I said nothing. Benedict had lied earlier. He didn't check the Facebook page of old girlfriends or if he did, he didn't do it with much enthusiasm. But once when I burst into his office—like him, I never knocked—I saw him using Facebook. I caught a quick glance and saw that the page he had up belonged to that same woman whose picture he carried in his wallet. Benedict quickly shut the browser down, but I bet that he checked that page a lot. Every day, even. I bet that he looked at every new photograph of the only woman he ever loved. I bet that he looked at her life now, her family maybe, the man who shared her bed, and that he stared at them the same way he stared at the photograph in his wallet. I don't have proof of any of this, just a feeling, but I don't think I'm too far off.

Like I said before, we all have our own brand of crazy.

"What are you trying to say?" I asked him.

"I'm just telling you that that whole 'them' stuff is over now."

"Natalie hasn't been a part of my life in a long time."

"You really believe that?" Benedict asked. "Did she make you promise to forget how you felt too?"

"I thought you were afraid of losing your best wingman."

"You're not that good-looking."

"Cruel bastard."

He rose. "We humanities professors know all."

Benedict left me alone then. I stood and walked over to the window. I looked out on the commons. I watched the students walk by and, as I often did when confronted with a life situation, I wondered what I'd advise one of them if they were in my shoes. Suddenly, without warning, it all came rushing in at once—that white chapel, the way she wore her hair, the way she held up her ring finger, all the pain, the want, the emotions, the love, the hurt. My knees buckled. I thought that I had stopped carrying a torch for her. She had crushed me, but I had picked up the pieces, put myself back together, and moved on with my life.

How stupid to have such thoughts now. How selfish. How inappropriate. The woman had just lost her husband, and prick that I am, I was worried about the ramifications for me. Let it go, I told myself. Forget it and her. Move on.

But I couldn't. I was simply not built that way.

I had last seen Natalie at a wedding. Now I would see her at a funeral. Some people would find irony in that—I was not one of them.

I headed back to the computer and booked a flight to Savannah.

Chapter 3

The first sign something was off occurred during the eulogy.

Palmetto Bluff was not so much a town as a gigantic gated community. The newly built "village" was beautiful, clean, nicely maintained, historically accurate—all of which gave the place a sterile, Disney-Epcot faux feel. Everything seemed a little too perfect. The sparkly white chapel—yep, another one—sat on a bluff so picturesque it appeared to be, well, a picture. The heat, however, was all too real—a living, breathing thing with humidity thick enough to double as a beaded curtain.

Another fleeting moment of reason questioned why I had come down here, but I swatted it away. I was here now, thus making the question moot. The Inn at Palmetto Bluff looked like a movie facade. I stepped into its cute bar and ordered a scotch straight up from a cute barmaid.

"You here for the funeral?" she asked me.

"Yep."

"Tragic."

I nodded and stared down at my drink. The cute barmaid picked up the hint and said no more.

I pride myself on being an enlightened man. I do not believe in fate or destiny or any of that superstitious nonsense, yet here I was, justifying my impulsive behavior in just such a manner. I am *supposed* to be here, I told myself. Compelled to board that flight. I didn't know why. I had seen with my own two eyes Natalie marry another man, and yet even now, I still couldn't quite accept it. There was still an innate need for closure. Six years ago, Natalie had dumped me with a note telling me she was marrying her old beau. The next day, I got an invitation to their wedding. No wonder it all still felt . . . incomplete. Now I was here in the hopes of finding, if not closure, completion.

Amazing what we can self-rationalize when we really want something.

But what exactly did I want here?

I finished my drink, thanked the cute barmaid, and carefully started toward the chapel. I kept my distance, of course. I might be horrible and callous and self-involved, but not so much as to intrude on a widow burying her husband. I stayed behind a large tree—a palmetto, what else?—not daring to so much as sneak a look at the mourners.

When I heard the opening hymn, I figured that the coast was as clear as it was going to be. A quick glance confirmed it. Everyone was inside the chapel now. I started toward it. I could hear a gospel choir singing. They were, in a word, magnificent. Not sure what exactly to do, I tried the chapel door, found it unlocked (well, duh), and pushed inside. I lowered my head as I entered, putting a hand to my face as though scratching an itch.

Talk about a poor man's disguise.

There was no need. The chapel was packed. I stood in the back with other late-arriving mourners who couldn't find a seat. The choir finished the spirited hymn, and a man—I don't know if he was a minister or priest or what—took to the pulpit. He began to talk about Todd as a "caring physician, good neighbor, generous friend, and wonderful family man." Physician. I hadn't known that. The man waxed eloquent on Todd's strengths—his charity work, his winning personality, his generosity of spirit, his ability to make every person feel special, his willingness to roll up his sleeves and pitch in whenever anyone, stranger or friend, needed a hand. I naturally wrote this off as familiar funeral narrative—we have a natural habit of overpraising the deceased—but I could see the tears in the eyes of the mourners, the way they nodded along with the words, as though it was a song only they could hear.

From my perch in the back I tried to glance up front for a glimpse of Natalie, but there were too many heads in the way. I didn't want to make myself conspicuous, so I stopped. Besides, I had come into the chapel and looked around and even listened to words of praise for the deceased. Wasn't that enough? What else was there to do here?

It was time to leave.

"Our first eulogy," the man at the pulpit said, "comes from Eric Sanderson."

A pale teen—I would guess that he was around sixteen—rose and moved to the pulpit. My first thought was that Eric must be Todd Sanderson's (and by extension, Natalie's) nephew, but that thought was quickly shot down by the boy's opening sentence.

"My father was my hero . . ."

Father?

It took me a few seconds. Minds have a habit of going on certain tracks and not being able to hop off. When I was a child, my father told me an old riddle that he thought would fool me. "A father and son get in a car accident. The father dies. The boy is rushed to the hospital. The surgeon says, 'I can't operate on this boy. He's my son.' How can that be?" This was what I mean about tracks. For my father's generation, this riddle was, I guess, mildly difficult to figure, but for people my age, the answer—the surgeon was his mother—was so obvious, I remember laughing out loud. "What next, Dad? Are you going to start using your eight-track player?"

Here was something similar. How, I wondered, could a man who has only been married to Natalie six years have a teenage son? Answer: Eric was Todd's son, not Natalie's. Either Todd had been married previously or at the very least had a child with another woman.

I tried again to see Natalie in the front row. I craned my neck, but the woman standing next to me gave me an exasperated sigh for invading her space. Up on the podium, Todd's son, Eric, was killing it. He spoke beautifully and movingly. There wasn't a dry eye in the chapel except, well, mine.

So now what? Just stand here? Pay my respects to the widow and, what, confuse her or disrupt her day of mourning? And what about selfish ol' me? Did I really want to see her face again, see her crying over the loss of the love of her life?

I didn't think so. I checked my watch. I had booked my flight out tonight. Yep, quick in and out. No muss, no fuss, no overnight, no hotel cost. Closure on the cheap.

There were those who would state the obvious about Natalie and me—that is, I had idealized our time together out of all rational proportion. I understand that. Objectively I see where that argument has validity. But the heart isn't objective. I, who worshipped the great thinkers, theorists, and philosophers of our time, would never stoop so low as to use an axiom as trite as, *I just know*. But I *do know*. I know what Natalie and I were. I can see it through clear eyes, nothing even slightly tinted, and because of that, I cannot compute what we've become.

In sum, I still don't get what happened to us.

As Eric finished up and took his seat, the sounds of sniffles and gentle sobs echoed through the sparkly white chapel. The clergyman who'd been running the funeral moved back to the pulpit and used the universal "please rise" hand gesture. When the congregation began to stand, I used the diversion to slip back outside. I moved across the way, back to the cover of the palmetto tree. I leaned against the trunk, staying out of sight of the chapel.

"Are you okay?"

I turned and saw the cute barmaid. "I'm fine, thanks."

"Great man, the doc."

"Yeah," I said.

"Were you close?"

I didn't answer. A few minutes later, the chapel doors opened. The coffin was rolled into the blazing sun. When it got near the hearse, the pallbearers, one of whom was his son, Eric, surrounded the casket. A woman with a big black hat came out next. She had one arm around a girl of maybe fourteen. A tall man stood next to her. She leaned on him. The man looked a bit like Todd. I guessed this was his brother and sister, but it was only a guess. The pallbearers lifted the coffin and slid it into the back of the hearse. The woman with the black hat and the girl were escorted to the first limousine. The tall maybe-brother opened the door for them. Eric got in after them. I watched the rest of the mourners start coming out.

No sign of Natalie yet.

I found that only mildly odd. I had seen it work both ways. Sometimes the wife was the first person to depart, trailing the coffin, sometimes resting a hand on it. And sometimes she was the last, waiting for the entire chapel to empty out before braving the walk up the aisle. I remembered my own mother hadn't wanted to deal with anyone at my father's funeral. She went so far as to slip out a side door to avoid the crush of family and friends.

I watched mourners exit. Their grief, like the southern heat, had become a living, breathing thing. It was genuine and palpable. These people were not here out of mere courtesy. They cared for this man. They were rocked by his death, but then again, what had I expected? Did I think Natalie would dump me for a loser? Wasn't it better to have lost out to this beloved healer instead of a swarthy douchebag?

Good question.

The barmaid was still standing next to me. "How did he die?" I whispered.

"You don't know?"

I shook my head. Silence. I turned toward her.

"Murdered," she said.

The word hung in the humid air, refusing to go away. I repeated it. "Murdered?"

"Yes."

I opened my mouth, closed it, tried again. "How? Who?"

"He was shot, I think. I'm not sure about that part. The police don't know who. They think it was a robbery gone wrong. You know, a guy broke in and didn't know someone was home."

Numbness crept in now. The flow of people had stopped coming out of the chapel. I stared at the door and waited now for Natalie to make her appearance.

But she didn't.

The man who'd led the service came out, closing the doors behind him. He got into the front of the hearse. The hearse started rolling out. The first limousine followed.

"Is there a side exit?" I asked.

"What?"

"To the chapel. Is there another door?"

She frowned. "No," she said. "There's only that one door."

The procession was under way now. Where the hell was Natalie?

"Aren't you going to the graveyard?" the barmaid asked me.

"No," I said.

She put a hand on my forearm. "You look like you could use a drink."

It was hard to argue with that. I half stumbled behind her toward the bar and half collapsed onto the same stool as before. She poured me another scotch. I kept my eyes on the procession, on the chapel door, on the little town square.

No Natalie.

"My name is Tess, by the way."

"Jake," I said.

"So how did you know Dr. Sanderson?"

"We went to the same college."

"Really?"

"Yes. Why?"

"You look younger."

"I am. It was an alumni connection."

"Oh, okay, that makes sense."

"Tess?"

"Yes?"

"Do you know Dr. Sanderson's family at all?"

"His son, Eric, used to date my niece. Good kid."

"How old is he?"

"Sixteen, maybe seventeen. Such a tragedy. He and his father were so close."

I didn't know how to broach the subject so I just asked: "Do you know Dr. Sanderson's wife?"

Tess cocked her head. "You don't?"

"No," I lied. "I never met her. We just knew each other through a few college events. He'd come alone."

"You seem awfully emotional for a guy who only knew him through a few college events."

I didn't know how to answer that one, so I stalled by taking a deep sip. Then I said, "It's just that, well, I didn't see her at the funeral."

"How would you know?"

"What?"

"You just said you never met her. How would you know?"

Man, I was really not good at this, was I? "I've seen photographs."

"They must not have been good ones."

"What do you mean?"

"She was right there. Came out right after the coffin with Katie."

"Katie?"

"Their daughter. Eric was one of the pallbearers. Then Dr. Sanderson's brother came out with Katie and Delia."

I remembered them, of course. "Delia?"

"Dr. Sanderson's wife."

My head started spinning. "I thought her name was Natalie."

She crossed her arms and frowned at me. "Natalie? No. Her name is Delia. She and Dr. Sanderson were high school sweethearts. Grew up right down the road here. They've been married for ages."

I just stared at her.

"Jake?"

"What?" I said.

"Are you sure you're even at the right funeral?"

Chapter 4

I headed back to the airport and took the next flight home. What else could I do? I guess I could have approached the grieving widow graveside and asked her why her dearly departed husband married the love of my life six years ago, but just then, that felt somewhat inappropriate. I'm sensitive like that.

So with a nonrefundable ticket on a professor's salary, plus classes tomorrow and students to see, I reluctantly ducked into one of those "express" jets that are too small for guys my size, folding my legs up so that my knees felt as though they were under my chin, and flew back to Lanford. I live in personality-imperiled campus housing made of washed-out brick. The décor might generously be dubbed "functional." It was clean and comfortable, I guess, with one of those couch-loveseat combos you see advertised in highway stores for $699. The overall effect is, I think, more apathetic than downright bad, but that also may just be what I tell myself. The small kitchen had a microwave and toaster oven—it had a real oven too, but I don't think I've ever used it—and the dishwasher breaks a lot. As you may have guessed, I don't entertain here too often.

This is not to say that I don't date or even have meaningful relationships. I do, though most of these relationships carry a three-month expiration date. Some might find insight in the fact that Natalie and I lasted a little over three months, but I wouldn't be one of them. No, I don't live in heartache. I don't cry myself to sleep or any of that. I am, I tell myself, over it. But I do feel a void, icky as that sounds. And—like it or not—I still think about her every single day.

Now what?

The man who had married the woman of my dreams was, it seemed, married to another woman—not to mention that he was, well, deceased. To put it another way, Natalie was not at the funeral of her husband. That seemed to warrant some kind of response on my part, didn't it?

I remembered my six-year-old promise. Natalie had said, "Promise me you'll leave us alone." Us. Not him or her. Us. At the risk of sounding cold and perhaps overly literal, there was no "us" anymore. Todd was dead. That meant, I firmly believed, that the promise, if it even could still exist because the "us" no longer existed, should be declared null and void.

I booted up the computer—yes, it was old—and typed Natalie Avery into the search engine. A list of links came up. I started going through them, but quickly got discouraged. Her old gallery page still had some of her paintings up. Nothing had been added in, well, six years. I found a few articles on art openings and the like, but again all of them were old. I clicked the button for more current links. There were two hits on white pages, but one woman named Natalie Avery was seventy-nine years old and married to a man named Harrison. The other was sixty-six and married to a Thomas. There were the other routine mentions you would find for pretty much any name—genealogy sites, high school and college alumni pages, that kind of thing.

But really, in the end, nothing appeared relevant.

So what happened to my Natalie?

I decided to try googling Todd Sanderson, see what I could find there. He was indeed a physician—more specifically, a surgeon. Impressive. His office was in Savannah, Georgia, and he was affiliated with Memorial University Medical Center. His specialty was cosmetic surgery. I didn't know if that meant serious cleft palates or boob jobs. I didn't know how that could possibly be relevant either. Dr. Sanderson was not big on social networking. He had no Facebook account or LinkedIn or Twitter, none of that.

There were a few mentions of Todd Sanderson and his wife, Delia, at various functions for a charity called Fresh Start, but for the most part there was very little to learn here. I tried throwing in his name with Natalie's. I got bupkis. I sat back and thought a moment. Then I leaned forward and tried their son, Eric Sanderson. He was only a kid, so I didn't think there'd be much, but I figured that he'd probably have a Facebook profile. I started there. Parents often choose not to have a Facebook page, but I've yet to meet a student who didn't have one.

A few minutes later, I hit bingo. Eric Sanderson, Savannah, Georgia.

The profile picture was, poignantly enough, a photograph of Eric and his late father, Todd. They both had wide smiles, trying to hold up a big fish of some kind, happily struggling with the weight. A father-son fishing trip, I figured with the pang of a man who wants to be a father. The sun was setting behind them, their faces in shadow, but you could feel the contentment radiate through my computer monitor. I was struck by a strange thought.

Todd Sanderson was a good man.

Yes, it was only a photograph and, yes, I was aware of how people could fake smiles or entire life scenarios, but I sensed goodness here.

I checked out the rest of Eric's photographs. Most were of Eric and his friends—hey, he was a teenager—at school, at parties, at sporting events, you know the drill. Why does everyone make pouty lips or hand gestures in photographs nowadays? What's up with that? Dumb thought but the mind goes where it goes.

There was an album simply titled FAMILY. The photos ran through a gamut of years. Eric was a baby in some. Then his sister joined. Then there was the trip to Disney World, other fishing vacations, family dinners, church confirmation, soccer games. I checked them all.

Todd never had long hair—not in any of them. He was never anything but clean-shaven.

So what did that mean?

Not a clue.

I clicked on Eric's wall or whatever you call that opening page. There were dozens of condolence messages.

"Your dad was the best, I'm so sorry."

"If there is anything I can do."

"RIP, Dr. S. You rocked."

"I'll never forget the time your dad helped out with my sister."

Then I saw one that made me pause:

"Such a senseless tragedy. I will never understand the cruelty of human beings."

I clicked for "older posts" to come up. There, six more down, I found another that caught my eye:

"I hope they catch the a&&hole who did this and fry him."

I brought up a news search engine and tried to find out more. It didn't take long to stumble across an article:

HOMICIDE IN SAVANNAH

Local Surgeon Murdered

Popular local surgeon and humanitarian Dr. Todd Sanderson was killed in his home last night in what police believe may have been a robbery gone wrong.

Someone tried my front door, but it was locked. I heard the rustling of the doormat—in a fit of originality, I hide my spare key beneath it—and then the key was in the lock and the door opened. Benedict came in.

"Hey," he said. "Surfing porn?"

I frowned. "No one uses the term 'surfing' anymore."

"I'm old-school." Benedict headed to the fridge and grabbed a beer. "How was your trip?"

"Surprising," I said.

"Do tell."

I did. Benedict was a great listener. He was one of those guys who actually listened to every single word and remained focused on you and only you and didn't talk over you. This isn't faked either, and he doesn't just save this for his closest friends. People fascinate him. I would list that as Benedict's greatest strength as a teacher but it would probably be more apropos to list it as his greatest strength as a Don Juan. Single women can fight off a lot of pickup routines, but a guy who genuinely cares about what they say? Gigolo wannabes, take note.

When I finished, Benedict took a swig of his beer. "Wow. I mean . . . wow. That's all I can say."

"Wow?"

"Yeah."

"Are you sure you're not an English professor?"

"You do know," he said slowly, "that there is probably a logical explanation for all this, right?"

"Such as?"

He rubbed his chin. "Maybe Todd is one of those guys with several families, but they don't know about each other."

"Huh?"

"Lotharios who have lots of wives and kids and one lives in, say,

Denver, and the other lives in Seattle, and he divides his time between them and they don't know. You see it on *Dateline* all the
time. They're bigamists. Or polygamists. And they can get away
with it for years."

I made a face. "If that's your logical explanation, I'd love to hear
your far-fetched one."

"Fair point. So how about I give you the most obvious one?"

"The most obvious explanation?"

"Yes."

"Go for it."

Benedict spread his hands. "It's not the same Todd."

I said nothing.

"You don't remember the guy's last name, right?"

"Right."

"So are you sure that it's the same guy? Todd isn't the most uncommon name in the world. Think about it, Jake. You see a picture
six years later, your mind plays a few tricks with you, and voilà,
you think it's your archenemy."

"He isn't my archenemy."

"*Wasn't* your archenemy. Dead, remember? That puts him in the
past tense. But seriously, you want the most obvious explanation?"
He leaned forward. "It's all a simple case of mistaken identity."

I had, of course, already considered this. I had even considered
Benedict's conning bigamist explanation. Both made more sense
than . . . than what? What else was there, really? What other
possible—obvious, logical, far-fetched—explanation was there?

"Well?" Benedict said.

"It makes sense."

"See?"

"This Todd—Todd Sanderson, MD—looked different from Natalie's Todd. His hair is shorter. His face is freshly shaven."

"So there you go."

I glanced away.

"What?"

"I'm not sure I buy it."

"Why not?"

"For one thing, the man was murdered."

"So? If anything, that backs my polygamist theory. He crossed the wrong gal and kapow."

"Come on, you don't really think that's the answer."

Benedict sat back. He started plucking at his lower lip with two fingers. "She left you for another man."

I waited for him to say more. When he didn't, I said, "Uh, yeah, Captain Obvious, I know."

"That was hard for you." He sounded sad now, wistful. "I get it. I get it more than you know." I thought now about the photograph, about the love he lost, about how many of us go around with some kind of heartache and never show it. "You two were in love. So you can't accept it—how could she dump you for another man?"

I frowned again, but I could feel the twang in my chest. "Are you sure you're not a psychology professor?"

"You want this so badly—this second chance, this chance at real redemption—that you can't see the truth."

"What truth is that, Benedict?"

"She's gone," he said, simple as that. "She dumped you. None of this changes that."

I swallowed, tried to swim through that crystal-clear reality. "I think there is more to it."

"Like what?"

"I don't know," I admitted.

Benedict considered that for a moment. "But you won't stop trying to find out, will you?"

"I will," I said. "But not today. And probably not tomorrow."

Benedict shrugged, rose, grabbed another beer. "So let's have it. What's our next step?"

Chapter 5

had no answer to that one, and it was getting late. Benedict suggested a bar and some late-night carousing. I thought that it might be an excellent distraction but I had essays to grade, so I begged off. I managed to get through about three of them before realizing that my mind wasn't there and grading papers now wouldn't be fair to my students.

I made a sandwich and tried looking up Natalie's name again, this time doing an "image" search. I saw an old bio picture of her. The image struck me hard in the chest so I clicked it off. I found some of her old paintings. Several of them were of my hands and torso. Painful memories didn't just ease back in—they shoved the door open hard, all of them and all at once. The way she tilted her head, the way the sunlight burst through the skylight of her studio, that look of concentration on her face, the playful smile when she took a break. The memories almost made me double over in pain. I missed her that much. I missed her with an ache that was physical and something beyond. I had blocked it on and off for six years, but suddenly the longing had flooded back, as strong as the day we last made love in that cabin at the retreat.

Screw it.

I wanted to see her and be damned the consequences. If Natalie could look me in the eye a second time and dismiss me, well, I would deal with it then. But not now. Not tonight. Right now, I simply needed to find her.

Okay, slow down. Let me think this through. What do I need to do here? First, I have to figure out if Todd Sanderson is Natalie's Todd. There was plenty of evidence to suggest, as Benedict had clearly explained, that this was simply a case of mistaken identity.

How should I go about proving it one way or the other?

I needed to know more about him. For example, what would Dr. Todd Sanderson, happily married father of two living in Savannah, be doing at an artist retreat in Vermont six years earlier? I needed to see more pictures of him. I needed to do more background, starting . . .

Starting here. At Lanford.

That was it. The school still maintains every student file, though they can only be viewed by the student or with the student's permission. I looked at my own a few years back. For the most part, there was nothing remarkable, but my professor in freshman year Spanish, a class I ended up dropping, suspected that I had "adjustment" problems and perhaps could benefit from seeing the school psychologist. That was crap, of course. I was terrible at Spanish—foreign languages are my academic Achilles' heel—and you're allowed a fresh-man drop to maintain your GPA. The note had been in the professor's own handwriting, and that somehow made it worse.

The point?

There could be something in Todd's file, if I could figure a way to finagle it, that would tell me something about him. You might ask, "Like what?" I might reply, "I have no friggin' idea." It still felt like a place to start.

So what else?

The obvious: Check in on Natalie. If I found her still happily married to her Todd, I would be able to drop this immediately. That was the most direct route here, wasn't it? The question was, how?

I continued an online search, hoping to stumble across an ad-dress or a clue, but there was absolutely nothing. I know that we supposedly live our entire lives online nowadays, but I have found this not to be the case. If a person wanted to stay in the shadows, they could. It took effort, but you really could remain off the grid.

The question might be, why would you expend the effort?

I debated calling her sister, if I could find the number, but what exactly would I say? "Hi, uh, this is Jake Fisher, your sister's old, uh, fling. Um, did Natalie's husband die?"

That might be a tough approach.

I remembered listening to a phone conversation between the two sisters where Natalie gushingly told Julie, "Oh man, wait till you meet my wonderful boyfriend . . ." And, yep, we did eventually meet. Sort of. At Natalie's wedding to another man.

Her father was dead. Her mom, well, that would be the same problem as with the sister. Friends of Natalie's . . . that was an issue

too. Natalie and I had spent our time together in retreats in Kraftboro, Vermont. I was at one to write my political science dissertation, Natalie was doing her art at the neighboring farm-cum-retreat.
I was supposed to stay six weeks. I stayed double that because, one,
I met Natalie, and two, I lost focus on my writing after I met Natalie. I had never visited her hometown in northern New Jersey, and
she had only come to campus for one brief visit. Our relationship
had stayed in that Vermont bubble.

I can almost see the head nods now. Ah, you think, that explains
it. It was a summer romance, built in an unreal world of no responsibilities or reality. Under those conditions, it is easy for love and
obsession to bloom without taking root, only to wither and die
when the cold of September rolled around. Natalie, being the more
insightful of us, saw and accepted that truth. I did not.

I understand that sentiment. I can only say that it is wrong.

Natalie's sister's name was Julie Pottham. Six years ago, Julie
had been married with an infant son. I looked her up online. This
time, it didn't take long. Julie lived in Ramsey, New Jersey. I wrote
down the phone number on a slip of paper—like Benedict, I can be
old-school—and stared at it. Outside my window I could hear students laughing. It was midnight. Too late to call. It might be best to
sleep on this decision anyway. In the meantime, there were papers I
needed to correct. There was a class tomorrow I had to prepare for.
There was a life I had to lead.

There was no point in trying to sleep. I focused on the
student essays. Most were numbingly tedious and expected, written

as though to fit a high school teacher's rote specifications. These
were top-level students who knew how to write "A+" high school
papers, what with their opening paragraph, introductory sentences,
supportive body, all that stuff that makes an essay solid and
ridiculously boring. As I mentioned earlier, my job is to get them to
think critically. That was always more important to me than having
them remember the specific philosophies of, say, Hobbes or Locke.
You could always look those up and be reminded of what they
were. Rather, what I really hoped was my students would learn to
both respect and piss all over Hobbes and Locke. I wanted them to
not only think outside the box, but to get to that outside by
smashing the box into little pieces.

Some were getting that. Most were not as of yet. But, hey, if they
all got it right away, what would be the point of my job?

At around four in the morning I headed to bed to pretend that
sleep would find me. It didn't. By 7:00 A.M., I had made up my
mind: I would call Natalie's sister. I remembered the robotic smile
in the white chapel, the pale face, the way Julie asked me if I was
okay, as if she truly understood. She might be an ally.

Either way, what did I have to lose?

It had been too late to call last night. It was too early now. I
showered and got ready for my 8:00 A.M. Rule of Law class over in
Vitale Hall. I would call Natalie's sister as soon as class ended.

I expected to sleepwalk through the class. I was obviously distracted and, let's face it, 8:00 A.M. was too early for most college
students. But not today. Today the class was beyond lively, with
hands shooting up, points and counterpoints worded strongly but
with no animosity. I took no sides, of course. I moderated and mar-
veled. The class was in the zone. Usually with the early class, the

clock's minute hand moved as though bathed in syrup. Today I wanted to reach up and grab that stupid hand and stop it from flying forward. I loved every moment. The ninety minutes passed in a blur, and I realized yet again how lucky I was to have this job.

Lucky in occupation, unlucky in love. Or something like that.

I headed to my office at Clark House to make the phone call. I stopped at Mrs. Dinsmore's desk and awarded her my best charm-yer-pants-off smile. She frowned and said, "That work with single women nowadays?"

"What, the charming smile?"

"Yeah."

"Sometimes," I said.

She shook her head. "And they say not to worry about the future." Mrs. Dinsmore sighed and straightened out some papers. "Okay, pretend you got me all hot and bothered. What do you want?"

I tried to shake away the hot-and-bothered image. It wasn't easy. "I need to get ahold of a student file."

"Do you have the student's permission?"

"No."

"Ergo the charming smile."

"Right."

"Is this one of your current students?"

I reloaded the smile. "No. He was never a student of mine."

She arched an eyebrow.

"In fact, he graduated twenty years ago."

"You're kidding, right?"

"Do I look like I'm kidding?"

"Actually, with that smile, you look kind of constipated. What's the student's name?"

"Todd Sanderson."

She sat back and crossed her arms. "Didn't I just read his obituary on the alumni page?"

"You did."

Mrs. Dinsmore studied my face. My smile was gone. A few seconds later, she slipped her reading glasses back on and said, "I'll see what I can do."

"Thank you."

I headed into my office and closed the door. No more excuses. It was nearly 10:00 A.M. now. I took out the piece of paper and looked at the number I'd jotted down last night. I picked up the phone, hit the button for an outside line, and dialed.

I had rehearsed what I would say, but nothing had sounded sane, so I figured that I would play it by ear. The phone rang two times, then three. Julie probably wouldn't answer. No one answered home phones anymore, especially when they came from an unfamiliar number. The caller ID would show Lanford College. I didn't know if that would encourage or discourage answering.

On the fourth ring, the phone was picked up. I gripped the receiver tighter and waited. A woman said a tentative "Hello?"

"Julie?"

"Who is this please?"

"It's Jake Fisher."

Nothing.

"I dated your sister."

"What's your name again?"

"Jake Fisher."

"Have we met?"

"Sort of. I mean, we were both at Natalie's wedding—"

"I don't understand. Who are you exactly?"

"Before Natalie married Todd, she and I were, uh, seeing each other."

Silence.

"Hello?" I said.

"Is this a joke?"

"What? No. In Vermont. Your sister and I—"

"I don't know who you are."

"You used to talk to your sister on the phone a lot. I even heard you two talking about me, in fact. After the wedding, you put your hand on my arm and asked me if I was okay."

"I have no idea what you're talking about."

I was gripping the receiver so tight I feared it might shatter. "Like I said, Natalie and I dated—"

"What do you want? Why are you calling me?"

Wow, that was a good question. "I wanted to talk to Natalie."

"What?"

"I just wanted to make sure that she was okay. I saw an obituary for Todd, and I thought that maybe I should reach out and just, I don't know, offer my condolences."

More silence. I let it last as long as I could.

"Julie?"

"I don't know who you are or what you're talking about, but never call here again. Do you understand? Never."

She hung up the phone.

Chapter 6

tried calling back, but Julie didn't answer.

I didn't understand. Had she really forgotten who I was? That seemed doubtful. Had I scared her with my call-out-of-the-blue? I didn't know. The whole conversation had been surreal and spooky. It would have been one thing to tell me that Natalie didn't want to hear from me or that I was wrong, Todd was still alive. Whatever. But she didn't even know who I was.

How was that possible?

So now what? Calm down, for one. Deep breaths. I needed to continue my two-prong attack: Figure out what the deal was with the late Todd Sanderson, and find Natalie. The second would, of course, negate the first. Once I found Natalie, I would know all. I wondered how to do that exactly. I had looked her up online and found nothing. Her sister, too, seemed to be a dead end. So where to go? I didn't know, but in this day and age, how hard would it be to get an address on her?

An idea came to me. I signed on to the campus website and checked the teaching schedules. Professor Shanta Newlin had a class in an hour.

I buzzed Mrs. Dinsmore.

"What, you expect me to have the file that fast?"

"No, it isn't that. I'm wondering if you know where Professor Newlin is."

"Well, well. This day gets more and more interesting. You know she's engaged, right?"

I should have known better. "Mrs. Dinsmore . . ."

"Don't get your panties in a bunch. She's having breakfast with her thesis students in Valentine."

Valentine was the campus cafeteria. I hurried across the quad toward it. It was an odd thing. A college professor always has to be on. You have to keep your head up. You have to smile or wave at every student. You have to remember every name. There was a strange sort of celebrity to walking around campus. I would claim that it didn't matter to me, but I confess that I liked the attention and took it pretty seriously. So even now, rushed and anxious and distracted as I was, I made sure that no student felt blown off.

I avoided the two main dining rooms. These were for students. The professors who sometimes chose to join them once again felt a little desperate to me. There were lines, and I admit that they are sometimes fuzzy and flimsy and arbitrary, but I still drew them and kept on my side of them. Professor Newlin, a class act all the way, would do likewise, which was why I was confident she'd be tucked away in one of the back private dining halls, reserved for such faculty-student interaction.

She was in Bradbeer dining hall. On campus, every building, room, chair, table, shelf, and tile is named after someone who gave money. Some people bristle at this. I like it. This ivy-covered institution is isolated enough, as it should be. There is no harm in letting a little real-world, cold-cash reality in every once in a while.

I peeked in through the window. Shanta Newlin caught my eye and held up a finger signaling one minute. I nodded and waited. Five minutes later the door opened and the students streamed out. Shanta stood in the doorway. When the students were gone, she said, "Walk with me. I have to be somewhere."

I did. Shanta Newlin had one of the most impressive résumés I'd ever seen. She graduated Stanford as a Rhodes Scholar and attended Columbia Law School. She then worked for both the CIA and FBI before serving in the last administration as an undersecretary of state.

"So what's up?"

Her manner was, as always, brusque. When she first came to campus we had dinner. It wasn't a date. It was a "let's see if we want to" date. There is a subtle difference. After that date, she chose not to pursue it, and I was okay with that.

"I need a favor," I said.

Shanta nodded, inviting me to make my request.

"I'm looking for someone. An old friend. I've tried all the usual methods—Google, calling the family, whatever. I can't get an address."

"And you figured that with my old contacts, I'd be able to help."

"Something like that," I said. "Well, yes, exactly like that."

"Her name?"

"I didn't say it was a she."

Shanta frowned. "Name?"

"Natalie Avery."

"When was the last time you saw her or had an address?"

"Six years ago."

Shanta kept walking, military style, ramrod back, very fast. "Was she the one, Jake?"

"Pardon?"

A small smile came to her lips. "Do you know why I never followed up on our first date?"

"It wasn't really a date," I said. "It was more a 'let's see if we want to' date."

"What?"

"Never mind. I figured that you didn't follow up because you had no interest."

"Uh, that would be a no. Here is what I saw that night: You're a great guy, you're funny, you're smart, you have a full-time job, and you have blue eyes to die for. Do you know how many single straight guys I'd met with that criteria?"

I wasn't sure what to say, so I stayed quiet.

"But I could sense it. That's part of being a trained detective, maybe. I study body language. I look for the little things."

"Sense what?"

"You're damaged goods."

"Gee, thanks."

She shrugged. "Some men carry torches for old loves, and then some guys—not many, but some—get completely consumed by the torch's flames. It makes them nothing but long-term trouble for the follow-ups."

I said nothing.

"So this Natalie Avery that you're suddenly desperate to find," Shanta said. "Is she that flame?"

What would be the point in lying? "Yes."

She stopped and looked way up at me. "And it hurt bad?"

"You have no idea."

Shanta Newlin nodded and started walking away, leaving me behind. "I'll have her address for you by the end of the day."

Chapter 7

On television, the detective always goes back to the scene of the crime. Or, come to think of it, maybe it's the criminal who does that. Whatever. I was at a dead end, so I figured that I'd go back to where it all happened.

The retreats in Vermont.

Lanford was only about forty-five minutes from the Vermont border, but then you had another two hours plus to get up to where Natalie and I first met. Northern Vermont is rural. I grew up in Philadelphia and Natalie was from northern New Jersey. We didn't know rural like this. Yes, an objective observer might again point out that in such a secluded venue, love would flourish in an unrealistic way. I might agree or I might point out that in the absence of other distractions—like, say, anything—love might suffocate under the weight of too much togetherness, thus making this proof of something far deeper than a summer fling.

The sun was starting to weaken by the time I passed my old retreat on Route 14. The six-acre "subsistence farm" was run by writer-in-residence Darly Wanatick, who offered critiques of the retreatees' work. For those who don't know, subsistence farming is farming that provides the basic needs for the farmer and his family without surpluses for marketing. In short, you grow it, you eat it, you don't sell it. For those who don't know what a writer in residence is or what qualifies him or her to critique your writing, it meant that Darly owned the property and wrote a weekly shopping column in the free local paper, the *Kraftboro Grocer*. The retreat housed six writers at a time. Each writer had a bedroom in the main house and a shack or "work cottage" in which to write. We all met up for dinner at night. That was it. There was no Internet, no TV, no phones, yes lights, but no motorcar, not a single luxury. Cows, sheep, and chickens meandered around the property. It started out soothing and relaxing and I enjoyed that unplugged, unconnected solitude for about, oh, three days and then my brain cells began to rust and corrode. The theory seemed to be if you make an author feel this numbingly bored, he or she will flock to the salvation of his legal pad or laptop and produce pages. It worked for a while and then it felt as though I'd been placed in solitary confinement. I spent one entire afternoon watching a colony of ants carry a bread crumb across the "writer cottage" floor. So enamored was I with this bit of entertainment I strategically placed more bread crumbs in various corners in order to create insect relay races.

Dinner with my fellow retreat scribes was not much of a reprieve. They were all precious pseudo-intellectuals writing the next great American novel, and when the subject of my nonfiction dissertation was tossed up, it landed upon the old kitchen table with the thud of a heaping pile of donkey dung. Sometimes these great American novelists did dramatic readings of their own work. The works were pretentious, tedious, self-involved crap written in a prose style one might best describe as "Look at me! *Please* look at me!" I never said any of this out loud, of course. When they read, I sat with my most studiously enraptured expression frozen to my face, nodding at regular intervals to appear wise and engaged and also to prevent myself from actually nodding off. One guy named Lars was writing a six-hundred-page poem on Hitler's last days in the bunker, written from the viewpoint of Eva Braun's dog. His first reading consisted of ten minutes of barking.

"It sets the mood," he explained, and he was correct if that mood was to punch him hard in the face.

Natalie's artist retreat was different. It was called the Creative Recharge Colony and had a decidedly more crunchy-granola, hemp, hippie-esque, "Kumbaya" commune feel to it. They took breaks by working in a garden that grew organic (and I am not just talking about food here). They gathered around a fire at night and sang songs of peace and harmony that would make Joan Baez gag. They were, interestingly enough, wary of strangers (perhaps because of what they "grew organic") and there was a guarded, cultish edge to some of the staff. The property was more than a hundred acres with a main house, true cottages with fireplaces and private decks, a swimming pool designed to look like a pond, a cafeteria with fantastic coffee and a wide variety of sandwiches that all tasted like sprouts covered in wood shavings—and on the border with the actual town of Kraftboro, a white chapel where one could, if they so desired, get married.

The first thing I noticed was that the entrance was now un-marked. Gone was the brightly painted CREATIVE RECHARGE sign, like something you'd see advertising a kids' summer camp. A thick chain blocked my car from heading up the drive. I pulled over, turned off the ignition, and got out of the car. There were several NO TRESPASSING signs, but those had always been there. With the new chain and without the Creative Recharge welcome, the no trespassing signs took on a more ominous tone.

I wasn't sure what to do.

I knew that the main house was about a quarter mile up the drive. I could leave my car here and walk it. See what's what. But what would be the point? I hadn't been up here in six years. The retreat probably sold the land, and the new owner probably craved privacy. That might explain all this.

Still it didn't feel right.

What would be the harm, I thought, in going up and knocking on the door of the main house? Then again, the thick chain and no trespassing signs were not exactly welcome mats. I was still trying to decide what to do when a Kraftboro police cruiser pulled up next to me. Two officers got out. One was short and stocky with bloated gym muscles. The other was tall and thin with slicked-back hair and the small mustache of a guy in a silent movie. Both wore aviator sunglasses, so you couldn't see their eyes.

Short and Stocky hitched up his pants a bit and said, "Can I help you?"

They both gave me hard stares. Or at least I think they were hard stares. I mean, I couldn't see their eyes.

"I was interested in visiting the Creative Recharge retreat."

"The what?" Stocky asked. "What for?"

"Because I need to creatively recharge."

"You being a smart mouth with me?"

His voice had a little too much snap in it. I didn't like the attitude. I didn't understand the attitude either, except for the fact that they were cops in a small town and I was probably the first guy they could hassle for something other than underage drinking.

"No, Officer," I said.

Stocky looked at Thin Man. Thin Man remained silent. "You must have the wrong address."

"I'm pretty sure this is the place," I said.

"There is no Creative Recharge retreat here. It closed down."

"So which is it?" I asked.

"Pardon me?"

"Is this the wrong address," I said, "or did the Creative Recharge retreat close down?"

Stocky didn't like that answer. He whipped off his sunglasses and used them to point at me. "Are you being a wiseass with me?"

"I'm trying to find my retreat."

"I don't know anything about any retreat. This land has been owned by the Drachman family for, what, Jerry, fifty years?"

"At least," Thin Man said.

"I was here six years ago," I said.

"I don't know nothing about that," Stocky said. "I only know that you're on private property and if you don't get off it, I'm going to bring you in."

I looked down at my feet. I wasn't on the driveway or any private property. I was on the road.

Stocky moved closer to me, getting into my personal space. I confess that I was scared, but I had learned something in my years of bouncing at bars. You never show fear. That was something you always heard about when it came to the animal kingdom, and trust me, there are no wilder animals than human beings "unwinding" at late-night bars. So even though I didn't like what was happening, even though I had no leverage and was trying to figure a safe way out of this, I didn't back away when Stocky got all up on me. He didn't like that. I held my ground and looked down at him. Way down. He really didn't like that.

"Let me see some ID, hotshot."

"Why?" I asked.

Stocky looked at Thin Man. "Jerry, go run the license plate through the system."

Jerry nodded and headed back to the squad car.

"For what?" I asked. "I don't understand. I'm just here for a retreat."

"You got two choices," Stocky said to me. "One"—he held up a pudgy finger—"you show me your identification without any more back talk. Two"—yep, another chubby digit—"I arrest you for trespassing."

None of this felt right. I glanced behind me at a tree and saw what looked like a security camera pointed down at us. I didn't like this. I didn't like this at all, but there was nothing to be gained by antagonizing a cop. I needed to keep my big mouth shut.

I started to reach into my pocket to get my wallet when Stocky held up a hand and said, "Steady. Slow down."

"What?"

"Reach into your pocket, but make no sudden moves."

"You're kidding, right?"

So much for keeping my big mouth shut.

"Do I look like I'm kidding? Use two fingers. Your thumb and your index finger. Move slowly."

My wallet was deep down in my front pocket. Extracting it with two fingers took longer than it should.

"I'm waiting," he said.

"Give me a second."

I finally got ahold of the wallet and handed it to him. He started to look through it, as though on a scavenger hunt. He stopped at my Lanford College ID, looked at the photograph, looked at me, then he frowned.

"This you?"

"Yes."

"Jacob Fisher."

"Everyone calls me Jake."

He frowned down at my photograph.

"I know," I said. "It is hard to capture my raw animal magnetism in photography."

"You have a college ID in here."

I didn't hear a question so I didn't answer one.

"You look kind of old to be a student."

"I'm not a student. I'm a professor. See where it says 'staff'?"

Thin Man came back from the car. He shook his head. I guessed that meant the license plate check came back negative.

"Why would a big-time professor be coming up to our little town?"

I remembered something that I saw on television once. "I need to reach into my pocket again. That okay?"

"What for?"

"You'll see."

I pulled out my smartphone.

"What do you need that for?" Stocky asked.

I pointed it at him and hit the video record button. "This is on a live feed to my home computer, Officer." That was a lie. It was only recording on my phone, but what the heck. "Everything you say and do can be seen by my colleagues." More lies, but good ones. "I'd very much like to know why you need to see my identification and are asking so many questions about me."

Stocky put the sunglasses back on as though that would mask the rage. He closed his lips so tight that they were quaking. He handed me back my wallet and said, "We had a complaint that you were trespassing. Despite finding you on a private property and listening to some story about a retreat that doesn't exist, we decided to let you off with just a warning. Please leave these premises. Have a nice day."

Stocky and Thin Man headed back to their squad car. They sat in the front and waited until I was back in mine. There was no other play here. I got into my car and drove away.

Chapter 8

I didn't go far.

I drove to the village of Kraftboro. If it had a big, sudden influx of new construction and cash, it might raise itself to the level of small-town America. It looked like something out of an old movie. I half expected to see a barbershop quartet in straw hats. There was a general store (the sign actually said GENERAL STORE), an old "stone mill" with an unmanned "visitor's center," a gas station that also housed a one-chair barbershop, and a bookstore café. Natalie and I had spent a lot of time in that bookstore café. It was small, so there wasn't much browsing, but there was a corner table and Natalie and I would sit there and read the paper and sip coffee. Cookie, a baker who'd escaped the big city, used to run the place with her partner, Denise. She always played *Redemption's*

Son by Joseph Arthur or Damien Rice's *O*, and after a while, Natalie and I started thinking of those—gag alert—as "our" albums. I wondered whether Cookie was still there. Cookie baked what Natalie considered the greatest scones in the history of the world. Then again, Natalie loved all scones. I, on the other hand, still have trouble differentiating scones from dry, rock-hard bread.

See? We had our differences.

I parked down the road and started journeying up the same path I had stumbled down six years earlier. The wooded trail ran for about a hundred yards. In the clearing I spotted the familiar white chapel on the edge of the property I had just been booted off. Some service or meeting was letting out. I watched the congregants blink their way back into the lowering sun. The chapel was, as far as I knew, nondenominational. It seemed more utilitarian, if you will, than Unitarian, a gathering place more than any sort of house of deeply religious worship.

I waited, smiling like I belonged, nodding like Mr. Friendly as about a dozen people walked past me and down the path. I checked the faces, but there was no one that I recognized from six years ago. No surprise really.

A tall woman with a severe hair bun waited by the chapel steps. I made my way over, maintaining the Mr. Friendly smile.

"May I help you?" she asked.

Good question. What did I hope to find here? It wasn't as though I had a plan.

"Are you looking for Reverend Kelly?" she asked. "Because he's not around right now."

"Do you work here?" I asked.

"Sort of. I'm Lucy Cutting, the registrar. It's a volunteer position."

I stood there.

"Is there something I can help you with?"

"I don't know how to put this . . . ," I began. And then: "Six years ago I attended a wedding here. I knew the bride, but not the groom."

Her eyes narrowed a bit, more curious than wary. I pushed ahead.

"Anyway, I recently saw an obituary for a man named Todd. That was the groom's name. Todd."

"Todd is a fairly common name," she said.

"Yes, of course, but there was also a photograph of the deceased. It looked like, I know how this sounds, but it looked like the same man I saw marry my friend. The problem is, I never learned Todd's last name so I don't know if it is him or not. And if it is, well, I'd like to pay my respects."

Lucy Cutting scratched her cheek. "Can't you just call?"

"I wish I could, but no." I was going with honesty here. It felt good. "For one thing I don't know where Natalie—that's the bride's name—I don't know where she lives now. She changed her last name to his, I think. So I can't find them. And also, to be completely up-front, I had a past with this woman."

"I see."

"So if the man I saw in the obituary wasn't her husband—"

"Your communication might be unwanted," she finished for me.

"Exactly."

She thought about that. "And if it was her husband?"

I shrugged. She scratched her cheek some more. I tried to look nonthreatening, even demure, which really doesn't play on a guy my size. I almost batted my eyelashes.

"I wasn't here six years ago," she said.

"Oh."

"But we can check the schedule books. They've always kept immaculate records—every wedding, baptism, communion, bris, whatever."

Bris? "That would be great."

She led me down the steps. "Do you remember the date of the wedding?"

I did, of course. I gave her the exact date.

We reached a small office. Lucy Cutting opened a file cabinet, thumbed through it, and pulled out one of those accounting books. As she flipped through it, I could see that she was right. The records were immaculate. There was a column for the date, type of event, participants, start and end times—all written in handwriting that could double as calligraphy.

"Let's see what we can find here . . ."

She made a production of putting on her reading glasses. She licked her index finger schoolmarm-like, flipped a few more pages, and found the one she wanted. The same finger started tracing down the page. When she frowned, I thought to myself, Uh-oh . . .

"Are you sure about the date?" she asked me.

"Positive."

"I don't see any wedding that day. There was one two days earlier. Larry Rosen married Heidi Fleisher."

"That's not it," I said.

"Can I help you?"

The voice startled us both.

Lucy Cutting said, "Oh, hello, Reverend. I didn't expect you back so soon."

I turned, saw the man, and nearly hugged him with joy. Pay dirt. It was the same minister with the shaved head who'd presided over Natalie's wedding. He reached out his hand to shake mine, a practiced smile at the ready, but when he saw my face, I saw the smile flicker.

"Hello," he said to me. "I'm Reverend Kelly."

"Jake Fisher. We've met before."

He made a skeptical face and turned back to Lucy Cutting. "What's going on, Lucy?"

"I was looking up a record for this gentleman," she began to explain. He listened patiently. I studied his face, but I wasn't sure what I was seeing, just that he was trying to control his emotions somehow. When she was done, he turned to me and raised both palms to the sky. "If it isn't in the records . . ."

"You were there," I said.

"Excuse me?"

"You presided over the wedding. That's where we met."

"I don't recall that. So many events. You understand."

"After the wedding, you were in front of the chapel with the bride's sister. A woman named Julie Pottham. When I walked by, you said it was a lovely day for a wedding."

He arched an eyebrow. "How could I have possibly forgotten that?"

Sarcasm does not normally wear well on men of the cloth, but it fit Reverend Kelly as though hand tailored. I pressed on. "The bride was named Natalie Avery. She was a painter at the Creative Recharge retreat."

"The what?"

"Creative Recharge. They own this land, right?"

"What are you talking about? The town owns this land."

I didn't want to argue deeds and boundaries right now. I tried another avenue. "The wedding. It was last-minute. Maybe that's why it isn't in the records."

"I'm sorry. Mr. . . . ?"

"Fisher. Jake Fisher."

"Mr. Fisher, first off, even if it was a last-minute wedding, it would certainly be recorded. Second, well, I'm confused what exactly you're looking for."

Lucy Cutting answered for me. "The groom's last name."

He gave her a quick glare. "We aren't in the information business, Miss Cutting."

She looked down, properly chastised.

"You have to remember the wedding," I said.

"I'm sorry I don't."

I stepped closer, looking down on him. "You do. I know you do."

I heard the desperation in my own voice, and didn't like it. Reverend Kelly tried to meet my eye, but he couldn't quite do it. "Are you calling me a liar?"

"You remember," I said. "Why won't you help me?"

"I don't remember," he said. "But why are you so anxious to find the wife of another man or, if your story is true, a recent widow?"

"To pay my respects," I said.

My hollow words hung in the air like thick humidity. No one moved. No one spoke. Finally Reverend Kelly broke the silence.

"Whatever your motive for finding this woman, we have no interest in being party to it." He stepped away and showed me the door. "I think it'd be best if you left immediately."

* * *

Once again, dazed by betrayal and heartbreak, I stumbled back down the path toward the village center. I could almost get the reverend's behavior. If he did remember the wedding—and I suspect he did—he wouldn't want to give Natalie's dumped boyfriend any information said boyfriend didn't already have. It seemed an extreme hypothesis on my part, but at least it kind of made sense. What I couldn't make sense of, what I couldn't figure out in any way, shape, or form, was why Lucy Cutting had found nothing in the neat-to-the-point-of-anal records on Natalie and Todd's nuptials. And why the hell had no one heard of the Creative Recharge retreat?

I couldn't get that to mesh.

So now what? I had come here in hopes of ... of what? Of learning Todd's last name for one thing. That could end this pretty quickly. If not, perhaps someone here still kept in touch with Natalie. That could end this all pretty quickly too.

"Promise me, Jake. Promise me you'll leave us alone."

Those were the last words the love of my life said to me. The very last. And here I was, six years later, going back to where it all began, to break my word. I waited to find irony in that, but irony would not come.

As I hit the town center, the gentle aroma of fresh pastries made me pull up. The Kraftboro Bookstore Café. Natalie's favorite scones. I thought about it and decided that it was worth a try.

When I opened the door, a little bell rang, but that sound was quickly forgotten. Elton John was singing that the child's name was Levon, and he'd be a good man. I felt a rush and a shiver. Both tables were taken, including, of course, our old favorite. I stared at it, just standing there like a big goof, and for a moment I swore I could hear Natalie's laugh. A man with a maroon baseball cap came in behind me. I was still blocking the door.

"Uh, excuse me," he said.

I moved to the side to let him pass. My eyes found the coffee bar. A woman with wildly curly hair wearing, yep, a purple tie-dyed shirt had her back to me. No doubt about it. It was Cookie. My heart picked up a step. She turned, saw me, and smiled. "Can I get you something?"

"Hi, Cookie."

"Hey."

Silence.

"Do you remember me?" I asked.

She was wiping frosting off her hands with a hand towel. "I'm bad with faces, but even worse with names. What can I get you?"

"I used to come in here," I said. "Six years ago. My girlfriend's name was Natalie Avery. We used to sit at the corner table."

She nodded but not like she remembered. She nodded like she wanted to appease the lunatic. "Lots of customers in and out. Coffee? Doughnut?"

"Natalie loved your scones."

"A scone it is. Blueberry?"

"I'm Jake Fisher. I was writing my dissertation on the rule of law. You used to ask me about it. Natalie was an artist from the retreat. She'd break out her sketchpad right in that corner." I gestured toward it, as though that mattered. "Six years ago. Over the summer. Heck, you were the one to point her out to me."

"Uh-huh," she said, her fingers toying with her necklace as though they were prayer beads. "See, that's the good part of being called Cookie. You don't forget a name like Cookie. It sticks in the mind. But the bad part is, since everyone remembers your name, they think you should do the same. You know what I mean?"

"I do," I said. Then: "You really don't remember?"

She didn't bother replying. I looked around the café. People at the tables were starting to stare. The guy with the maroon baseball cap was over by the magazines, pretending he wasn't hearing a thing. I turned back to Cookie.

"Small coffee, please."

"No scones?"

"No thanks."

She grabbed a cup and started to fill it.

"Are you still with Denise?" I asked.

Her body stiffened.

"She used to work at the retreat up the hill too," I said. "That's how I knew her."

I saw Cookie swallow. "We never worked at the retreat."

"Sure you did. The Creative Recharge, right up the path. Denise would bring in the coffee and your scones."

She finished pouring the coffee and put it on the counter in front of me. "Look, mister, I have work to do."

I leaned closer to her. "Natalie loved your scones."

"So you said."

"You two used to talk about them all the time."

"I talk to a lot of people about my scones, okay? I'm sorry I don't remember you. I probably should have been polite and faked it and been all, 'Oh sure, you and your scone-loving girlfriend, how you guys doing?' But I didn't. Here's your coffee. Can I get you something else?"

I took out my card with all my phone numbers on it. "If you remember anything . . ."

"Can I get you something else?" she asked, more bite in her voice now.

"No."

"Then that's a buck fifty. Have a nice day."

Chapter 9

now understand when someone says they feel as though they're being followed.

How did I know? Intuition maybe. My lizard brain could sense it. I could feel it in almost a physical way. That, plus the same car—a gray Chevy van with a Vermont license plate—had been behind me since I left the town of Kraftboro.

I couldn't swear to it, but I thought that maybe the driver was wearing a maroon baseball cap.

I wasn't sure what to do about this. I tried to make out the license plate number, but it was too dark now. If I slowed down, he'd slow down. If I picked up speed, well, you get the drift. An idea came to me. I pulled over at a rest stop to see what the tail would do. I saw the van slow and then drive on. From that point on, I didn't see the van again.

So maybe he wasn't following me.

I was about ten minutes away from Lanford when my cell phone rang. I had the phone set up to go through the car Bluetooth—something it took me much too long to figure out—so I could see on the radio screen that it was Shanta Newlin. She had promised to get back to me by the end of the day with Natalie's address. I answered the call with a press of a button on the steering wheel.

"It's Shanta," she said.

"Yeah, I know. I got that caller ID thing up."

"And I think my years at the FBI make me special," she said. "Where are you?"

"I'm driving back to Lanford."

"Back from where?"

"It's a long story," I said. "Did you find her address?"

"That's why I called," Shanta said. I could hear something in the background—a man's voice maybe. "I don't have it yet."

"Oh?" I said, because what else was I going to say to that. "Is there a problem?"

"I need you to give me until the morning, okay?"

"Sure," I said. Then I repeated: "Is there a problem?"

There was a pause that lasted a beat too long. "Just give me till morning." She hung up.

What the hell?

I hadn't liked the tone. I hadn't liked the fact that a woman with enormous contacts in the FBI needed until morning to find the address of a random woman. My smartphone dinged, signaling that I was getting a new e-mail. I ignored it. I am not a goody-goody or any of that, but I never text or e-mail and drive. Two years ago, a student at Lanford had been seriously injured while texting and driving. The eighteen-year-old woman in the passenger seat, a freshman in my Rule of Law class, died in the crash. Even before that, even before the wealth of obvious information about the downright stupidity if not criminal negligence in texting while driving, I was not a fan. I like driving. I like the solitude and the music. In spite of my earlier misgivings about technological seclusion, we all need to disconnect more often. I realize that I sound like a grumpy old man, complaining that whenever I see a table of college "friends" sitting together they are inevitably texting with unseen others, searching, always searching, I guess, for something that might be better, a perpetual life hunt for digital greener grass, an attempt to smell roses that are elsewhere at the expense of the ones in front of you, but there are few times that I feel more at peace, more in tune, more Zen, if you will, than when I force myself to unplug.

Right now I was flipping stations, settling on one that played 1st Wave music from the eighties. General Public asked, where is the tenderness? I wondered that too. Where is the tenderness? For that matter, where is Natalie?

I was getting loopy.

I parked in front of my housing—I didn't call it my house or my apartment because it was and felt like campus housing. Night had fallen, but because we are a college campus, there was plenty of artificial illumination. I checked the new e-mail and saw it was from Mrs. Dinsmore. The subject read:

Here's the student file you requested

Good work, you sexy beast, I thought. I clicked on the message. It read in its entirety:

> How much elaboration do you need on "Here's the student file you requested"?

Clearly the answer was, none.

My phone's screen was too small to see the attached file, so I hurried up the walk in order to view it on my laptop. I put my key in the lock, opened the front door, and flipped on the lights. For some reason I expected, I don't know, to find the place in shambles, as though someone had ransacked the joint, as they say. I had seen too many movies. My apartment remained, at kindest, nondescript.

I rushed over to my computer and jumped on the e-mail. I opened the one from Mrs. Dinsmore and downloaded the attachment. As I mentioned earlier, I saw my student file years ago. It was, I thought, a tad disturbing, reading professors' comments that had not been shared with me. I guess at some point the school decided that it was too much to store all these old records so they'd scanned them into digital forms.

I started with Todd's freshman year. There was nothing particularly spectacular there except that Todd was, well, spectacular. Straight A+'s across the board. No freshman got straight A+'s. Professor Charles Powell noted that Todd was "an exceptional student." Professor Ruth Kugelmass raved, "A special kid." Even Professor Malcolm Hume, never one easy with praise, commented: "Todd Sanderson is almost supernaturally gifted." Wow. I found this strange. I had been a good student here, and the only note I'd found in my file was negative. The only ones I'd ever written were negative. If all was okay, the professor just left it alone and let the grade suffice. The rule of thumb in student files seemed to be, "If you have nothing negative to say, don't say anything at all."

But not with good ol' Todd.

First-semester sophomore year followed the same pattern—incredible grades—but then things changed abruptly. Next to second semester was a big "LOA."

Leave of Absence.

Hmm. I checked for a reason and it only said, "Personal." That was bizarre. We rarely, if ever, leave it at just that—"Personal" in a student file—because the file is closed and confidential. Or supposed to be. We write openly in here.

So why be so circumspect about Todd's LOA?

Usually the "personal" reason involves some kind of financial hardship or an illness, either the student's or a close family member's, either physical or mental. But those reasons are always listed in the private student files. None was listed here.

Interesting.

Or not. For one thing they were probably more discreet about personal issues twenty years ago. But second . . . well, who cared? What on earth could Todd's taking time off as a sophomore have to do with his marrying Natalie and then dying and leaving behind a different wife?

When Todd came back to school, there were now more professor comments—not the ones a student would long for. One professor described him as "distracted." Another said that Todd was "clearly bitter" and "not the same." Another suggested that Todd should take more time off to deal with "the situation." No one mentioned what the situation was.

I clicked to the next page. Todd had been brought up to the disciplinary board. Some schools have students deal with disciplinary issues, but we have a three-professor rotating panel. I did it for a two-month stint last year. Most of the cases that came before us dealt with two campus epidemics: underage drinking and cheating. The rest were a smattering of thefts or threats of violence or some variety of sexual assault or aggression that didn't meet the standard for law enforcement.

The case that came before the disciplinarian board involved an altercation between Todd and another student named Ryan McCarthy. McCarthy ended up hospitalized with contusions and a broken nose. The school was calling for a heavy suspension or even expulsion, but the three-professor panel gave Todd a total pass. That surprised me. There were no details or minutes on the actual hearing or the subsequent deliberations. That surprised me too.

The handwritten decision had been scanned into the file:

Todd Sanderson, a superior member of the Lanford College community, has had a tough blow in his life, but we think he is on the way back. He has recently worked with a faculty member to create a charity to make amends for his recent actions. He understands the ramifications of what he has done, and due to the highly unusual extenuating circumstances in this case, we have agreed that Todd Sanderson should not face expulsion.

My eyes traveled down to the bottom of the page to see the professor who had signed the panel's opinion. I made a face. Professor Eban Trainor. I should have known. I knew Trainor well enough. We were not what one would call friendly.

If I wanted to learn more about this "tough blow" or indeed this decision, I would need to talk to Eban. I wasn't looking forward to that.

It was late, but I wasn't worried about waking Benedict. He only used a cell phone and turned it off when sleeping. He answered on the third ring.

"What?"

"Eban Trainor," I said.

"What about him?"

"He still hate my guts?"

"I would assume so. Why?"

"I need to ask him about my buddy Todd Sanderson. Do you think you can smooth it out?"

"Smooth it out? Sure. Why do you think they call me the Sandman?"

"Because you put your students to sleep?"

"You really know how to butter a guy up when you're asking for a favor. I'll call you in the morning."

We hung up. I sat back, unsure what to do next, when my monitor dinged that I had received a new e-mail. I was going to ignore it. Like most people I knew, I got too many irrelevant e-mails during all hours of the day. This would undoubtedly be yet another.

Then I saw the sender's e-mail address:

RSbyJA@ymail.com

I stared at it until my eyes watered. There was a rushing in my ears. Everything around me was silent and too still. I kept staring, but the letters didn't change.

RSbyJA.

It took me no time to see what those letters meant: *Redemption's Son* by Joseph Arthur—the album Natalie and I listened to in the café.

The subject was empty. My hand found the mouse. I tried to get the cursor over the e-mail so I could open it, but first I had to control my shake. I took a deep breath and willed my hand still. The room remained a hushed quiet, almost expectantly so. I moved the cursor over the e-mail and clicked on it.

The e-mail stopped my heart.

There, on my screen, were four words. That was all, just four words, but those four words sliced through my chest like a reaper's scythe, making it nearly impossible to breathe. I collapsed back on the chair, lost, as the four words on the screen stared back at me:

You made a promise.

Chapter 10

The e-mail wasn't signed. Didn't matter.

I quickly hit the reply button and typed:

Natalie? Are you okay? Please just let me know that.

I hit send.

I would explain to you how time slowed to a crawl as I waited for her next e-mail, but that wasn't really what happened. There was no time for it, I guess. Three seconds later, my new-e-mail-ding sounded. My heart raced until I saw the sender's name:

MAILDAEMON

I clicked open but I already knew what I would find:

This e-mail address doesn't exist . . .

I almost smacked the computer in frustration, as if it were a candy machine that wouldn't dispense the Milky Way. I actually shouted "No way!" out loud. I didn't know what to do. I sat there and I started drowning. I felt as though I were sinking and couldn't even flail my way back to the surface.

I went back to googling. I tried the e-mail and different variations, but it was just a waste of time. I read her e-mail again:

You made a promise.

I had, hadn't I? And when you stopped and thought about it, why did I break that promise? A man had died. Maybe it was her husband. Maybe it wasn't. Still, was that a reason to go back on my promise to her? Maybe. Maybe it was at first. But now she had made it clear. That was the purpose of the e-mail. Natalie was calling me on it. She was reminding me of the promise because she knew that I don't make promises idly.

It was why she had made me promise to stay away in the first place.

I thought about that now. I thought about the funeral and the visit to Vermont and this student file. What did it all add up to? I don't know. If it had originally warranted going back on my word, I now had proof that I could no longer justify it. Natalie's message couldn't have been clearer.

You made a promise.

With a tentative finger, I touched the words on the screen. My heart crumbled anew. Too bad, tough guy. So okay, heartbreak notwithstanding, I would let it go. I would back off. I would keep my word.

I headed to bed and fell asleep almost immediately. I know. I was surprised by that too, but I think all the blows since reading that obituary, the swirl of memory and emotion, of heartbreak and confusion, wore me down like a boxer taking body shots for twelve solid rounds. Eventually, I just folded.

Unlike Benedict, I often forget to turn my cell phone off. His call at 8:00 A.M. woke me up.

"Eban has reluctantly agreed to meet with you."

"Did you tell him what it's about?"

"You didn't tell me what it's about."

"Oh. Right."

"You got a nine A.M. class. He'll be waiting for you at his house when you're done."

I felt the pang deep in my chest. "His house?"

"Yeah, I didn't think you'd like that. He insisted."

"Douchebag move."

"He isn't so bad."

"He's a lecherous creep."

"And that's bad because?"

"You don't do what he does."

"You don't know what he does. Go. Be nice. Get what you need."

Benedict hung up. I checked my e-mail and texts. Nothing. This whole strange episode in my life had taken on a surreal, dream-like quality. I worked hard to dismiss it. I did indeed have a 9:00 A.M. class on Law and the Constitution. That was my priority again. Yep, I'd put it behind me. I actually sang in the shower. I dressed and walked across campus with my smile wide and my head high. There was a little hop in my step. The sun bathed the campus in a warm, celestial beacon. I kept smiling. I smiled at the brick buildings longing for ivy. I smiled at the trees, at the lush grass, at the statues of famous alumni, at the view of the athletic fields down the hill. When students said hello to me, I greeted them with a level of enthusiasm that made one fear I was suddenly into religious conversion.

When class started, I stood in the front of the room and shouted "Good morning, everyone!" like a born-again cheerleader on too much Red Bull. The students gave me curious looks. I was starting to scare myself, so I tried to dial it back.

You made a promise.

And what about you, Natalie? Wasn't there at least an implied promise to me in your words and actions? How do you just capture a heart and crush it like that? Yes, I'm a big boy. I get the risks of falling in love. But we said things. We felt things. They weren't lies. And yet. You dumped me. You invited me to your wedding. Why? Why would anyone be that cruel, or were you trying to hammer home the fact that it was time for me to move on?

I did move on. You reached into my chest, plucked out my heart, tore it up, and walked away, but I picked up the shreds and moved on.

I shook my head. Picked up the shreds? Sheesh, that was horrible. That's the problem with falling in love. It makes you start talking like a bad country song.

Natalie had e-mailed me. Or at least, I thought it was Natalie. Who else could it be? But either way, even though she was telling me to stay away, it was communication. It was her reaching out to me. Reaching? Sure. But she had used that e-mail address. RSbyJA. She had remembered it. It had meant something to her, something that still resonated, and that gave me—I don't know—hope. Hope is cruel. Hope reminds me of what almost was. Hope makes the physical ache return.

I called on Eileen Sinagra, one of my brightest students. She began to explain one of the finer points of Madison and *The Federalist Papers*. I nodded, encouraging her to continue, when I saw something out of the corner of my eye. I moved closer to the window for a better look. I stopped.

"Professor Fisher?"

In the parking lot was a gray Chevy van. I checked the license plates. I couldn't make out the numbers from here, but I could see the color and pattern.

Vermont plates.

I didn't think twice. I didn't consider that it probably meant absolutely nothing, that gray Chevy vans are hardly rare, that there are plenty of Vermont license plates in western Massachusetts. None of that made any difference.

I was already sprinting toward the door when I shouted, "I'll be right back, stay here." I started down the corridor. The floor had just been mopped. I skidded around the WET sign and slammed open the door. The parking lot was across the commons. I hurdled a bush and ran full speed across the grass. My students must have thought that I'd gone off the deep end. I didn't really care.

"Go, Professor Fisher! I'll hit you!"

A student, mistaking my running for desire to participate, actually threw me a Frisbee. I let it land and kept running.

"Dude, you gotta work on your catches."

I ignored the voice. I was getting closer to the Chevy van when I saw its lights go on.

The driver had started up the van.

I ran even faster. That bright beacon of sun shone off the front windshield, blocking my view of the driver. I lowered my head and pumped my legs, but the Chevy van was backing out of the space now. I was too far away. I wasn't going to make it.

The van shifted into drive.

I pulled up and tried to get a look at the driver. No go. Too much glare, but I thought I saw . . .

A maroon baseball cap?

There was no way to be sure. I did, however, memorize the license plate—like that would help, like that would do any good—and then I stood, panting, as the van sped away.

Chapter 11

Professor Eban Trainor sat on the lemonade porch in front of a gorgeous Second-Empire Victorian. I knew the house well. For half a century it had been home to Professor Malcolm Hume, my mentor. A lot of good times had been had in this house. Poly-sci wine tastings, staff parties, late-night cognac, philosophical arguments, literary discussions—all things academia. But, alas, God has an interesting sense of humor. Professor Hume's wife passed away after forty-eight years of marriage, and his health followed. Eventually he could not take care of this great old house by himself. He now resided in a gated community in Vero Beach, Florida, while Professor Eban Trainor, the closest thing I had to an enemy on campus, had purchased this beloved dwelling, making himself the new lord of the manor.

I felt my phone buzz in my pocket. It was a text from Shanta:

JUDIE'S. 1:00 P.M.

Quite the wordsmith, but I knew what she meant. We should meet at Judie's Restaurant on Main Avenue at 1:00 P.M. Okay, fine. I put the phone away and started up the porch steps.

Eban rose and offered me a condescending smile. "Jacob. So good to see you."

His handshake felt greasy. His fingernails were manicured. Women found him handsome in an aging-playboy sort of way, what with the long unruly hair and big green eyes. His skin was waxy, as though his face were either melting or still recovering from some kind of skin treatment. I suspected Botox. He wore slacks a size too tight and a dress shirt that could have used one more closed button. His cologne smelled like too many European businessmen jammed into a morning elevator.

"Do you mind sitting on the porch?" he asked. "It's so beautiful out."

I readily agreed. I didn't want to go inside and see what he'd done with the place. I knew the work had been extensive. Gone, I was sure, were the dark woods, the cognac and cigar feel, traded in for blond wood and couches in colors like "eggshell" and "churned butter" and gatherings that only served white wine and Sprite because they wouldn't stain the upholstery.

On cue, he offered me white wine. I politely declined. He had his in hand. It wasn't even noon. We both sat on wicker chairs with big pillows.

"So what can I do for you, Jacob?" he asked.

I had taken a class with him sophomore year on Mid-Twentieth-Century Drama. He wasn't a bad teacher. He was both effective and affected, the kind of teacher who loves nothing more than the sound of his voice and while he is rarely boring—the kiss of death in any class—the lessons are all a tad professor-centric. He spent one week reading Genet's *The Maids* in its entirety out loud, taking on each character, reveling in his own performance, not to mention the S&M scenes. The performance was good, no doubt, but, alas, it was all him.

"I wanted to ask you about a student," I said

Eban raised both eyebrows as though my words were both intriguing and surprising. "Oh?"

"Todd Sanderson."

"Oh?"

I saw him stiffen. He didn't want me to see it. But I did. He looked off and stroked his chin.

"You remember him," I said.

Eban Trainor stroked his chin some more. "The name rings a bell, but . . ." A few more strokes and then Eban shrugged in surrender. "I'm sorry. So many years, so many students."

Why didn't I believe him?

"You didn't have him in class," I said.

"Oh?"

Again with the oh.

"He came up before the discipline committee when you were in charge. This would have been about twenty years ago."

"And you expect me to still remember?"

"You helped keep him on campus after an altercation. Here, let me show you." I pulled out my laptop and brought up the scan of his handwritten decision. I held out the laptop. Eban hesitated as though it might contain explosives. He took out his reading glasses and examined the letter.

"Wait, where did you get this?"

"It's important, Eban."

"This is from a student's confidential file." A small smile crossed his lips. "Isn't reading this file breaking the rules, Jacob? Wouldn't you say you were crossing boundaries?"

So there it was. Six years ago, just a scant few weeks before I headed up to that retreat in Vermont, Professor Eban Trainor hosted a graduation party at his then-house. Trainor frequently hosted parties at his house. In fact, he was somewhat legendary for both throwing and attending them. When I was a sophomore, there had been a rather famous incident at Jones College, the nearby all-women institution, during which a fire alarm went off at three in the morning, forcing a dorm to evacuate, and there stood Professor Trainor, half-dressed. True, the coed he'd been seeing that particular night was of legal age and not one of his students. But this was typical Trainor. He was a letch and a drunk, and I didn't like him.

The graduation party six years ago was mostly attended by students, many of whom were underclassmen and thus underage. Alcohol had been served. A lot of it. Campus police were called. Two students were taken to the hospital for alcohol poisoning, something that happens with increasing frequency on college campuses. Or maybe that's what I tell myself because I like to think that it was not as bad in "my day."

Professor Trainor was brought up before the administration for his actions. There were calls for his resignation. He refused. He claimed that, yes, he had offered alcohol to the attendees but only seniors who were over twenty-one years old were invited. If underclassmen crashed the party, he should not be held responsible. He also suggested that much of the alcohol had been consumed before his party began, at a nearby fraternity kegger.

The professors on campus govern themselves. We rarely do more than slap one another on the wrist. Like with the student discipline committee, professors rotate through. As luck would have it, I was on the committee when this incident occurred. Trainor had tenure and couldn't be fired, but I firmly believed that he deserved some sort of disciplinary action. We took a vote to have Trainor removed as chairman of the English department. I argued in favor of the punishment. There were simply too many incidents of this kind of behavior in his past. Interestingly enough, my beloved mentor, Malcolm Hume, did not agree.

"Are you really going to blame Eban for students drinking too much?" he had asked me.

"There are reasons why we have rules about fraternizing with students when alcohol is served."

"The extenuating circumstances don't mean anything to you?"

They might have, I guessed, if I hadn't already seen Eban's pattern of obvious bad behavior and poor choices. This wasn't a court of law or a question of rights; this was a great job and a privilege. In my view, his actions warranted termination—we expel students for far less and with far less evidence—but at the very least, he deserved a demotion. Despite my mentor's urging, I voted in favor of taking away his chairmanship, but I was outvoted by a wide margin.

Those hearings might be long over, but the resentment lasts. I had used those exact terms—"broken rules," "crossed boundaries"—

during the supposedly closed debates. Nice to have my own words thrown back at my face, but maybe that was fair.

"This particular student," I said, "is dead."

"So his confidential file is now fair game?"

"I'm not here to argue legal minutiae with you."

"No, no, Jacob, you're a big-picture guy, aren't you?"

This was a waste of time. "I don't really understand your reticence."

"That surprises me, Jacob. You're usually such a rules follower. The information you're asking for is confidential. I'm protecting Mr. Sanderson's privacy."

"But again," I said, "he's dead."

I did not want to sit here, on this lemonade porch where my beloved mentor spent so many wonderful hours, another moment. I rose and reached for my laptop. He did not hand it back to me. He started doing the chin rub again.

"Sit," he said.

I did.

"Would you tell me why a case this old would have relevance to you now?"

"It would be very hard to explain," I said.

"But it is clearly very important to you."

"Yes."

"How did Todd Sanderson die?"

"He was murdered."

Eban closed his eyes as though that revelation made it all so much worse. "By whom?"

"The police don't know yet."

"Ironic," he said.

"How so?"

"That he would die by violence. I remember the case. Todd Sanderson injured a fellow student in a violent altercation. Well, that's not really an adequate way of stating it. In truth, Todd Sanderson nearly killed a fellow student."

Eban Trainor looked off again and took a gulp of wine. I waited for him to say more. It took some time, but eventually he continued. "It happened at a Thursday night kegger at Chi Psi."

Chi Psi sponsored a kegger every Thursday night for as long as anyone could remember. The powers that be tried to stop it twelve years ago, but a wealthy alum simply bought a house off campus specifically for their use. He could have donated the money to a worthy cause. Instead he bought a party house for his younger frat brothers to imbibe in. Go figure.

"Naturally both participants were drunk," Eban said. "Words were exchanged, but there was little doubt that Todd Sanderson turned this verbal altercation into something horribly physical. When all is said, the other student—I'm sorry, I don't remember his name, it may have been McCarthy or McCaffrey, something like that—had to be hospitalized. He had a broken nose and a crushed cheekbone. But that wasn't the worst part."

He stopped again. I picked up the hint.

"What was the worst part?" I asked.

"Todd Sanderson nearly choked the other student to death. It took five people to pull him off. The other student was unconscious. He had to be resuscitated."

"Wow," I said.

Eban Trainor shut his eyes for a moment. "I can't see how this matters anymore. We should let him rest in peace."

"I'm not asking out of some kind of prurient interest."

The thin smile crossed his lips again. "Oh, I know, Jacob. You are, if nothing else, a righteous man. I'm sure your interest here is nothing but the healthiest and most well-meaning."

I let that pass.

"So why was Sanderson let off?" I asked.

"You read my decision."

"I did," I said. "Something about 'highly unusual extenuating circumstances.'"

"That's correct."

I waited again, figuring my follow-up question was obvious. When Trainor didn't say anything, I gave the proper prompt: "What were the extenuating circumstances?"

"The other student—McCarthy. That was his name. I remember now." Trainor took a deep breath. "Mr. McCarthy made derogatory comments about a certain incident. When Sanderson heard the comments, he more or less—yet understandably—lost control." Eban held a hand up in my face as though I were about to object, which I wasn't about to do at all. "Yes, Jacob, I know that we do not excuse violence under any circumstances. That would be your stand, I am certain. But we looked at this unusual case from every level. We heard from several Todd Sanderson supporters. One, in particular, defended him with great gusto."

I met his eyes and saw something mocking in them. "Who would that be, Eban?"

"Hint: He used to own this house."

That surprised me. "Professor Hume defended Todd Sanderson?"

"What's the word attorneys always use?" He rubbed his chin

again. "*Vigorously*. He even helped him set up a charity when the case was over."

I tried to put it together. Hume detested violence in all forms. He was one of those people who felt too much. Cruelty on any level made him cringe. If you hurt, he hurt.

"I confess," Eban continued, "that I was surprised too, but your mentor has always understood extenuating circumstances, hasn't he?"

We weren't talking about Todd Sanderson anymore, so I brought the topic back to him.

"And what were the extenuating circumstances in this case?"

"Well, for one thing, Todd Sanderson had just come back from a long leave. He had missed the prior semester for personal reasons."

I had just about had enough. "Eban?"

"Yes?"

"Could we stop dancing around here? What happened to Todd Sanderson? Why did he leave campus? What were the extenuating circumstances that would cause a man as anti-violence as Malcolm Hume to defend such an extreme assault?"

"It's not in the file?"

"You know it's not. Everything but the decision was kept off the record. So what happened to him?"

"Not to him," Trainor said. "To his father."

He reached behind him for a glass and handed it to me. He didn't ask; he just handed me the glass. I took it and let him pour the wine into it. It was still not yet noon, but I figured that this would be the wrong time to comment on morning drinking. I accepted it and hoped that it would loosen his tongue.

Eban Trainor sat back and crossed his legs. He stared into his wineglass as though it were a crystal ball. "Do you remember the Martindale Little League incident?"

Now it was my turn to look at the wine. I took a sip. "The pedophilia scandal?"

"Yes."

It had to be fifteen, maybe even twenty years ago, but I remembered because it was one of the first cases that received a lot of press. "The coach or head of a Little League was raping young boys, right?"

"That was the accusation, yes."

"It wasn't true?"

"No," Eban said slowly, taking yet another deep sip. "It wasn't true."

We just sat there.

"So what does that have to do with Todd Sanderson?"

"Not him." There was a slur now in Eban's voice. "But the coach or head of the Little League, as you just described him."

I saw it now. "It was his father?"

Eban pointed at me. "Bingo."

I didn't know what to say to that.

"Todd Sanderson skipped that semester to help his father," Eban said. "He supported his family financially—his father was fired as a schoolteacher, of course—offered moral support, did whatever he could."

I was surprised and confused, but it all just raised the central question in this whole line of questioning: What could any of this possibly have to do with my Natalie?

"I don't remember the case that well," I said. "How did it end? Did Todd's father serve any time?"

"No. He was found innocent."

"Oh?" I said.

"The outcome didn't really get much press. That's part of our process. The accusation gets page one. The retraction not so much."

"So he was found not guilty?"

"That's correct."

"Big difference though between not guilty and innocent."

"True," Eban said, "but not in this case. During the first week of trial, it came to light that a vindictive parent made it up because Todd's father wouldn't let his son pitch. The lie just snowballed. But in the end Todd's father was cleared of all charges."

"And Todd returned to school?"

"Yes."

"And I assume the derogatory comment had something to do with the accusations against Todd's father?"

Eban raised an unsteady hand in mock toast. "You are correct, sir. You see, despite the new evidence, many believed, as you did, that where there was smoke there was fire. Mr. Sanderson must have done *something*. Maybe not this. But something. Especially after what happened after the trial."

"What happened after the trial?"

He stared at his glass again. I was losing him.

"Eban?"

"I'm getting to it."

I waited, gave him his space.

"Todd Sanderson came from a small Southern town. His father had lived there his entire life. But now, well, you could imagine. He couldn't get a job. His friends wouldn't talk to him. See, no one had truly believed him. You can't unring that bell, Jacob. We teach that here, don't we? Only one person still believed in him."

"Todd," I said.

"Yes."

"Weren't there other family members? Todd's mother?"

"Long dead."

"So what happened?"

"His father was crushed, of course, but he insisted that Todd go back to school. Did you read Todd's transcript?"

"Yes."

"Then you know already. Todd was a magnificent student, one of the finest ever to attend Lanford. He had a bright future. His father saw that too. But Todd wouldn't come back. He saw it as abandoning his father in his hour of most need. Todd flat-out refused to return until the situation at home got better. But of course, as we know all too well, situations like this don't get better. So Todd's father did the only thing he thought he could to end his own pain and free his son to continue his studies."

Our eyes met. His were wet now.

"Oh no," I said.

"Oh yes."

"How . . . ?"

"His father broke into the school where he used to work and shot himself in the head. See, he didn't want his son to be the one who found his body."

Chapter 12

Three weeks before Natalie dumped me, when we were madly in love, we sneaked down from our retreats in Kraftboro to visit Lanford. "I want to see this place that means so much to you," she said.

I remember the way her eyes lit up when she walked with me on that campus. We held hands. Natalie wore a big straw hat, which was both endearing and odd, and sunglasses. She looked a bit like a movie star in disguise.

"When you were a student here," she asked me, "where did you take the hot coeds?"

"Straight to bed."

Natalie playfully slapped my arm. "I'm serious. And hungry."

So we headed to Judie's Restaurant on Main Avenue. Judie made a wonderful popover and apple butter. Natalie loved it. I watched her take it all in—the artwork, the décor, the young waitstaff, the menu, everything. "So this is where you took your ladies?"

"The classy ones," I said.

"Wait, where did you take the, uh, classless ones?"

"Barsolotti's. The dive bar next door." I smiled.

"What?"

"We used to play condom roulette."

"Excuse me?"

"Not with girls. I was kidding about that. I'd go there with friends. There was a condom dispenser in the men's room."

"A condom dispenser?"

"Yep."

"Like a condom vending machine."

"Exactly," I said.

Natalie nodded. "Classy."

"I know, right?"

"So what are the rules of condom roulette?"

"It's silly."

"Oh, you're not getting off that easy. I want to hear."

There was that smile that knocked me back a step.

"Okay," I said. "You play with four guys . . . this is so stupid."

"Please? I love it. Come on. You play with four guys . . ." She gestured for me to continue.

"The condoms come in four colors," I explained. "Midnight Black, Cherry Red, Lemon Yellow, Orange Orange."

"You're making up those last two."

"Something like that. The point is, they came in four colors, but you never knew which one you'd get. So see, we'd each put three bucks in the pot and choose a color. Then one of us would go to the dispenser and bring back the wrapped condom. Again, you didn't know the color until you actually open the wrapper. Someone would do a drumroll. Another guy would do the play-by-play like it was an Olympic event. Finally, the package was opened, and whoever picked the right color got the money."

"Oh, that's too awesome."

"Yeah, well," I said. "Of course, the winner had to buy the next pitcher of beer, so there wasn't much of a financial windfall. Eventually Barsy—that's the guy who owned the place—made it a full-fledged game with rules and league play and a leader board."

She took my hand. "Could we play?"

"What, now? No."

"Please."

"No way."

"After the game," Natalie whispered, giving me a look that singed my eyebrows, "we could use the condom."

"I call Midnight Black," I said.

She laughed. I could still hear that sound as I entered Judie's, as if her laugh were still here, still echoing, still mocking me. I hadn't been back to Judie's in, well, six years. I looked over at the table where we'd sat. It was empty.

"Jake?"

I spun toward my right. Shanta Newlin sat at a quiet table over by the bay windows. She didn't wave or nod. Her body language, usually fully loaded with confidence, seemed all wrong. I sat across from her. She barely looked up.

"Hi," I said.

Still staring at the table, Shanta said, "Tell me the whole story, Jake."

"Why? What's going on?"

Her eyes came up, pinning me interrogator-style. I could see the FBI agent now. "Is she really an old girlfriend?"

"What? Yes, of course."

"And why do you all of a sudden want to find her?"

I hesitated.

"Jake?"

The e-mail came back to me:

You made a promise.

"I asked you a favor," I said.

"I know."

"So you can either let me know what you found or we can just forget it. I'm not sure I get why you need to know more."

The young waitress—Judie always hired college kids—gave us menus and asked if we would like drinks. We both ordered iced teas. When she left, Shanta turned the hard eyes back on me.

"I'm trying to help you, Jake."

"Maybe we should just let it go."

"You're kidding, right?"

"No," I said. "She asked me to leave her alone. I should probably have listened."

"When?"

"When what?"

"When did she ask you to leave her alone?" Shanta asked.

"What difference does that make?"

"Just tell me, okay? It could be important."

"How?" Then, figuring, what was the harm, I added: "Six years ago."

"You said that you were in love with her."

"Yes."

"So was this when you broke up?"

I shook my head. "It was at her wedding to another man."

That made her blink. My words diffused the hard glare, at least for the moment. "Just so I'm clear on this, you went to her wedding—were you still in love with her? Dumb question. Of course you were. You still are. So you went to her wedding, and while you were there, Natalie told you to leave her alone?"

"Something like that, yes."

"That must have been some scene."

"It wasn't like it sounds. We had just broken up. She ended up choosing another guy over me. An old boyfriend. They got married a few days later." I tried to shrug it off. "It happens."

"You think?" Shanta said with the confused head tilt of a freshman. "Go on."

"Go on with what? I went to the wedding. Natalie asked me to accept her choice and leave them be. I said I would."

"I see. Have you had any contact with her during the past six years?"

"No."

"None at all?"

I realized now how good Shanta was at this. I had taken the position that I wouldn't talk, and now you pretty much couldn't get me to shut up. "Right, none at all."

"And you're sure her name is Natalie Avery?"

"That's not the kind of thing you make a mistake about. Enough questions. What did you find, Shanta?"

"Nothing."

"Nothing?"

The waitress came back with a big smile and our iced teas. "Here are some of Judie's fresh popovers." Her voice was the happy song of youth. The popover scent rose from the table and took me back to my last visit here, yep, six years ago.

"Any questions about the menu?" the perky waitress asked.

I couldn't answer.

"Jake?" Shanta said.

I swallowed. "No questions."

Shanta ordered a grilled portobello mushroom sandwich. I went with the turkey BLT on rye. When the waitress was gone, I leaned across the table. "What do you mean you found nothing?"

"What part of 'nothing' is confusing you, Jake? I found nothing on your ex—zippo, *nada*, zilch. No address, no tax returns, no bank account, no credit card statement. Not-a-thing, no thing, nothing. There is not one shred of evidence that your Natalie Avery even exists anymore."

I tried to take this in.

Shanta put her hands on the table. "Do you know how hard it is to live off the grid like that?"

"Not really, no."

"In this day and age with computers and all the technology? It's pretty close to impossible."

"Maybe there's a reasonable explanation," I said.

"Like what?"

"Maybe she moved overseas."

"Then there's no record of her going there. No passport issued. No entry or exit in the computer. Like I said before—"

"Nothing," I finished for her.

Shanta nodded.

"She's a person, Shanta. She exists."

"Well, she existed. Six years ago. That was the last time we had an address on her. She has a sister named Julie Pottham. Her mother, Sylvia Avery, is in a nursing home. Do you know all this?"

"Yes."

"Who did she marry?"

Should I answer that one? I saw little harm. "Todd Sanderson."

She jotted the name down. "And why did you want to look her up now?"

You made a promise.

"It doesn't matter," I said. "I should just let it be."

"Are you serious?"

"I am. It was a whim. I mean, it's been six years. She married another man and made me promise to leave her alone. So what exactly am I looking for anyway?"

"But that's what makes me curious, Jake."

"What does?"

"You kept this promise for six years. Why did you suddenly break it?"

I didn't want to answer that, and something else was starting to gnaw at me. "Why are you so interested?"

She didn't reply.

"I asked you to look a person up. You could have just told me that you didn't find anything. Why are you asking me all these questions about her?"

Shanta seemed taken aback. "I was just trying to help."

"You're not telling me something."

"Neither are you," Shanta said. "Why now, Jake? Why are you looking for your old love now?"

I stared down at the popover. I thought about that day in this restaurant six years ago, the way Natalie tore off small pieces of her popover, the look of concentration as she buttered it, the way she simply enjoyed everything. When we were together, even the smallest thing took on significance. Every touch brought pleasure.

You made a promise.

Even now, even after all that had happened, I couldn't betray her. Stupid? Yep. Naive? Oh, several steps south of that. But I couldn't do it.

"Talk to me, Jake."

I shook my head. "No."

"Why the hell not?"

"Who ordered turkey BLT?"

It was another waitress, this one less perky and more harried. I raised my hand.

"And the grilled portobello sandwich?"

"Wrap it for me," Shanta said, rising. "I lost my appetite."

Chapter 13

The first time I met Natalie she was wearing sunglasses indoors. To make matters worse, it was nighttime.

I rolled my eyes, thinking it was for effect. I figured that she fancied herself an Artiste with a capital *A*. We were attending a mixer of sorts, the art colony and the writers' retreat, sharing one another's work. This was my first time attending, but I soon learned that it was a weekly gathering. The art was displayed in the back of Darly Wanatick's barn. Chairs were set up for the readings.

The woman in the sunglasses—I hadn't met her yet—sat in the last row, her arms crossed. A bearded man with dark curly hair sat next to her. I wondered whether they were together. Remember the blowhard named Lars who was writing poetry from the perspective of Hitler's dog? He began to read. He read for a long time. I began to fidget. The woman in the sunglasses remained still.

When I could listen no longer, rude or not, I wandered toward the back of the barn and started to check out the various art on display. Most of it, well, I will be kind. I didn't "get it." There was an installation piece called *Breakfast in America* that featured spilled boxes of cold cereal on a kitchen table. That was it. There were boxes of Cap'n Crunch, Cap'n Crunch with Peanut Butter (one person actually muttered, "Notice there is no Cap'n Crunch with Crunch Berries—why?—what is the artist saying?"), Lucky Charms, Cocoa Puffs, Sugar Smacks, even my old favorite, Quisp. I looked at the spilled cereal coating the table. It did not speak to me, though my stomach grumbled a little.

When one person asked, "What do you think?" I was tempted to say that it needed a little milk.

As I kept walking, only one artist's work gave me real pause. I stopped at a painting of a small cottage on top of a hill. There was a soft morning glow hitting the side—the pinkness that comes with the first light of day. I couldn't tell you why but it choked me up. Maybe it was the dark windows, as though the cottage had once been warm but it was abandoned now. I don't know. But I stood in front of the painting and felt lost and moved. I stepped slowly from one painting to the next. They all delivered a blow of some kind. Some made me melancholy. Some made me nostalgic, whimsical, passionate. None left me indifferent.

I will spare you the "big reveal" that the paintings were done by Natalie.

A woman was smiling at my reaction. "Do you like them?"

"Very much," I said. "Are you the artist?"

"Heavens no. I run the bakery and coffee shop in town." She offered me her hand. "They call me Cookie."

I shook it. "Wait. Cookie runs a bakery?"

"Yeah, I know. Too precious, right?"

"Maybe a tad."

"The artist is Natalie Avery. She's right over there."

Cookie pointed to the woman with the sunglasses.

"Oh," I said.

"Oh what?"

With the sunglasses-indoors look, I had her pegged as the creator of *Breakfast in America*. Lars had just finished his reading. The crowd gave him a small golf-clap, but Lars, sporting an ascot, bowed as though it were a thunderous standing ovation.

Everyone quickly rose except for Natalie. The man with the beard and curly hair whispered something to her as he stood, but still she didn't move. She stayed with her arms crossed, still lost, it seemed, in the essence of Hitler's dog.

I approached her. She looked right through me.

"The cottage in your painting. Where is it?"

"Huh?" she said, startled. "Nowhere. What painting?"

I frowned. "Aren't you Natalie Avery?"

"Me?" She seemed befuddled by the question. "Yeah, why?"

"The painting of the cottage. I really loved it. It . . . I don't know. It moved me."

"Cottage?" She sat up, took off the sunglasses, and rubbed her eyes. "Sure, right, a cottage."

I frowned again. I was not sure what reaction I expected, but something a bit more demonstrative than this. I looked down at her. Sometimes I am not the sharpest knife in the drawer but when she rubbed her eyes again, the realization hit me.

"You were sleeping!" I said.

"What?" she said. "No."

But she rubbed her eyes some more.

"Holy crap," I said. "That's why you're wearing the sunglasses. So no one can tell."

"Shh."

"You were sleeping this whole time!"

"Keep it down."

She finally looked up at me and I remembered thinking that she had a beautiful, sweet face. I would soon learn that Natalie had what I'd call a slow beauty, the kind you don't really notice at first and then it knocks you back and grows on you and she gets more beautiful every time you see her and then you can't believe that you ever thought that she was anything less than completely stunning. Whenever I saw her, my entire body reacted, as though it were the first time or better.

"Was I that obvious?" she asked in a whisper.

"Not at all," I said. "I just thought you were being a pretentious ass."

She arched an eyebrow. "What better disguise to blend in with this crowd?"

I shook my head. "And I thought you were a genius when I saw your paintings."

"Really?" She seemed caught off guard by the compliment.

"Really."

She cleared her throat. "And now that you see how deceptive I can be?"

"I think you're a *diabolical* genius."

Natalie liked that. "You can't fault me. That Lars guy is like human Ambien. He opens his mouth, I'm out."

"I'm Jake Fisher."

"Natalie Avery."

"So do you want to grab a cup of coffee, Natalie Avery? Looks like you could use one."

She hesitated, studying my face to the point where I think I started to redden. She tucked a ringlet of black hair behind her ear and stood. She moved closer to me, and I remember thinking that she was wonderfully petite, smaller than I had imagined when she'd been sitting. She looked way up at me, and a smile slowly came to her face. It was, I must say, a great smile. "Sure, why not?"

That image of that smile held in my brain for a beat before it mercifully dissolved away.

I was out at the Library Bar with Benedict. The Library Bar was pretty much exactly that—an old, dark-wood campus library that had recently been converted into a retro-trendy drinking establishment. The owners were clever enough to change very little of the old library. The books were still on the oak shelves, sorted in alphabetical order or the Dewey Decimal System or whatever the librarians had used. The "bar" was the old circulation desk. The coasters were old card files that had been laminated. The lights were green library lamps.

The young female bartenders wore their hair in severe buns and sported fitted conservative clothes and, of course, horn-rimmed glasses. Yep, the fantasy librarian hottie. Once an hour, a loud librarian *shush* would play over the loudspeaker and the bartenders would rip off their glasses, let loose their bun, and unbutton the top of their blouse.

Cheesy but it worked.

Benedict and I were getting properly oiled. I threw my arm loosely around him and leaned in close. "You know what we should do?" I asked him.

Benedict made a face. "Sober up?"

"Ha! Good one. No, no. We should set up a rousing tournament of condom roulette. Single elimination. I'm thinking sixty-four teams. Like our own March Madness."

"We aren't in Barsolotti's, Jake. This place doesn't have a condom vending machine."

"It doesn't?"

"No."

"Shame."

"Yeah," Benedict said. Then he whispered, "Pair of red-hot spank-worthy honeys at three o'clock."

I was about to turn to my left, then to my right, and suddenly the concept of three o'clock made no sense to me. "Wait," I said, "where's my twelve o'clock again?"

Benedict sighed. "You're facing twelve o'clock."

"So three o'clock would be . . . ?"

"Just turn to your right, Jake."

You may have guessed that I do not handle spirits well. This surprises people. When they see someone my size, they expect me to drink smaller folks under the table. I can't. I hold my liquor about as well as a freshman coed at her first mixer.

"Well?"

I knew the type before my eyes even had a chance to settle on them. There sat two blondes who looked good-to-great in low Library Bar light and ordinary-to-frightful in the light of the morning sun. Benedict slid toward them and started chatting them up. Benedict could chat up a file cabinet. The two women looked past him and at me. Benedict signaled for me to join them.

Why the hell not?

You made a promise.

Damn straight I did. Thanks for the reminder. Might as well keep it and try to score me a honey, right? I weaved my way toward them.

"Ladies, meet the legendary Professor Jacob Fisher."

"Wow," one of the blondes said, "he's a big boy," and—because Benedict couldn't help but be obvious—he winked and said, "You got no idea, sweetheart."

I bit back the sigh, said hello, and sat. Benedict "macked" on them with pickup lines, specifically handpicked for this bar: "It's a library so it's perfectly okay to check you out." "Will I be fined if I keep you out late?" The blondes loved it. I tried to join in, but I have never been great with superficial banter. Natalie's face kept appearing. I kept pushing it away. We ordered more drinks. And more.

After a while we all stumbled to couches near the former children's section. My head lolled back, and I may have passed out for a bit. When I woke up, one of the blondes started talking to me. I introduced myself.

"My name is Windy," she said.

"Wendy?"

"No, Windy. With an *i* instead of an *e*." She said this as though she had said it a million times before, which, I guessed, she had.

"Like the song?" I asked.

She looked surprised. "You know the song? You don't look old enough."

"'*Everyone knows it's Windy,*'" I sang. Then: "My dad loved the Association."

"Wow. My dad too. That's how I got the name."

It turned into, surprisingly enough, a real conversation. Windy was thirty-one years old and worked as a bank teller, but she was getting her degree in pediatric nursing, her dream job, at the community college down the road. She took care of her handicapped brother.

"Alex has cerebral palsy," Windy said, showing me the picture of her brother in a wheelchair. The boy's face was radiant. I stared at it, as if somehow the goodness could come out of the picture and be a part of me. Windy saw it, nodded, and said in the softest voice: "He's the light of my life."

An hour passed. Maybe two. Windy and I chatted. During nights like these, there is always a time when you know if you are going to, ahem, close the sale (or, to stay within the library metaphors, if you are going to get your library card punched) or not. We were at that time now, and it was clear that the answer was yes.

The ladies left to powder their noses. I felt overly mellow from drink. Part of me wondered whether I'd be able to perform. Most of me didn't really care.

"You know what I like about both of them?" Benedict pointed to a shelf of books. "They're stacked. Get it? Library, books, stacked?"

I groaned out loud. "I think I'm going to be sick."

"Amusing," Benedict said. "By the way, where were you last night?"

"I didn't tell you?"

"No."

"I went up to Vermont," I said. "To Natalie's old retreat."

He turned toward me. "Whatever for?"

It was an odd thing, but when Benedict talked after drinking too much, a hint of a British accent came through. I assumed that it was from his prep school days. The more he drank, the more pronounced the accent.

"To get answers," I said.

"And did you get any?"

"Yep."

"Do tell."

"One"—I stuck a finger in the air—"no one knows who Natalie is. Two"—another finger—"no one knows who I am. Three"—you get the point with the fingers—"there is no record at the chapel Natalie ever got married. Four, the minister I saw conducting the wedding swears it never happened. Five, the lady who owned the coffee shop we used to go to and who first pointed Natalie out to me had no idea who I was and didn't remember either Natalie or me."

I put my hand down.

"Oh, and Natalie's art retreat?" I said. "The Creative Recharge Colony? It's not there and everyone swears it never existed and that it's always been a family-run farm. In short, I think I'm losing my mind."

Benedict turned away and started sipping his beer.

"What?" I said.

"Nothing."

I gave him a little shove. "No, come on. What is it?"

Benedict kept his head lowered. "Six years ago, when you went up to that retreat, you were in pretty bad shape."

"Maybe a little. So?"

"Your father had died. You felt alone. Your dissertation wasn't going well. You were upset and on edge. You were angry about Trainor getting off with nary a slap."

"What's your point?"

"Nothing," he said. "Forget it."

"Don't give me that. What?"

My head was really swimming now. I should have stopped several glasses ago. I remembered once when I had too much to drink my freshman year and I started walking back to my dorm. I never quite arrived. When I woke up, I was lying on top of a bush. I remembered staring up at the stars in the night sky and wondering why the ground felt so prickly. I had that sway now, like I was on a boat in a rough sea.

"Natalie," Benedict said.

"What about her?"

He turned those glass-magnified eyes toward me. "How come I never met her?"

My vision was getting a little fuzzy. "What?"

"Natalie. How come I never met her?"

"Because we were in Vermont the whole time."

"You never came to campus?"

"Just once. We went to Judie's."

"So how come you didn't bring her by to meet me?"

I shrugged with a little too much gusto. "I don't know. Maybe you were away?"

"I was here all that summer."

Silence. I tried to remember. Had I tried to introduce her to Benedict?

"I'm your best friend, right?" he said.

"Right."

"And if you married her, I would have been the best man."

"You know it."

"So don't you find it bizarre that I never met her?" he asked.

"When you put it that way . . ." I frowned. "Wait, are you trying to make a point here?"

"No," he said quietly. "It's just odd is all."

"Odd how?"

He said nothing.

"Odd like I-made-her-up odd? Is that what you mean?"

"No. I'm just saying."

"Saying what?"

"That summer. You needed something to hold on to."

"And I found it. And lost it."

"Okay, fine, drop it."

But, no, that would not do. Not right now. Not with my anger and the drink talking. "And speaking of which," I said, "how come I never met the love of your life?"

"What are you talking about?"

Oh man, I was drunk. "The picture in your wallet. How come I never met her?"

It looked as though I'd slapped him across the face. "Leave it alone, Jake."

"I'm just saying."

"Leave. It. Alone."

I opened my mouth, closed it. The ladies reappeared. Benedict gave his head a shake and suddenly the smile was back on it.

"Which one do you want?" Benedict asked me.

I looked at him. "For real?"

"Yes."

"Windy," I said.

"Which one is that?"

"Seriously?"

"I'm not good with names," Benedict said.

"Windy is the one I've been talking to all night."

"In other words," Benedict said, "you want the hotter one. Fine, whatever."

I went back to Windy's place. We took it slow until we took it fast. It wasn't full-on bliss, but it was awfully sweet. It was around 3:00 A.M. when Windy walked me to the door.

Not sure what to say, I stupidly went with "Uh, thank you."

"Uh, you're welcome?"

We kissed lightly on the lips. It wasn't something that would last, we both knew that, but it was a small, quick delight, and sometimes in this world, there was nothing wrong with that.

I stumbled back across campus. There were students still out. I tried to stay in the shadows, but Barry, the student who visits my office weekly, spotted me and cried out, "Taking the walk of shame, Teach?"

Caught.

I gave him a good-hearted wave and continued serpentine-style to my humble abode.

A sudden head rush hit me as I entered. I stayed still, waiting for my legs to come back to me. When the dizziness receded, I headed into the kitchen and grabbed a glass of ice water. I drank it in big gulps and poured another. I would be hurting tomorrow, no question about it.

Exhaustion weighed down my bones. I stepped into my bedroom and flicked on the light. There, sitting on the edge of my bed, was the man with the maroon baseball cap. I jumped back, startled.

The man gave me a friendly wave. "Hey, Jake. Sheesh, look at you. Have you been out carousing?"

For a second, no more, I just stood there. The man smiled at me as though this were the most natural encounter in the history of the world. He even touched the front of his cap at me, as though he were a professional golfer acknowledging the gallery.

"Who the hell are you?" I asked.

"That's not really relevant, Jake."

"Like hell it isn't. Who are you?"

The man sighed, let down, it seemed, by my seemingly irrational insistence on knowing his identity. "Let's just say I'm a friend."

"You were in the café. In Vermont."

"Guilty."

"And you followed me back here. You were in that van."

"Guilty again. Man, you smell like cheap booze and cheaper sex. Not that there's anything wrong with that."

I tried to keep from swaying. "What do you want?"

"I want us to take a ride."

"Where?"

"Where?" He arched an eyebrow. "Let's not play games here, Jake. You know where."

"I don't have the slightest idea what you're talking about," I said. "How did you get in here anyway?"

The man almost rolled his eyes at that one. "Oh, right, Jake, that's what we want to waste time discussing—how I managed to get past that piece-of-crap excuse for a lock on your back door. You'd be better off sealing it closed with Scotch tape."

I opened my mouth, closed it, tried again. "Who the hell are you?"

"Bob. Okay, Jake? Since you don't seem to be able to get past this name issue, my name is Bob. You're Jake, I'm Bob. Now can we get moving, please?"

The man stood. I braced myself, ready to relive my bouncer days. There was no way I was letting this guy out of here without an explanation. If the man was intimidated, he was doing a pretty good job of hiding it.

"Are we ready to go now," he asked me, "or do you want to waste more time?"

"Go where?"

Bob frowned as though I were putting him on. "Come on, Jake. Where do you think?" He gestured toward the door behind me. "To see Natalie, of course. We better hurry."

Chapter 14

The van was parked in the faculty lot behind Moore dormitory.

The campus was still now. The music had ceased, replaced by the incessant chirping of crickets. I could see the silhouettes of a few students in the distance, but for the most part, 3:00 A.M. seemed to be the witching hour.

Bob and I walked side by side, two buddies out for a night stroll. The drink was still canoodling with certain brain synapses, but the combination of night air and surprise visitor was sobering me up pretty rapidly. As we neared the now-familiar Chevy van, the back door slid open. A man stepped out.

I didn't like this.

The man was tall and thin with cheekbones that could dice tomatoes and perfectly coiffed hair. He looked like a male model, right down to that vaguely knowing scowl. During my years as a bouncer, I developed something of a sixth sense for trouble. It just happens after you work a job like that long enough. A man walks by you and the danger comes off in hot waves, like those squiggly lines in a cartoon. This guy gave off hot danger-waves like an exploding supernova.

I pulled up. "Who's this?"

"Again with the names?" Bob said. Then, with a dramatic sigh, he added, "Otto. Jake, meet my friend Otto."

"Otto and Bob," I said.

"Yes."

"Two palindromes."

"You college professors and your fancy words." We had reached the van. Otto stepped to the side to let me in, but I didn't move. "Get in," Bob said.

I shook my head. "My mommy told me not to get in cars with strangers."

"Yo, Teach!"

My eyes flew open as I turned toward the voice. Barry was semi-running toward us. He had clearly imbibed, and so the steps made him look like a marionette with twisted strings. "Yo, Teach, a quick question if I—?"

Barry never finished his sentence. Without warning or hesitation, Otto stepped forward, reared back, and punched Barry square in the face. I stood there for a moment, shocked by the suddenness of it. Barry went horizontal in the air. He landed on the asphalt with a hard thud, his head lolling back. His eyes were closed. Blood streamed from his nose.

I dropped to one knee. "Barry?"

He didn't move.

Otto took out a gun.

I positioned my body to the left a bit, so I could shield Barry from Otto's gun.

"Otto won't shoot you," Bob said in the same calm voice. "He'll just start shooting students until you get in the van."

I cradled Barry's head. I could see that he was breathing. I was about to check his pulse when I heard a voice cry out.

"Barry?" It was another student. "Where are you, bro?"

Fear seized me as Otto raised his gun. I debated making a move, but as though reading my mind, Otto took a step farther away from me.

Another student yelled, "I think he's over there—by that van. Barry?"

Otto aimed the gun toward the voice. Bob looked at me and gave a half shrug.

"Okay!" I whisper-shouted. "I'm going! Don't shoot anyone."

I quickly rolled into the back of the van. The seats had all been cleared out. There was a bench against one side—that was it for seating. Otto lowered the gun and slid in next to me. Bob took the driver's seat. Barry was still out cold. The students were getting closer as we pulled away. I heard one cry out, "What the . . . oh my God! Barry?"

If Bob and Otto were worried about someone spotting the license plate, they didn't show it. Bob drove the van at an aggravatingly slow speed. I didn't want that. I wanted Bob to hit the gas. I wanted him to hurry. I wanted to get Otto and Bob as far away from the students as possible.

I turned to Otto. "Why the hell did you hit him like that?"

Otto looked back at me with eyes that sent a chill straight through my heart. They were lifeless eyes, not the slightest hint of light behind them. It was as though I were looking into the eyes of an inanimate object—the eyes of an end table, maybe, or a cardboard box.

From the front seat, Bob said, "Toss your wallet and phone into the front passenger seat, please."

I did as he asked. I took a quick inventory of the back of the van and didn't like what I saw. The carpeting had been ripped out, revealing a bare metal floor. There was a rusty toolbox by Otto's feet. I had no idea what was in it. There was a bar welded into the van wall across from me. I swallowed hard when I saw the handcuffs. One loop of the handcuff was fastened to the bar. The other handcuff loop was open, waiting perhaps for a wrist.

Otto kept the gun on me.

When we hit the highway, Bob began to steer casually with his palms, like my father used to when we'd head to the hardware store for a weekend home project. "Jake?" Bob called to me.

"Yes."

"Where to?"

"Huh?" I said.

"It's simple, Jake," Bob said. "You're going to tell us where Natalie is."

"Me?"

"Yep."

"I don't have the slightest idea where she is. I thought you said—"

That was when Otto sucker punched me deep in the gut. The air rushed from my lungs. I folded at the waist like a suitcase. My knees dropped hard to the metal floor of the van. If you have ever had the wind knocked out of you, you know how it completely paralyzes you. You feel as though you're going to suffocate. All you can do is curl up in a ball and pray for oxygen to return.

Bob's voice: "Where is she?"

I couldn't give an answer, even if I had one. My breath was gone. I tried to ride it out, tried to remember that if I didn't struggle, the air would return, but it was as though someone was holding my head underwater and I was supposed to trust that he would eventually let me go.

Bob's voice again: "Jake?"

Otto kicked me hard in the side of the head. I rolled onto my back and saw stars. My chest started hitching, my breaths finally coming in small, grateful sips. Otto kicked my head again. Blackness seeped into my edges. My eyes rolled back. My stomach roiled. I thought that I might be sick and, because the mind works weirdly, I actually thought that it was a good thing that they had pulled out the carpet so the mess would be easier to clean.

"Where is she?" Bob asked again.

Scuttle-crawling to the far side of the van, I managed to spit out, "I don't know, I swear!"

I pressed my back against the van wall. That bar with the handcuff was above my left shoulder. Otto kept the gun on me. I didn't move. I was trying to buy time, catch my breath, recover, think straight. The booze was still there, still making everything a bit of a haze, but pain was an efficient way to bring clarity and focus back into your life.

I pulled my knees in to my chest. As I did, I felt something small and jagged against my leg. A small shard of glass, I figured, or maybe a rough pebble. I looked down at the ground, and with mounting dread, I saw that it was neither.

It was a tooth.

My breath caught in my throat. I looked across and saw a hint of a smile on Otto's model face. He opened the box, revealing a set of rusted tools. I saw a set of pliers, a hacksaw, a box cutter—and then I stopped looking.

Bob: "Where is she?"

"I already told you. I don't know."

"That answer," Bob said. I could see the back of his head shaking. "It's very disappointing."

Otto remained impassive. He kept the gun aimed at me, but his gaze kept sneaking a loving look at his tools. The dead eyes would light up when they landed on the pliers, the hacksaw, the box cutter.

Bob again: "Jake?"

"What?"

"Otto is going to cuff you now. You won't do anything stupid. He has a gun, and hey, we can always drive back to campus and use your students for target practice. You understand me?"

I swallowed again, my mind whirling. "I don't know anything."

Bob gave an overdramatic sigh. "I didn't ask you if you knew anything, Jake. Well, I mean, yes, I asked you that before, but right now, I'm asking if you understand what I said—about the handcuffs and the student target practice. Did you understand all that, Jake?"

"Yes."

"Okay, so stay still." Bob used his blinker and slid into the left lane. We were still on the highway. "Go ahead, Otto."

I didn't have much time. I knew that. Seconds maybe. Once the handcuff was in place—once I was fastened to the van wall—I was finished. I looked down at the tooth.

A good reminder of what was about to come.

Otto came at me from near the back door. He still held the gun. I could rush him, I guess, but he'd be expecting that. I considered trying to open the side door and roll out, take my chances with this van moving more than sixty miles per hour on a highway. But the door locks were down. I'd never get one open in time.

Otto finally spoke: "Grab the bar next to the cuff with your left hand. Use all your fingers to hold on."

I got why. I'd have one hand occupied. Only one to watch. Not that it would matter. It would take him a mere second to snap the cuff into place, and then, well, game over. I gripped the bar—and an idea came to me.

It was a long shot, maybe even an impossibility, but once the cuff snapped down and I was locked into place and Otto went to work on me with his little toolbox . . .

I had no choice.

Otto was prepared for me to rush at him. What he wasn't prepared for was my going in the other direction.

I tried to relax. Timing was everything here. I was tall. Without that, I didn't have a chance. I was also counting on the fact that Otto wouldn't want to shoot me, that they truly did want me—as Bob had implied with his threat about shooting students instead of me—alive.

I would have a second. Less. Tenths of a second maybe.

Otto reached toward the cuff. When his fingers found it, I made my move.

Using the hand gripping the bar for leverage, I swung my legs up—but not to kick Otto. That would be pointless and expected. Instead, I pushed off, making my long body horizontal. I wasn't exactly flying across the van like some veteran martial artist, but with my height and all those damn core exercises I'd been doing, I was able to snap my leg around like a whip.

I aimed the heel of my shoe for the side of Bob's head.

Otto reacted fast. At the exact moment my heel hit pay dirt, Otto tackled me in midair, dropping me hard to the ground. He grabbed me around the neck and started to squeeze.

But he was too late.

My kick had landed on Bob's skull with force, jerking his head to the side. Bob's hands instinctively leapt off the steering wheel. The car veered sharply, sending Otto and me—and the gun—into a rolling heap.

It was on.

Otto still had his arm around my neck, but without the gun, it was just man against man. He was a good, experienced fighter. I was a good, experienced fighter. He was probably six feet tall and 180 pounds. I'm nearly six-six and weigh 230.

Advantage: Me.

I smashed him hard against the back of the van. His grip on my neck loosened. I smashed him again. He let go. My eyes searched the van floor for the gun.

I couldn't see it.

The van was still veering right, then left, as Bob tried to regain control.

I stumbled forward, landing on my knees. I heard a skittering noise, and there, in the corner in front of me, I saw the gun. I crawled toward it, but Otto grabbed me by the leg and pulled me back. We had a brief tug-of-war, me trying to get closer to the gun, him pulling me back. I tried to stomp on his face, but I missed.

Then Otto lowered his head and bit hard into my leg.

I let out a howl of pain.

He held on to the meaty part of my calf by the teeth. Panicked, I kicked out harder. He held on. The pain was making my vision grow cloudy again. The van mercifully swerved again. Otto flew to the right. I rolled to the left. He landed near the tool chest. His fingers disappeared inside of it.

Where the hell was that gun?

I couldn't find it.

From the front, Bob said, "Give up now and we won't hurt more students."

But I wasn't listening to that crap. I looked left and right. No sign of the gun.

Otto pulled his hand back into view. He had the box cutter now. He hit the button with his thumb. The blade popped out.

Suddenly my size advantage was irrelevant.

He started toward me, leading with the sharp edge. I was cornered and trapped. No sign of the gun. No real chance of jumping him without getting sliced up good. That left me with only one option.

When in doubt, go with what has already worked.

I turned and punched Bob in the back of the head.

Once again the van swerved, sending both Otto and me airborne. When I landed, I saw an opening. I lowered my head and dived at him. Otto still had the box cutter. He lashed out at me, but I grabbed his wrist. Once again I tried to use my weight advantage.

Up front, Bob was having a tougher time controlling the car.

Otto and I started rolling. I kept one hand on his wrist. I

wrapped my legs around his body. I jammed my free forearm into the crook of Otto's neck, trying to get at his windpipe. He lowered his chin to block. Still I had my forearm against his neck. If I could just worm my arm in a little deeper . . .

That was when it happened.

Bob slammed on the brakes. The van stopped short. The momentum lifted Otto and me into the air and sent us crashing hard against the floor. The thing was, my forearm stayed pinned against his throat throughout. Think about it. My weight plus the velocity of the car and the sudden stop—it all turned my forearm into a pile driver.

I heard a horrible crinkling sound, like dozens of damp twigs snapping. Otto's windpipe gave way like wet papier-mâché. My arm hit something hard—I could actually feel the floor of the van through the skin and cartilage of his neck. Otto's entire body went slack. I looked down at the pretty-boy face. The eyes were open, and now they did not just appear lifeless—they genuinely were.

I almost hoped for a blink. There was none.

Otto was dead.

I rolled off him.

"Otto?"

It was Bob. From the driver's seat, I saw him reach into his pocket. I wondered whether he was reaching for a gun, but I was not in the mood to hang around and find out. I grabbed the lock on the back door of the van and pulled it up. I pulled the handle and took one last look back as the back door opened.

Yep, Bob had a gun, and it was aimed right at me.

I ducked as the bullet landed above my head. So much for not wanting me dead. I rolled out of the back of the van and landed hard on my right shoulder. I saw headlights heading toward me. My eyes widened. A car was headed directly for me.

I ducked and rolled yet again. Tires screeched. The car passed so close to me I felt the dirt kick up into my face. Horns began to honk. Someone cursed.

Bob's van began to move. The feeling of relief flooded my veins. I clawed my way to the relative safety of the left shoulder. With all the cars flying by, I figured Bob would drive away.

He didn't.

The van was now on the same shoulder, maybe twenty yards from where I lay sprawled.

With the gun still in his hand, Bob jumped out of the driver's-side door. I was spent. I didn't think I could move, but here's the thing: When someone has a gun, stuff like pain and exhaustion become, at best, secondary.

Again I had only one option.

I leapt straight into the bush off the side of the road. I didn't look first. I didn't test it out. I just leapt. In the darkness I hadn't seen the incline. I tumbled down through the brush, letting gravity take me farther away from the road. I expected to reach the bottom soon, but it seemed to take a long time.

I tumbled long and hard. My head smacked against a rock. My legs hit a tree. My ribs hit . . . I don't even know what. I kept rolling. I tumbled through the thicket, tumbled and tumbled until my eyes began to close and the world turned black and still.

Chapter 15

When I saw the headlights, I let out a gasp and tried yet again to roll away. The headlights followed me.

"Sir?"

I lay flat on my back, staring straight up in the air. That was curious. How could a car be approaching me head-on if I was facing the sky? I raised my arm to block the light. A thunderbolt of pain ripped down my shoulder socket.

"Sir, are you okay?"

I shielded my eyes and squinted. The two headlights merged into one flashlight. The person pointing it moved the beam away from my eyes. I blinked up and saw a cop standing over me. I sat up slowly, my entire body crying out in protest.

"Where am I?" I asked.

"You don't know where you are?"

I shook my head, trying to clear it. It was pitch-dark. I was lying in shrubbery of some kind. For a moment I flashed back to my freshman year of college, that time I ended up in a bush after a night of too much inexperienced drinking.

"What's your name, sir?" the cop asked.

"Jake Fisher."

"Mr. Fisher, have you been drinking tonight?"

"I was attacked," I said.

"Attacked?"

"Two men with guns."

"Mr. Fisher?"

"Yes?"

The cop had that condescending-patient-cop tone. "Have you been drinking tonight?"

"I was. Much earlier."

"Mr. Fisher, I'm State Trooper John Ong. You appear to have some injuries. Would you like us to take you to a hospital?"

I was trying hard to focus. Every brain wave seemed to travel through some kind of shower-door distortion. "I'm not sure."

"We will call for an ambulance," he said.

"I don't think that's necessary." I looked around. "Where am I?"

"Mr. Fisher, may I see some identification, please?"

"Sure." I reached into my back pocket, but then I remembered that I had tossed my wallet and phone into the front passenger seat next to Bob. "They stole it."

"Who?"

"The two men who attacked me."

"The guys with the guns?"

"Yes."

"So it was a robbery?"

"No."

The images flashed across my eyes—my forearm against Otto's neck, the box cutter in his hand, the tool chest, the handcuff, that naked, horrible, paralyzing fear, the sudden stop, the squelching sound as his windpipe collapsed like a twig. I closed my eyes and tried to make them go away.

Then, almost more to myself than State Trooper Ong, "I killed one of them."

"Excuse me?"

There were tears in my eyes now. I did not know what to do. I had killed a man, but it had been both an accident and in self-defense. I needed to explain that. I couldn't just keep that to myself. I knew better. Many of the students who majored in political science were also pre-law. Most of my fellow professors had even gotten their JDs and passed the bar. I knew a lot about the Constitution and rights and how our legal system worked. In short, you need to be careful about what you say. You cannot "unring" that bell. I wanted to talk. I needed to talk. But I couldn't just blurt out admissions of murder.

I heard sirens and saw the ambulance pull up.

State Trooper John Ong shone the light back in my eyes. That couldn't have been an accident. "Mr. Fisher?"

"I'd like to call my attorney," I said.

*   *   *

I don't have an attorney.

I am a single college professor with no criminal record and very few resources. What would I need an attorney for?

"Okay, I have good news and bad news," Benedict said.

I had instead called Benedict. Benedict wasn't a member of the bar, but he had gotten a law degree at Stanford. I sat on one of those gurneys covered with what seemed to be butcher paper. I was in the ER of a small hospital. The doctor on duty—who looked almost as exhausted as I felt—had told me that I had probably suffered a concussion. My head ached like it. I also had various contusions, cuts, and maybe a sprain. He didn't know what to make of the teeth marks. With the adrenaline spikes ebbing away, the pain was gaining ground and confidence. He promised to prescribe some Percocet for me.

"I'm listening," I said.

"The good news is, the cops think you've gone completely nuts and don't believe a word of what you say."

"And the bad news?"

"I tend to agree with them, though I add the strong possibility of an alcohol-induced hallucination."

"I was attacked."

"Yes, I get that," Benedict said. "Two men, guns, a van, something about power tools."

"Tools. No one said anything about power."

"Right, whatever. You also drank a lot and then you got some strange."

I pulled up my calf to reveal the bite mark. "How do you explain that?"

"Wendy must have been wild."

"Windy," I corrected him. This was pointless. "So what now?"

"I don't like to brag," Benedict said, "but I have some top-drawer legal advice for you, if you'd like to hear it."

"I do."

"Stop confessing to killing another human being."

"Wow," I said, "and you didn't want to brag."

"It's also in a lot of the law books," Benedict said. "Look, the license plate number you gave? It doesn't exist. There is no body or signs of violence or a crime—only a minor misdemeanor because you, admittedly drunk, trespassed into a man's backyard by falling down a hill. The cops are willing to let you go with just a ticket. Let's just get home and then we can figure it out, okay?"

It was hard to argue with that logic. It would be wise for me to get out of this place, to get back on campus, to rest and regroup and recover, to consider everything that had happened in the sober light of familiar day. Plus, I had taught Constitution 101 one semester. The Fifth Amendment protects you against self-incrimination. Maybe I should use that right now.

Benedict drove. My head spun. The doc had given me a shot that had lifted me up and dropped me in the middle of Loopy Land. I tried to focus, but putting aside the drinking and drugs, the threat to life was hard to shake. I had literally had to fight for survival. What was going on here? What could Natalie have to do with all this?

As we pulled into the staff parking lot, I saw a campus police car near my front door. Benedict looked a question at me. I shrugged and stepped out of the car. The head rush as I stood nearly floored me. I made my way to a standing position and started gingerly up the path. Evelyn Stemmer was the head of campus security. She was a petite woman with a ready smile. The ready smile wasn't there right now.

"We've been trying to reach you, Professor Fisher," she said.

"My cell phone was stolen."

"I see. Do you mind coming with me?"

"Where?"

"President's house. President Tripp needs to speak with you."

Benedict stepped between us. "What's this about, Evelyn?"

She looked at him as though he'd just plopped out of a rhino's rectum. "I'd rather let President Tripp do the talking. Me, I'm just an errand girl."

I was too out of it to protest. What would be the point anyway? Benedict wanted to come with us, but I really didn't think it would behoove my position to have my best friend visit my boss with me. The front seat of the campus police car had some kind of computer in it. I had to sit in the back like a real-life perp.

The president lived in a twenty-two-room, 9,600-square-foot stone residence, done up in a style that the experts called "re-strained Gothic Revival." I was not sure what that meant, but it was a pretty impressive structure. I also didn't see the need for the squad car—the villa sat on a hilltop overlooking the athletic fields, maybe four hundred yards from the staff parking lot. Fully reno-vated two years ago, the home could now play host to not only the president's young family but, more importantly, to a full potpourri of fund-raising events.

I was escorted into an office that looked exactly like a college president's office, just sleeker and more polished. Come to think of it, so did the new president. Jack Tripp was sleek and polished and corporate with floppy hair and capped teeth. He tried to fit in by dressing in tweed, but the tweed was far too tailored and costly to be bona fide professorial. His patches were too evenly cut. The students derisively referred to him as a "poser." Again I wasn't sure exactly what that meant, but it seemed apropos.

I have learned that human beings are all about incentives, so I cut the president some slack. His job, though couched in haughty terms of academia and higher learning, was all about raising money. Period. That was, and perhaps should be, his main concern. The best presidents, I had learned, were often the ones who understood this and thus came in with the least lofty agenda. By that definition, President Tripp was doing a pretty good job.

"Sit, Jacob," Tripp said, looking past me to Officer Stemmer. "Evelyn, close the door on your way out, would you?"

I did as Tripp asked. Evelyn Stemmer did too.

Tripp sat at the ornate desk in front of me. It was a big desk. Too big and corporate and self-important. When I am feeling unkind, I often note that a man's desk, like his car, often seems to involve, uh, compensation. Tripp folded his hands on a desktop large enough to land a helicopter and said, "You look like hell, Jacob."

I bit back the "you should see the other guy" because, in this case, the rejoinder was in serious bad taste. "I had a late night."

"You look injured."

"I'm fine."

"You should get it looked at."

"I have." I shifted in the seat. The meds were making everything hazy, as though my eyes were covered in thin strips of gauze. "What's this about, Jack?"

He spread his hands for a moment and then brought them back to the desk. "Do you want to tell me about last night?"

"What about last night?" I asked.

"You tell me."

So we were playing that game. Fair enough. I'd go first. "I went drinking with a friend at a bar. Had too much. When I came back to my place, two men jumped me. They, uh, kidnapped me."

His eyes widened. "Two men kidnapped you?"

"Yes."

"Who?"

"They said their names were Bob and Otto."

"Bob and Otto?"

"That's what they said."

"And where are these men now?"

"I don't know."

"Are they in custody?"

"No."

"But you've reported the matter to the police?"

"I have," I said. "Do you mind telling me what this is about?"

Tripp lifted his hand, as if he'd suddenly realized the desktop was sticky. He placed the lower parts of his palms together and let the fingertips bounce off one another. "Do you know a student named Barry Watkins?"

My heart skipped a beat. "Is he okay?"

"You know him?"

"Yes. One of the men who grabbed me punched him in the face."

"I see," he said, as though he didn't see at all. "When?"

"We were standing by the van. Barry called out to me and ran over. Before I could so much as turn around, one of the guys punched him. Is Barry okay?"

The fingertips bounced some more. "He is in the hospital with facial fractures. That punch did serious damage."

I sat back. "Damn."

"His parents are rather upset. They are talking about a lawsuit."

Lawsuit—the word that strikes terror in the heart of every bureaucrat. I half expected some lame horror-movie music to start up.

"Barry Watkins also doesn't recall two other men. He remembers calling out to you, running toward you, and that's it. Two other students recall seeing you flee in a van."

"I didn't flee. I got in the back."

"I see," he said in that same tone. "When these other two students arrived, Barry was lying on the ground bleeding. You drove off."

"I wasn't driving. I was in the back."

"I see."

Again with the "I see." I leaned closer to him. The desk was completely bare except for one too-neat stack of papers and, of course, the requisite family photograph with the blond wife, two adorable kids, and a dog with floppy hair like Tripp's. Nothing else. Big desk. Nothing on it.

"I wanted to get them as far away from campus as possible," I said, "especially after that display of violence. So I quickly cooperated."

"And by them, you mean the two men who . . . were they abducting you?"

"Yes."

"Who were these men?"

"I don't know."

"They were just, what, kidnapping you for ransom?"

"I doubt it," I said, realizing how crazy it all sounded. "One had broken into my home. The other waited in the van. They insisted I come with them."

"You are a very large man. Powerful. Physically intimidating."

I waited.

"How did they persuade you to go with them?"

I skipped the part about Natalie and dropped the bombshell instead. "They were armed."

The eyes widened again. "With guns?"

"Yes."

"For real?"

"They were real guns, yes."

"How do you know?"

I decided not to mention that one had taken shots at me. I wondered whether the police might find bullets near the highway. I'd have to check.

"Did you tell anyone else about this?" Tripp asked when I didn't answer.

"I told the cops, but I'm not sure that they believe me."

He leaned back and started picking at his lip. I knew what he was thinking: How would the students, their parents, and important alumni react if they knew that gunmen had been on campus? Not only had they been on campus, but if I were telling the truth—questionable at best—they had kidnapped a professor and assaulted a student.

"You were quite inebriated at the time, were you not?"

Here we go. "I was."

"We have a campus security camera in the middle of the quad. Your walk was rather more of a weave."

"That's what happens when you have too much to drink."

"We also have reports that you left the Library Bar at one A.M. . . . and yet you weren't seen weaving across campus until three."

Again I waited.

"Where were you for those two hours?"

"Why?"

"Because I'm investigating an assault on a student."

"That we know took place after three A.M. What, you think I planned it for two hours?"

"I see very little need for sarcasm, Jacob. This is a serious matter."

I closed my eyes and felt the room spin. He had a point. "I left with a young lady. It's totally irrelevant. I'd never punch Barry. He visits my office every week."

"Yes, he defended you too. He said that you're his favorite professor. But I have to look at the facts, Jacob. You understand that, don't you?"

"I do."

"Fact: You were drunk."

"I'm a college professor. Drinking is practically a job requirement."

"That's not funny."

"But true. Heck, I've been to parties right here. You're not afraid to hoist a glass or two yourself."

"You're not helping yourself."

"I'm not trying to. I'm trying to get at the truth."

"Then, fact: While you are being vague, it appears as though after drinking you had a one-night stand."

"We shouldn't be vague," I said. "That's exactly what I'm saying. She was over thirty and does not work for the college. So what?"

"So after these episodes, a student got assaulted."

"Not by me."

"Still, there is a connection," he said, leaning back. "I don't see where I have any choice but to ask for you to take a leave of absence."

"For drinking?"

"For all of it," he said.

"I'm in the middle of teaching classes—"

"We will find coverage."

"And I have a responsibility to my students. I can't just abandon them."

"Perhaps," he said, with an edge in his voice, "you should have thought of that before you got drunk."

"Getting drunk isn't a crime."

"No, but your actions afterward . . ." His voice trailed off, and a smile came to his lips. "Funny," he said.

"What?"

"I heard about your run-in with Professor Trainor years ago. How can you not see the parallel?"

I said nothing.

"There is an old Greek saying," he went on. "The humpback never sees the hump on his own back."

I nodded. "Deep."

"You're making jokes, Jacob, but do you really think you're blameless here?"

I wasn't sure what to think. "I didn't say I was blameless."

"Just a hypocrite?" He sighed a little too deeply. "I don't like doing this to you, Jacob."

"I hear a but."

"You know the but. Are the police investigating your claim?"

I wasn't sure how to answer so I went with the truth. "I don't know."

"Then maybe it's best that you take a leave of absence until this is resolved."

I was about to protest, but then I pulled up. He was right. Forget all the political mumbo jumbo or legal claims here. The truth was, I was indeed putting students in harm's way. My actions *had*, in fact, already gotten one student seriously injured. I could make all the excuses I wanted to, but if I had kept my promise to Natalie, Barry would not be lying in a hospital bed with facial fractures.

Could I take the risk of letting it happen again?

Lest I forgot, Bob was still out there. He might want vengeance for Otto or, at the very least, to finish the job or silence the witness. By staying, wouldn't I be endangering the welfare of my students?

President Tripp started sorting the papers on his desk, a clear sign we were done here. "Pack your things," he said. "I'd like you off campus within the hour."

Chapter 16

By noon the next day, I was back in Palmetto Bluff.
I knocked on the door of a home located on a quiet cul-
de-sac. Delia Sanderson—Todd Sanderson's, uh, widow, I
guess—opened it with a sad smile. She was what some might call a
handsome woman in a sinewy, farmhand kind of way. She had
strong facial features and big hands.

"Thank you so much for making the trip, Professor."

"Please," I said, feeling a small ping of guilt, "call me Jake."

She stepped aside and invited me inside. The house was nice,
done up in that modern faux-Victorian style that seemed to be the
rage of these spanking new developments. The property backed
onto a golf course. The atmosphere was both green and serene.

"I can't tell you how much I appreciate you coming all this way."

Another ping. "Please," I said, "it's an honor."

"Still. For the college to send a professor all this way . . ."

"It's not a big deal, really." I tried to smile. "It's nice to get away too."

"Well, I'm grateful," Delia Sanderson said. "Our children aren't home right now. I made them go back to school. You need to grieve but you need to do something, you know what I mean?"

"I do," I said.

I hadn't been specific when I made the call yesterday. I just told her that I was a professor at Todd's alma mater and that I hoped to stop by the house to talk about her late husband and offer condolences. Did I hint that I was sort of coming on behalf of the college? Let us say I didn't discourage that thinking.

"Would you like some coffee?" she asked.

I've found that people have a tendency to relax more when they are doing simple tasks and feeling as though they are making their guests feel comfortable. I said yes.

We were standing in the foyer. The formal rooms, where you'd normally take guests, were on the right. The lived-in rooms—den and kitchen—were on the left. I followed her into the kitchen, figuring that the more casual setting might also make her more apt to open up.

There were no signs of the recent break-in, but what exactly did I think I'd find? Blood on the floor? Overturned furniture? Open drawers? Yellow police tape?

The sleek kitchen was expansive with great flow into an even more expansive "media" room. An enormous television hung on the wall. The couch was littered with remotes and Xbox controllers. Yes, I know Xbox. I have one. I love to play Madden. Sue me.

She headed toward one of those coffeemakers that use individual pods. I took a seat on a stool at the kitchen's granite island. She showed me a surprisingly large display of coffee-pod options.

"Which would you like?" she asked.

"You tell me," I said.

"Are you a strong-coffee guy? I bet you are."

"You'd win that bet."

She opened the machine's mouth and put in a pod called Jet Fuel. The machine seemed to eat the pod and piss out the coffee. Appetizing imagery, I know. "Do you take it black?" she asked.

"Not that much a strong-coffee guy," I said, asking for a little milk and sweetener.

She handed me the cup. "You don't look like a college professor."

I get that a lot.

"My tweed jacket is at the cleaner." Then: "I'm sorry for your loss."

"Thank you."

I took a sip of the coffee. Why was I here exactly? I needed to figure out if Delia Sanderson's Todd was Natalie's Todd. If he was the same man, well, how was that possible? What did his death mean? And what secrets was this woman in front of me maybe keeping?

I had no idea, of course, but I was willing to take some chances now. That meant that I might have to push her. I didn't relish that—prodding a woman who was so clearly grieving. Whatever else I thought might be going on here—and really I didn't have a clue—Delia Sanderson was in obvious pain. You could see the pull in her face, the subtle slump in the shoulders, the shatter in the eyes.

"I don't know how to ask this delicately . . . ," I began.

I stopped, hoping she'd take the bait. She did. "But you want to know how he died?"

"If I'm prying . . ."

"It's okay."

"The papers say it happened during a break-in."

Her face lost color. She spun back toward the coffeemaker. She fiddled with a pod, picked one up, dropped it, chose another.

"I'm sorry," I said. "We don't need to go into this."

"It wasn't a break-in."

I stayed quiet.

"I mean, they didn't steal anything. Isn't that unusual? If it was a break-in, wouldn't you take something? But they just . . ."

She slammed down the mouth of the coffeemaker.

I said, "They?"

"What?"

"You said 'they.' There was more than one burglar?"

She still had her back to me. "I don't know. The police won't speculate. I just don't see how one guy could have done . . ." Her head dropped. I thought that maybe I saw her knees buckle. I started to rise and move toward her, but really, who the hell was I? I stopped and quietly slid back onto the stool.

"We were supposed to be safe here," Delia Sanderson said. "A gated community. It was supposed to keep the bad out."

The development was huge, acres upon acres of cultivated remoteness. There was a gate of sorts, a little hut at the development's entrance, a steel arm that had to be lifted to drive through, a rent-a-cop who nodded and pushed a button. None of that could keep the bad out, not if the bad was determined. The gate was possibly a deterrent for easygoing trouble. It maybe added an extra layer of hassle so that trouble chose to find an easier mark. But true protection? No. The gate was more for show.

"Why do you think there was more than one?" I asked.

"I guess . . . I guess I don't see how one man could cause that much damage."

"What do you mean?"

She shook her head. Using one finger, she wiped one eye, then the other. She turned around and faced me. "Let's talk about something else."

I wanted to push it, but I knew that wouldn't play here. I was a college professor visiting from her late husband's alma mater. Plus, well, I was still a human being. It was time to back up and try another route.

I stood as gently as I knew how and moved toward the refrigerator. There were dozens of family photographs done up in a magnetic collage. The photographs were wonderfully unspectacular, almost too expected: fishing trip, Disney visit, dance recitals, beach-Christmas photograph, school holiday concerts, graduations. The refrigerator missed none of life's little yard markers. I leaned in and studied Todd's face in as many of them as I could.

Was he the same man?

In every image on the refrigerator, he was clean-shaven. The man I had met had that fashionably annoying stubble. You could grow that in a few days, of course, but I found it odd. So again, I wondered: Was this the man I saw marry Natalie?

I could feel Delia's eyes on my back.

"I met your husband once," I said.

"Oh?"

I turned toward her. "Six years ago."

She picked up her coffee—evidently she took it black—and sat at another stool. "Where?"

I kept my eyes on her as I said, "In Vermont."

There was no big jolt or anything like that, but her face did scrunch up a bit. "Vermont?"

"Yes. In a town called Kraftboro."

"You're sure it was Todd?"

"It was in late August," I explained. "I was staying at a retreat."

Now she looked openly confused. "I don't recall Todd ever going to Vermont."

"Six years ago," I said again. "In August."

"Yes, I heard you say that the first time." There was a hint of impatience in her tone now.

I pointed back toward the refrigerator. "He didn't look exactly like this though."

"I'm not following you."

"His hair was longer," I said, "and he had stubble."

"Todd?"

"Yes."

She considered that and a small smile found her lips. "I get it now."

"Get what?"

"Why you came all this way."

This I was anxious to hear.

"I couldn't figure it out. Todd hadn't been an active member of the alumni or anything like that. It wasn't as though the college would have much more than a passing interest in him. Now all this talk about a man from Vermont . . ." She stopped and shrugged. "You mistook my husband for another man. For this Todd you met in Vermont."

"No, I'm pretty certain it was—"

"Todd has never been to Vermont. I'm sure of that. And every August for the past eight years, he traveled to Africa to perform surgery on the needy. He also shaved every day. I mean, even on a lazy Sunday. Todd never went a day without shaving."

I took another look at the photographs on the refrigerator. Could that be? Could it be that simple? I had the wrong man. I had considered that possibility before but now, finally, I was sort of believing it.

In a sense, that didn't change much anymore. There was still the e-mail from Natalie. There was still Otto and Bob and all that happened. But now, maybe, I could put this connection to rest.

Delia was openly studying me now. "What's going on? Why are you really here?"

I reached into my pocket and plucked out the photograph of Natalie. Strangely enough, I have only one. She didn't like photographs, but I had snapped this one while she was asleep. I don't know why. Or maybe I do. I handed it to Delia Sanderson and waited for a reaction.

"Strange," she said.

"What?"

"Her eyes are closed." She looked up at me. "Did you take this picture?"

"Yes."

"While she was sleeping?"

"Yes. Do you know her?"

"No." She stared down at the photograph. "She means something to you, doesn't she?"

"Yes."

"So who is she?"

The front door opened. "Mom?"

She put down the photograph and started toward the voice. "Eric? Is everything okay? You're home early."

I followed her down the corridor. I recognized her son from his eulogy at the funeral. He looked past his mother, his gaze boring into me. "Who's this?" he asked. His tone was surprisingly hostile, as though he suspected that I'd come here to hit on his mom or something.

"This is Professor Fisher from Lanford," she said. "He came to ask about your father."

"Ask what?"

"Just paying my respects," I said, shaking the young man's hand. "I'm very sorry for your loss. The entire college is."

He shook my hand and said nothing. We all stood in that front foyer like three awkward strangers who hadn't yet been introduced at a cocktail party. Eric broke the deadlock. "I couldn't find my cleats," he said.

"You left them in the car."

"Oh, right. I'll just grab them and head back."

He rushed back out the door. We both watched him, perhaps with the same thoughts about his fatherless future looming in front of us. There was nothing more to learn here. It was time for me to let this family be.

"I better be going," I said. "Thank you for your time."

"You're welcome."

As I turned toward the door, my line of vision swung past the living room.

My heart stopped.

"Professor Fisher?"

My hand was on the doorknob. Seconds passed. I don't know how many. I didn't turn the knob, didn't move, didn't even breathe. I just stared into the living room, across the Oriental rug, to a spot above the fireplace.

Delia Sanderson again: "Professor?"

Her voice was very far away.

I finally let go of the knob and moved into the living room, across the Oriental carpet, and stared up above the fireplace. Delia Sanderson followed me.

"Are you okay?"

No, I wasn't okay. And I hadn't been wrong. If I had questions before, they all ended now. No coincidence, no mistake, no doubt: Todd Sanderson was the man I saw marry Natalie six years ago.

I felt rather than saw Delia Sanderson standing next to me. "It moves me," she said. "I can stand here for hours and find something new."

I understood. There was the soft morning glow hitting the side, the pinkness that comes with the new day, the dark windows as though the cottage had once been warm but was now abandoned.

It was Natalie's painting.

"Do you like it?" Delia Sanderson asked me.

"Yes," I said. "I like it very much."

Chapter 17

sat on the couch. Delia Sanderson didn't offer me coffee this time. She poured two fingers' worth of Macallan. It was early and as we've already learned I am not much of a drinker, but I gratefully accepted it with a shaking hand.

"Do you want to tell me what this is about?" Delia Sanderson asked.

I wasn't sure how to explain this without sounding insane, so I started with a question. "How did you get that painting?"

"Todd bought it."

"When?"

"I don't know."

"Think."

"What's the difference?"

"Please," I said, trying to keep my voice steady. "Could you just tell me when and where he bought it?"

She looked up, thinking about it. "The where I don't remember. But the when . . . it was our anniversary. Five, maybe six years ago."

"It was six," I said.

"Again with six," she said. "I don't understand any of this."

I saw no reason to lie—and worse, I saw no way to say this in a way that would soften the blow. "I showed you a photograph of a sleeping woman, remember?"

"It was only two minutes ago."

"Right. She painted that picture."

Delia frowned. "What are you talking about?"

"Her name is Natalie Avery. That was her in the photograph."

"That . . ." She shook her head. "I don't understand. I thought you taught political science."

"I do."

"So are you some kind of art historian? Is that woman a Lanford alum too?"

"No, it's not like that." I looked back at that cottage on the hill. "I'm looking for her."

"The artist?"

"Yes."

She studied my face. "Is she missing?"

"I don't know."

Our eyes met. She didn't nod, but she didn't have to. "She means a great deal to you."

It wasn't a question, but I answered it anyway. "Yes. I realize that this is making no sense."

"It isn't," Delia Sanderson agreed. "But you believe that my husband knew something about her. That's why you're really here."

"Yes."

"Why?"

Again I saw no reason to lie. "This will sound insane."

She waited.

"Six years ago, I saw your husband marry Natalie Avery in a small chapel in Vermont."

Delia Sanderson blinked twice. She rose from the couch and started to back away from me. "I think you better leave."

"Please just listen to me."

She closed her eyes, but, hey, you can't close your ears. I talked fast. I explained about going to the wedding six years ago, about seeing Todd's obituary, about coming to the funeral, about believing that maybe I was mistaken.

"You were mistaken," she said when I finished. "You have to be."

"So that painting. It's a coincidence?"

She said nothing.

"Mrs. Sanderson?"

"What are you after?" she asked in a soft voice.

"I want to find her."

"Why?"

"You know why."

She nodded. "Because you're in love with her."

"Yes."

"Even though you saw her marry another man six years ago."

I didn't bother responding. The house was maddeningly quiet. We both turned and looked back at that cottage on the hill. I wanted it to change somehow. I wanted the sun to rise a little higher or to see a light on in one of the windows.

Delia Sanderson moved a few yards farther away from me and took out her phone.

"What are you doing?" I asked.

"I googled you yesterday. After you called me."

"Okay."

"I wanted to make sure that you were who you said you were."

"Who else would I be?"

Delia Sanderson ignored my question. "There was a picture of you on the Lanford website. Before I opened the door, I checked through the peephole to make sure."

"I'm not following."

"Better to be safe than sorry, I figured. I worried that maybe whoever murdered my husband . . ."

I understood now. "Would come back for you?"

She shrugged.

"But you saw it was me."

"Yes. So I let you in. But now I'm wondering. I mean, you came here under false pretenses. How do I know that you aren't one of them?"

I wasn't sure what to say.

"So for right now I'm keeping my distance, if that's okay with you. I'm standing pretty close to the front door. If I see you start to rise, I hit this button for nine-one-one and run. Do you understand?"

"I'm not with—"

"Do you understand?"

"Of course," I said. "I won't move from this seat. But can I ask you a question?"

She gestured for me to go ahead.

"How do you know I don't have a gun?"

"I've been watching since you entered. There'd be no place for you to conceal it in that outfit."

I nodded. Then I said, "You don't really believe I'm here to hurt you, do you?"

"I don't. But like the saying goes, better safe than sorry."

"I know that story about a wedding in Vermont sounds crazy," I said.

"It does," Delia Sanderson said. "And yet, it's too crazy to be a lie."

We gave it another moment. Our eyes wandered back to that cottage up on the hill.

"He was such a good man," Delia Sanderson said. "Todd could have made a fortune in private practice, but he worked almost exclusively for Fresh Start. You know what that is?"

The name was not entirely unfamiliar, but I couldn't place it. "I'm afraid that I don't."

She actually smiled at that. "Wow, you really didn't do your homework before you came. Fresh Start is the charity Todd founded with some other Lanford graduates. It was his passion."

I remembered it now. There had been a mention of it in his obituary, though I didn't know it had any connection to Lanford. "What did Fresh Start do?"

"They operated on cleft palates overseas. They worked on burns and scars and performed various other necessary cosmetic surgeries. The procedures were life-changing. Like the name, they gave people a fresh start. Todd dedicated his life to it. When you said that you saw him in Vermont, I knew that couldn't be true. He was working in Nigeria."

"Except," I said, "he wasn't."

"So you're telling this widow that her husband lied to her."

"No. I'm telling her that Todd Sanderson was in Vermont on August twenty-eighth, six years ago."

"Marrying your ex-girlfriend, the artist?"

I didn't bother replying.

A tear ran down her cheek. "They hurt Todd. Before they killed him. They hurt him badly. Why would someone do something like that?"

"I don't know."

She shook her head.

"When you say they hurt him," I said slowly, "do you mean that they did more than kill him?"

"Yes."

Again I didn't know how to ask the question with any sort of sensitivity, so I settled on directness: "How did they hurt him?"

But even before she replied, I thought that maybe I knew the answer.

"With tools," Delia Sanderson said, a sob coming to her throat. "They cuffed him to a chair and tortured him with tools."

Chapter 18

When my plane landed back in Boston, there was a message on my new phone from Shanta Newlin. "I heard you got kicked off campus. We should talk."

I called her back as I walked through the airport terminal. When Shanta picked up, she asked me where I was.

"Logan Airport," I said.

"Nice trip?"

"Delightful. You said we needed to talk."

"In person. Come straight to my office from the airport."

"I'm not welcome on campus," I said.

"Oh, right, I forgot for a second. Judie's again? Be there in an hour."

Shanta was sitting at the corner table when I arrived. She had a drink in front of her. The drink was bright pink and had a pineapple on top. I pointed at it.

"All you're missing is a little umbrella," I said.

"What, you figured me as more a scotch-and-soda girl?"

"Minus the soda."

"Sorry. With me, the fruitier the drink, the better."

I slid into the chair across from her. Shanta picked up the drink and took a sip from the straw.

"I heard you were involved in a student attack," she said.

"Are you working for President Tripp now?"

She frowned over her fruity drink. "What happened?"

I told her the whole story—Bob and Otto, the van, the self-defense killing, the escape from the van, the roll down the hill. Her expression didn't change, but I could see the wheels moving behind her eyes.

"You told the police this?"

"Sort of."

"What do you mean, sort of?"

"I was pretty drunk. They seem to think I fabricated the bit about being kidnapped and killing a guy."

She looked at me as though I were perhaps the biggest fool ever to inhabit this planet. "Did you really tell the police that part?"

"At first. Then Benedict reminded me that maybe it wasn't the best idea to admit to killing a man, even if it was in self-defense."

"You get your legal advice from Benedict?"

I shrugged. Once again I thought about keeping my mouth shut. I had been warned, hadn't I? There was also the promise. Shanta sat back and sipped her drink. The waitress came over and asked what I wanted. I pointed at the fruity drink and indicated that I wanted a "virgin" one of those too. I don't know why. I hate fruity drinks.

"What did you really learn about Natalie?" I asked.

"I told you."

"Right, nothing, zippo, zilch. So why did you want to see me?"

The portobello sandwich came for her, the turkey BLT on rye for me. "I took the liberty of ordering for you," she said.

I didn't touch the sandwich.

"What's going on, Shanta?"

"That's what I want to know. How did you meet Natalie?"

"What difference does that make?"

"Humor me."

Once again she was asking all the questions, and I was giving all the answers. I told her how we met at the retreats in Vermont six years ago.

"What did she tell you about her father?"

"Just that he was dead."

Shanta kept her eyes on mine. "Nothing else?"

"Like what?"

"Like, I don't know"—she took a deep sip and shrugged theatrically—"that he used to be a professor here."

My eyes widened. "Her father?"

"Yep."

"Her father was a professor at Lanford?"

"No, at Judie's Restaurant," Shanta said with an eye roll. "Of course at Lanford."

I was still trying to clear my head. "When?"

"He started about thirty years ago. He taught here for seven years. In the political science department."

"You're kidding?"

"Yes, that's why I called you here. Because I'm such a top-notch kidder."

I did the math. Natalie would have been very young when her father started teaching here—and still a kid when he left. Maybe she didn't remember being here. Maybe that was why she didn't say anything. But wouldn't Natalie have at least known about it? Wouldn't she have said, "Hey, my father taught here too. Same department as you."

I thought about how she came to campus with those sunglasses and hat on, how she wanted to see so much of it, how she had grown pensive during the walks on the commons.

"Why wouldn't she tell me?" I asked out loud.

"I don't know."

"Was he fired? Where did they go afterward?"

She shrugged. "A better question might be, why did Natalie's mom start using her maiden name?"

"What?"

"Her father's name was Aaron Kleiner. Natalie's mother's maiden name was Avery. She changed it back. And she changed Natalie and Julie's name to her maiden name too."

"Wait, when did her father die?"

"So Natalie never told you?"

"I just got the impression it was a long time ago. Maybe that's it. Maybe he died and that's why they left campus."

Shanta smiled. "I don't think so, Jake."

"Why?"

"Because here's where it gets really interesting. Here's where Daddy is just like his little girl."

I said nothing.

"There is no report he ever died."

I swallowed. "So where is he?"

"Like father, like daughter, Jake."

"What the hell does that mean?" But maybe I already knew.

"I looked into where Professor Aaron Kleiner is now," Shanta said. "Guess what I found?"

I waited.

"That's right—zippo, *nada*, zilch, nothing. Since he left Lanford a quarter century ago, there has been absolutely no sign of Professor Aaron Kleiner."

Chapter 19

found old yearbooks in the school library.

They were in the basement. The books smelled of mold. The glossy pages stuck together as I tried to flip through them. But there he was. Professor Aaron Kleiner. The picture was fairly unremarkable. He was a nice-enough-looking man with the usual posed smile, aiming for happiness but landing somewhere closer to awkward. I stared at his face to see if I could spot any resemblance to Natalie. There might have been. Hard to say. The mind can play tricks, as we all know.

We have a tendency to see what we want to see.

I stared at his face as though it would give me some kind of answer. It didn't. I checked through the other yearbooks. There was nothing more to learn. I scanned through the political science pages and stopped at a group picture taken in front of Clark House. All of the professors and support staff were there. Professor Kleiner stood right next to department chair Malcolm Hume. The smiles in this photograph were more relaxed, more natural. Mrs. Dinsmore still looked to be about a hundred years old.

Wait. Mrs. Dinsmore . . .

I tucked one of the yearbooks under my arm and hurried toward Clark House. It was after hours, but Mrs. Dinsmore lived at the office. Yes, I had been suspended and was supposed to be off campus, but I doubted that campus police would open fire. So I walked across the quad where the students roamed, with a book I hadn't checked out of the library. Look at me, living on the edge.

I remembered walking here that day six years ago with Natalie. Why hadn't she said anything? Had there been any sign? Did she grow quiet or slow her step? I didn't remember. I just remember yapping happily away about the campus like some freshman tour guide after too many Red Bulls.

Mrs. Dinsmore looked up at me over her half-moon reading glasses. "I thought you were out of here."

"Maybe in body," I said, "but am I ever far from your heart?"

She rolled her eyes. "What do you want?"

I put the yearbook down in front of her. It was open to the group picture. I pointed at Natalie's father. "Do you remember a professor named Aaron Kleiner?"

Mrs. Dinsmore took her time. The reading glasses were mounted to a chain around her neck. She removed them, cleaned them with quaking hands, and put them back on again. Her face was still as stone.

"I remember him," she said softly. "Why do you ask?"

"Do you know why he was fired?"

She looked up at me. "Who said he was fired?"

"Or why he left? Is there anything you can tell me about what happened to him?"

"He hasn't been here in twenty-five years. You were maybe ten when he left."

"I know."

"So why are you asking?"

I didn't even know how to dance around that question. "Do you remember his children?"

"Little girls. Natalie and Julie."

No hesitation. That surprised me. "You remember their names?"

"What about them?"

"Six years ago I met Natalie at a retreat in Vermont. We fell in love."

Mrs. Dinsmore waited for me to say more.

"I know this sounds crazy, but I'm trying to find her. I think she may be in danger, and maybe it has something to do with her father, I don't know."

Mrs. Dinsmore kept her eyes on me another second or two. She let her reading glasses drop back to her chest. "He was a good professor. You'd have liked him. His classes were lively. He was terrific at energizing the students."

Her gaze dropped back to the photograph in the yearbook.

"In those days, some of the younger professors doubled as dorm monitors. Aaron Kleiner was one of them. He and his family lived on the bottom floor of the Tingley dormitory. The students loved them. I remember one year, the students chipped in and bought a swing set for the girls. They all built it on a Saturday morning in the courtyard behind Pratt."

She looked off wistfully. "Natalie was an adorable little girl. How does she look now?"

"She's the most beautiful woman in the world," I said.

Mrs. Dinsmore gave me a wry smile. "You're a romantic."

"What happened to them?"

"A few things," she said. "There were rumors about their marriage."

"What kind of rumors?"

"What kind are there always on a college campus? Young kids, distracted wife, attractive man on a campus with impressionable coeds. I tease you about the young girls who stop by your office, but I've seen too many lives ruined by that temptation."

"He had an affair with a student?"

"Maybe. I don't know. Those were the rumors. Have you heard of Vice Chair Roy Horduck?"

"I've seen his name on some plaques."

"Aaron Kleiner accused Horduck of plagiarism. The charges were never brought, but vice chair is a pretty powerful position. Aaron Kleiner got demoted. Then he got involved in a cheating scandal."

"A professor cheated?"

"No, of course not. He made accusations against a student, maybe two. I don't remember the details anymore. That might have been his downfall, I don't know. He started to drink. He behaved more erratically. The rumors started."

She stared down at the photograph again.

"So they asked him to resign?"

"No," Mrs. Dinsmore said.

"Then what happened?"

"One day, his wife walked through that very door." She pointed behind her. I knew what door. I had walked through it a thousand times, but I still looked, as though Natalie's mom might walk through it again. "She was crying. Hysterical, really. I was sitting right where I am now, at this very spot, at this very desk . . ."

Her words faded away.

"She wanted to see Professor Hume. He wasn't here so I called him on the phone. He hurried over. She told him that Professor Kleiner was gone."

"Gone?"

"He'd packed his things and run off with another woman. A former student."

"Who?"

"I don't know. Like I said, she was hysterical. There were no cell phones back in those days. We had no way to reach him. We waited. I remember he had a class that afternoon. He never showed. Professor Hume had to cover that day. The other professors took turns covering until the semester ended. The students were really upset. Parents called, but Professor Hume placated them all by giving everyone an A." She shrugged, pushed the yearbook back toward me, and pretended to get back to work.

"We never heard from him again."

I swallowed. "So what happened to his wife and daughters?"

"The same, I guess."

"What does that mean?"

"They moved away at the end of the semester. I never heard from them again. I always hoped that they all ended up at another college—that they patched things up. But I guess that wasn't what happened, was it?"

"No."

"So what happened to them?" Mrs. Dinsmore asked.

"I don't know."

Chapter 20

Who would know?

Answer: Natalie's sister, Julie. She had blown me off on the phone. I wondered whether I'd have better luck in person.

I was heading back to my car when my cell phone rang. I checked the number on the caller ID. The area code was 802.

Vermont.

I answered the phone and said hello.

"Um, hi. You left your card at the café."

I recognized the voice. "Cookie?"

"We should talk," she said.

My grip on the phone tightened. "I'm listening."

"I don't trust phones," Cookie said. There was a quake in her voice. "Can you get back up here?"

"I can drive up right now if you want."

Cookie gave me directions to her home, not far from the café. I took 91 north and tried unsuccessfully not to speed. My heart pounded in my chest, keeping beat, it seemed, with whatever song was on the radio. By the time I reached the state line, it was near midnight. I had started that morning flying down to see Delia Sanderson. It had been a long day and for just a second, I could feel the exhaustion. I flashed back to the first time I saw Natalie's painting of that cottage on the hill—to Cookie coming up behind me and asking if I liked it.

Why, I asked myself again, had Cookie acted as though she didn't remember me when I stopped in the café?

There was something else that came back to me. Everyone else I met said that there had never been a Creative Recharge retreat, but when Cookie made her denial, she said, "We never worked at the retreat."

I hadn't caught that at the time, but if there had never been a retreat up that hill, wouldn't your response be something like, "Huh? What retreat?"

I slowed as I passed Cookie's bookshop café. There were only two streetlights, both casting long, menacing shadows. No people were present. The small town center was perfectly still, too still, like that scene in a zombie film before the hero gets surrounded by the flesh-eaters. I made a right at the end of the block, drove half a mile, made another right. There were no streetlights now. The only illumination at all came from my headlights. If I was passing houses or buildings, all the lights had been turned off there too. I guess no one out here left their lights on a timer to deter burglars. Smart move. I doubted in this darkness that burglars could find the homes.

I checked my GPS and saw that I was half a mile from my destination. Two more turns. Something akin to dread started seeping into my chest. We have all read about how certain animals and sea creatures can sense danger. They can actually feel threats or even oncoming natural disasters, almost as though they had survival radar or invisible tentacles reaching out and around corners. Somewhere, of course, primitive man must have had this ability too. That sort of survival stuff stays with us. It may lie dormant. It may wither away from lack of use. But that instinctive Neanderthal man is always there, lurking under our khakis and dress shirt.

Right now, to use vernacular from my comic-book youth, my Spidey senses were tingling.

I turned off the headlights and slowed to the curb in pitch darkness practically by sense of touch. There were no stones framing the street. The pavement just gave way to the grass. I didn't know what I was about to do, but the more I thought about this, the more I thought that maybe some measure of care was in order.

I could walk from here.

I slipped out of the car. Once I closed the door, once all the light was gone, I realized just how dark it really was. The night seemed to be a living thing, consuming me, covering my eyes. I waited a minute or two, just standing there, letting my eyes adjust. Eyes adjusting to darkness—another one of those talents we undoubtedly inherited from primitive man. When I could see at least a few feet in front of me, I started on my way. I had my smartphone too. It was loaded up with apps I never used, but the one I did, the one that was probably the most useful and least techie, was the simple flashlight. I debated turning it on but decided against it.

If there was danger here—and I couldn't imagine what that danger might be or what form it might take—I didn't want to give it a heads-up with a shining flashlight. That had been the whole point of parking and sneaking up, right?

I flashed back to being trapped in the back of that van. I had no qualms about what I'd been forced to do to escape—I would do it again, of course, a thousand times over—but there was also no doubt that Otto's final moments would haunt my sleep until the day I died. I would always hear the wet crack of that neck snapping, would always remember the feel of bone and cartilage giving way, ending a life. I had killed someone. I had snuffed out a human being.

Then my thoughts turned to Bob.

I slowed my step. What did Bob do after I escaped down the hill? He must have gotten back in his van, driven away, probably dumped Otto's body someplace, and then . . .

Would he maybe try to find me again?

I thought about the strain in Cookie's voice. What did she want to tell me? And why was it suddenly so urgent? Why call me up here now, late at night, not giving me a chance to think it all through?

I was on Cookie's block now. Small lights were on in a few of the windows, giving the houses a spooky, jack-o'-lantern glow. The house at the end of the cul-de-sac had more lights on than the others.

Cookie's.

I moved to the left to stay out of sight. Her front porch lights were on, so that wouldn't be the way to approach. Not if I wanted to stay unseen. The house was a sprawling one-level, unnaturally long and slightly uneven, as though additions had been stuck on without much forethought. Staying low, I circled toward the side of the house. I tried to stay in the dark. I literally crawled the last ten yards toward the window with the brightest light.

Now what?

I was under the window on all fours. I stayed still and tried to listen. Nothing. There is silence, and then there is rural silence, silence you could feel and reach out and touch, silence with texture and distance. That was what surrounded me now. Real, true, rural silence.

I shifted my weight slightly. My knees cracked, the sound seemingly screaming through the stillness. I got my feet beneath me, my knees deeply bent, my hands on my thighs. I readied to push myself up like a human piston, so that I could take a peek in the window.

Keeping most of my face out of sight, I rose toward the corner of the window so that only one eye and the top right quadrant of my face would be exposed. I blinked in the sudden light and looked into the room.

Cookie was there.

She sat on the couch. Cookie's back was ramrod straight. Her mouth was set. Denise, her partner, sat next to her. They were holding hands, but their faces were pale and drawn. The tension came off them in waves.

You didn't have to be an expert in body language to see that they were nervous about something. It took me a few more moments to realize what that something was.

A man sat in the chair across from them.

His back was to me so that at first I could only see the top of his head.

My first thought was a panicked one: Could it be Bob?

I raised myself up a few more inches, trying to get a better look at the man. No luck. The chair was big and plush. The man sank deep into it, vanishing from view. I moved to the other side of the window, changing my exposed face quadrant to the upper left. Now I could see the hair was salt-and-pepper curly.

Not Bob. Definitely not Bob.

The man was speaking. The two women listened intently, nodding in unison to whatever he was saying. I turned and pressed my ear against the window. The glass was cold. I tried to make out what the man was saying, but it was still too muffled. I glanced back into the room. The man in the chair leaned a little forward, trying to make a point. Then he tilted his chin just enough so I could see his profile.

I may have gasped out loud.

The man had a beard. That was the key. That was how I was able to recognize him—the beard and the curly hair. I flashed back again to that very first time I saw Natalie, sitting in the chair with her sunglasses on. And next to her, seated to her right, had been a man with a beard and curly hair.

This man.

What the . . . ?

The bearded guy rose out of the plush chair. He started to pace, gesturing wildly. Cookie and Denise tensed up. They held hands so tightly I swore that I could see their knuckles whiten. That was when I noticed something else that sent me reeling—something that made me realize with a stunning thud the importance of running this little reconnaissance mission before walking blindly into the situation.

The bearded man had a gun.

I froze in my half squat. My legs started to shake, from fear or exertion, I wasn't sure which. I lowered myself back down. Now what?

Flee, dopey.

Yep, that seemed the best play. Flee back to my car. Call the cops. Let them handle it. I tried to picture how that scenario would play out. First off, how long would it take the cops to get here? Wait, would they even believe me? Would they call Cookie and Denise first? Would a SWAT team come out? And now that I really thought about it, what was happening here exactly? Did Beardy kidnap Cookie or Denise and make them call me—or were they all in cahoots together? And if they were in cahoots, what would happen after I called? The cops would show up, and Cookie and Denise would deny everything. Beardy would hide his gun and claim ignorance.

Then again, what was the alternative? I had to bring in the cops, right?

Beardy continued to pace. The tension in the room made it pound out like a heart. Beardy checked his watch. He took out his mobile phone and held it in a walkie-talkie manner. He barked something into it.

Who was he talking to?

Whoa, I thought. What if there were others? It was time to go. Call the cops, don't call the cops, whatever. That guy was armed. I wasn't.

Hasta luego, mofos.

I was taking one last look through the window when I heard the dog bark come from behind me. I froze at the sound. Beardy did not. His head snapped toward the barking—and by extension, me—as though pulled on a string.

Our eyes locked through the window. I saw his widen in surprise. For the briefest of moments—a hundredth of a second, maybe two of them—neither of us moved. We just stared in shock, unsure of what to make of each other, until Beardy raised the gun, pointed it at me, and pulled the trigger.

I fell backward as the bullet crashed through the window.

I dropped to the ground. Shards of glass rained down on me. The dog kept barking. I rolled over, cutting myself on the glass, and got to my feet.

"Stop!"

It was another man's voice coming from my left. I didn't recognize the voice, but the guy was outside. Oh man, I had to get out of there. No time to think or hesitate. I ran full throttle in the other direction. I turned the corner, legs pumping, nearly in the clear.

Or so I thought.

Earlier I had credited my attuned Spidey senses with gifting me the premonition of danger. If that was the case, those same senses had just failed me miserably.

Another man was standing right around the corner. He'd been waiting for me, baseball bat at the ready. I managed to stop my legs, but there was no time for anything else. The meat of the bat came toward me. No chance for me to react. No chance for me to do anything but stand there stupidly. The blow landed flush on my forehead.

I dropped to the ground.

He may have hit me with the bat again. I don't know. My eyes rolled back, and I was gone.

Chapter 21

First thing when I woke up: pain.

That was all I could think of: massive, all-consuming pain and how to lessen it. It felt as though my skull had been shattered, that tiny fragments of bone were loose, that their jagged edges were ripping through my most sensitive brain tissue.

I moved my head slightly to the side, but that just made those jagged edges angrier. I stopped, blinked my eyes, blinked them again in an attempt to open them, gave up.

"He's awake."

The voice belonged to Cookie. I tried once more to pry my eyes open. I almost used my fingers against my eyelids. I swam past the hurt. It took a few seconds, but I finally got there. It took a few more seconds to focus and start to take in my new surroundings.

I wasn't outside anymore.

That much was for certain. I looked up at the exposed wooden beams of a roof. I also wasn't in Cookie's house. She had a one-level ranch. This looked more like a barn or old farmhouse. There was a wooden floor underneath me, not dirt, so I ruled out the barn.

Cookie was there. So was Denise. Beardy came over and looked down at me with pure, unfiltered hatred. I had no idea why. I saw a second man standing by a door to my left. A third man sat in front of a computer screen. I didn't recognize either of them.

Beardy waited, glaring down at me. He probably thought that I would say something obvious like, "Where am I?" I didn't. I used the time to calm myself and try to gather my thoughts.

I had no idea what was going on.

I kept my eyes moving, trying to get a sense of the room. I searched for an escape route. I saw one door and three windows, all closed. The door was guarded too. I remembered that at least one of them was armed with a gun.

I needed to be patient.

"Talk," Beardy said to me.

I didn't. He kicked me in the ribs. I let out a groan, but I didn't move.

"Jed," Cookie said, "don't."

Beardy Jed stared down at me. There was rage behind his eyes. "How did you find Todd?"

That threw me. I don't know what I'd expected him to ask, but it wasn't that. "What?"

"You heard me," Jed said. "How did you find Todd?"

My head was swimming. I didn't see where a lie here would help me, so I went with the truth. "His obituary."

Jed looked at Cookie. Now I saw confusion on their faces.

"I saw his obituary," I continued. "It was on the college website. That's how I got to his funeral."

Jed wound up to kick me again, but Cookie stopped him with a shake of her head. "I'm not talking about that," Jed spat. "I'm talking about before."

"What before?"

"Don't play dumb. How did you find Todd?"

"I don't know what you're talking about," I said.

The rage behind his eyes exploded. He pulled out the gun and pointed it at me. "You're lying."

I said nothing.

Cookie moved closer to him. "Jed?"

"Back off," he snapped. "You know what he did? Do you?"

She nodded and did as she was asked. I stayed perfectly still.

"Talk," he said to me again.

"I don't know what you want me to say."

I glanced at the guy sitting by the computer. He looked scared. So did the guy by the door. I thought back to Bob and Otto. They hadn't looked scared. They looked ready and experienced. These guys didn't. I wasn't sure what, if anything, that meant, except that either way, I was in huge trouble.

"One more time," Jed began through gritted teeth. "How did you find Todd?"

"I already told you."

"You killed him!" Jed shouted.

"What? No!"

Jed dropped to his knees and put the muzzle of the gun against my temple. I closed my eyes and waited for the blast. He moved his lips close to my ear.

"If you lie again," he whispered, "I will kill you right here and now."

Cookie: "Jed?"

"Shut up!"

He pressed the muzzle hard enough against my temple to leave an indentation. "Talk."

"I didn't . . ." His eyes told me that another denial would seal my fate. "Why would I kill him?"

"You tell us," Jed said. "But first I want to know how you found him."

Jed's hand was shaking, the muzzle jangling against my temple. His spittle was getting tangled up in his beard. My pain was gone now, replaced by naked fear. Jed wanted to pull that trigger. He wanted to kill me.

"I told you how," I said. "Please. Listen to me."

"You're lying!"

"I'm not—"

"You tortured him, but he wouldn't talk. Todd couldn't help you anyway. He didn't know. He was just helpless and brave, and you, you bastard . . ."

I was seconds from death. I could hear the torment in his voice and knew that he wouldn't listen to reason. I had to do something, had to risk going for the gun, but I was flat on my back. Any move would take too long.

"I never hurt him, I swear."

"And I guess you'll also tell us you didn't visit his widow today."

"No, I did," I said quickly, happy to agree with him.

"But she didn't know anything either, did she?"

"Know about what?"

Again the muzzle dug in a little deeper. "Why did you go down to talk to the widow?"

I met his eye. "You know why," I said.

"What were you looking for?"

"Not what," I said. "Who. I was looking for Natalie."

He nodded now. A chilly smile came to his face. The smile told me that I had given him the right answer—and the wrong one. "Why?" he asked.

"What do you mean, why?"

"Who hired you?"

"No one hired me."

"Jed!"

It wasn't Cookie this time. It was the guy at the computer screen.

Jed turned, annoyed by the interruption. "What?"

"You better take a look at this. We have company."

Jed pulled the gun away from my head. I let out a long breath of relief. The guy by the computer twisted the monitor so Jed could see the screen. It was a surveillance video in black-and-white.

"What are they doing here?" Cookie asked. "If they find him here . . ."

"They're our friends," Jed said. "Let's not worry until—"

I didn't wait for more. I saw my chance and I took it. Without warning I jumped to my feet and ran toward the guy blocking the door. It seemed as though I were moving in slow motion, as if it were taking much too long to get to that door. I lowered my shoulder, ready to ram into him.

"Stop!"

I was maybe two steps from the guy guarding the door. He was in a crouch, bracing himself for my attack. My brain kept working, calculating and recalculating. In something quicker than seconds—quicker than nanoseconds—I laid out the whole upcoming scenario. How long would it take me to put the guy down? At best, two or three seconds. Then I had to reach for the knob, turn it, fling the door open, run outside.

How long would that all take?

Conclusion: Too long.

Two other men and maybe two women would be on me by then. Or maybe Jed would just shoot. In fact, if he reacted fast enough, he could probably fire a round before I even reached the guy.

In short, calculating the odds, I realized that I had no chance of getting out through the door. Yet here I was, still running toward my adversary with a full head of steam. He was ready for me. He expected me to go for him. So, I assumed, did Jed and the others.

That wouldn't do then, would it?

I needed to surprise them. At the last possible moment, I veered my body right and without so much as a backward glance or even the slightest hesitation, I leapt forward and dived straight through the window.

Still airborne, with yet another window shattering around me, I heard Jed shout, "Get him!"

I tucked my arms and head, landing on the roll, hoping to use my momentum to get smoothly back on my feet. That was a fantasy. I did manage to roll up to my feet, but the momentum didn't suddenly stop. It kept me going, knocking me back to the ground, sending me tumbling. When I finally stopped, I struggled to get back up.

Where the hell was I?

No time to think. I was in the backyard, I guessed. I saw woods. The driveway and front, I assumed, were behind me. I started in that direction, but then I heard the front door open. The three men appeared.

Uh-oh.

I turned and ran into the woods. The darkness swallowed me whole. I couldn't see more than a few feet in front of me, but slowing down wasn't an option. There were men—at least one of whom had a gun—behind me.

"Over there!" I heard someone yell.

"We can't, Jed. You saw what was on the screen."

So I ran. I ran into those woods hard and fast, and eventually I ran face-first into a tree. It was like when Wile E. Coyote runs into a rake—a dull thud followed by vibrations. My brain started shaking. The blow stopped me cold, and I fell to the ground. My already aching head screamed in pain.

I saw the beam of a flashlight coming closer to me.

I tried to roll into some kind of hiding spot. My side hit another tree or, hell, maybe it was the same one. My head screamed in protest. I rolled in the other direction, trying to stay as flat as possible. The flashlight beam sliced through the air right above me.

I could hear footsteps moving closer.

Had to move.

Back toward the house I heard the crunch of tires on gravel. A car was coming up the drive.

"Jed?"

It was a harsh whisper. The flashlight stopped moving. I heard someone call out to Jed again. Now the flashlight went off. I was back in the pure darkness. I heard the footsteps recede.

Get up and run, dumb ass!

My head wouldn't let me. I lay still another moment and then looked back toward the old farmhouse in the distance. Now I could finally see it from the outside for the first time. I stayed still and stared. Once again, the floor beneath me seemed to fall away.

It was the main house of the Creative Recharge retreat.

I was being held in the place where Natalie had stayed.

What the hell was going on?

The car came to a stop. I rose just enough to get a look. When I did, when I saw the car, I felt an entirely new sense of relief.

It was a police squad car.

Now I understood their panic. Jed and his group had a surveillance camera by the entrance. They had seen the cop car coming to my rescue and had panicked. It made sense now.

I started toward my saviors. Jed and his followers wouldn't kill me now. Not in front of cops who had come to rescue me. I was almost to the edge of the woods, maybe thirty yards from the cop car, when another thought entered my head.

How had the cops known where I was?

For that matter, how had the cops known I was in trouble? And why, if they were here to rescue me, had the car driven up at such an unhurried pace? Why had Jed made that comment about their being "our friends"? As I slowed down, the relief now ebbing away, a few more questions entered my head. Why was Jed walking toward the squad car with a big smile and casual wave? Why were the two cops getting out of the car waving back just as casually?

Why were they all shaking hands and exchanging backslaps like old buddies?

"Hey, Jed," one called out.

Oh damn. It was Stocky. The other cop was Thin Man Jerry. I decided to stay where I was.

"Hey, fellas," Jed said. "How are you guys?"

"Good, man, when did you get back?"

"A couple of days ago. What's up?"

Stocky said, "You know a guy named Jake Fisher?"

Whoa. So maybe they were here to rescue me?

"No, don't think so," Jed said. The others were all outside now. More handshakes and backslaps. "Guys, you know a . . . what was the name again?"

"Jacob Fisher."

They all shook their heads and muttered their lack of knowledge.

"There's an APB out on him," Stocky said. "College professor. Seems he killed a man."

My blood went cold.

Thin Man Jerry added, "The dope confessed to it even."

"He sounds dangerous," Jed said, "but I don't get what that has to do with us."

"First off, we spotted him trying to get on your land a couple days back."

"My land?"

"Yep. But that's not why we're here now."

I ducked down in the brush, not sure what to do here.

"See, we got a GPS working a trace on a cell phone," Stocky said.

"And," Thin Man Jerry added, "the coordinates are leading us right up here."

"I don't understand."

"Simple, Jed. We can track his iPhone. Not that hard nowadays. Hell, I got a tracker on my kid's phone, for crying out loud. It tells us that our perp is here on your property at this very moment."

"A dangerous killer?"

"Could be, yep. Why don't you all wait inside now?" He looked back toward his partner. "Jerry?"

Jerry reached back into the car and pulled some sort of hand-held device into view. He studied it for a few moments, hit the touch screen, and then declared, "He's within fifty yards—in that direction."

Thin Man Jerry pointed right to where I was hiding.

Several scenarios flew through my brain. One, the most obvious: Surrender. Throw my hands up, walk out of the woods with them held high, and shout, "I give up," as loud as I can. Once I was in police custody I was, if nothing else, safe from Jed and his group.

I was seriously considering doing that—raising my arms, calling out, surrendering—when I saw Jed take out his gun.

Uh-oh.

Stocky said, "Jed, what are you doing?"

"It's my gun. I own it legally. And we're on my property, right?"

"Right, so?"

"So this murderer you're after . . . ," Jed began.

Now I was a murderer.

"He might be armed and dangerous. We aren't letting you guys go after him without backup."

"We don't need backup, Jed. Put that away."

"This is still my property, right?"

"It is."

"So if it's all the same to you, I'm staying right here."

The obvious scenario suddenly didn't seem so obvious. Jed was intent on killing me for two reasons. One, he thought that I had something to do with Todd's murder. That was the reason they had grabbed me in the first place. But now, two, dead men tell no tales. If I surrendered, I could tell the cops what had happened tonight, how they had kidnapped me and fired shots at me. It might be my word against theirs, but there'd be the bullet at Cookie's house matching his gun. There'd be the phone records of Cookie calling me. It might be a tough sell, but I bet Jed didn't want to take the risk.

But if Jed shot me now—even if he fired as I tried to surrender— it could be viewed as either self-defense or, at worst, a jumpy trigger finger. He would shoot and kill me and say that he thought I had a gun or something like that and, really, I already killed one man, according to Stocky and Thin Man Jerry. And all of these Vermont buddies would back Jed's story and the only guy who would contradict them—yours truly—would be worm food.

There was more to consider. If I surrendered, how long would I be jammed up with the police? I was getting closer to the truth. I could feel it. They thought that I killed someone. Heck, I sort of confessed to it. How long could they hold me? A while, I bet.

If they nabbed me now, I'd probably never have a chance to confront Natalie's sister, Julie.

"This way," Thin Man Jerry said.

They started walking to me. Jed lifted his gun, keeping it very much at the ready.

I started to backpedal. My head felt as though it'd been encased in molasses.

"If someone is in those woods," Stocky shouted, "come out now with your hands up."

They moved closer. I slid backward a few more steps and ducked behind a tree. The woods were thick. If I could get deep enough in them, I'd be safe at least for a bit. I picked up a rock and hurled it as far as I could to my left. All eyes turned. Flashlights came on and shone in that direction.

"Over there," someone yelled.

Jed led the way, gun pointed.

Surrender? Oh, I don't think so.

Stocky moved next to Jed. Jed hurried his step, nearly running, but Stocky put up an arm to stop him. "Move slow," Stocky said. "He might be armed."

Jed, of course, knew better, didn't he?

Thin Man Jerry didn't budge. "This thing says he's still over here."

Again he pointed in my direction. They were forty, fifty yards away. Staying low in the thicket, I quickly buried the phone—my second lost in the past three days—under a pile of leaves and hurried away, trying to make as little noise as possible. I started moving backward, deeper into the woods, again trying my best not to make any noise. I kept a few rocks in my hand. I'd throw them if I needed to distract.

The others gathered back around Jerry, all moving slowly toward the phone.

I picked up my pace, getting deeper and deeper into the trees. I couldn't see them anymore, just the flashlights.

"He's close by," Thin Man Jerry said.

"Or," Jed added, seeing the light, I guess, "his cell phone is."

I kept moving, kept low. I really didn't have a plan here. I had no idea what direction to take or how far the woods went. I might be able to escape them, might be able to keep moving, but eventually, unless I found a way out of here, I didn't have a clue how I'd get out of this.

Maybe, I thought, I could double-back to the house.

I heard voices mumbling. They were now too far for me to see them. That was a good thing. I could see the movement stop. The flashlight was lowered.

"He's not here," someone said.

Stocky, annoyed: "I can see that."

"Maybe your tracker is off."

They were, I guessed, right on top of where I'd haphazardly buried the phone. I wondered how long that gave me. Not much time, but probably enough. I rose to keep running and then it happened.

I'm not a doctor or a scientist, so I really can't tell you how adrenaline works. I only know that it does. It had helped me move past the pain from that blow to the head, from my jumping through a window, from my landing hard on the ground. It helped me recover from running face-first into that tree, even as I felt my lip fatten, could taste the bitter blood on my tongue.

What I do know—what I was learning at that very moment—was that adrenaline is not limitless. It was a finite hormone found within our bodies, nothing more. It may be the most potent surge we know, but the effects, as I was quickly experiencing, were only short-term.

That surge eventually peters out.

The pain didn't so much ebb back in as announce itself with the thrash of a reaper's scythe. A bolt of pain ripped through my head, knocking me to my knees. I actually had to cover my mouth with my hand to prevent myself from crying out.

I heard another car coming up the drive. Had Stocky called for backup?

In the distance, I could hear voices:

"It's his phone!"

"What the . . . he buried it!"

"Spread out!"

I could hear rustling behind me. I wondered how much of a lead I had and how well that lead would stand up to flashlights and bullets. Probably not very big or well. I once again considered the idea of surrendering and taking my chances. I once again didn't like it.

I heard Stocky say, "Just back off, Jed. We can handle this."

"It's my land," Jed replied. "Too much land for you two to cover."

"Still—"

"My property, Jerry." There was snap in Jed's voice. "You're on it without a warrant."

"A warrant?" It was Stocky. "You serious? We're just worried about your safety."

"Me too," Jed answered. "You got no idea where this murderer is hiding, right?"

"Well—"

"For all you know, he could be in the house. Hiding. Waiting for us. No way, bro—we are staying out here with you."

Silence.

Get *up*, I told myself.

"I want everyone to stay in sight," Stocky said. "No heroes. You see something, you scream for help."

I heard murmurs of agreement, then flashlights sliced through the dark. They were spreading out. I couldn't see people in the dark, just the bouncing beams of light. It was enough to know that I was really screwed.

Get up, dumb ass!

My head reeled in agony, but I managed to get to my feet. I stumbled forward like some kind of stiff-legged movie monster. I had made it about three steps, maybe four, when the flashlight sliced across my back.

I quickly jumped behind a tree.

Had I been spotted?

I waited for someone to call out. No one did. I kept my back against the bark. The only sound now was my own breath. Did that beam of light hit me? I was pretty sure that it had. But I didn't know for sure. I stayed where I was and waited.

Footsteps coming toward me.

I wasn't sure what to do. If someone had spotted me, I was finished. There was no way I could get away. I waited for someone to shout for help.

Nothing, except for the approaching footsteps.

Wait a second. If I had been spotted, why hadn't anyone called out? Maybe I was okay. Maybe I had been mistaken for a tree or something.

Or maybe no one was calling out because they wanted to shoot me?

I tried to coldly consider that for a moment. Suppose, for example, it was Jed. Would he call out? No. If he called out, I might run and then Stocky and Thin Man Jerry would be on me too and it would be harder to kill me. But suppose he had spotted me with his flashlight. What then? If he had indeed seen me, if he knew that I was hiding behind this very tree, well, maybe Jed could sneak up on me alone, gun at the ready, and . . .

Ka-boom.

The footsteps were growing louder.

My brain tried to do that quick-calculating-reptilian thing again—it had already saved me, right?—but after a second or two of neuron burning, I came to a rather startling yet obvious conclusion:

I was finished. There was no way out.

I tried to gather my strength for a big-time sprint, but really, what would that do? I'd expose myself for certain and in the condition I was in I'd never get far. I'd either get shot or captured. Come to think of it, those seemed to be my only two choices now: shot or captured. I preferred captured, thank you very much. The question now was, how could I maximize my chances of captured over shot?

I didn't have a clue.

A beam of light danced in front of me. I pressed my back into the tree and went up on my tippy-toes. Like that was going to help. The footsteps were getting closer. Judging by the sound and the brightness of the light, I would guess that someone was within ten yards of me.

Options flew in and out of my brain. I could stay here and jump the guy. If it was Jed, for example, I could disarm him. But any struggle on my part would not only reveal my location for sure, but if it wasn't Jed—if it was, for example, Stocky—then it would be open season on using deadly force on me.

So what to do?

Hope that I hadn't been spotted.

Of course, hope wasn't a plan or even an option. It was wishing. It was fanciful thinking. It was leaving my fate in the hands of, well, fate.

The footsteps were only a yard or two away now. I braced myself, unsure what to do, leaving it to that reptilian part of my brain, when I heard a whisper.

"Don't say a word. I know you're behind the tree."

It was Cookie.

"I'm going to walk past you," she said, her voice low. "When I do, get right behind me and walk. Get as close to my back as possible."

"What?"

"Just do it." Her tone left no room for discussion. "Right up close."

Cookie walked past my tree, nearly knocking into it, and kept going. I didn't hesitate. I fell in line right behind her and followed. I could see flashlights in the distance, both on my left and on my right.

"That wasn't an act, was it?" Cookie said.

I didn't know what she meant.

"You loved Natalie, didn't you?"

"Yes," I whispered.

"I'm going to walk you as far as I can. We will hit a path. Take it to the right. Stay low and out of sight. The path will lead to the clearing where the white chapel is. You'll know how to get away from there. I will try to keep them occupied. Get as far away as you can. Don't go home. They'll find you there."

"Who will find me?"

I tried to move in sync with her, matching footstep for footstep like an annoying kid copying another.

"You need to stop, Jake."

"Who will find me?"

"This is bigger than you can imagine. You have no idea what you're up against. None at all."

"Tell me."

"If you don't stop, you'll kill us all." Cookie veered left. I kept with her. "The path is up ahead. I will turn left, you head down to the right. Understand?"

"Where's Natalie? Is she alive?"

"In ten seconds, we will be on the path."

"Tell me."

"You're not listening to me. You've got to leave this alone."

"Then tell me where Natalie is."

In the distance I could hear Stocky yell out something, but I couldn't make out the words. Cookie slowed her step.

"Please," I said.

Her voice was distant, hollow. "I don't know where Natalie is. I don't know if she's dead or alive. Neither does Jed. Neither do any of us."

We hit a path made of crumbled stone. She began to turn to the left. "One last thing, Jake."

"What?"

"If you come back, I won't be the one saving your life." Cookie showed me the gun in her hand. "I'll be the one who ends it."

Chapter 22

I recognized the path.

There was a small pond to the right. Natalie and I had gone swimming there late one night. We got out, panting, lying naked in each other's arm, skin against skin. "I never had this," she said slowly. "I mean, I've had this, but . . . never *this*."

I understood. I hadn't either.

I passed the old park bench where Natalie and I used to sit after having coffee and scones at Cookie's. Up ahead, I could see the faint outline of the chapel. I barely glanced at it, didn't need those memories slowing me down right now. I took the path down into town. My car was less than half a mile away. I wondered whether the cops had located it yet. I didn't see how. I wouldn't be able to drive it very long—there was probably an

APB on it too—but I didn't see any other way of getting out of town. I'd have to risk it.

The street remained so dark that I was only able to find my car via memory. I practically walked right into it. When I opened the door, the car's interior light burst through the night. I quickly slipped inside and closed the door. Now what? I was, I guessed, a guy on the run. I remembered seeing on some TV show where the fugitive switched license plates with another car. Maybe that would help. Maybe I could find a parked car and do that. Right, sure, except, of course, I didn't have a screwdriver. How could I do it without a screwdriver? I searched my pocket and pulled out a dime. Would that work as a screwdriver?

It would take too long.

I did have a destination in mind. I drove south, careful not to drive too fast or too slowly, constantly hitting the gas and brake, as though the proper speed would somehow make me invisible. The roads were dark. That would probably help. I had to keep in mind that an APB wasn't all-powerful. I probably had some time on my hands if I could keep off main roads.

My iPhone was, of course, gone. I felt naked and impotent without it. Funny how attached we get to those devices. I continued south.

Now what?

I had only sixty dollars on me. That wouldn't get me far. If I used a credit card, the cops would see it and pick me up right away. Well, not right away. They'd have to see the charge come in and then dispatch a squad car or whatever. I don't know how long that took but I doubt it would be instantaneous. Cops are good. They aren't omnipotent.

No choice really. I had to take a calculated risk. Interstate 91, the main highway in this area, was just up ahead. I took it to the first rest area and parked near the back in the least-lit spot I could find. I actually cinched up my collar, as if that would disguise me, and headed inside. When I walked past the small rest-stop convenience store, something snagged my gaze.

They sold pens and markers. Not a lot of them, but maybe . . .

I thought about it for a second, maybe two, and then I headed into the shop. When I checked the small selection of writing utensils, the disappointment hit me harder than I expected.

"Can I help you?"

The girl behind the counter couldn't have been more than twenty. She had blond hair with streaks of pink in it. Yep, pink.

"I like your hair," I said, ever the charmer.

"The pink?" She pointed at the streaks. "It's for breast cancer awareness. Say, are you okay?"

"Sure, why?"

"You got a big bump on your head. I think it's bleeding."

"Oh, that. Right. I'm fine."

"We sell a first aid kit, if you think that'll help."

"Yeah, maybe." I turned back to the pens and markers. "I'm looking for a red marker, but I don't see any here."

"We don't carry any. Just black."

"Oh."

She studied my face. "I got one here though." She reached into a drawer and picked out a red Sharpie marker. "We use it for inventory, to cross out stuff."

I tried not to show how anxious I was. "Is there any way I can purchase it from you?"

"I don't think we're supposed to do that."

"Please," I said. "It is really important."

She thought about it. "Tell you what. You buy the first aid kit and promise to take care of that bump, and I'll throw in the pen."

I made the deal and hurried into the men's room. The clock had to be ticking. A police car would eventually drive by major rest stops and check cars, right? Or wrong? I didn't have a clue. I tried to keep my breathing even and smooth. I checked my face in the mirror. Ugh. There was swelling on my forehead, and an open gash above my eye. I cleaned it out as much as I could, but a big bandage would make me stick out like a sore thumb.

The ATM was next to the vending machines, but that would have to wait a few more minutes.

I rushed out to my car. My car license plate read "704 LI6." The lettering in Massachusetts is red. Using the marker I turned the 0 into an 8, the L into an E, the I into a T, the 6 into an 8. I took a step back. It would never stand up to close inspection, but from any sort of distance, the plate did read "784 ET8."

I would have smiled at my ingenuity, but there was no time. I headed back toward the ATM and debated how to approach the machine. I knew that all ATMs had cameras—who didn't?—but even if I avoided being seen, the authorities would know it was my credit card.

Speed seemed more important here. If they had a picture of me, they had a picture of me.

I have two credit cards. I took out the max on both and hurried back to my car. I got off the highway at the next exit and started taking side roads. When I reached Greenfield, I parked the car on a side street in the center of town. I considered taking the nearest bus, but that would be too obvious. I found a taxi and took it to Springfield. Naturally I paid cash. I took the Peter Pan bus from there to New York City. Throughout all of this travel, my eyes kept shifting all over the place, waiting for—I don't know—a cop or a bad guy to spot and nab me.

Paranoid much?

Once in Manhattan I hired another taxi to take me out to Ramsey, New Jersey, where I knew Julie Pottham, Natalie's sister, lived.

When we reached Ramsey, the driver said, "Okay, bud, where to?"

It was four in the morning—clearly too late (or, depending on your point of view, too early) to visit Natalie's sister. Plus I needed rest. My head hurt. My nerves were shot. I could feel my body quake from exhaustion.

"Let's find a motel."

"There's a Sheraton up this way."

They'd require identification and probably a credit card. "No. Something . . . cheaper."

We found one of those no-tell motels designed for truckers, adulterers, and us fugitives. It was aptly named the Fair Motel. I liked that honesty: We aren't great, we aren't even good, we're "fair." A sign above the awning announced "Hourly Rates" (just like a Ritz-Carlton), "Color TV" (mocking those competitors who still use black-and-white), and my favorite part: "Now Featuring Towels!"

This place wouldn't require ID or credit card or even a pulse.

The woman behind the desk was in her seventies. She looked at me with seen-it-all eyes. Her name tag read MABEL. Her hair had the consistency of hay. I asked for a room in the back.

"Do you have a reservation?" she asked me.

"You're kidding, right?"

"Yeah, I am," Mabel said. "But the rooms in the back are full. Everyone wants a room in the back. Must be the view of the Dumpster. I got a nice room overlooking a Staples store, if you'd like."

Mabel gave me a key to room 12, which ended up not being as nightmarish as I imagined. The place looked *fair*ly clean. I tried not to think what this room had probably witnessed during its lifetime, but then again, if I stopped and thought about it, I wouldn't like to think about that in a Ritz-Carlton either.

I collapsed into bed with my clothes still on and fell into one of those sleeps where you don't remember falling asleep and have no idea what time it is when you wake up. When morning hit, I reached for my iPhone on the night table but, alas, I remembered that I didn't have it anymore. The police did. Were they going through it? Were they seeing all the places I had searched, all the texts I had sent, all the e-mails I had mailed out? Were they doing the same at my house on campus? If they had gotten a warrant to track me down via my iPhone, wouldn't it stand to reason that they also had enough to search my place? But then again, so what? They wouldn't find anything incriminating. Embarrassing maybe, but who didn't have some Internet searches that were embarrassing?

My head still hurt. A lot. I smelled like a goat. A shower would help but not if I had to change into these same clothes. I stumbled into the bright morning sunlight, shielding my eyes like a vampire or one of those guys who spent too much time in a casino. Mabel was still behind the desk.

"Wow, what time do you get off?" I asked.

"Are you hitting on me?"

"Uh, no."

"Because you might want to clean up a little before you make your big move. I got standards."

"Do you have any aspirin or Tylenol?"

Mabel frowned, reached into her purse, and pulled out a small arsenal of painkillers. Tylenol, Advil, Aleve, Bayer. I chose the Tylenol, downed two, and thanked her.

"The Target down the road has a big-n-tall section," Mabel said. "Maybe you want to buy some new clothes."

Great suggestion. I headed over and bought a pair of jeans and a flannel shirt, not to mention a few undergarments. I also bought a travel-size toothbrush, toothpaste, and deodorant. My plan was not to stay on the run for very long, but there was still one thing I wanted to do before I surrendered to the authorities.

Talk to Natalie's sister in person.

Last purchase: A disposable cell phone. I called Benedict's cell, home, and office. No answer at any of them. It was probably too early for him. I wondered who else I should try and decided to call Shanta. She answered on the first ring.

"Hello?"

"It's Jake."

"What's this phone number you're calling from?"

"It's a disposable phone," I said.

There was a pause. "Do you want to tell me what's going on?"

"Two Vermont cops were looking for me."

"Why?"

I quickly explained.

"Wait," Shanta said, "you ran away from cops?"

"I didn't trust the situation. I thought those people would kill me."

"So surrender now."

"Not quite yet."

"Jake, listen to me. If you're a fugitive, if law enforcement officials are looking for you—"

"I just need to do something first."

"You need to surrender."

"I will, but . . ."

"But what? Are you out of your mind?"

Maybe. "Uh, no."

"Where the hell are you?"

I said nothing.

"Jake? This isn't a game. Where are you?"

"I'll call you back."

I quickly hung up, mad at myself. Calling Shanta had been a mistake. She was a friend, but she also had other responsibilities and agendas here.

Okay, deep breath. Now what?

I called Natalie's sister.

"Hello?"

It was Julie. I hung up. She was home. That was all I needed to know. The phone number for a taxi service had been prominently displayed in my motel room. I guess a lot of people don't like to come to or leave the Fair Motel with their real cars. I called that number and asked for a cab to pick me up at Target. I ducked into the men's room, did as much washing as a sink would allow, and changed into my new duds.

Fifteen minutes later, I rang Julie Pottham's doorbell.

She had one of those screen-glass doors in front of the wooden one, so she could open one, see who it was, but still be locked behind the glass. When Julie saw who was standing on her front stoop, her eyes grew big and her hand fluttered toward her mouth.

"Do you still want to pretend you don't know who I am?" I asked.

"If you don't leave right now, I am going to call the cops."

"Why did you lie to me, Julie?"

"Get off my property."

"No. You can call the cops, and they can drag me away, but I will come back. Or I'll follow you to work. Or I'll come back at night. I'm not going away until you answer my questions."

Julie's eyes darted left and then right. Her hair was still mousy brown. She hadn't changed much in the past six years. "Leave my sister alone. She's happily married."

"To whom?"

"What?"

"Todd is dead."

That slowed her down. "What are you talking about?"

"He was murdered."

Her eyes widened. "What? Oh my God, what did you do?"

"What? Me? No. You think . . . ?" This conversation was quickly spinning out of control. "It has nothing to do with me. Todd was found in the home he shared with his wife and two kids."

"Kids? They don't have kids."

I looked at her.

"I mean, she would have told me . . ." Julie's voice drifted off. She looked shell-shocked. I hadn't expected that. I figured that she knew what was going on, was part of it, whatever the hell "it" was.

"Julie," I said slowly, trying to get her refocused, "why did you pretend you didn't know me when I called?"

Her voice was still far away. "Where?" she asked.

"What?"

"Where was Todd murdered?"

"He lived in Palmetto Bluff, South Carolina."

She shook her head. "That makes no sense. You've made a mistake. Or you're lying."

"No," I said.

"If Todd was dead—murdered, according to you—Natalie would have told me."

I licked my lips, tried to keep the desperation out of my voice. "So you're in touch with her?"

No answer.

"Julie?"

"Natalie worried this might happen."

"What might happen?"

Her eyes finally found focus. They hit mine like a laser. "Natalie thought you'd come to me someday. She even told me what to say if you did."

I swallowed. "What did she say?"

"'Remind him of his promise.'"

Silence.

I took a step closer to her. "I kept that promise," I said. "I kept it for six years. Let me in, Julie."

"No."

"Todd is dead. If there was a promise, I kept it. It's over now."

"I don't believe you."

"Check the Lanford website. You'll see an obituary."

"What?"

"On the computer. Todd Sanderson. Check his obituary. I'll wait."

Without another word, she stepped back and closed the door. I didn't know what that meant. I didn't know if that meant she was going to check the website or if she had had enough. I had nowhere else to go. I stayed there, facing the door, waiting. Ten minutes later Julie was back. She unlocked the screen door and gestured for me to come inside.

I sat on the couch. Julie sat across from me, stunned. Her eyes looked like shattered marbles.

"I don't understand," she said. "It says he's married with kids. I thought . . ."

"You thought what?"

She shook her head sharply. "Why are you so interested in this anyway? Natalie dumped you. I saw you at the wedding. I thought you'd never show up, but Natalie knew you would. Why? Are you some kind of masochist?"

"Natalie knew I'd show?"

"Yes."

I nodded.

"What?" she asked.

"She knew I'd have to see for myself."

"Why?"

"Because I didn't believe it."

"That she could fall in love with another man?"

"Yes."

"But she did," Julie said. "And she made you promise to stay away."

"I knew that promise was wrong. Even as I made it, even as I watched her exchange vows with another man, I never believed that Natalie stopped loving me. I know that sounds delusional. I know that sounds like I'm wearing the thickest pair of rose-tinted glasses in the history of mankind or I'm some sort of egomaniac who can't accept the truth. But I know. I know how I felt when I was with her—and I know how she felt. All that stuff we scoff at about two hearts beating as one, about sun shining on a cloudy day, about a connection that went beyond physical, beyond spiritual—now suddenly I got it. Natalie and I had it all. You can't lie about that. If there is a false note in that kind of love, you hear it. There were too many moments that stole my breath. I lived for her laugh. When I looked into her eyes, I could see forever. When I held her, I knew—once in a lifetime, if you're lucky. We'd found a place rare and special, a place with color and texture, and if you're this lucky, you regret any moment of your life that you're not in this place because it feels like a sad waste. You pity others because they will never know these continuous bursts of passion. Natalie made me feel alive. She made everything around us crackle and surprise. That's how I felt—and I *know* that Natalie felt the same. We weren't blinded by love. Just the opposite. It made us both clear-eyed and that was why it will never let me go. I should never have made that promise. There was confusion in my head but never my heart. I should have kept listening to my heart."

There were tears running down my face when I finished.

"You really believe that, don't you?"

I nodded. "No matter what you tell me."

"And yet—" Julie said.

I finished the thought for her. "And yet Natalie broke it off with me and married her old boyfriend."

Julie made a face. "Old boyfriend?"

"Yes."

"Todd wasn't an old boyfriend."

"What?"

"They'd just met. It was all ridiculously sudden."

I tried to clear my head. "But she said that they'd dated before, that they even lived together and were in love and they'd broken it off and then realized that they belonged together . . ."

But Julie was shaking her head. The floor underneath me gave way.

"It was a whirlwind romance," she said. "That was what Natalie told me. I couldn't understand the sudden rush to get married. But Natalie, well, she was an artist. She was unpredictable. She had, as you put it, these bursts of passion."

It made no sense. None of this made any sense. Or maybe, for the first time, the confusion was leading to some kind of clarity.

"Where is Natalie?" I asked.

Julie tucked her hair behind her ear and looked off.

"Please tell me."

"I don't get any of this," Julie said.

"I know. I want to help."

"She warned me. She warned me not to tell you anything."

I didn't know how to reply to that.

"I think it's best if you go now," Julie said.

No chance, but maybe it was time to circle in from another direction, keep her off balance. "Where is your father?" I asked her.

When I'd first confronted her at the door, a slow stun had come to her face. Now it looked as though I'd slapped her. "What?"

"He taught at Lanford—in my department even. Where is he now?"

"What does he have to do with anything?"

Good question, I thought. Great question even. "Natalie never told me about him."

"She didn't?" Julie gave a halfhearted shrug. "Maybe you two weren't as close as you thought."

"She came with me to campus and she never said one word about him. Why?"

Julie considered that for a moment. "He left us twenty-five years ago, you know. I was five years old. Natalie was nine. I barely remember him."

"Where did he go?"

"What difference does it make?"

"Please. Where did he go?"

"He ran off with a student, but that didn't last. My mother . . . She never forgave him. He got remarried and started a new family."

"Where are they?"

"I don't know and I don't care. My mother said he moved out west someplace. That's all I know. I had no interest."

"And Natalie?"

"What about her?"

"Did she have an interest in her father?"

"An interest? It wasn't up to her. He ran off."

"Did Natalie know where he was?"

"No. But . . . I think he's the reason Natalie was always so screwed up when it came to men. When we were little, she was convinced that one day Dad would come back and we'd be a family. Even after he remarried. Even after he had other kids. He was no good, Mom said. He was dead to her—and me."

"But not to Natalie."

Julie didn't reply. She seemed lost in a thought.

"What?" I asked.

"My mother is in a home now. Complications due to diabetes. I tried to care for her but . . ." Her voice faded away. "See, Mom never remarried. She never had a life. My father took all that away from her. And yet Natalie still longed for some kind of reconciliation. She still thought, I don't know, that it wasn't too late. Natalie was such a dreamer. It's like finding Dad would prove a point—like then she could meet a man that would never leave and that would prove that Dad didn't mean to leave us either."

"Julie?"

"What?"

I made sure that she was looking directly into my eyes. "She met that man."

Julie looked out her back window, blinked hard. A tear ran down her cheek.

"Where is Natalie?" I asked.

Julie shook her head.

"I won't leave until you tell me. Please. If she still has no interest in seeing me—"

"Of course she has no interest," Julie snapped, suddenly angry. "If she had an interest, wouldn't she have contacted you on her own? You were right before."

"About what?"

"About being delusional. About wearing those rose-tinted glasses."

"Then help me take them off," I said, unfazed. "Once and for all. Help me see the truth."

I don't know if my words reached her. I would not be dissuaded. I looked at her and maybe she saw that. Maybe that was why she finally caved.

"After the wedding, Natalie and Todd moved to Denmark," Julie said. "That was their home, but they traveled a lot. Todd worked as a doctor for a charity. I forget the name of it. Something about beginnings maybe."

"Fresh Start."

"Yes, that's it. So they traveled to poorer countries. Todd would do medical procedures on the needy. Natalie would do her artwork and teach. She loved it. They were happy. Or so I thought."

"When was the last time you saw her?"

"At the wedding."

"Wait. You haven't seen your sister in six years?"

"That's right. After the wedding, Natalie explained to me that her life with Todd was going to be a glorious journey. She warned me that it might be a long time before I saw her again."

I couldn't believe what I was hearing. "And you've never gone over and visited? She's never come back?"

"No. Like I said, she warned me. I get postcards from Denmark. That's it."

"How about e-mail or talking on the phone?"

"She doesn't have either. She thought that modern technology was clouding her thinking and harming her work."

I made a face. "She told you that?"

"Yes."

"And you bought it? What if there was an emergency?"

Julie shrugged. "This was the life she wanted."

"Didn't you find this arrangement odd?"

"Yes. In fact, I made a lot of the arguments you're making now. But what could I do? She made it clear—this was what she wanted. This was the start of a whole new journey. Who was I to stand in the way?"

I shook my head in disbelief and to clear it. "When was the last time you got a postcard from her?"

"It's been a while. Months, maybe half a year."

I sat back. "So in reality, you don't know where she is, do you?"

"I would say Denmark, but in truth, no, I guess I don't. I also don't understand how her husband could have been living with another woman in South Carolina or any of this. I mean, nothing makes sense anymore. I don't know where she is."

A sharp knock on the door startled us both. Julie actually reached for my hand as though she needed comfort. There was a second knock and then a voice called out.

"Jacob Fisher? This is the police. The house is surrounded. Come out with your hands in the air."

Chapter 23

refused to say a word until my attorney—Benedict—was present.

That took some time. The lead officer identified himself as Jim Mulholland of the New York Police Department. I couldn't figure out that jurisdiction. Lanford College is in Massachusetts. I had killed Otto along Route 91 still within that state. I had ventured into Vermont and when they picked me up I was in New Jersey. Other than taking public transportation through Manhattan, I could not figure out how the NYPD could possibly be involved in this mess.

Mulholland was a burly man with a thick mustache that brought on visions of Magnum PI. He stressed that I was not under arrest and that I could leave anytime, but boy, they would really, *really* appreciate my cooperation. He chatted politely, if not inanely, as he drove me to a Midtown precinct. He offered me soda, coffee, sandwiches, whatever I wanted. I was suddenly hungry and accepted. I was about to dig in when I remembered that it was guilty men who ate in custody. I had read that somewhere. The guilty man knows what is going on, so he can sleep and eat. It is the innocent man who is too confused and nervous to do either.

Then again, which was I?

I ate the sandwich and even enjoyed every bite. Every once in a while, Mulholland or his partner, Susan Telesco, a tall blonde with jeans and a turtleneck, would try to engage me in conversation. I would shake them off and remind them that I had invoked my right to counsel. Three hours later, Benedict showed up. The four of us—Mulholland, Telesco, Benedict, and yours truly—sat around a table in an interrogation room that had been done up to not be overly intimidating. Of course it wasn't as though I had a lot of experience in interrogation rooms, but I always expected them to be somewhat stark. This one was more a soft beige.

"Do you know why you're here?" Mulholland asked.

Benedict frowned. "Really?"

"What?"

"How did you expect us to answer that exactly? With a confession perhaps? 'Oh yes, Detective Mulholland, I assume you've arrested me because I shot up two liquor stores'? Can we skip amateur hour and just get to the heart of this?"

"Listen," Mulholland said, adjusting himself in the chair, "we're on your side."

"Oh boy."

"No, I mean it. We just need to clean up some details, and then we all go home better people for what happened."

"What are you talking about?" Benedict asked.

Mulholland nodded at Telesco. She opened a folder and slid a sheet of paper across the table. When I saw the mug shots—front view, side view—my blood hummed in my veins.

It was Otto.

"Do you know this man?" Telesco asked me.

"Don't answer." I wasn't about to, but Benedict put a hand on my arm just in case. "Who is he?"

"His name is Otto Devereaux."

The name sent a chill through me. They had shown me their faces. They had used at least Otto's real name. That could only mean one thing—they never intended for me to leave that van alive.

"Recently, your client stated that he had an altercation with a man matching Otto Devereaux's description on a highway in Massachusetts. In that statement, your client said that he had been forced to kill Mr. Devereaux in self-defense."

"My client retracted that statement. He was disoriented and under the influence of alcohol."

"You don't understand," Mulholland said. "We aren't here to bust his chops. If we could, we'd give him a medal." He spread his hands. "We are all on the same side here."

"Oh?"

"Otto Devereaux was a career scumbag of almost biblical proportions. We could show his full oeuvre, but it would take too long. Let's just lead with some of the highlights. Murder, assault, extortion. His nickname was Home Depot because he liked using tools on his victims. He enforced for the legendary Ache brothers until someone decided that he was too violent for them. Then he worked on his own or for whatever desperate bad guy needed a true sicko."

He smiled at me. "Look, Jake, I don't know how you got the drop on this guy, but what you did was a blessing for society."

"So," Benedict said, "theoretically speaking, you're here to thank us?"

"Nothing theoretical about it. You're a hero. We want to shake your hand."

No one shook hands.

"Tell me," Benedict said, "where did you find his body?"

"That's not important."

"What was the cause of death?"

"That's not important either."

Benedict said, smiling broadly, "Is this really the way to treat your hero?" He nodded toward me. "If there is nothing else, I think we will be leaving now."

Mulholland glanced over at Telesco. I thought that I saw a small smile on her face. I didn't like it. "Okay," he said, "if that's how you want to play it."

"Meaning?"

"Meaning nothing. You're free to go."

"Sorry we couldn't help," Benedict said.

"Don't worry about it. Like I said, we just wanted to thank the man who took this guy out."

"Uh-huh." We were both standing now. "We can find our way out."

We were nearly out the door when Susan Telesco said, "Oh, Professor Fisher?"

I turned.

"Do you mind if we show you one more photograph?"

They both looked up at me as though they couldn't be bothered, as though they had all the time in the world and my answer was meaningless. I could look at the picture or I could walk out the door. No biggie. I didn't move. They didn't move.

"Professor Fisher?" Telesco said.

She slid the photograph out of the folder facedown, as if we were playing blackjack in a casino. I could see the glint in her eye now. The room dropped ten degrees.

"Show me," I said.

She flipped over the photograph. I froze.

"Do you know this woman?" she asked.

I didn't reply. I stared at the photograph. Yes, of course, I knew the woman.

It was Natalie.

"Professor Fisher?"

"I know her."

The photograph was black-and-white. It looked like a still frame from some kind of surveillance video. Natalie was hurrying down a corridor.

"What can you tell me about her?"

Benedict put a hand on my shoulder. "Why are you asking my client?"

Telesco pinned me down with her eyes. "You were visiting her sister when we found you. Would you mind telling us what you were doing there?"

"And again," Benedict said, "why are you asking my client?"

"The woman's name is Natalie Avery. We've previously spoken at length to her sister, Julie Pottham. She claims that her sister lives in Denmark."

I spoke this time. "What do you want with her?"

"I'm not at liberty to discuss that."

"Then neither am I," I said.

Telesco looked at Mulholland. He shrugged. "Okay, then. You're free to go."

We all stood there, playing this game of chicken. To mix metaphors, I had no cards here so I was the first to blink. "We used to date," I said.

They waited for more.

Benedict said, "Jake . . . ," but I waved him off.

"I'm looking for her."

"Why?"

I glanced at Benedict. He seemed to be as curious as the cops. "I loved her," I said. "I never really got over her. So I was hoping . . . I don't know. I was hoping for some kind of reconciliation."

Telesco wrote something down. "Why now?"

That anonymous e-mail came back to me:

You made a promise.

I sat back down and pulled the photograph closer. I swallowed hard. Natalie's shoulders were hunched. Her beautiful face . . . I could feel myself well up . . . she looked terrified. My finger found her face, as if somehow she could feel my touch and would find comfort. I hated this. I hated seeing her so scared.

"Where was this taken?" I asked.

"It's not important."

"The hell it isn't. You're looking for her, aren't you? Why?"

They looked at each other again. Telesco nodded. "Let's just say," Mulholland began slowly, "that Natalie is a person of interest."

"Is she in trouble?"

"Not from us."

"What's that supposed to mean?"

"What do you think it means?" For the first time, I saw the facade drop and could see a flash of anger on Mulholland's face. "We've been looking for her"—he grabbed the photograph of Otto—"but so were he and his friends. Who would you rather found her first?"

I stared at the photograph, my vision blurring and clearing, when I noticed something else. I tried not to move, tried not to change the expression on my face. In the bottom right-hand corner, there was a time-date stamp. It read: 11:47 P.M., May 24 . . . six years ago.

This picture had been taken a few weeks before Natalie and I met.

"Professor Fisher?"

"I don't know where she is."

"But you're looking?"

"Yes."

"Why now?"

I shrugged. "I missed her."

"But why now?"

"It could have been a year ago. It could have been a year later. It was just the time."

They didn't believe me. Too bad.

"Have you had any luck?"

"No."

"We can help her," Mulholland said.

I said nothing.

"If Otto's friends find her first . . ."

"Why are they looking for her? Hell, why are you looking for her?"

They changed subjects. "You were in Vermont. Two police officers identified you and we found your iPhone up there. Why?"

"It is where we dated."

"She stayed at that farm?"

I was talking too much. "We met in Vermont. She got married in the chapel up there."

"And how did your phone end up there?"

"He must have dropped it," Benedict said. "By the way, can we get it back?"

"Sure. That can be arranged, no problem."

Silence.

I looked at Telesco. "Have you been searching for her for the last six years?"

"In the beginning. But not so much in recent years, no."

"Why not?" I asked. "I mean, well, the same question you asked me: Why now?"

Again they exchanged a glance. Mulholland said to Telesco, "Tell him."

Telesco looked at me. "We stopped looking for her because we were sure that she was dead."

I had somehow expected that answer. "Why did you think that?"

"It doesn't involve you. You need to help us here."

"I don't know anything."

"If you tell us what you know," Telesco said, her voice suddenly hard, "we forget all about Otto."

Benedict: "What the hell is that supposed to mean?"

"What do you think it means? Your client claims self-defense."

"So?"

"You asked about the cause of death. Here's your answer: He snapped a man's neck. I have news for you. A broken neck is rarely the result of self-defense."

"First off, we deny that he had anything to do with the death of this felon—"

She put her hand up. "Save it."

"It doesn't matter," I said. "You can make all the threats you want. I don't know anything."

"Otto didn't believe that, did he?"

Bob's voice: *"Where is she?"*

Mulholland leaned close to me. "Are you dumb enough to think this is the end of it? You think they'll just forget about you now? They underestimated you the first time. They won't do that again."

"Who are 'they'?" I asked.

"Some seriously bad men," he said. "That's all you need to know."

"That makes no sense," Benedict said.

"Listen to me closely. They can find Natalie first," Mulholland said, "or we can. It's your choice."

Again I said, "I really don't know anything."

Which was true enough. But more than that, Mulholland had left off one last option, much as it might seem like a long shot.

I could find her.

Chapter 24

Benedict drove. "You want to fill me in?"

"It's a long story," I said.

"It's a long drive. Speaking of which, where am I going to drop you off?"

Good question. I couldn't go back to campus, not only because I was unwelcome, but as Detectives Mulholland and Telesco reminded me, some very bad people might be interested in finding me. I wondered whether Jed and Cookie were part of the same bad people as Bob and Otto or if I had two different groups of bad people after me. Doubtful. Bob and Otto were cool professionals. Grabbing me had been another day at the office. Jed and Cookie were bumbling amateurs—unsure, angry, scared. I wasn't sure what that meant, but I suspected that it was important.

"I'm not sure."

"I'll start back toward campus, okay? You fill me in on what's going on."

So I did. Benedict kept his eyes on the road, nodding every once in a while. His face remained set, his hands always at ten and two. When I finished he said nothing for several seconds. Then: "Jake?"

"Yes?"

"You need to stop this," Benedict said.

"I'm not sure I can."

"A lot of people want to kill you."

"I was never popular to begin with," I said.

"True enough, but you've stumbled into some serious doo-doo."

"You humanities professors and your big words."

"I'm not joking," he said.

I knew that.

"These people in Vermont," Benedict said. "Who were they?"

"Old friends, in a way. I mean, that's the weirdest part. Jed and Cookie were both there the first time I met Natalie."

"And now they want to kill you?"

"Jed thinks that I had something to do with Todd Sanderson's murder. But I can't figure out why he'd care or how he knew Todd. There has to be some connection between them."

"A connection between this Jed guy and Todd Sanderson?"

"Yes."

"The answer is obvious, isn't it?"

I nodded. "Natalie," I said.

"Yep."

I thought about that. "The first time I saw Natalie, she was sitting next to Jed. I even had a passing thought that maybe they were dating."

"Well then," Benedict said, "now it sounds like all three of you have something of a connection."

"Meaning?"

"Carnal knowledge of Natalie."

I didn't like that. "You don't know that for sure," I protested weakly.

"May I state the obvious?"

"If you must."

"I've known my share of women," Benedict said. "At the risk of bragging, some might even call me an expert on the subject."

I made a face. "Risk?"

"Some women are just trouble. You understand what I'm saying?"

"Trouble."

"Right."

"And I guess you're going to tell me Natalie is one of these women."

"You, Jed, Todd," Benedict said. "No offense, but there is only one explanation for all this."

"And that is?"

"Your Natalie is a big ol' can of crazy."

I frowned. We drove a little more.

"I have that guest cottage I use as an office," Benedict said. "You can stay there until this all cools down."

"Thank you."

We drove a little more.

"Jake?"

"Yeah?"

"We always fall harder for the crazy ones," Benedict said. "That's our problem as men. We all claim we hate the drama, but we don't."

"That's deep, Benedict."

"Can I ask you one more thing?"

"Sure."

I thought I saw his grip tighten on the wheel. "How did you happen to see Todd's obituary?"

I turned to face him. "What?"

"His obituary. How did you see it?"

I wondered if the confusion was showing on my face. "It was on the front page of the college website. What exactly are you trying to ask?"

"Nothing. I was just wondering, that's all."

"I told you about it in my office—and you encouraged me to go down to the funeral, remember?"

"I do," Benedict said. "And now I'm encouraging you to let this go."

I didn't reply. We drove for a while in silence. Benedict interrupted it.

"One other thing that's bothering me," he said.

"What's that?"

"How do you think the police found you at Natalie's sister's house?"

I had wondered the same thing, but now I realized the answer was obvious. "Shanta."

"She knew where you were?"

I explained about my calling her and my stupidity in keeping the disposable phone. If the police can track you by your phone, it stood to reason that if they knew the number (which would have popped up on Shanta's caller ID), they could track you by a disposable phone too. I still had it in my pocket and debated chucking it out the window. No need. The cops weren't the ones I was worried about anymore.

After President Tripp requested my departure, I had packed a suitcase and my laptop and stored them in my office at Clark House. I wondered whether someone might be, I don't know, staking out my campus house or that office. It seemed like overkill, but what the heck. Benedict had the idea of having us park far away. We looked to see if there was anything suspicious. There wasn't.

"We can send a student in to pick up your stuff," he said.

I shook my head. "I already got one student hurt in this."

"There's no risk here."

"Still."

Clark House was closed. I carefully entered via the back entrance. I grabbed my stuff and hurried back toward Benedict's car. No one shot me. Score one for the good guys. Benedict drove to the back of his property and dropped me off at the guest cottage.

"Thank you," I said.

"I got a bunch of papers to grade. You'll be all right?"

"Sure."

"You should see a doctor about your head."

I did have a residual headache. If it was from some kind of concussion, exhaustion, stress, or some combination of those, I had no idea. Either way I didn't think a doctor could help. I thanked Benedict again and settled into the room. I took out my laptop and set it up on the desk.

It was time, I thought, to do some cyber-sleuthing.

You may wonder what qualifies me to be a top-notch investigator or how I would know how to cyber-sleuth. I'm not and I don't. But I know how to type stuff in a Google search field. That was what I started to do now.

First, I searched for a date: May 24, six years ago.

That had been the date on the surveillance photograph the NYPD had shown me. It stood to reason that whatever had happened that day, well, it was probably a crime. It might have been reported in the news. Was that a long shot? I guess. But it could be a start.

When I hit the return button, a bunch of hits about a tornado in Kansas popped up first. I would need to narrow this down. I added "NYC" into the search field and hit the return button again. The first story told me that the New York Rangers had lost to the Buffalo Sabres 2 to 1. Second link: the New York Mets beat the Arizona Diamondbacks 5 to 3. Man, we are a sports-obsessed society.

I finally located a site that ran daily New York newspapers and their archives. Over the past two weeks, the front pages of many newspapers were discussing the brazen string of bank robberies in New York City. They hit at night and left no clue and had earned the nickname "the Invisibles." Catchy. Then I hit the link for the archives for May 24 six years ago and started cyber-paging through the metro sections.

Top stories for that day: An armed man attacked the French consulate. Police took down a heroin ring operated by a Ukrainian gang. A cop named Jordan Smith accused of rape was having his day in court. A house fire in Staten Island had been deemed suspicious. A hedge fund manager from Solem Hamilton had been indicted in some kind of Ponzi scheme. A state comptroller was accused of ethics violations.

This didn't help. Or maybe it did. Maybe Natalie had been part of the Ukrainian gang. Maybe she knew the hedge fund manager— the surveillance photo looked like the lobby of an office building— or the state comptroller. Where was I on that day six years ago? May 24. School would have been coming to a close. In fact, classes would probably be over right around then.

Six years ago.

My life had been in turmoil, as Benedict had recently reminded me at the Library Bar. My father had died of a heart attack a month earlier. My thesis wasn't going well. May 24. That would have been right around the time Professor Trainor had thrown his graduation party with the underage drinking. I had wanted him seriously censured, putting a bit of tension between Professor Hume and myself.

But my life wasn't the point here. Natalie's was.

The surveillance photograph had been taken May 24. I thought about that for a moment. Suppose there had been some kind of crime or incident on May 24. Okay, right, that was certainly the possibility I had been going on, but now I was following through on the thought. If the incident took place on May 24, when would the papers report it?

May 25, not May 24.

This was not a brilliant insight, but it did make some sense. I found the papers for May 25 and again searched the metro sections. Top stories: Local philanthropist Archer Minor was gunned down. A fire in Chelsea kills two. An unarmed teen was shot by police. Man kills his ex-wife. High school principal arrested for embezzling school funds.

This was a waste of time.

I closed my eyes and rubbed them. Giving up sounded really good right now. I could lie down and close my eyes. I could keep my promise and honor the wishes, it seemed, of the woman I thought was my true love. Of course, as Benedict had pointed out, maybe Todd and Jed thought that Natalie was their true love. A flush of something primordial—let's call it jealousy—whooshed through me.

Sorry, I didn't buy it.

Jed wasn't attacking me as a jealous lover. Todd . . . I didn't know what the hell was going on there, but it didn't matter. I couldn't back away. I wasn't built that way—who is, really? How could any reasonable person live with so many questions left unanswered?

A small voice in my head replied: Well, at least you'd *live*.

Didn't matter. Couldn't be done. I had been attacked, threatened, assaulted, arrested, and I had even killed a man . . .

Whoa, hold the phone. I had killed a man—and now I knew his name.

I leaned forward and googled a name: Otto Devereaux.

I expected to find an obituary on top. I didn't. The first hit was a forum for "gangster enthusiasts." Yes, for real. I clicked into the discussion boards, but you had to create a profile. I quickly did.

There was a topic called "RIP, OTTO." I hit the link:

Holy crap! Otto Devereaux, one of the toughest mob hit men and extortionists, got his neck snapped! His body was dumped on the side of Saw Mill Parkway like some piece of garbage. Respekt, Otto. You knew how to kill, bro.

I shook my head. What next—a fan site for convicted pedophiles?

There were about a dozen comments from people remembering some of Otto's most horrible deeds and, yes, praising his work. They say that you can find any sort of depravity on the Internet. I had stumbled across a site devoted to admirers of violent gangsters. Some world.

On the fourteenth comment, I hit pay dirt:

> Otto is being laid to rest at the Franklin Funeral Home in Queens this Saturday. The funeral is private, so you can't go to pay your respects, but admirers can still send flowers. Here's the address.

The post listed an address in Flushing, Queens.

There was a sketchpad on the desk. I grabbed a pencil and leaned back with it. I wrote down Natalie's name on the left. I wrote down Todd's beneath it. I jotted down other names—mine, Jed, Cookie, Bob, Otto—any name I could come up with at all. Delia Sanderson; Eban Trainor; Natalie's father, Aaron Kleiner, and mother, Sylvia Avery; Julie Pottham; Malcolm Hume even. All of them. Then on the right side of the page, I drew a timeline from top to bottom.

Go back as far as I could. Where did this first start?

I didn't know.

So back to the beginning.

Twenty-five years ago, Natalie's father, who taught here at Lanford, had run off with a student. According to Julie Pottham, dear old Dad had relocated and remarried. The only problem was, there was no sign of him anywhere. How had Shanta put it? Like father, like daughter. Both Natalie and her father had seemingly vanished into thin air. Both were completely off the grid.

I drew a line connecting Natalie and her father.

How could I learn more about this connection? I thought about what Julie had said. Her information about her father's remarriage came from her mother. Maybe Mom knew more than she was saying. Maybe she had an address for Dad. Either way, I needed to talk to her. But how? She was in a home. That was what Julie had said. I didn't know which home and somehow I doubted that Julie would be forthcoming. Still, it couldn't be too difficult to track Mrs. Avery down.

I circled Sylvia Avery, Natalie's mother.

Back to the timeline. I moved up through the years until I reached twenty years ago when Todd Sanderson was a student. He had nearly been expelled after his father's suicide. I thought back to his student file and his obituary. Both had mentioned that Todd had made amends by launching a charity.

I wrote down *Fresh Start* on my pad.

One, Fresh Start had been birthed on this very campus in the wake of Todd's personal turmoil. Two, six years ago, Natalie told her sister that she and Todd were going to travel around the world doing good works for Fresh Start. Three, Delia Sanderson, Todd's real wife, told me that Fresh Start had been her husband's passion. Four, Professor Hume, my very own beloved mentor, had been the faculty adviser during Fresh Start's creation.

I started tapping the paper with my pencil. Fresh Start was all over this. Whatever "this" was.

I needed to look into that charity. If Natalie had indeed traveled for Fresh Start, someone there might at the very least have a lead on where she was. Again I started doing web searches. Fresh Start helped people get new starts, though the work seemed a bit unfocused. They worked with kids who needed cleft palates repaired, for example. They helped with political dissidents who needed asylum. They helped people with bankruptcy issues. They helped you find new employment, no matter what issues you've had in the past.

In short, as the mantra on the bottom of the home page said, "We help anyone who truly, desperately needs a fresh start."

I frowned. Could that be more vague?

There was a link to donate. Fresh Start was a 501(c)(3) charity, so all contributions were tax deductible. No officers were listed— no mention of Todd Sanderson or Malcolm Hume or anyone. There was no office address. The phone number had an 843 area code—South Carolina. I dialed the number. An answering machine picked up. I didn't leave a message.

I found a company online that investigates various charities "so that you may give with confidence." For a small fee, they would send you a complete report on any charity, including an IRS Form 990 (whatever that was) and a "comprehensive analysis with full financial data, mission-driven decisions, officers' biographies, charity holdings, money spent on fund-raising and all other activities." I paid the small fee. An e-mail came to me saying that the report would be in my e-mail the following day.

I could wait that long. My head throbbed like a stubbed toe. My craving for sleep was overwhelming, emanating from the marrow of my bones. Tomorrow morning I would head to Otto Devereaux's funeral, but for now, the body needed rest and nourishment. I took a shower, grabbed a bite to eat, and slept the sleep of the dead, which, based on what was going on around me, seemed apropos.

Chapter 25

Benedict leaned into the car window of his own car. "I don't like this."

I didn't bother responding. We had been through this a dozen times already. "Thanks for letting me borrow your car."

I had left my car with its altered license plate on the street in Greenfield. At some point I would have to figure out a way to retrieve it, but it could wait.

"I can go with you," Benedict said.

"You have a class."

Benedict didn't argue. We never miss class. I had hurt enough students, in ways small and big, by taking up this bizarre quest. I wouldn't allow more to pay even a minor price.

"So your plan is to show up at this gangster's funeral?"

"More or less."

"Sounds like less to me."

Hard to argue. I planned on staking out Otto Devereaux's funeral. My hope was that I could somehow learn why he attacked me, who he worked for, why they were searching for Natalie. I wasn't big on the details—like how I'd accomplish this—but I had no job right now and sitting around idly waiting to be found by Bob or Jed didn't seem like a terrific alternative either.

Better to be proactive. That was what I would tell my students.

Route 95 in Connecticut and New York is basically a series of construction areas masquerading as an interstate highway. Still I made decent time. The Franklin Funeral Home was located on Northern Boulevard in the Flushing section of Queens. For some odd reason, the picture on their website was of Central Park's beloved Bow Bridge, a place you've seen lovers get married in pretty much every romantic comedy that takes place in Manhattan. I had no idea why they had that, as opposed to the photographs of their actual funeral home, until I pulled up to it.

Some final resting spot.

The Franklin Funeral Home looked as though it'd been built to house two dentists' offices with maybe room for a proctologist, circa 1978. The facade was the yellowing stucco of a smoker's teeth. Weddings, parties, celebrations often reflect the celebrants. Funerals rarely do. Death is truly the great equalizer, so much so that all funeral services, except the ones in movies, end up being the same. They are always colorless and rote and offer not so much solace and comfort as formula and ritual.

So now what? I couldn't just go in. Suppose Bob was there? I could try to stay in the back, but guys my size do not blend well.

There was a man in a black suit directing people where to park. I pulled up and tried to smile as though I was heading for a funeral, whatever that meant. The man in the black suit asked, "Are you here for the Devereaux or Johnson funeral?"

Because I was quick on my feet, I said, "Johnson."

"You can park on the left."

I pulled into the spacious lot. The Johnson funeral, it seemed, was taking place by the front entrance. There was a tent set up out back for Devereaux's. I found a parking spot in the right corner. I backed into it, giving me a perfect view of the Devereaux tent. If by some chance someone in the Johnson party or the Franklin Funeral staff noticed me, I could pull off being bereaved and needing a moment.

I thought back to the last time I was at a funeral, just six days ago in that small white chapel in Palmetto Bluff. If I still had my timeline on me, there would be a six-year gap between a wedding in one white chapel and a funeral in another. Six years. I wondered how many of those days passed without Natalie in some way crossing my mind, and I realized that the answer was none.

But right now, the bigger question was, what had those six years been like for her?

A stretch limousine pulled up to the front of the tent. Another strange death ritual: The one time we all get to ride in cars we equate with luxury and excess is when we are mourning the death of a beloved. Then again, when better? Two dark-suited men came over and opened the limo doors, red-carpet style. A slender woman in her mid-thirties was helped out. She was holding hands with a long-haired little boy who looked to be six or seven. The little boy wore a black suit, which struck me as borderline obscene. Little boys should never wear black suits.

The obvious had not dawned on me until this very moment: Otto might have had a family. Otto might have had a slender wife who shared his bed and dreams. He might have had a long-haired son who loved him and played ball with him in the yard. Other people poured out of the car. An elderly woman wept hard in a handkerchief kept crumpled up in her fist. She had to be half carried toward the tent by a couple in their thirties. Otto's mother and maybe siblings, I didn't know. The family made a receiving line by the front of the tent. They greeted mourners, the devastation obvious in their bearings and on their faces. The little boy looked lost, confused, scared, like someone had sneaked up on him and punched him in the stomach.

That someone being me.

I sat perfectly still. I had thought about Otto as some contained entity. I thought killing him was merely a personal tragedy, the end of one isolated human life. But none of us are truly contained. Death ripples, echoes.

In the end though, hard as it might have been to watch the result of my actions, it didn't change the fact that my actions were justified. I sat a little straighter and kept a closer eye on the mourners. I expected that the line would look like a casting call for *Sopranos* extras. There were some of those, no question about it, but the crowd was a pretty varied bunch. They shook hands with the family, embraced them, offered kisses. Some held the hugs a long time. Some did the quick back-pat and release. At one point, the woman I pegged as Otto's mother nearly fainted, but two men caught her.

I had killed her son. The thought was both obvious and surreal. Another stretch limousine pulled up and stopped directly in front of the receiving line. Everyone seemed to freeze for a moment. Two men who looked like New York Jets offensive linemen opened the back door. A tall, skinny man with slicked-down hair stepped out. I saw the crowd start whispering. The man was in his seventies, I'd guess, and looked vaguely familiar, but I couldn't place him. The man didn't wait at the end of the line—the line parted for him like the Red Sea for Moses. The man had one of those thin mustaches that looked as though it'd been sketched on with a pencil. He nodded as he approached the family, accepting handshakes and greetings.

Whoever this guy was, he was important.

The thin man with the thin mustache stopped and greeted each family member. One—a guy I pegged as Otto's brother-in-law—took a knee. The thin man shook his head, and the man apologetically stood back up. One of the offensive linemen stayed a step in front of the thin man. The other stayed a step behind him. No one followed them down the receiving line.

When the thin man shook hands with Otto's mother, the final person on the line, he turned and headed back toward his limo. One of the offensive linemen opened the back door. The thin man slid inside. The door closed. One offensive lineman drove. The other sat in the passenger seat. The stretch limousine was put in reverse. Everyone stayed still as the thin man made his exit.

For a full minute after he was gone, no one moved. I saw one woman cross herself. Then the line started up again. The family accepted condolences. I waited, wondering who the thin man was and if it mattered. Otto's mother started sobbing again.

As I watched, her knees buckled. She fell into the arms of a man, sobbing into his chest. I froze. The man helped her back up and let her cry. I could see him stroke her back and offer her words of condolence. She held on for a long time. The man stood and waited with extreme patience.

It was Bob.

I ducked down in my seat, even though I was probably a solid hundred yards away. My heart started pounding. I took a deep breath and risked another look. Bob was gently pulling Otto's mom off him. He smiled at her and moved toward a group of men standing maybe ten yards away.

There were five of them. One produced a pack of cigarettes. All the men took a cigarette, except Bob. Good to know my gangster was somewhat health conscious. I took out my phone, found the camera app, and zoomed onto Bob's face. I snapped four photos.

So now what?

Wait here, I guessed. Wait for the funeral and then follow Bob home.

And then?

I didn't know. I really didn't. The key was to find out his real name and identity and hope that led to his motive for asking about Natalie. He had clearly been the boss. He'd have to know the reasons, right? I could also just watch him get in his car and then I could write down his license plate number. Maybe Shanta would help track down his real name from that, except that I no longer fully trusted her and for all I knew, Bob had driven to the funeral with his smoker pals.

Four of the men peeled off the group and headed inside, leaving Bob alone with one guy. The guy was younger and wore a suit so shiny it looked like a disco ball. Bob seemed to be giving Shiny Suit instructions. Shiny Suit nodded a lot. When Bob was done, he headed into the funeral. Shiny Suit did not. Instead he swaggered with almost cartoon exaggeration in the other direction, toward a bright white Cadillac Escalade.

I bit my lower lip, trying to decide what to do. The funeral would take some time—half an hour, hour, something like that. There was no reason to just sit here. I might as well follow Shiny Suit and see where it led.

I started up the car and pulled onto Northern Boulevard behind him. This felt weird—"tailing a perp"—but it seemed a day for the weird. I didn't know how far to stay behind the Escalade. Would he spot me following him? I doubted it, even though I had a Massachusetts license plate in the state of New York. He made a right onto Francis Lewis Boulevard. I stayed two cars behind him. Crafty. I felt like Starsky and Hutch. One of them anyway.

When I'm nervous, I tell myself a lot of dumb jokes.

Shiny Suit pulled off at a mega-nursery called Global Garden. Great, I thought. He's picking up flower arrangements for Otto's funeral. Another weird thing about funerals: Wear black but kill something as colorful as flowers to decorate. The store, however, was closed. I wasn't sure what to make of that, so I didn't make anything of it yet. Shiny Suit pulled in to the back. I did likewise, though I stayed to the side, at a pretty good distance. Shiny Suit stepped down from the driver's seat of the Escalade and swaggered over toward the store's back door. Shiny Suit was big on the swagger. I didn't want to prejudge but based on the company he kept, the glistening of his suit, and the poser-like swagger, I somehow suspected that Shiny Suit was what the students today technically refer to as a douchebag. He rapped on the back door with his pinkie ring and waited, bouncing on his feet like a boxer listening to the ring introduction. I thought the bouncing around was for show. It wasn't.

A kid—he could have been one of my students—wearing a bright green store apron and a backward-facing Brooklyn Nets baseball cap opened the door, stepped out, and Shiny Suit sucker-punched him in the face.

Oh man. What had I stumbled across?

The cap flew to the ground. The kid followed, holding his nose. Shiny Suit grabbed him by the hair. He lowered his face so that I feared he might bite the kid's probably-broken nose and started yelling at him. Then he stood back up and threw a kick in the kid's ribs. The kid rocked back and forth in pain.

Okay, enough.

Working on a rather heady albeit dangerous blend of fear and instinct, I opened my car door. The fear could be controlled. I had learned how to do that during my years as a bouncer. Anyone with an iota of humanity experiences fear during physical altercations. That is how we are built. The key is harnessing it, not letting it paralyze or weaken you. Experience helps.

"Stop!" I shouted, and then—here was where the instinct part came in—I added, "Police!"

Shiny Suit's head spun toward me.

I reached into my pocket and took out my wallet. I flipped it open. No, I don't have a badge, but he would be too far away to see. My attitude would sell it. I stayed firm, calm.

The kid scrambled back toward the door. He stopped to scoop up his Brooklyn Nets baseball cap, jammed it onto his head with the bill facing back, and disappeared into the building. I didn't care. I closed my wallet and started walking toward Shiny Suit. He, too, must have had some experience in this. He didn't run. He didn't look guilty. He didn't try to explain. He just waited patiently for me to approach.

"I have one question for you," I said. "If you answer it, we forget all about this."

"All about what?" Shiny Suit replied. He smiled. His tiny teeth looked like Tic Tacs. "I don't see anything to forget, do you?"

The iPhone was in my hand, displaying the clearest photo I had of Bob. "Who is this man?"

Shiny Suit looked at it. He smiled at me again. "Let me see your badge."

Uh-oh. So much for attitude selling it.

"Just tell me—"

"You ain't no cop." Shiny Suit found this funny. "You know how I know?"

I didn't respond. The door to the shop opened a crack. I could see the kid peeking out. He met my eye and nodded his gratitude.

"If you were a cop, you'd know who that is."

"So just tell me his name and . . ."

Shiny Suit started to reach into his pocket. He could have been reaching for a gun. He could have been reaching for a knife. He could have been reaching for a tissue. I didn't know which. I didn't ask. I probably didn't care.

I had had enough.

Without saying a word or issuing a warning of any sort, I snapped my fist into his nose. I could hear the cracking sound, like I'd stepped on a big beetle. Blood ran down his face. Even through the small crack in the door, I could see the kid smiling.

"What the—?"

I snapped another punch, aiming again for the definitely-broken nose. "Who is he?" I asked. "What's his name?"

Shiny Suit cupped his nose as though it were a dying bird he wanted to save. I swept his leg. He went down in almost the exact spot the kid had been in less than a minute earlier. Behind him, the crack in the door disappeared. The kid wanted no part of this, I guessed. I didn't blame him. The blood was messing up my man's shiny suit. I bet it would wipe right off like vinyl. I bent down with my fist cocked.

"Who is he?"

"Oh man." Shiny Suit's voice had a tinge of awe in the nasal. "You're such a dead man."

That almost slowed me down. "Who is he?"

I showed him the fist again. He held up his hand in a pitiful defensive move. I could punch right through it.

"Okay, okay," he said. "Danny Zuker. That's who you're messing with, pal. Danny Zuker."

Unlike Otto, Bob hadn't used his real name.

"You're a dead man, bro."

"I heard you the first time," I snapped, but even I could hear the fear in my voice.

"Danny ain't a forgiving guy either. Oh man, you are so dead. You hear what I'm saying? You know what you are?"

"A dead man, yeah, I got it. Lie on your stomach. Put your right cheek on the pavement."

"Why?"

I cocked the fist again. He lay on his stomach and put the wrong cheek down. I told him that. He turned his head the other way. I grabbed his wallet out of his back pocket.

"You robbing me now?"

"Shut up."

I checked his ID and read his name out loud: "Edward Locke from right here in Flushing, New York."

"Yeah, so?"

"So now I know your name. And where you live. See, two can play at that game."

He chuckled at that.

"What?"

"No one plays that game like Danny Zuker."

I dropped his wallet onto the pavement. "So you plan to tell him about our little altercation?" I asked.

"Our little what?"

"Are you going to tell him about this?"

I could see him smile through the blood. "The minute you're gone, bro. Why, you wanna threaten me some more?"

"No, not at all, I think you should tell him," I said, using my calmest voice. "But, well, how will it look?"

With his face still on the pavement, he frowned. "How will what look?"

"You, Edward Locke, just got taken down by some chump you don't know. He broke your nose, ruined your nice suit—and how did you save yourself from a bigger beating? Well, you sung like a bird."

"What?"

"You sold out Danny Zuker after two punches."

"I did not! No way I'd ever—"

"You gave me his name after only two punches. Do you think that will impress Danny? You seem to know him pretty well.

How do you think he'll react to your story of selling him out like that?"

"I didn't sell him out!"

"Think he'll see it that way?"

Silence.

"Up to you," I said, "but here's what I might suggest. If you say nothing, Danny will never know about this. He won't know you messed up. He won't know someone got the jump on you. He won't know that you sold him out after only two punches."

More silence.

"We understand each other, Edward?"

He didn't reply and I didn't bother pushing for one. It was time to leave now. I doubted that Edward would be able to see the license plate from here—Benedict's license plate—but I didn't want to take any chances.

"I'm going to leave now. Keep your face down until I'm gone and then all this goes away."

"Except for my broken nose," he pouted.

"That'll heal too. Just stay down."

Keeping an eye on him, I walked backward to the car. Edward Locke never so much as budged. I got in my car and drove away. I felt pretty good about myself, which, ironically, was not something I was proud of. I got back on Northern Boulevard and drove past the funeral home. No reason to stop there. I had stirred up enough trouble for now. When I stopped at the next traffic light, I quickly checked my e-mail. Bingo. There was one from the website who investigated charities. The subject read:

Here is your complete analysis on Fresh Start

It could wait till I was back, couldn't it? Or maybe . . . I kept my
eyes peeled. It didn't take long. Two blocks up I spotted a place
called the Cybercraft Internet Café. It was far enough away from
the funeral home, not that I thought that they'd go searching
nearby parking lots for me.

The place looked like an overcrowded tech department. There
were dozens of computers lined up in narrow cubbies along the
wall. They were all taken. No customer, other than yours truly,
looked older than twenty.

"It's going to be a wait," a pure slacker yah-dude with more
piercings than teeth told me.

"That's okay," I said.

It could indeed wait. I wanted to get home. I was just about to
leave when a group of what had to be gamers let out a shout,
slapped one another on the back, offered up complicated handshakes of congratulations, and rose from the terminals.

"Who won?" Slacker Yah-Dude asked.

"Randy Corwick, man."

Slacker Yah-Dude liked that. "Pay up." Then to me he said,
"How long you need a terminal for, Pops?"

"Ten minutes," I said.

"You got five. Use terminal six. It's hot, man. Don't cool it down
with something lame."

Terrific. I quickly signed on and opened up my e-mail. I downloaded the financial report on Fresh Start. It was eighteen pages.
There was an income statement, expense graphs, revenue graphs,
profitability graphs, liquidity graphs, a graph on useful versus depre-
ciated life of building and equipment, something about liability com-
position, a balance sheet, something called a comparables analysis . . .

I teach political science. I do not understand business or numbers.

Toward the back I found a history of the organization. It had indeed been founded twenty years ago by three people. Professor Malcolm Hume was listed as the academic adviser. Two students were listed as copresidents. One was Todd Sanderson. The other was Jedediah Drachman.

My blood chilled. What's a common nickname for someone named Jedediah?

Jed.

I still had no idea what was going on, but it was all about Fresh Start.

"Time's up, Pops." It was Slacker Yah-Dude. "Another terminal will be open in fifteen."

I shook my head. I paid the rental fee and stumbled back to my car. Was my mentor somehow involved in this? What kind of good works did Fresh Start do that involved trying to kill me? I didn't know. It was time to head home and maybe discuss this all with Benedict. Maybe he'd have a clue.

I started up Benedict's car and, still dazed, headed west on Northern Boulevard. I had programmed the address for the Franklin Funeral Home into the GPS, but for the ride back, I figured that I could just hit "Previous Destinations" and Benedict would have his home in there. So when I hit the next red light, I turned the knob and clicked on "Previous Destinations." I was about to scan down for Benedict's address in Lanford, Massachusetts, but my gaze stopped cold at the first address, the place Benedict had most recently visited. The address didn't read Lanford, Massachusetts.

It read Kraftboro, Vermont.

Chapter 26

My world tilted, teetered, rocked, and flipped itself upside down.

I just stared at the GPS. The full address was listed as 260 VT-14, Kraftboro, Vermont. I knew the address. I had put it in my own GPS not long ago.

It was the address of the Creative Recharge Colony.

My best friend had visited the retreat where Natalie had stayed six years ago. He had visited the place where she married Todd. He had visited the place where, most recently, Jed and his gang had tried to kill me.

For several seconds, maybe longer, I could not move. I sat in the car. The car radio was on, but I couldn't tell you what was playing. It felt as though the world had shut down. It took reality a while to get through my haze, but when it did, it hit me like a surprise left hook.

I was alone.

Even my best friend had lied—check that: was *still* lying—to me.

Wait, I said to myself. There had to be a reasonable answer.

Like what? What possible explanation could there be for having that address in Benedict's GPS? What the hell was going on? Who could I trust?

I only knew the answer to that last question: No one.

I'm a big guy. I consider myself pretty independent. But right here, right now, I didn't think that I had ever felt so small or such gut-wrenching loneliness.

I shook my head. Okay, Jake, snap out of it. Enough with the self-pity. Time to act.

First I checked through the rest of the addresses in Benedict's GPS. There was nothing of interest. I did find his home address, so I set it up to lead me home. I started on my way. I flipped stations on the radio, searching for that ever-elusive perfect song. Never found it. I whistled along with what crappy song came on. It didn't help. The construction sites on Route 95 pounded the hell out of what was left of my psyche.

I spent most of the ride having imaginary conversations with Benedict. I actually rehearsed how I'd approach him, what I'd say, what he might answer, how I'd counter.

My grip on the wheel tightened when I pulled onto Benedict's street. I checked the time. He had a seminar for another hour, so he wouldn't be home. Good. I parked by the guest cottage and started toward his house. Again I debated what to do. The truth was, I needed more information. I wasn't ready to interrogate him yet. I didn't know enough. The simple Francis Bacon axiom, one we constantly stressed to our students, applied here: Knowledge is power.

Benedict hid a spare house key in a fake rock by his garbage can. One may wonder how I know this, so I will tell you: We are best friends. We have no secrets from each other.

Another voice in my head: Was it all a lie? Was our friendship never real?

I thought what Cookie had whispered to me in those dark woods: *"If you don't stop, you'll kill us all."*

It was not meant to be hyperbole and yet here I was, not stopping, risking in a way I could still not fathom "all" these lives. Who was "all"? Was I always, in a sense, risking them? Was Benedict supposed to, I don't know, keep an eye on me or something?

Let's not get completely paranoid here.

Right, okay, a step at a time. There was still the possibility of an innocent explanation for the Vermont address being on his GPS. I was not the most creative fellow. I have a habit of seeing things linearly. Maybe someone else borrowed his car, for example. Maybe someone even stole it. Maybe one of his late-night conquests wanted to visit an organic farm. Maybe I was once again practicing self-delusion.

I put the key in the lock. Was I really about to cross this line? Was I really going to snoop on my closest friend?

Bet your ass.

I entered through the back door. My apartment would kindly be described as functional. Benedict's resembled a third-world prince's harem. The den featured dozens of upscale, brightly hued beanbag chairs. There were vibrant tapestries on the walls. Slim African sculptures stood tall in all four corners. The room was over the top in a thousand ways, but I had always felt comfortable here. The big yellow beanbag was my favorite. I had watched a lot of football on that. I had played a lot of Xbox there.

The Xbox controllers were lying on it now. I stared down at them, though I didn't really think the controllers would offer up much information. I wondered what I was looking for. A clue, I guess. Something that would tell me why Benedict would have driven up to that farm/retreat/kidnapper-hideout in Kraftboro, Vermont. What that might be, I didn't have the slightest.

I started going through the drawers. I searched the ones in the kitchen first. Nothing. I took the spare bedroom next. Nothing. I tried the closet and bureau in the den. More nothing. I headed into the bedroom and tried there. Nothing. Benedict had a desk in there with a computer on it. I checked the drawers underneath it. Nothing.

I found a file drawer. I checked the file cabinet. There were routine bills. There were student papers. There were class schedules. As far as anything truly personal, there was—drum roll, please—nothing.

Absolutely nothing.

I thought about that. Who doesn't have anything personal in their house? Then again what would you find in my house? More than this, certainly. There would be some old photographs, a few personal letters, something that indicated my past.

Benedict had none of that. So what?

I kept looking. I was hoping to find something that would link Benedict to the Creative Recharge Colony or Vermont or anything really. I tried to sit at his desk. Benedict is a lot smaller than I am, so my knees couldn't fit under the desk. I leaned forward and hit a key on the computer. The screen lit up. Like most people, Benedict had not shut down his computer. I suddenly realized how old-fashioned my house search had been thus far. No one keeps secrets in their drawers anymore.

We keep them on the computer.

I opened up his Microsoft Office and looked for the most recent documents. The first listed was a Word document called VBM-WXY.doc. Strange name. I clicked on it.

The file wouldn't open. It was password protected.

Whoa.

There was no point in trying to guess the password. I didn't have a clue. I tried to think of another way around that. Nothing came to mind. The rest of the files under "Recent" were student recommendations. Two were for medical schools, two for law schools, one for business school.

So what was in the password-protected one?

No idea. I clicked on the Mail icon on the bottom. The mail, too, required a password to enter. I looked around the desk for a slip of paper with a password—lots of people did that—but I found nothing. Another dead end.

Now what?

I clicked on his web browser. His Yahoo! news page popped up. Not much to learn here. I clicked the history page and finally hit something approaching pay dirt. Benedict had been on Facebook recently. I clicked the link. A profile for a man named, believe it or not, John Smith, came up. John Smith had no photograph of himself. He had no friends. He had no status reports. His address was listed as New York, NY.

This computer was signed in to this Facebook under the name John Smith.

Hmm. I thought about that. It was a fake account. I know a lot of people have them. A friend of mine uses a music service that goes through Facebook, showing all his friends every song he listens to. He didn't like that, so he created a dummy account like this one. Now no one can see what songs he likes.

The fact that Benedict had a dummy account meant nothing. What was more interesting though, as I typed his name into the search engine, was that Benedict Edwards didn't have a real Facebook account. There were two Benedict Edwardses listed in the Facebook directory. One was a musician from Oklahoma City, the other was a dancer from Tampa, Florida. Neither was my Benedict Edwards.

Again, so what? A lot of people don't have Facebook accounts. I had one set up, but I've almost never used it. My profile picture was the yearbook photograph. I accepted friends maybe once a week. I probably had about fifty of them. I had originally signed up because people were sending me links to photographs and the like and the only way I could view them was to sign in to a Facebook account. Other than that, social media in general held very little appeal to me.

So maybe that was what Benedict had done. We were on many of the same e-mail lists. He had probably set up the dummy account so he could view Facebook links.

When I looked down the history page, that theory immediately imploded. The first listing was for a man on Facebook named Kevin Backus. I clicked the link. For a second, I thought that maybe it was another dummy account for Benedict, that Kevin Backus was merely an online pseudonym. But that wasn't the case. Kevin Backus was just some nondescript guy. He wore sunglasses in his profile picture and posed with his thumb up. I frowned at that.

I racked my brain. Kevin Backus. Neither his name nor his face was familiar.

I hit the "about" page. It was blank. It didn't list a home, a school, an occupation, any of that. The only thing that had been filled out was "in a relationship." He was, according to this, in a relationship with a woman named Marie-Anne Cantin.

I rubbed my chin. Marie-Anne Cantin. That name didn't ring a bell either. So, why had Benedict been on this Kevin Backus's page? I didn't know, but I suspected it was hugely important. I could start googling him. I looked again at the name Marie-Anne Cantin. It was typed in blue, meaning that she also had a profile. I only had to click on her name.

That was what I did.

When her page came up—when I saw Marie-Anne Cantin's profile photograph—I recognized the face almost immediately.

Benedict carried her picture in his wallet.

Oh man. I swallowed, sat back, caught my breath. Now I got it. I could almost feel Benedict's pain. I had lost the great love of my life. Benedict, it seemed, had done the same. Marie-Anne Cantin was indeed a stunning woman. I would describe her as high-cheekboned, regal, African American except, as I looked closer at her profile, that last part would be inaccurate.

She wasn't African American. She was, well, African. Marie-Anne Cantin, according to her Facebook page, lived in Ghana.

This fact was, I guess, interesting, albeit in a not-my-business way. Somewhere along the way, Benedict had met this woman. He had fallen in love with her. He carried a torch for her. What that could possibly have to do with his visiting Kraftboro, Vermont . . .

Hold the phone.

Hadn't I, too, fallen in love with a woman? I, too, still carried a torch for her. And I, too, had been up in Kraftboro, Vermont.

Was Kevin Backus Benedict's very own Todd Sanderson?

I frowned. That felt like a stretch. And wrong. Still, wrong as it felt, I needed to investigate this. Marie-Anne Cantin was the only lead I had right now. I clicked her "about" link. It was impressive. She had studied economics at Oxford University and had received a law degree at Harvard. She was legal counsel for the United Nations. She both lived in and was from Accra, the capital of Ghana. She was, as I already knew, "in a relationship" with Kevin Backus.

Now what?

I clicked on her pictures, but they were set on private. No way to view them. An idea came to me. I hit the back arrow until I was on Kevin Backus's page again. His photographs were not set on private. I could see them all. Okay, good. I started clicking through them. I don't know why. I don't know what I expected to find.

Kevin Backus had his photographs in various albums. I started with the one simply titled "Happy Times." There were twenty, twenty-five pictures of either my boy Kevin with his main squeeze, Marie-Anne, or just Marie-Anne alone, obviously snapped by Kevin. They looked happy. Check that. She looked happy. He looked deliriously happy. I pictured Benedict sitting here, clicking through these photographs of the woman he loved with this Kevin guy. I could see the glass of scotch in his hand. I could see the room growing dark. I could see the blue light of the screen bouncing off Benedict's oversize Ant-Man glasses. I could see a lone tear running down his cheek.

Too much?

Facebook loved to torture ex-loves by keeping them front and center. You couldn't escape your exes anymore. Their lives were right here for you to see. Man, that sucked. So this was what Benedict did at night—tormented himself. I didn't know any of this for certain, of course, but I was pretty sure that was how it played out. I remembered that drunken night in the bar, the way he carefully took out the well-creased photograph of Marie-Anne. I could still hear the agony in his slurred words:

"The only girl I'll ever love."

Benedict, you poor bastard.

Poor bastard perhaps, but I still didn't have a clue what this meant or how it related to Benedict's recent visit to Vermont. I clicked through some more albums. There was one titled "Family." Kevin had two brothers and a sister. His mother appeared in a number of photographs. I didn't see any sign of a father. There was an album called "Kintampo Falls" and another for "Mole National Park." Most of the photographs there were shots of wildlife and natural wonders.

The last album was called "Oxford Graduation." Curious. That was where Marie-Anne Cantin had studied economics. Could Kevin and Marie-Anne have attended together? Could they be college sweethearts? I doubted it. It seemed like a long time to be "in a relationship," but, hey, who knew?

The photographs in this album were considerably older. Judging by the hairstyles, clothing, and Kevin's face, I would say at least fifteen, maybe twenty years earlier. I would bet that these photographs predated digital cameras. Kevin had probably scanned them into his computer. I skimmed through the thumbs, not expecting to see anything of interest, when a photograph in the second row made me pull up.

My hand was shaking. I grabbed the mouse, managed to move the cursor so that it hovered over the image, and clicked. The photograph grew bigger. It was a group photograph. Eight people, all in black graduation gowns, stood with big smiles on their faces. I recognized Kevin Backus. He stood on the far right next to a woman I didn't know. Their body language suggested that they were a couple. In fact, as I looked closer, it appeared that I was looking at four couples on their graduation day. I couldn't be sure, of course. It could have been that they were just lined up boy-girl, but I didn't think that was all.

My eye was immediately drawn to the woman on the left. It was Marie-Anne Cantin. She wore a killer smile, absolutely devastating. It was a smile that could twist a man's heart. A man could fall in love just being on the receiving end of that smile. A man would want to see the smile every day and be the one who could make it appear. He would want it all to himself.

Man, I got it, Benedict. I really, truly got it.

Marie-Anne was gazing lovingly at a man I didn't recognize.

At least, not at first.

He, too, was African or African American. His head was shaved. He had no facial hair. He did not wear glasses. That was why I didn't recognize him at first. That was why, even when I looked hard, I couldn't be sure. Except it was the only thing that made sense.

Benedict.

There were only two problems. One, Benedict hadn't graduated from Oxford University. Two, the name underneath the picture didn't read Benedict Edwards. It read Jamal W. Langston.

Huh?

Maybe it wasn't Benedict. Maybe Jamal W. Langston just looked like Benedict.

I frowned. Yeah, right, sure, that made sense. And maybe Benedict just happened to be carrying a torch for a woman who had long ago dated a man who looked just like him!

Dopey theory.

So what other theory did I have? The obvious: Benedict Edwards was really Jamal W. Langston.

I didn't get it. Or maybe I did. Maybe the pieces were finally, if not coming together, all on the same table. I googled Jamal W. Langston. The first link came from a newspaper called the *Statesman*. It was, according to the link, "Ghana's oldest mainstream newspaper—Founded in 1949."

I clicked the article. When I saw what it was—when I read the headline—I nearly screamed out loud, and yet, at the same time, some of those puzzle pieces were starting to come together.

It was Jamal W. Langston's obituary.

How could that be . . . ? I started reading, my eyes growing wide as a few of the puzzle pieces finally started to click into place.

From behind me, a tired voice sent a chill straight down my spine: "Man, I wish you hadn't seen that."

I slowly turned toward Benedict. He had a gun in his hand.

Chapter 27

If I'd been ranking the many surreal moments I'd been experiencing in recent days, having my best friend point a gun at me would have just elbowed its way into the top spot. I shook my head. How had I not seen it or sensed anything? His eyeglasses and their frames were beyond ridiculous. The haircut almost dared me to question his sanity or personal space-time continuum.

Benedict stood there wearing a green turtleneck, beige corduroys, and a tweed jacket—with a gun in his hand. Part of me wanted to laugh out loud. I had a million questions for him, but I started with the one I had been asking repeatedly from the beginning.

"Where's Natalie?"

If he was surprised by what I'd asked, his face didn't show it. "I don't know."

I pointed at the gun in his hand. "Are you going to shoot me?"

"I took an oath," he said. "I made a promise."

"To shoot me?"

"To kill anyone who learned my secret."

"Even your maybe best friend?"

"Even him."

I nodded. "I get it, you know."

"Get what?"

"Jamal W. Langston," I said, gesturing toward the screen. "He was a crusading prosecutor. He took on the deadly drug cartels of Ghana without worry about his own safety. He brought them down when no one else could. The man died a hero."

I waited for him to say something. He didn't.

"Brave guy," I said.

"Foolish guy," Benedict corrected.

"The cartels swore vengeance on him—and if the article is to be believed, they got it. Jamal W. Langston was burned alive. But he wasn't, was he?"

"Depends."

"Depends on what?"

"No, Jamal wasn't burned alive," Benedict said. "But the cartels still got their vengeance."

The proverbial veil was being lifted from my eyes. Well, no, it felt more like a camera coming into focus. The indistinguishable blob in the distance was gaining shape and form. Turn by turn—or in this case, moment by moment—the focus was growing sharper. Natalie, the retreat, our sudden breakup, the wedding, the NYPD, that surveillance photo, her mysterious e-mail to me, the promise she forced me to make six years ago . . . it was all coming together now.

"You faked your own death to save this woman, didn't you?"

"Her," he said. "And me too, I guess."

"But mostly her."

He didn't respond. Instead Benedict—or should I call him Jamal?—moved toward the computer screen. His eyes were moist as he reached his finger out and gently touched Marie-Anne's face.

"Who is she?" I asked.

"My wife."

"Does she know what you've done?"

"No."

"Wait," I said, my head spinning with the realization. "Even she thinks you're dead?"

He nodded. "Those are the rules. That's part of the oath we take. It is the only way to make sure everyone stays safe."

I thought again about him sitting here, looking up that Facebook page, staring at those photographs, her status, her life updates—like the one about her being "in a relationship" with another man.

"Who is Kevin Backus?" I asked.

Benedict managed something like a smile. "Kevin is an old friend. He waited a long time for his chance. It's okay. I don't want her to be alone. He's a good man."

Even the silence pierced the heart.

"Are you going to tell me what's going on?" I asked.

"Nothing to tell."

"I think there is."

He shook his head. "I already told you. I don't know where Natalie is. I've never met her. I've never even heard her name except through you."

"I'm having trouble believing that."

"Too bad." He still had the gun in his hand. "What made you suspect me?"

"The GPS in your car. It showed you'd gone to the retreat in Kraftboro, Vermont."

He made a face. "Dumb of me."

"Why did you drive up there?"

"Why do you think?"

"I don't know."

"I was trying to save your life. I pulled into Jed's farm right after the cops. Seems you didn't need my help."

I remembered now—that car coming up the driveway as the cops found my buried phone.

"Are you going to shoot me?" I asked.

"You should have listened to Cookie."

"I couldn't. You of all people should understand that."

"Me?" There was something akin to fury in his voice now. "Are you out of your mind? You said it before. I did all this to keep the woman I loved safe. But you? You're trying to get her killed."

"Are you going to shoot me, yes or no?"

"I need you to understand."

"I think I do," I said. "Like we said before, you worked as a prosecutor. You put some really bad people in jail. They tried to seek vengeance on you."

"They did more than try," he said softly, gazing again at Marie-Anne's photograph. "They took her. They even . . . they even hurt her."

"Oh no," I said.

His eyes filled with tears. "It was a warning. I managed to get her back. But that was when I knew for certain that the two of us had to leave."

"So why didn't you?"

"They'd find us. The Ghana cartel smuggles for the Latin Americans. Their tentacles can reach anyplace. Wherever we'd go, they'd track us down. I thought about faking both of our deaths, but . . ."

"But what?"

"But Malcolm said they'd never buy it."

I swallowed. "Malcolm Hume?"

He nodded. "See, Fresh Start had people in the area. They heard about my situation. Professor Hume was put in charge of me. He went off protocol though. Sent me here because I thought I could be of value as both a teacher and, if they needed me, someone to help others."

"You mean, someone like Natalie?"

"I don't know about that."

"Yeah, you do."

"It is very compartmentalized. Different people deal with different aspects and different members. I only worked with Malcolm. I spent some time in that training facility in Vermont, but until a few days ago I never knew about Todd Sanderson, for example."

"So our friendship," I said. "Was that part of your work? Were you supposed to keep an eye on me?"

"No. Why would we need to keep an eye on you?"

"Because of Natalie."

"I told you. I never met her. I don't know anything about her case."

"But she does have a case, doesn't she?"

"You don't get it. I don't know." He shook his head. "No one has ever said anything to me about your Natalie."

"But it makes sense, right? You'll grant me that?"

He didn't respond.

"You didn't call it a retreat," I said. "You called it a training center. How brilliant, really. Disguising it as some kind of artist retreat in such a remote area. Who'd suspect, right?"

"I've said too much already," Benedict said. "It isn't important."

"Like hell it isn't. Fresh Start. I should have guessed by the name. That's what they do. They give people who need it a fresh start. A drug cartel wanted you dead. So they saved you. Gave you a fresh start. I don't know what that entails—fake IDs, I guess. A plausible reason for a person to vanish. A dead body in your case. Or maybe you paid off a coroner or a cop, I don't know. Maybe some kind of training on how to behave, learn a language or a new accent, maybe wear a disguise like yours. By the way, can you take those stupid glasses off now?"

He almost smiled. "Can't. I used to wear contact lenses."

I shook my head. "So six years ago, Natalie is up at this training center. I don't know why yet. I assume that it has something to do with that surveillance photograph the NYPD showed us. Maybe she committed a crime, but my guess is, she witnessed something. Something big."

I stopped. Something here wasn't adding up, but I pushed on.

"We met," I said. "We fell in love. That was probably frowned upon or maybe, I don't know, she was up there for another reason when we started our relationship. I don't really get what happened exactly, but all of a sudden Natalie had to vanish. She had to vanish fast. If she wanted to take me too, how would your organization have reacted?"

"Not positively."

"Right. Like with you and Marie-Anne." I barely stopped to think about it now, the pieces just falling into place. "But Natalie also knew me. She knew how I felt about her. She knew that if she just broke up with me, I'd never buy it. She knew if she suddenly disappeared, vanished, I'd follow her to the ends of the earth. That I'd never give up on her."

Benedict just stared at me, not saying a word.

"So what happened next?" I went on. "I guess that your organization could have faked her death, like with you, but nobody would buy it in her case. If guys like Danny Zuker and the NYPD were looking for her, they'd need some pretty solid proof that she was dead. They'd need to see her body and with DNA, well, I don't know. It wouldn't work. So she staged that fake wedding. In many ways it was perfect. It would convince me and, at the same time, it would convince her sister and close friends. Several birds, one stone. She told me that Todd was an old boyfriend that she had recently decided was her true love. That was a lot more plausible than a guy she'd just met. But when I asked Julie about him, she said she had never met Todd. She just thought it was a whirlwind romance. Either way, even if we all felt it was odd, what could we do about it? Natalie was married and gone."

I looked up at him.

"Am I right, Benedict? Or Jamal? Or whatever the hell your name is? Am I at least close?"

"I don't know. I'm not lying. I know nothing about Natalie."

"Are you going to shoot me?"

He still had the gun in hand. "No, Jake, I don't think so."

"Why not? What about your precious oath?"

"The oath is for real. You have no idea how real." He reached into his pocket and pulled out a small box. My grandmother used to keep her pills in one just like it. "We all carry one of these."

"What's in it?" I asked.

He opened it. There was only one black-and-yellow capsule inside. "Cyanide," he said simply, the word chilling the room. "Whoever grabbed Todd Sanderson, well, he must have caught Todd off guard, before he had a chance to jam it in his mouth." He took a step toward me. "You see now, don't you? You see why Natalie made you promise?"

I just stood there, unable to move.

"If you find her, you kill her. It is as simple as that. If the organization is compromised, a lot of people will die. Good people. People like your Natalie and my Marie-Anne. People like you and me. Do you understand now? Do you understand why you have to let it go?"

I did. But I still raged against the machine. "There has to be another way."

"There isn't."

"You just haven't thought of it yet."

"I have," he said in the gentlest voice I have ever heard. "More times than you can imagine. For years and years. You have no idea."

He put the pillbox back in his pocket.

"You know what I'm saying is the truth, Jake. You are my best friend. With the exception of a woman I will never get to see or touch again, you are the most important person in my life. Please, Jake. Please don't make me kill you."

Chapter 28

almost bought it.

Check that: I did buy it for a long while. At first blush, Benedict—he wanted to make sure that I always called him that, that there would never be any slipup—seemed to be absolutely right. I had to back off.

I didn't know all the details, of course. I didn't know what the full deal was with Fresh Start. I didn't know for certain why Natalie had vanished or where she had gone. Truth was, I didn't even know if she was alive. The NYPD had suspected that she was dead. I didn't know why, but they probably surmised that if guys like Danny Zuker and Otto Devereaux want you dead, someone like Natalie doesn't survive and stay out of sight for six years.

There was more I didn't know. I didn't know how Fresh Start

worked or about the training center doubling as a retreat or about Jed or Cookie or what role everyone played in this organization. I didn't know how many people they'd helped vanish or when they had started, though according to that charity report, it all began twenty years ago, when Todd Sanderson was a student. I could probably build a comfortable house with what I didn't know. That no longer mattered. What did matter, of course, was that lives were at stake. I understood the oath. I understood that those who had made such sacrifices and taken such risks would kill to protect themselves and their loved ones.

There was also tremendous comfort in knowing that my relationship with Natalie had not been a lie, that she had, it seemed, sacrificed the truest love I'd ever known in order to save our lives. But that knowledge and its accompanying utter helplessness tore a hole straight through my heart. The pain was back—different maybe, but even more potent.

How to lessen that pain? Yep, you guessed it. Benedict and I hit the Library Bar. We didn't pretend the arms of a stranger would help this time. We knew that only friends like Jack Daniel's and Ketel One could blot out or at least blur images this searing.

We were pretty deep into our Jack-Ketel friendship when I asked one simple question. "Why can't I be with her?"

Benedict didn't reply. He was suddenly fascinated by something at the bottom of his drink. He hoped that I'd let it go. I didn't.

"Why can't I vanish too and live alone with her?"

"Because," he said.

"Because?" I repeated. "What are you, five years old?"

"You'd be willing to do that, Jake? Give up teaching, your life here, all of it?"

"Yes." There was no hesitation. "Of course I would."

Benedict stared back down at his drink. "Yeah, I get that," he said in the saddest voice.

"So?" I said.

Benedict closed his eyes. "Sorry. You can't."

"Why not?"

"Two reasons," he said. "One, it isn't done. That's just part of our protocol, part of how we compartmentalize. It's too dangerous."

"But I could do it," I said, hearing the pleading in my voice coming right through the slur. "It's been six years. I say I'm moving overseas or—"

"You're talking too loudly."

"Sorry."

"Jake?"

"Yes?"

He met my eye and held it. "This is the last time we talk about this. Any of this. I know how hard it is, but you have to promise me you won't raise it again. Do you understand?"

I didn't reply directly. "You said there were two reasons I couldn't be with her."

"Right."

"What's the second?"

He dropped his eyes and finished his drink in one enormous gulp. He held the liquor in his mouth and signaled to the bartender for another. The bartender frowned. We had been keeping him busy.

"Benedict?"

He lifted his glass, tried to drain out the last drops. Then he said, "No one knows where Natalie is."

I made a face. "I get that there's secrecy—"

"Not just secrecy." He kept an impatient eye toward the bartender now. "No one knows where she is."

"Come on. Someone must."

He shook his head. "That's part of it. That's our saving grace. That's what's keeping our people alive right now. Or so I hope. Todd was tortured. You know that, right? He could give up certain things—the retreat in Vermont, some members—but not even he knows where they go after they get their"—he made quote marks in the air—"'fresh start.'"

"But they know who you are."

"Only Malcolm does. I was the exception because I came from overseas. The rest? Fresh Start set them up. They are given all the tools. Then, for everyone's safety, they go out on their own and tell no one where they end up. That's what I mean by compartmentalizing. We all know just enough—and not any more than that."

Nobody knew where Natalie was. I tried to let that sink in. It wouldn't. Natalie was in danger, and I could do nothing about it. Natalie was out there alone, and I couldn't be with her.

Benedict shut down then. He had explained as much as he ever would. I knew that now. As we left the bar and staggered back to the house, I made my own promise of sorts. I would back off. I would let it go. I could deal with this pain—I had dealt with it in other forms for six years—in exchange for the safety of the woman I loved.

I could live without Natalie, but I couldn't live if I did something that would put her in danger. I had been warned repeatedly. Now it was time to listen.

I was out of it.

That was what I told myself as I stumbled into the guest cottage.

That was what I planned to do as my head hit the pillow and I closed my eyes. That was what I believed when I flipped onto my back and watched the ceiling spin from too much drink. That was what I was sure was the truth up until—according the bedside digital alarm clock—6:18 A.M., when I remembered something that had almost escaped my mind:

Natalie's father.

I sat up in bed, my entire body suddenly rigid.

I still didn't know what happened to Professor Aaron Kleiner.

There was, I supposed, the off chance that Julie Pottham was right, that her father ran off with a student and then remarried, but if that was the case, Shanta would have found him with no problem. No, he had vanished.

Just like his daughter Natalie would some twenty years later.

Perhaps there was a simple explanation. Perhaps Fresh Start had helped him too. But, no, Fresh Start had been created twenty years ago. Could Professor Kleiner's disappearance have been the organization's precursor? Malcolm Hume knew Natalie's father. In fact, Natalie's mother had come to him when Aaron Kleiner first abandoned the family. So maybe my mentor helped him vanish and then, what, years later, formed a group under the guise of a charity to help others like him?

Maybe.

Except twenty years later, his daughter suddenly had to vanish too? Does that make sense?

It didn't.

And why would the NYPD have shown me a surveillance photograph from six years ago? How could that relate to Natalie's father? What about Danny Zuker and Otto Devereaux? How could whatever was going on now, with Natalie, be related to her father who vanished twenty-five years ago?

Good questions.

I got out of bed and debated my next move. But what next move? I had promised Benedict that I would stay out of this. Moreover, I now understood in a very real, very concrete way the dangers of continuing this quest, not only for me but for the woman I loved. Natalie had chosen to vanish. Whether it was to protect herself or me or both, I had to not only respect her wishes but her judgment. She had scrutinized her predicament with more knowledge than I had, weighed the pros and cons, and decided that she had to disappear.

Who was I to mess that up?

So once again, I was about to let it go, was about to surrender to living with this horrible albeit necessary frustration, when another thought struck me so hard I almost stumbled. I stayed perfectly still, mulling it over in my mind, looking at it from every conceivable angle. Yes, it was there—something we had all overlooked. Something that changed the very nature of what Benedict had convinced me to do.

Benedict was heading to class when I sprinted outside. When he saw the look on my face, he froze too. "What's wrong?"

"I can't let it go."

He sighed. "We went over this."

"I know," I said, "but we were missing something."

His eyes moved from side to side as though he were afraid someone nearby might be eavesdropping. "Jake, you promised—"

"It didn't start with me."

"What?"

"This new danger. The NYPD asking questions. Otto Devereaux and Danny Zuker. Fresh Start under siege. It didn't start with me. I didn't kick that all up by trying to find Natalie. That's not how it started."

"I don't understand what you're talking about."

"Todd's murder," I said. "That's what got me involved. You guys keep thinking that I'm the one who breached your group. I'm not. Someone already knew. Someone found out about Todd and tortured and killed him. That's how I got involved—when I saw Todd's obituary."

"That doesn't change anything," Benedict said.

"Of course it does. If Natalie was tucked away safely someplace, okay, I get it. I should leave it alone. But don't you see? She's in danger. Someone knows that she didn't really get married and disappear overseas. Someone went so far as to kill Todd. Someone is after her—and Natalie doesn't even know it."

Benedict started rubbing his chin.

"They're looking for her," I said. "I can't just back away. Don't you see?"

He shook his head. "I don't see." His voice was so weary, so broken and exhausted. "I don't see how you can do anything but get her killed. Listen to me, Jake. I get your point, but we've circled the wagons. We've protected the group. Everyone has gone underground until this blows over."

"But Natalie is—"

"Is safe, as long as you leave it alone. If you don't—if we are all discovered—it could mean death not only to her but to Marie-Anne and me and many, many others. I get what you're saying, but you're not seeing straight. You don't want to accept the truth. You want her so badly that you're twisting the facts into a call for action. Don't you see that?"

I shook my head. "I don't. I really don't."

He glanced at his watch. "Look, I have to go to class. Let's talk about this later. Don't do anything until then, okay?"

I said nothing.

"Promise me, Jake."

I promised. This time, however, I kept the promise for closer to six minutes than six years.

Chapter 29

I hit the bank and took out four thousand dollars in cash. The window teller had to get permission from the head teller, who had to find the bank manager. I tried to remember the last time I had used a bank teller rather than the ATM, but I couldn't dredge up the memory.

I stopped at CVS and bought two disposable phones. Knowing that the cops could trace your phone anytime it was on, I powered down my iPhone and stuck it back in my pocket. If I needed to make calls, I'd use the disposables and keep them off as much as possible. If the cops could trace these phones, so, I figured, might a guy like Danny Zuker. I didn't know this for a fact, but my paranoia level was justifiably at an all-time high.

I might not be able to stay off the grid long, but if I could for a few days, that would be all I'd need.

First things first. Benedict said that no one involved with Fresh Start knew where Natalie was. I wasn't so sure. The organization had started at Lanford at the behest, in part anyway, of one Professor Malcolm Hume.

It was time to call my old mentor.

The last time I saw the man whose office I now inhabit was two years ago at a poly-sci seminar on Constitutional abuses. He flew up from Florida looking robust and tan. His teeth were shockingly white. Like many retired Floridians, he appeared rested and happy and very old. We had a nice time, but there was a distance between us now. Malcolm Hume could be like that. I loved the man. Aside from my own father, he was the closest thing I had to a role model. But he had made it clear that retirement was an ending. He had always detested the academic hangers-on, those elderly professors and administrators who stayed on well past their expiration date, like aging ballplayers who won't face the inevitable. Once he left our hallowed halls, Professor Hume didn't enjoy returning. He didn't buy into nostalgia or living off past laurels. Even at the age of eighty, Malcolm Hume was a forward-looking guy. The past was just that to him. The past.

So despite what I considered our rich history, we didn't speak regularly. This part of his life was over. Malcolm Hume now enjoyed golf and his mystery book club and his bridge group down in Florida. Fresh Start, too, might have been something he put behind him. I didn't know how he'd respond to my call—if it would agitate him or not. I didn't much care either.

I needed answers.

I dialed his phone number down in Vero Beach. After five rings his machine picked up. Malcolm's booming recorded voice, graveled a bit with age, invited me to leave a message. I was about to, but then I realized that I didn't really have a callback number, what with my phone off most of the time. I would try him again later.

Now what?

My brain started buzzing again, settling for the umpteenth time on Natalie's father. He was the key here. Who, I wondered, could possibly shine some light on what happened to him? The answer was fairly obvious: Natalie's mom.

I considered calling Julie Pottham and asking her if I could speak to her mother, but again that felt like a complete waste of time. I headed to the local library and signed in to use the Internet. I searched for Sylvia Avery. The address listed was Julie Pottham's in Ramsey, New Jersey. I leaned back for a second and considered that. I brought up the Yellow Pages website and asked for all assisted-living facilities in the Ramsey area. Three came up. I called them and asked to speak to Sylvia Avery. All three said that they had no "resident" (they all used that term) with that name. I headed back to the computer and spread out the search to Bergen County, New Jersey. Too many came up. I brought up the map and started calling the ones closest to Ramsey. On the sixth call, the operator at Hyde Park Assisted Living said, "Sylvia? I believe she's doing crafts with Louise. Would you like to leave a message?"

Crafts with Louise. Like she was a child at summer camp. "No, I'll call back, thanks. Do you have visiting hours?"

"We prefer that guests come between eight A.M. and eight P.M."

"Thank you."

I hung up. I checked the Hyde Park Assisted Living website.

They had a daily schedule online. Crafts with Louise was listed. According to the itinerary, Scrabble Club was next, followed by Armchair Travel Social—I had no idea what that meant—and then Baking Memories. Tomorrow, there would be a three-hour outing to the Paramus Park Mall, but today, nope, everything was in house. Good.

I headed over to the rent-a-car dealership and asked for a mid-size. I got a Ford Fusion. I had to use a credit card, but that couldn't be helped. Time for another road trip—this time to visit Natalie's mother. I wasn't too worried about her not being there when I arrived. Residents in assisted living rarely take unscheduled trips. If by some chance she did, it would be brief. I could wait. I had nowhere else to go anyway. Who knows? Maybe another delightful evening with Mabel at the Fair Motel was in the cards.

When I had just hit Route 95, my mind immediately went to my ride on this very road just . . . wow, it'd been yesterday. I thought about that. I pulled over and took out my iPhone. I turned it on. There were e-mails and phone calls. I noticed three from Shanta. I ignored them. I brought up the web and did a quick Google search for Danny Zuker. There was a famous one working in Hollywood who dominated the hits. I tried putting in the name and the word *mobster*. Nothing. I brought up the forum for gangster enthusiasts. There was nothing on Danny Zuker.

Now what?

I could be spelling the name wrong. I tried Zucker and Zooker and Zoocker. Nothing significant. The exit toward Flushing was nearby. It would be a detour but not a horrible one. I decided to take a chance. I pulled off and found Francis Lewis Boulevard. The Global Garden mega-nursery and garden shop, the place where I had smacked Edward around, was open. I thought about those punches. I had always prided myself on being a rule follower, and I had self-justified my violence of yesterday by claiming that I was rescuing that kid, but the truth was, I didn't have to punch Edward in the nose. I needed information. I broke laws to get it. One could easily rationalize what I had done. The case for obtaining that information while giving Edward a touch of comeuppance was certainly compelling.

But more to the point—and this was something I would need to explore when I had the time—I wondered whether part of me enjoyed it. Did I really need to punch Edward to get the information? Not really. There were other ways. And awful as it was to even let the thought enter my head, hadn't a small part of me taken some pleasure in Otto's death? In my classes, I often talk about the importance of primitive instincts in philosophy and political theory. Did I think I was immune? Maybe the rules that I cherish aren't there to protect others so much as they're there to protect us from ourselves.

In his class on Early Political Thought, Malcolm Hume loved to explore the fine lines. I had balked at such talk. There is right. There is wrong.

So which side of the line was I on now?

I parked near the front, passed a big sale on "Perennials and Pottery," and headed inside. The store was huge. The pungent odor of mulch filled the air. I started toward the left, circled through fresh flowers, shrubbery, home accessories, patio furniture, soil, peat moss—whatever that was. My eyes checked out everyone with the bright green worker's apron. It took about five minutes, but I found the kid, interestingly enough, working in the fertilizer section.

There was a bandage on his nose. His eyes were black. He still wore the Brooklyn Nets baseball cap with the brim facing back. He was helping a customer, loading bags of fertilizer into a cart. The customer was telling him something. The kid nodded with enthusiasm. He had an earring. The hair that peeked out from under the cap looked streaky blond, probably something out of a bottle. The kid worked hard, smiling the entire time, making sure all the customer's needs were being met. I was impressed.

I moved so that I was standing behind him and waited. I tried to figure out an angle of approach so that the kid couldn't make a run for it. When he finished with this current customer, he immediately started looking for someone else to help. I moved up behind him and tapped him on the shoulder.

He turned, the smile at the ready. "Can I . . . ?"

He stopped when he saw my face. I was ready for him to break into a sprint. I wasn't sure what I'd do about it. I was close enough to grab him if he tried, but that would draw the wrong kind of attention. I braced myself and waited for his reaction.

"Dude!" He threw his arms around me, pulling me in tight for a hug. I had not expected that, but I went with it. "Thank you, man. Thank you so much."

"Um, you're welcome."

"Oh man, you're my hero, you know that? Edward is such a dickweed. Picks on me because he knows I ain't that tough. Thanks, man. Thanks a lot."

I said he was welcome again.

"So what's your deal?" he asked. "You ain't a cop. I know that. So are you, like, I don't know, a superhero or something?"

"Superhero?"

"I mean, you hang out and rescue people and stuff. And then you ask about his MM contact?" His face suddenly darkened. "Man, I hope you got a whole Avengers group behind you or something if you're gonna take him on."

"That's what I wanted to ask you," I said.

"Oh?"

"Edward works for a guy named Danny Zuker, right?"

"You know it."

"Who is Danny Zuker?"

"Sickest dude ever. He'd kill a puppy because it got in his way. You can't believe the psycho-crazy in that guy. He makes Edward pee in his pants. For real."

Terrific. "Who does Danny work for?"

The kid took half a step back. "You don't know?"

"No. That's why I'm here."

"For real?"

"Yes?"

"I was joking, dude—about you being a superhero. I figured, hey, you saw me getting the crap beaten out of me and, I don't know, you're a big dude and you hate bullies and stuff. That wasn't it?"

"No. I need some information."

"I hope one of your superpowers is that you're bulletproof. If you mess with those guys . . ."

"I'll be careful," I said.

"I don't want you to get hurt or nothing, just because you did me a solid, you know?"

"I know," I said, trying my best competent professorial tone. "Just tell me what you know."

The kid shrugged. "Eddie is my bookie. That's all. I'm behind, and he enjoys hurting people. But he's small-time. Like I said, he works for Danny Z. Danny's way high up in MM."

"What's MM?"

"I'd bend my nose with my finger to show you what I mean, but my nose is friggin' killing me."

I nodded. "So Danny Z is with the Mafia? Is that what you're trying to say?"

"I don't know if they call it that. I mean, I only heard that word in really old movies and whatever. I can only tell you Danny Z works directly for the head of MM. That guy is a legend."

"What's his name?"

"You for real? You don't know? How do you live here and not know?"

"I don't live here."

"Oh."

"Are you going to tell me?"

"I owe you. So sure. Like I said, Danny Z is like the right-hand man for MM."

"And MM is?"

An elderly woman stepped between us. "Hello, Harold."

He gave her a big smile. "Hello, Mrs. H. How did those petunias work out for you?"

"You were so right about the placement in the window box. You're a genius with arrangements."

"Thank you."

"If you have time . . ."

"Let me just finish with this gentleman and I'll be right with you."

Mrs. H shuffled away. Harold watched her, smiling all the way.

"Harold," I said, trying to get him back on topic, "who is MM?"

"Come on, man, don't you read the papers? MM. Danny Z reports directly to the biggest, baddest boy of them all—Maxwell Minor."

Something clicked. My face must have shown it because Harold said, "Whoa, dude, you okay?"

My pulse raced. My blood started humming in my ears. I could have looked it up on my iPhone, but I really needed a full screen. "I need to use a computer."

"Owner doesn't let anyone use the Internet here. It's all blocked off."

I thanked him and hurried out. Minor. I had heard that name before in connection to all this. I drove like a madman to Northern Boulevard. I found the same Cybercraft Internet Café. The same yah-dude was behind the desk. If he recognized me, he didn't show it. There were four terminals open. I grabbed one and quickly typed in the address for the New York local newspapers. Clicking on archives, I asked for May 25 again—the day after the surveillance photograph of Natalie had been taken. The computer seemed to be taking forever to grant my search request.

Come on, come on . . .

And then the headline popped up:

PHILANTHROPIST GUNNED DOWN

Archer Minor Executed in His Office

I wanted to shout "Eureka!" out loud, but I controlled myself. Minor. Oh, that couldn't be a coincidence. I clicked the article and read:

Archer Minor, son of reputed mob leader Maxwell Minor and victim's rights advocate, was executed in his high-rise law office on Park Avenue last night, apparently the victim of a hit authorized by his own father. Known as the Minor son who's gone straight, Archer Minor worked with crime victims, even going so far as to publicly denounce his father in recent weeks and promising the DA's office to provide proof of his familial wrongdoings.

The article didn't have too many other details. I went back to the search engine and looked up Archer Minor. There was at least an article a day for the next week. I started sifting through them, looking for some kind of clue, some kind of connection between Archer Minor and Natalie. An article that came out two days after the shooting snagged my attention:

NYPD SEARCHING FOR WITNESS IN MINOR SLAY

A source inside the NYPD claims that the department is currently looking for a woman who may have witnessed the murder of local gangster's-kid-turned-hero Archer Minor. The NYPD would not comment directly. "We are actively seeking out many leads," Anda Olsen, department spokesperson, said. "We expect to have a suspect in custody soon."

It fit. Or it sort of fit.

I conjured up that surveillance photo of Natalie in what looked

like the lobby of an office building. Okay, so now what? Put it together. Somehow, Natalie had been there that night, in Minor's law
office. She saw the murder. That would explain the fear on her face.
She ran off, hoping it would go away, but then the NYPD must
have gone through the surveillance video and found her walking
through the lobby.

There was still something big here, something I was missing. I
kept reading:

> When asked for a motive for the crime, Olsen said, "We
> believe that Archer Minor was killed because he wanted
> to do the right thing." Today, Mayor Bloomberg called Ar-
> cher Minor a hero. "He overcame his family name and
> history to be one of the great New Yorkers. His tireless
> work on behalf of victims and in bringing those who com-
> mit violent crimes to justice will never be forgotten."
>
> Many are wondering why Archer Minor, who had re-
> cently denounced his father, Maxwell Minor, and his re-
> puted organized-crime syndicate known as MM, was not
> placed in protective custody. "It was at his request," Olsen
> said. A source close to Minor's widow said that her hus-
> band had worked his whole life to make up for his father's
> crimes. "Archer started out just wanting to get a good ed-
> ucation and go straight," the source said, "but no matter
> how fast he ran, Archer could never do enough to escape
> that horrible shadow."
>
> It was not for a lack of trying. Archer Minor was a
> vocal advocate for crime-victims' rights. After attending
> Columbia Law School, he worked closely with law en-

forcement officials. He represented victims of violent crimes, trying to get lengthier sentences for those convicted and restitution for his clients' suffering.

The NYPD would not speculate, but one popular albeit shocking theory of the crime is that Maxwell Minor put out a hit on his own son. Maxwell Minor has not directly denied the charge, but he did release the following brief statement: "My family and I are devastated by the death of my son Archer. I ask the media to allow my family to mourn in private."

I licked my lips and hit the "next page" link. When I saw the photograph of Maxwell Minor, I wasn't the least bit surprised. It was the man with the thin mustache from Otto Devereaux's funeral.

It was coming together now.

I realized that I'd been holding my breath. I sat back and tried to relax for a moment. I put my hands behind my head and closed my eyes. My mental timeline/connection sheet had all kinds of new little lines on it. Natalie had been there the night of Archer Minor's high-profile murder. She had, I theorized, witnessed the crime. At some point, the NYPD realized it was Natalie in that surveillance video. Natalie, fearing for her life, decided to hide.

I would continue to check, but it was a pretty safe bet that no one had ever been convicted of Archer Minor's murder. That was why the NYPD, all these years later, was still looking for Natalie.

So what happened next?

Natalie hooked up with Fresh Start. How did that happen? I had no idea. But, really, how did anyone hook up with Fresh Start?

The organization kept an eye out, I supposed. Like with Benedict né Jamal. They approached those they felt needed and deserved their help.

Anyway, Natalie was sent up to the Creative Recharge Colony, which was, at least in part, a front for the organization. A brilliant one, I might add. Perhaps some of the attendees were really there for artistic reasons. Certainly Natalie was able to do both. Talk about hiding in plain sight. Natalie was probably told to hide there until they saw how the Archer Minor case played out. Maybe the cops would be able to make an arrest without her, and then she could return to her normal life. Maybe the NYPD wouldn't, or at least hadn't yet been able to, identify the woman in the photograph. Whatever. I was guessing here, but I was probably close.

At some point, reality reared its ugly head, crashing in and killing any hope of staying put with her new boyfriend. The choice became clear: Vanish or die.

So she vanished.

I read a few more articles on the case, but there wasn't much new. Archer Minor was portrayed as something of a heroic enigma. He'd been raised to be the baddest of bad guys. His older brother had been executed "gangland style" as the papers called it, while Archer was still in college. Archer was then supposed to take over the family business. It almost reminded me of *The Godfather* movie, except this particular good son never caved. Archer Minor not only flat-out refused to join MM, he worked tirelessly to take it down.

Again I wondered what would have led my sweet Natalie to be in that law office late at night. She could have been a client, I supposed, but that wouldn't explain being there so late. She may have known Archer Minor, but I had no clue how. I was just about to

give up on that, chalk up her visit to random chance, when I read a
small, colorless obituary.

What the . . . ?

I actually had to close my eyes, rub them, and then read the
obituary from the top again. Because this couldn't be. Just when
things had been starting to make sense—just when I thought I was
making some progress—I once again got smacked down from my
blind side:

> Archer Minor, age 41, of Manhattan, formerly of Flush-
> ing, Queens, New York. Mr. Minor was a senior partner
> at the law firm of Pashaian, Dressner and Rosenburgh,
> located in the Lock-Horne Building at 245 Park Avenue in
> New York City. Archer received many awards and cita-
> tions for his charitable work. He attended Saint Francis
> Prep and was graduated summa cum laude from Lanford
> College . . .

Chapter 30

Through the phone line, I heard Mrs. Dinsmore sigh. "Aren't you supposed to be on suspension?"

"You miss me. Admit it."

Even in the midst of this ever-growing combination of horror and confusion, Mrs. Dinsmore made me feel grounded. There were few constants. Messing around with Mrs. Dinsmore was one of them. It was comforting to hold on to my own version of ritual while the rest of the world spun madly on.

"Suspension probably includes calling college support staff," Mrs. Dinsmore said.

"Even if it's just for phone sex?"

I could feel her disapproving glare from 160 miles away. "What do you want, funny man?"

"I need a huge favor," I said.

"And in return?"

"Didn't you hear what I said about phone sex?"

"Jake?"

I don't think she had ever called me by my first name.

"Yes?"

Her voice was suddenly tender. "What's wrong? Getting suspended is not like you. You're a role model here."

"It's a really long story."

"You were asking me about Professor Kleiner's daughter. The one you're in love with."

"Yes."

"Are you still looking for her?"

"Yes."

"Does your suspension have something to do with that?"

"It does."

Silence. Then Mrs. Dinsmore cleared her throat.

"What do you need, Professor Fisher?"

"A student file."

"Again?"

"Yes."

"You need the student's permission," Mrs. Dinsmore said. "I told you that last time."

"And like last time, the student is dead."

"Oh," she said. "What's his name?"

"Archer Minor."

There was a pause.

"Did you know him?" I asked.

"As a student, no."

"But?"

"But I remember reading in the *Lanford News* that he was murdered a few years ago."

"Six years ago," I said.

I started up the car, keeping the phone to my ear.

"Let me see if I understand this," Mrs. Dinsmore said. "You're looking for Natalie Avery, correct?"

"Correct."

"And in searching for her, you've needed to look at the personal files of not one but two murdered students."

Strangely enough, I hadn't thought of it that way. "I guess that's true," I said.

"If I may be bold, this isn't sounding like much of a love story."

I said nothing. A few seconds passed.

"I'll call you back," Mrs. Dinsmore said before hanging up.

The Hyde Park Assisted Living facility resembled a Marriott Courtyard.

A nice one, grant you, upscale with one of those Victorian gazebos in front, but everything screamed chain, impersonal, prefab. The main building was three stories with faux turrets on the corners. An oversize sign read ASSISTED LIVING ENTRANCE. I followed the path, walked up a wheelchair ramp, and opened the door.

The woman at the desk had a helmety beehive hairdo last seen on a senator's wife circa 1964. She hit me with a smile so wooden I could have knocked on it for luck.

"May I help you?"

I smiled and spread my arms. I had read somewhere that spreading your arms makes you appear more open and trusting while folded arms make you seem the opposite. I didn't know if that was true. It felt as though I might swoop someone up and carry him away. "I'm here to see Sylvia Avery," I said.

"Would she be expecting you?" Beehive asked.

"No, I don't think so. I just happened to be in the neighborhood."

She looked doubtful. I couldn't blame her. I doubt too many people just happen to drop in on assisted-living facilities. "Do you mind signing in?"

"Not at all."

She spun an oversize guestbook, the kind I usually associate with weddings, funerals, and hotels in old movies, toward me and handed me a large quill pen. I signed my name. The woman spun the guestbook back toward her.

"Mr. Fisher," she said, reading the name very slowly. She looked up at me and blinked. "May I ask how you know Miss Avery?"

"Through her daughter Natalie. I thought it'd be nice to visit."

"I'm sure Sylvia will appreciate that." Beehive gestured to her left. "Our living room is available and inviting. Would it be okay if you met there?"

Inviting? "Sure," I said.

Beehive stood. "I'll be right back. Make yourself comfortable."

I moved into the available, inviting living room. I realized what was up. Beehive wanted the meeting in a public place just in case I wasn't on the up-and-up. Made sense. Better safe than sorry and all that. The couches looked nice enough, what with their floral prints, and yet they didn't look like something that could make one comfortable. Nothing here did. The décor resembled that of a model home perfectly laid out to accentuate the positives, but the smell of antiseptic, industrial-strength cleaner, and—yes, dare I say it—the elderly was unmistakable. I stayed standing. There was an old woman with a walker and tattered bathrobe standing in the corner. She was talking to a wall, gesturing wildly.

My new disposable number started buzzing. I looked at the caller ID, but I had only given this number to one person: Mrs. Dinsmore. There was a sign about no cell phone use, but as I've now learned, I sometimes live on the edge. I moved into a corner, turned my face to the wall, à la the old woman with the walker, and whispered, "Hello?"

"I have Archer Minor's file," Mrs. Dinsmore said. "Do you want me to e-mail it to you?"

"That would be great. Do you have it right there?"

"Yes."

"Is there anything strange about it?"

"I didn't look at it yet. Strange how?"

"Would you mind taking a quick peek?"

"What am I looking for?"

I thought about that. "How about a connection between the two murder victims. Were they in the same dorm? Did they take any of the same classes?"

"That one is easy. No. Archer Minor was graduated before Todd Sanderson even matriculated here. Anything else?"

As I did the math in my head, a cold hand reached into my chest.

Mrs. Dinsmore said, "Are you still there?"

I swallowed. "Was Archer Minor on campus when Professor Kleiner ran off?"

There was a brief pause. Then Mrs. Dinsmore said in a faraway voice: "I think he would have been a freshman or sophomore."

"Could you check to see if—?"

"One step ahead of you." I could hear file pages being flipped. I glanced behind me. From across the room the old woman with the walker and tattered bathrobe winked at me suggestively. I winked back with equal suggestion. Why not?

Then Mrs. Dinsmore said, "Jake?"

Again she used my first name.

"Yes?"

"Archer Minor was enrolled in Professor Kleiner's class called Citizenship and Pluralism. According to this, he received an A."

Beehive returned, pushing Natalie's mother in a wheelchair. I recognized Sylvia Avery from the wedding six years ago. The years hadn't been so kind to her up until then and judging by what I was seeing now, that hadn't gotten any better.

With the phone still to my ear, I asked Mrs. Dinsmore, "When?"

"When what?"

"When did Archer Minor take that class?"

"Let me see." Then I heard Mrs. Dinsmore's small gasp, but I already knew the answer. "It was the semester Professor Kleiner resigned."

I nodded to myself. Ergo the A. Everyone got them that semester.

My mind was whirling a thousand ways to Sunday. Still reeling, I thanked Mrs. Dinsmore and hung up as Beehive rolled Sylvia Avery right to me. I had hoped that we would be alone, but Beehive waited. I cleared my throat.

"Miss Avery, you may not remember me—"

"Natalie's wedding," she said without hesitation. "You were the mopey guy she dumped."

I looked toward Beehive. Beehive put her hand on Sylvia Avery's shoulder. "Are you okay, Sylvia?"

"Of course I'm okay," she snapped. "Go away and leave us alone."

The wooden smile did not so much as flicker, but then again wood never does. Beehive moved back to the desk. She gave us one more look as though to say, *I may not be sitting right with you but I'll be watching.*

"You're too tall," Sylvia Avery said to me.

"Sorry."

"Don't be sorry. Just sit the hell down so I don't strain my neck."

"Oh," I said. "Sorry."

"Again with the sorry. Sit, sit."

I sat on the couch. She studied me for a bit. "What do you want?"

Sylvia Avery looked small and wizened in that wheelchair, but then again who looks big and hardy in them? I answered her with a question of my own.

"Have you heard from Natalie at all?"

She gave me the suspicious stink eye. "Who wants to know?"

"Uh, me."

"I get cards now and then. Why?"

"But you haven't seen her?"

"Nope. That's okay though. She's a free spirit, you know. When you set a free spirit free, it flies off. That's what it's supposed to do."

"Do you know where this free spirit landed?"

"Not that it's any of your business, but she lives overseas. Happy as can be with Todd. I'm looking forward to those two having kids one day." Her eyes narrowed a bit. "What's your name again?"

"Jake Fisher."

"You married, Jake?"

"No."

"Ever been married?"

"No."

"You got a serious girlfriend?"

I didn't bother answering.

"Shame." Sylvia Avery shook her head. "Big, strong man like you. You should be married. You should be making a girl feel safe. You shouldn't be alone."

I didn't like where this conversational route was taking us. It was time to change it up.

"Miss Avery?"

"Yes?"

"Do you know what I do for a living?"

She looked me up and down. "You look like a linebacker."

"I'm a college professor," I said.

"Oh."

I turned my body so that I could get a clearer look at her reaction to what I was about to say. "I teach political science at Lanford College."

Whatever color had remained in her cheeks drained away.

"Mrs. Kleiner?"

"That's not my name."

"It was though, wasn't it? You changed it back after your husband left Lanford."

She closed her eyes. "Who told you about that?"

"It's a long story."

"Did Natalie say something?"

"No," I said. "Never. Not even when I brought her to campus."

"Good." Her quivering hand came up to her mouth. "My God, how can you know about this?"

"I need to speak to your ex-husband."

"What?" Her eyes widened in fright. "Oh no, this can't be . . ."

"What can't be?"

She sat there, hand on mouth, saying nothing.

"Please, Miss Avery. It is very important I talk to him."

Sylvia Avery squeezed her eyes shut tight like a little kid wishing away a monster. I glanced over her shoulder. Beehive was watching us with open curiosity. I forced up a smile as fake as hers to show that all was okay.

Sylvia Avery's voice was a whisper. "Why are you bringing this up now?"

"I need to speak to him."

"It was such a long, long time ago. Do you know what I had to do to move past that? Do you know how painful this is?"

"I don't want to hurt anyone."

"No? Then stop. Why on earth would you need to find that man? Do you know what his running off did to Natalie?"

I waited, hoping that she'd say more. She did.

"You need to understand. Julie, well, she was young. She barely remembered her father. But Natalie? She never got over it. She never let him go."

Her hand fluttered back toward her face. She looked off. I waited some more, but it was clear that Sylvia Avery had stopped talking for the moment.

I tried to stay firm. "Where is Professor Kleiner now?"

"California," she said.

"Where in California?"

"I don't know."

"Los Angeles area? San Francisco? San Diego? It's a big state."

"I said, I don't know. We don't speak."

"So how do you know he's in California?"

That made her pause. I saw something skitter across her face. "I don't," she said. "He may have moved."

A lie.

"You told your daughters he remarried."

"That's right."

"How did you know?"

"Aaron called and told me."

"I thought you didn't speak."

"Not in a very long time."

"What's his wife's name?"

She shook her head. "I don't know. And I would not tell you if I did."

"Why not? Your daughters, okay, I get that. You were protecting them. But why wouldn't you tell me?"

Her eyes shifted from left to right. I decided to bluff.

"I checked the marital records," I said. "You two were never divorced."

Sylvia Avery let out a small groan. There was no way Beehive could have heard it, but her ears still perked up like a dog's hearing a sound no one else could. I gave Beehive the same "all's fine" smile.

"How did your husband remarry if you two were never divorced?"

"You'll have to ask him."

"What happened, Miss Avery?"

She shook her head. "Let it be."

"He didn't run away with a coed, did he?"

"Yes, he did," she said. Now it was her turn to try to sound firm. But it wasn't there. It was too defensive, too practiced. "Yes, Aaron ran off and left me."

"Lanford College is a small campus, you know that, right?"

"Of course I know it. I lived there for seven years. So what?"

"A female student quitting to run off with a professor would have made news. Her parents would have called. There would have been staff meetings. Something. I checked the records. No one dropped out when your husband vanished. No female student dropped her classes. No female student was unaccounted for."

This again was a bluff but a good one. Campuses as small as Lanford do not keep secrets well. If a student ran off with a professor, everyone, especially Mrs. Dinsmore, would know her name.

"Maybe she was at Strickland. That state college down the street. I think she went there."

"That's not what happened," I said.

"Please," Miss Avery said. "What are you trying to do?"

"Your husband vanished. And now, twenty-five years later, so has your daughter."

That got her attention. "What?" She shook her head too firmly, reminding me of a stubborn child. "I told you. Natalie lives overseas."

"No, Miss Avery. She doesn't. She never married Todd. That was a ruse. Todd was already married. Someone murdered him a little more than a week ago."

It was one bombshell too many. Sylvia Avery's head lolled first to the side and then down as though her neck had turned to rubber. Behind her, I saw Beehive pick up the phone. She kept her eye on me and started talking to someone. The wooden smile was gone.

"Natalie was such a happy girl." Her head was still down, her chin on her chest. "You can't imagine. Or maybe you can. You loved her. You got to see the real her, but that was much later. After so much changed back."

"Changed back from what?"

"See, when Natalie was little, my God, that girl lived for her father. He'd come through the door after class, and she'd run to him screaming with joy." Sylvia Avery finally lifted her head. There was a distant smile on her face, her eyes seeing the long-ago memory. "Aaron would pick her up and twirl her and she'd laugh so hard . . ."

She shook her head. "We were all so damn happy."

"What happened, Miss Avery?"

"He ran off."

"Why?"

She shook her head. "It doesn't matter."

"Of course it does."

"Poor Natalie. She couldn't let it go and now . . ."

"Now what?"

"You don't understand. You can never understand."

"Then make me understand."

"Why? Who the hell are you?"

"I'm the man who loves her," I said. "I'm the man she loves."

She didn't know how to react to that. Her eyes were still on the floor, almost as though she didn't have the strength to lift even her gaze. "When her father ran off, Natalie changed. She grew so sullen. I lost that little girl. It was like Aaron took her happiness with him. She couldn't accept it. Why would her father abandon her? What did she do wrong? Why didn't he love her anymore?"

I pictured this, my Natalie as a child, feeling lost and abandoned by her own father. I could feel the pain in my chest.

"She had trust issues for so long. You have no idea. She pushed everyone away and yet she never gave up hope." She looked up at me. "Do you know anything about hope, Jake?"

"I think I do," I said.

"It's the cruelest thing in the world. Death is better. When you're dead, the pain stops. But hope keeps raising you way up high, only to drop you to the hard ground. Hope cradles your heart in its hand and then it crushes it with a fist. Over and over. It never stops. That's what hope does."

She put her hands on her lap and looked at me hard. "So, you see, I tried to take that hope away."

I nodded. "You tried to make Natalie forget about her father," I said.

"Yes."

"By saying he ran off and abandoned all of you?"

Her eyes began to well up. "I thought that was best. Do you see? I thought that would make Natalie forget him."

"You told Natalie that her father got remarried," I said. "You told her that he had other children. But all that was a lie, wasn't it?"

Sylvia Avery wouldn't answer. The expression on her face hardened.

"Miss Avery?"

She looked up at me. "Leave me alone."

"I need to know—"

"I don't care what you need to know. I want you to leave me alone."

She started to wheel back. I grabbed hold of her chair. The chair came to a sudden halt. The blanket on her lap fell toward the floor. When I looked down, my hand released the chair without any command from her. Half of her right leg had been amputated. She pulled the blanket up, slower than she had to. She wanted me to see.

"Diabetes," she said to me. "I lost it three years ago."

"I'm sorry."

"Believe me, it was nothing." I reached out again, but she knocked my hand away. "Good-bye, Jake. Leave my family alone." She started to wheel back. No choice now. I had to go nuclear.

"Do you remember a student named Archer Minor?"

Her chair stopped. Her mouth went slack.

"Archer Minor was enrolled in your husband's class at Lanford," I said. "Do you remember him?"

"How . . . ?" Her lips moved but no words came out for a few moments. Then: "Please." If her voice had sounded merely frightened before, she was downright terrified now. "Please leave this alone."

"Archer Minor is dead, you know. He was murdered."

"Good riddance," she said, and then she shut her mouth tightly, as though she regretted the words the moment they came out.

"Please tell me what happened."

"Let it go."

"I can't."

"I don't understand what this has to do with you. It isn't your business." She shook her head. "It makes sense."

"What does?"

"That Natalie would fall for you."

"How's that?"

"You're a dreamer, like her father. He couldn't let things go either. Some people can't. I'm an old woman. Listen to me. The world is messy, Jake. Some people want it to be black-and-white. Those people always pay a price. My husband was one of them. He couldn't let it go. And you, Jake, are heading down that same path."

I heard distant echoes in her past, from Malcolm Hume and Eban Trainor, from Benedict too. I thought about my own recent thoughts, about what it had felt like to punch and even kill a man.

"What happened with Archer Minor?" I asked.

"You won't quit. You'll keep digging until everyone dies."

"It will stay between you and me," I said. "It won't leave this room. Just tell me."

"And if I say no?"

"I'll keep digging. What happened with Archer Minor?"

She looked off again, fingers plucking at her lip as though in deep thought. I sat up a little straighter, trying to meet her eye.

"You know how they say the apple doesn't fall far from the tree?"

"Yes," I said.

"That kid tried. Archer Minor wanted to be the apple that fell and rolled away. He wanted to be good. He wanted to escape what he was. Aaron understood that. He tried to help him."

She took her time adjusting the blanket in her lap.

"So what happened?" I asked.

"Archer was in over his head at Lanford. In high school his father could pressure the teachers. They gave him A's. I don't know if he really earned that high SAT score on his résumé. I don't know how he got past admissions, but academically, that boy was in over his head."

She stopped again.

"Please go on."

"There's no reason," she said.

Then I remembered something Mrs. Dinsmore had said when I first asked her about Professor Aaron Kleiner.

"There was a cheating scandal, wasn't there?"

Her body language told me that I'd hit pay dirt.

"Did it involve Archer Minor?" I asked.

She didn't reply. She didn't have to.

"Miss Avery?"

"He bought a term paper from a student who'd graduated the year before. The other student had gotten an A on it. Archer just retyped it and handed it in as his own. Didn't change one single word. He figured there'd be no way Aaron would remember. But Aaron remembers everything."

I knew the school rules. That sort of cheating was an automatic expulsion at Lanford.

"Did your husband report him?"

"I told him not to. I told him to give Archer a second chance. I didn't care about the second chance, of course. I just knew."

"You knew his family would be upset."

"Aaron reported it anyway."

"To whom?"

"The chairman of the department."

My heart sank. "Malcolm Hume?"

"Yes."

I sat back. "What did Malcolm say?"

"He wanted Aaron to drop it. He said to go home and think about it."

I thought back to my case with Eban Trainor. He had said something similar to me, hadn't he? Malcolm Hume. You do not get to be secretary of state without compromise, without cutting deals and negotiating terms and understanding that the world was loaded up with gray.

"I'm very tired, Jake."

"I don't understand something."

"Let it go."

"Archer Minor was never reported. He graduated summa cum laude."

"We started getting threatening phone calls. A man visited me. He came into the house when I was in the shower. When I came out, he was just sitting on my bed. He was holding pictures of Natalie and Julie. He didn't say anything. He just sat on my bed and held the pictures. Then he got up and left. Can you imagine what that was like?"

I thought about Danny Zuker breaking in and sitting on my own bed. "You told your husband?"

"Of course."

"And?"

She took her time on this one. "I think he finally understood the danger. But it was too late."

"What did he do?"

"Aaron left. For our sake."

I nodded, seeing it now. "But you couldn't tell Natalie that. You couldn't tell anyone. They'd be in danger. So you told them he ran off. Then you moved away and changed your name."

"Yes," she said.

But I was missing something. I was missing a lot, I suspected. There was something that wasn't adding up here, something niggling at the back of my brain, but I couldn't see it yet. How, for example, did Natalie come across Archer Minor twenty years later?

"Natalie thought her father abandoned her," I said.

She just closed her eyes.

"But you said that she wouldn't let it go."

"She wouldn't stop pressing me. She was so sad. I should have never told her that. But what choice did I have? Everything I did, I did to protect my girls. You don't understand. You don't understand what a mother has to do sometimes. I needed to protect my girls, you see?"

"I do," I said.

"And look what happened. Look what I did." She put her hands to her face and started to sob. The old woman with the walker and tattered bathrobe stopped talking to the wall. Beehive looked like she was readying herself to intervene. "I should have made up some other story. Natalie just kept pressing me, demanding to know what happened to her father. She never stopped."

I saw it now. "So you eventually told her the truth."

"It ruined her life, don't you see? Growing up thinking your father did that to you. She needed closure. I never gave her that. So, yes, I finally told her the truth. I told her that her father loved her. I told her that she didn't do anything wrong. I told her that he would never, ever, abandon her."

I nodded along with her words. "So you told her about Archer Minor. That was why she was there that day."

She didn't say anything. She just sobbed. Beehive was having no more of this. She was on her way over.

"Where is your husband now, Miss Avery?"

"I don't know."

"And Natalie? Where is she?"

"I don't know that either. But, Jake?"

Beehive was by her side. "I think that's enough."

I ignored her. "What, Miss Avery?"

"Let it go. For all our sakes. Don't be like my husband."

Chapter 31

When I reached the highway, I flipped on my iPhone. I didn't think anyone was tracking me but if they were, they'd find me on Route 287 near the Palisades Mall. I didn't think that would help them very much. I pulled over to the right. There were two more e-mails and three calls from Shanta, each more urgent than the last. That added up to five. In the first two e-mails, she politely asked me to contact her. In the next two, her request was more urgent. In the final, she threw out the big net:

To: Jacob Fisher
From: Shanta Newlin

Jake,

Stop ignoring me. I found an important connection between Natalie Avery and Todd Sanderson.

Shanta

Whoa. I took the Tappan Zee Bridge and pulled over at the first
exit. I turned off the iPhone and picked up one of the disposables. I
dialed Shanta's number and waited. She answered on the second
ring.

"I get it," she said. "You're mad at me."

"You gave the NYPD that disposable number. You helped them
track me down."

"Guilty, but it was for your own good. You could have gotten
shot or picked up for resisting arrest."

"Except I didn't resist arrest. I ran away from some nut jobs
who were trying to kill me."

"I know Mulholland. He's a good guy. I didn't want some hot-
head taking a shot at you."

"For what? I was barely a suspect."

"It doesn't matter, Jake. You don't have to trust me. That's fine.
But we need to talk."

I put the car in park and turned off the engine. "You said you
found a connection between Natalie Avery and Todd Sanderson."

"Yep."

"What is it?"

"I'll tell you when we talk. In person."

I thought about that.

"Look, Jake, the FBI wanted to bring you in for a full-fledged interrogation. I told them I could better handle it for them."

"The FBI?"

"Yep."

"What do they want with me?"

"Just come in, Jake. It's fine, trust me."

"Right."

"You can talk to me or the FBI." Shanta sighed. "Look, if I tell you what it's about, do you promise you'll come in and talk to me?"

I thought about it. "Yes."

"Promise?"

"Cross my heart. Now what's this about?"

"It's about bank robberies, Jake."

The new rule-breaking, live-on-the-edge me broke plenty of speed laws on the way back to Lanford, Massachusetts. I tried sorting out some of what I learned, putting it in order, testing out various theories and suppositions, rejecting them, trying again. In some ways, it was all coming together; in others, there were pieces that felt too forced for a natural fit.

I was still missing a lot, including the biggie: Where was Natalie?

Twenty-five years ago, Professor Aaron Kleiner had gone to his department chairman, Professor Malcolm Hume, because he caught a student plagiarizing (really, just outright buying) a term paper. My old mentor asked him, in so many words, to let it go—just as he had asked me to do with Professor Eban Trainor.

I wondered whether it was Archer Minor himself who threatened Aaron Kleiner's family or had it been hired hands of MM? It didn't matter. They intimidated Kleiner to the point where he knew that he had to make himself disappear. I tried to put myself in his place. Kleiner probably felt scared, cornered, trapped.

Who would he go to for help?

First thought again: Malcolm Hume.

And years later, when Kleiner's daughter was in the same situation, scared, cornered, trapped . . .

My old mentor's fingerprints were all over this. I really had to talk to him. I dialed Malcolm's number in Florida and again got no answer.

Shanta Newlin lived in a brick town house that my mother would have described as "cutesy." There were overflowing flower boxes and arched windows. Everything was perfectly symmetrical. I walked up the stone walk and rang the doorbell. I was surprised to see a little girl come to the door.

"Who are you?" the little girl said.

"I'm Jake. Who are you?"

The kid was five, maybe six years old. She was about to answer when Shanta came rushing over with a harried look on her face. Shanta had her hair tied back, but strands were falling in her eyes. Sweat dotted her brow.

"I have it, Mackenzie," Shanta told the little girl. "What did I tell you about answering the door without an adult around?"

"Nothing."

"Well, yes, I guess that's true." She cleared her throat. "You should never open a door unless an adult is around."

She pointed at me. "He's around. He's an adult."

Shanta gave me an exasperated look. I shrugged. The kid had a point. Shanta invited me in and told Mackenzie to play in the den.

"Can I go outside?" Mackenzie asked. "I want to go on the swing."

Shanta glanced at me. I shrugged again. I was getting good with the shrugs. "Sure, we can all go out back," Shanta said with a smile so forced I worried it required staples.

I still had no idea who Mackenzie was or what she was doing there, but I had bigger concerns. We headed into the yard. There was a brand-new cedar-wood swing set complete with rocking horse, sliding board, covered fort, and sandbox. As far as I knew, Shanta lived by herself, making this something of a curiosity. Mackenzie jumped on the rocking horse.

"My fiancé's daughter," Shanta said in a way of explanation.

"Oh."

"We're getting married in the fall. He's moving in here."

"Sounds nice."

We watched Mackenzie rock the horse with gusto. She gave Shanta the stink eye.

"That kid hates me," Shanta said.

"Didn't you read fairy tales when you were a kid? You're the evil stepmother."

"Thanks, that helps." Shanta turned her eyes up toward me. "Wow, you look awful."

"Is this the part where I say, 'You should see the other guy'?"

"What are you doing to yourself, Jake?"

"I'm looking for someone I love."

"Does she even want to be found?"

"The heart doesn't ask questions."

"The penis doesn't ask questions," she said. "The heart usually has a little more intelligence."

True enough, I thought. "What is this about a bank robbery?"

She shaded her eyes from the sun. "Impatient, are we?"

"Not in the mood for games, that's for sure."

"Fair enough. Do you remember when you first asked me to check on Natalie Avery?"

"Yes."

"When I put her name through the systems it got two hits. One involved the NYPD. That was the big one. She was a person of great importance to them. I was sworn to secrecy about it. You are my friend. I want you to trust me. But I'm also a law enforcement officer. I'm not allowed to tell friends about ongoing investigations. You get that, right?"

I gave the smallest nod I could muster, more so she'd move on than to signal agreement.

"At the time, I barely noticed the other one," Shanta said. "They weren't interested in finding her or even talking to her. It was the most casual of mentions."

"What was it?"

"I'll get to that in a second. Just let me play it out, okay?"

I gave another small nod. First the shrugs, now the nods.

"I'm going to offer up a show of good faith here," she said. "I don't have to, but I spoke to the NYPD, and they gave me permission. You have to understand. I'm not breaking any legal confidences here."

"Just friends' confidences," I said.

"Low blow."

"Yeah, I know."

"And unfair. I was trying to help you."

"Okay, I'm sorry. What's up with the NYPD?"

She gave me a second or two to stew. "The NYPD believe that Natalie Avery witnessed a murder—that she, in fact, saw the killer and can positively identify him. The NYPD further believe that the perp is a major figure in organized crime. In short, your Natalie has the ability to put away one of the leading mob figures in New York City."

I waited for her to say more. She didn't.

"What else?" I asked.

"That's all I can tell you."

I shook my head. "You must think I'm an idiot."

"What?"

"The NYPD questioned me. They showed me a surveillance video and said that they needed to talk to her. I knew all that already. More to the point, *you* knew that I knew that already. A show of good faith. Come off it. You're hoping to gain my confidence by telling me what I already knew."

"That's not true."

"Who's the murder victim?"

"I'm not at liberty—"

"Archer Minor, son of Maxwell Minor. The police believe that Maxwell put out the hit on his own kid."

She looked stunned. "How did you know that?"

"It wasn't hard to figure out. Tell me one thing."

Shanta shook her head. "I can't."

"You still owe me the show of good faith, right? Does the NYPD know why Natalie was there that night? Just tell me that."

Her eyes moved back to the swing set. Mackenzie was off the rocking horse and heading up toward the slide. "They don't know."

"No idea?"

"The NYPD went through the Lock-Horne Building's security footage. It is pretty state-of-the-art. The first video they got was of your girlfriend running down the corridor on the twenty-second floor. There was also footage of her on the elevator, but the clearest shot—the one they showed you—was when she was exiting out the lobby on the ground floor."

"Any video of the killer?"

"I can't tell you more."

"I would say, 'can't or won't,' but that's such a hoary cliché."

She frowned. I thought that she was frowning at what I said, but I could see that wasn't it. Mackenzie was standing on top of the sliding board. "Mackenzie, that's dangerous."

"I do it all the time," the girl retorted.

"I don't care what you do all the time. Please sit down and slide."

She sat down. She didn't slide.

"The bank robbery?" I asked.

Shanta shook her head—again this action was not directed at what I had said, but at the stubborn girl at the top of the sliding board. "Have you heard anything about the rash of bank robberies in the New York area?"

I recalled a few articles I'd read. "The banks get hit at night when they're closed. The media calls the robbers the Invisibles or something."

"Right."

"What does Natalie have to do with them?"

"Her name came up in connection with one of the robberies—specifically the one on Canal Street in downtown Manhattan two weeks ago. It had been considered to be safer than Fort Knox. The thieves got twelve thousand in cash and busted open four hundred safety-deposit boxes."

"Twelve thousand doesn't sound like a ton."

"It's not. Despite what you see in the movies, banks don't store millions of dollars in vaults. But those safety-deposit boxes could be worth a fortune. That's where these guys are cleaning up. When my grandmother died, my mother put her four-carat diamond ring in a safety-deposit box to give me one day. That ring is probably worth forty grand alone. Who knows how much stuff is there? The insurance claim for one of their earlier robberies was three-point-seven million. Of course people lie. All of a sudden some expensive family heirloom happened to be in the box. But you see my point."

I saw her point. I didn't much care about it. "And Natalie's name came up with respect to this Canal Street robbery."

"Yes."

"How?"

"In a very, very small way." Shanta put her index finger and thumb half an inch apart to indicate how small. "Almost meaningless, really. It wouldn't be anything to care about on its own."

"But you do care."

"Now I do, yes."

"Why?"

"Because so much of what's surrounding your true love makes no sense anymore."

I couldn't argue with that.

"So what do you make of that?" she asked.

"Make of what? I don't know what to say here. I don't even know where Natalie is, much less how she might be connected in a very, very small way to a bank robbery."

"That's my point. I didn't think it mattered either, until I started looking up the other name you mentioned. Todd Sanderson."

"I didn't ask you to look him up."

"Yeah, but I did anyway. Got two hits on him too. Naturally the big hit surrounded the fact that he was murdered a week ago."

"Wait, Todd is also linked to this same bank robbery?"

"Yes. Did you ever read Oscar Wilde?"

I made a face. "Yes."

"He has a wonderful quote: 'To lose one parent may be regarded as a misfortune; to lose both looks like carelessness.' "

"From *The Importance of Being Earnest*," I said because I am an academic and can't help myself.

"Right. One of the people you asked about comes up in a bank robbery? That's nothing to get excited about. But two? That's not a coincidence."

And, I thought, a week or so after the bank robbery, Todd Sanderson was murdered.

"So was Todd's connection to the bank robbery also very, very small?" I asked.

"No. It was just small, I'd say."

"What was it?"

"Mackenzie!"

I turned toward the scream and saw a woman who looked a bit

too much like Shanta Newlin for my taste. Same height, same relative weight, same hairstyle. The woman had her eyes wide open as though a plane had suddenly crashed in the backyard. I followed her gaze. Mackenzie was back standing on the slide.

Shanta was mortified. "I'm so sorry, Candace. I told her to sit down."

"You *told* her?" Candace repeated incredulously.

"I'm sorry. I was watching her. I was just talking to a friend."

"And that's an excuse?"

Mackenzie, with a smile that said, *My work is done here*, sat, slid down the slide, and ran toward Candace. "Hi, Mommy."

Mommy. No surprise there.

"Let me show you out," Shanta tried.

"We're already out," Candace said. "We can just go around the front."

"Wait, Mackenzie drew the nicest picture. It's inside. I bet she'll want to take it home."

Candace and Mackenzie were already heading toward the front of the house. "I have hundreds of my daughter's drawings," Candace called back. "Keep it."

Shanta watched them both disappear into the front yard. Her normal military posture was gone. "What the hell am I doing, Jake?"

"Trying," I said. "Living."

She shook her head. "This will never work."

"Do you love him?"

"Yes."

"It'll work. It'll just be messy."

"How did you get to be so wise?"

"I was educated at Lanford College," I said, "and I watch a lot of daytime talk shows."

Shanta turned and looked back toward the swing set. "Todd Sanderson had a safety-deposit box at the Canal Street bank," she said. "He was one of the victims of the robbery. That's all. On the surface of it, he's pretty meaningless too."

"But a week later, he gets murdered," I said.

"Yes."

"Wait, does the FBI think he has something to do with the robberies?"

"I'm not privy to the full investigation."

"But?"

"I didn't see how it could be connected—the bank robbery in Manhattan and his murder down in Palmetto Bluff."

"But now?"

"Well, your Natalie's name came up too."

"In a very, very small way."

"Yes."

"How small?"

"After a robbery like this, the FBI does an inventory of everything. I mean, everything. So when the safety-deposit boxes are blown up, most people have all kinds of important papers in them. Stocks and bonds, powers of attorney, deeds to homes, all that. A lot of that ended up on the floor, of course. Why would a thief want any paperwork? So the FBI goes through all that and catalogs it. So, for example, one guy was holding his brother's car deed. The brother's name goes on the list."

I was trying to keep up with what she was saying. "So let me see if I follow. Natalie's name was on one of those documents from the safety-deposit box?"

"Yes."

"But she didn't have a box of her own there?"

"No. It was found in a box belonging to Todd Sanderson."

"So what was it? What's the document?"

Shanta turned and met my eye. "Her last will and testament."

Chapter 32

The FBI, Shanta said, wanted to know what I knew about all of this. I told her the truth: I knew nothing. I asked Shanta what the will and testament said. It was pretty simple: All of her assets should be split equally between her mother and sister. She had also left a request to be cremated, and interestingly enough, she wanted her ashes to be spread in the woods overlooking the quad at Lanford College.

I thought about the will and testament. I thought about where it had been found. The answer wasn't yet in my grasp, but it felt as though I were circling right above it.

As I started to leave, Shanta asked, "Are you sure you don't have any thoughts about this?"

"I'm sure," I said.

But I thought now that maybe I did. I just didn't want to share them with Shanta or the FBI. I trusted her as far as I could trust anyone who had openly told me that her first allegiance was to law enforcement. To tell her about Fresh Start, for example, would be catastrophic. But more to the point—and this was key—Natalie had not trusted law enforcement.

Why?

It was something I had never really considered before. Natalie could have trusted the cops and testified and gone into witness protection or something like that. But she didn't. Why? What did she know that prevented her from doing that? And if she didn't trust the cops, why on earth should I?

Once again I took out my cell phone and tried Malcolm Hume's number in Florida. Once again there was no answer. Enough. I hurried over to Clark House. Mrs. Dinsmore was just settling into her desk. She looked up at me over the half-moon reading glasses. "You're not supposed to be here."

I didn't bother defending or cracking wise. I told her about trying to reach Malcolm Hume.

"He's not in Vero Beach," she said.

"Do you know where he is?"

"I do."

"Could you tell me?"

She took her time shuffling papers and sliding a paperclip into place. "He's staying at his cabin off Lake Canet."

I had been invited once many years ago for a fishing trip, but I didn't go. I hate fishing. I didn't get it, but then again I was never one for ease-back, Zen-type activities. I have trouble turning myself off. I'd rather read than relax. I'd rather keep the mind engaged. But I remembered that the property had been in Mrs. Hume's family for generations. He joked that he liked to feel like an interloper, that it made it more like a vacation spot.

Or like a spot perfect for hiding.

"I didn't know he still owned a place up here," I said.

"He comes up a few times a year. He enjoys the seclusion."

"I didn't know."

"He doesn't tell anyone."

"He tells you."

"Well," Mrs. Dinsmore said, as though that were the most obvious thing in the world. "He doesn't like company there. He needs to be alone so he can write and fish in peace and quiet."

"Yeah," I said. "Escape that hectic, jam-packed life at the gated community in Vero Beach."

"Funny."

"Thanks."

"You're on paid leave," she said. "So maybe you should, uh, leave."

"Mrs. Dinsmore?"

She looked up at me.

"You know all of the stuff I've been asking about lately?"

"You mean like murdered students and missing professors?"

"Yes."

"What about it?"

"I need you to give me the address of the lake house. I need to talk to Professor Hume in private."

Chapter 33

The life of a college professor, especially one who lives on a small campus, is pretty contained. You stay in the surreal world of so-called higher learning. You are comfortable there. You have very little reason to leave it. I owned a car, but probably drove it no more than once a week. I walked to all my classes. I walked into the town of Lanford to visit my favorite shops, haunts, cinema, restaurants, what have you. I worked out at the school's state-of-the-art weight room. It was an isolated world, not just for the students but also for those who have made such places our livelihood.

You tend to live in a snow globe of liberal-arts academia.

It alters your mind frame, of course, but on a purely physical level, I had probably done more traveling in the week-plus since seeing Todd Sanderson's obituary than I had done in the previous six years combined. That may be an exaggeration, but not much of one. The violent altercations, combined with the stiffness of sitting for hours in these car and plane rides, were sapping my energy. I'd been flying high on adrenaline, of course, but as I had learned the hard way, that resource was not unlimited.

As I turned off Route 202 and started climbing toward the rural area along the Massachusetts–New Hampshire border, my back started to seize up. I stopped at Lee's Hot Dog Stand to stretch a bit. A sign in the front promoted their fried haddock sandwich. I went instead with a hot dog, cheese fries, and a Coke. It all tasted wonderful, and for a second, heading up to this remote cabin, I thought about the notion of a last meal. That couldn't be a healthy mind frame. I ate ravenously, bought and downed another hot dog, and got back in the car. I felt strangely renewed.

I drove past Otter River State Forest. I was only about ten minutes from Malcolm Hume's house. I didn't have his cell phone number—I don't even know if he had one—but I wouldn't have called it anyway. I wanted to just show up and see what was what. I didn't want to give Professor Hume time to prepare. I wanted answers, and I suspected my old mentor had them.

I didn't really need to know it all. I knew enough. I only needed to be sure that Natalie was safe, that she understood some very bad people were back on her trail, and if possible, I wanted to see if I could run away and be with her. Yes, I had heard about Fresh Start's rules and oaths and all that, but the heart doesn't know from rules and oaths.

There had to be a way.

I almost missed the small sign for Attal Drive. I made a left onto the dirt road and started up the mountain. When I reached the top, Lake Canet was laid out below me, still as a mirror. People toss around the word *pristine*, but that word was taken to a new level of purity when I saw the water. I stopped the car and got out. The air had that kind of freshness that lets you know even one breath could nourish the lungs. The silence and stillness were almost devastating. I knew that if I called out, my shout would echo, would keep echoing, would never fully dissipate. The shout would live in these woods, growing dimmer and dimmer but never dying, joining the other past sounds that somehow still echoed into that low hum of the great outdoors.

I looked for a house on the lake. There was none. I could see two docks. There were canoes tied to both of them. Nothing else. I got back in my car and drove to the left. The dirt road was not as well paved here. The car bounced on the rough terrain, testing the shocks and finding them wanting. I was glad I took the insurance out on the rental, which was a bizarre thing to think about at a time like this, but the mind goes where it goes. I remembered Professor Hume had owned a four-by-four pickup truck, not exactly standard liberal-arts driving fare. Now I knew why.

Up ahead I saw two pickup trucks parked side by side. I pulled my car behind them and got out. I couldn't help but notice that there were several sets of tire tracks in the dirt. Either Malcolm had gone back and forth repeatedly or he had company.

I wasn't sure what to make of that.

When I looked up the hill and saw the small cottage with the dark windows, I could feel my eyes start to well up.

There was no soft morning glow this time. There was no pinkness from the start of a new day. The sun was setting behind it, casting long shadows, turning what had appeared empty and abandoned into something more black and menacing.

It was the cottage from Natalie's painting.

I started up the hill toward the front door. There was something dream-like about this trek, something almost Alice in Wonderland-ish, as though I were leaving the real world and entering Natalie's painting. I reached the door. There was no bell to press. When I knocked, the sound ripped through the stillness like a gunshot.

I waited, but I heard no returning sound.

I knocked again. Still nothing. I debated my next move. I could walk down to the lake and see if Malcolm was on it, but that stillness I had witnessed earlier seemed to indicate that no one was down there. There was also the matter of all those tire tracks.

I put my hand on the knob. It turned. Not only was the door left unlocked, there was, I could see now, no actual lock on it—no hole in either the knob or the door to place a key. I pushed the door open and stepped inside. The room was dark. I flicked on the lights.

No one.

"Professor Hume?"

Once I'd graduated, he had insisted that I call him Malcolm. I never could.

I checked the kitchen. It was empty. There was only one bedroom. I headed toward it, tiptoeing for some odd reason across the floor.

When I stepped into the bedroom, my heart dropped like a stone.

Oh no . . .

Malcolm Hume was on the bed, lying on his back, dried foam

on his face. His mouth was half open, his face twisted in a final, frozen scream of agony.

My knees buckled. I used the wall to support me. Memories rushed at me, nearly knocking me over: the first class I took with him freshman year (Hobbes, Locke, and Rousseau), the first time I met with him in that office I now called my own (we discussed depictions of law and violence in literature), the hours working on my thesis (subject: The Rule of Law), the way he bear-hugged me the day I graduated, with tears in his eyes.

A voice behind me said, "You couldn't leave it alone."

I spun around to see Jed pointing a gun at me.

"I didn't do this," I said.

"I know. He did it to himself." Jed stared at me. "Cyanide."

I remembered Benedict's pillbox now. All the members of Fresh Start, he said, carried one.

"We told you to leave it alone."

I shook my head, trying to keep it together, trying to tell the side of me that just wanted to collapse and grieve that there'd be time for that later. "This whole thing started before I got involved. I didn't know a damn thing about any of this until I saw Todd Sanderson's obituary."

Jed suddenly looked exhausted. "It doesn't matter. We asked you to stop in a million different ways. You wouldn't. It doesn't make a difference if you're guilty or innocent. You know about us. We took an oath."

"To kill me."

"In this case, yes." Jed looked again toward the bed. "If Malcolm was committed enough to do this to himself, shouldn't I be committed enough to kill you?"

But he didn't fire. Jed no longer relished shooting me. I could see that now. He had when he thought I'd been the one to kill Todd, but the idea of killing me just to keep me quiet was weighing on him. He looked back down at the body in the end.

"Malcolm loved you," Jed said. "He loved you like a son. He wouldn't want . . ." His voice just drifted off. The gun dropped to his side.

I took a tentative step toward him. "Jed?"

He turned to me.

"I think I know how Maxwell Minor's men found Todd in the first place."

"How?"

"I need to ask you something first," I said. "Did Fresh Start begin with Todd Sanderson or Malcolm Hume or, well, you?"

"What does that have to do with anything?"

"Just . . . trust me for a second, okay?"

"Fresh Start began with Todd," Jed said. "His father was accused of a heinous crime."

"Pedophilia," I said.

"Yes."

"His father ended up killing himself over it," I said.

"You can't imagine what that did to Todd. I was his college roommate and best friend. I watched him fall apart. He railed against the unfairness of it all. If only his father could have moved away, we wondered. But of course, even if he had, that kind of accusation follows you. You can never escape it."

"Except," I said, "with a fresh start."

"Exactly. We realized that there were people who needed to be rescued—and the only way to rescue them was to give them a new life. Professor Hume understood too. He had a person in his life that could have used a fresh start."

I thought about that. I wondered whether that "person" could very well have been Professor Aaron Kleiner.

"So we joined up," Jed continued. "We formed this group under the guise of a legitimate charity. My father was a federal marshal. He hid people in witness protection. I knew all the rules. I inherited that family farm from my grandfather. We made it into a retreat. We trained people how to act when they change identities. If you love gambling, for example, you don't go to Vegas or the track. We worked with them psychologically so they realized that disappearing was a form of suicide and renewal—you kill one being to create another. We created flawless new identities. We used misinformation to lead their stalkers down the wrong path. We added distracting tattoos and disguises. In certain instances, Todd performed cosmetic surgery to change a subject's appearance."

"So then what?" I asked. "Where did you relocate the people you rescued?"

Jed smiled. "That's the beauty. We didn't."

"I don't understand."

"You keep searching for Natalie, but you don't listen. None of us knows where she is. That's how it works. We couldn't tell you even if we wanted to. We give them all the tools and at some point, we drop them off at a train station and have no idea where they end up. That's part of how we keep it safe."

I tried to push through what he was saying, the notion that there was absolutely no way I could find her, no way that we could ever be together. It was simply too crushing to think that all of this had been futile from the start.

"At some point," I said, "Natalie came to you guys for help."

Again Jed looked down at the bed. "She came to Malcolm."

"How did she know him?" I asked.

"I don't know."

But I did. Natalie's mother had told her daughter about Archer Minor's cheating scandal and how her father had been forced to vanish. She would have tried to track her father down, so naturally Malcolm Hume would be one of the first people she would visit. Malcolm would have befriended her, the daughter of the beloved colleague who had been forced to disappear. Had Malcolm helped her father run from Archer Minor's family? I don't know. I suspected that he probably did. Either way, Aaron Kleiner was Malcolm's impetus for joining Fresh Start. His daughter would be someone he'd immediately care about and take under his wing.

"Natalie came to you guys because she witnessed a murder," I said.

"Not just any murder. The murder of Archer Minor."

I nodded. "So she witnesses the murder. She goes to Malcolm. Malcolm brings her to your retreat."

"First he brought her here."

Of course, I thought. The painting. This place inspired it.

Jed was smiling.

"What?"

"You don't get it, do you?"

"Get what?"

"You were so close to Malcolm," he said. "Like I said. He loved you like a son."

"I'm not following."

"Six years ago, when you needed help writing your dissertation,

Malcolm Hume was the one who suggested the Vermont retreat to you, didn't he?"

I felt a small coldness seep into my bones. "Yeah, so?"

"Fresh Start isn't just the three of us, of course. We have a committed staff. You met Cookie and some of the others. There aren't many, for obvious reasons. We have to trust each other completely. At one point, Malcolm thought that you'd be an asset to the organization."

"Me?"

"That was why he suggested that you attend that retreat. He hoped to show you what Fresh Start was doing so that you'd join us."

I didn't know what to say, so I went with the obvious: "Why didn't he?"

"He realized that you wouldn't be a good fit."

"I don't understand."

"We work in a murky world, Jake. Some of the things we do are illegal. We make our own rules. We decide who is deserving and who is not. The line between innocence and guilt isn't so clear with us."

I nodded, seeing it now. The black-and-white—and the grays. "Professor Eban Trainor."

"He broke a rule. You wanted him punished. You couldn't see the extenuating circumstances."

I thought about how Malcolm had defended Eban Trainor after the party where two students had been rushed to the hospital for alcohol poisoning. Now I saw the truth. Professor Hume's defense of Trainor had been, in part, a test—one that in Malcolm's mind I had failed. He was right though. I believe in the rule of law. If you start down that slippery slope, you take all of what makes us civilized with you.

At least, that was how I felt before this week.

"Jake?"

"Yes?"

"Do you really know how the Minors found Todd Sanderson?"

"I think so," I said. "You keep some paperwork on Fresh Start, right?"

"Only on a web cloud. And you needed two of the three of us—Todd, Malcolm, or me—to access it." He blinked, looked away, blinked some more. "I just realized. I'm the only one left. The paperwork is gone forever."

"But there must be something physical you store, no?"

"Like what?" he asked.

"Like their last will and testament?"

"Well, yes, those, but they're kept someplace where no one can find them."

"You mean like a safety-deposit box on Canal Street?"

Jed's mouth dropped open. "How can you know that?"

"It was broken into. Someone got into the safety-deposit boxes. I can't say what happened for sure, but Natalie was still a huge priority for the Minor family. If you found her, it could mean big bucks. So my guess is, someone—the thieves, a cop on the take, whatever—recognized her name. They reported it to the Minors. The Minors saw that the box was taken out by a guy named Todd Sanderson who lived in Palmetto Bluff, South Carolina."

"My God," Jed said. "So they paid him a visit."

"Yes."

"Todd was tortured," Jed said.

"I know."

"They made him talk. A man can only stand so much pain. But

Todd didn't know where Natalie or anyone else was. See? He could only tell them what he knew."

"Like about you and the retreat in Vermont," I said.

Jed nodded. "That's why we had to close it down. That's why we had to run away and pretend that there was nothing there but a farm. Do you understand?"

"I do," I said.

He looked back down at Malcolm's body. "We need to bury him, Jake. You and me. Out here in this place he loved."

And then I realized something else that chilled me to the bone. Jed could see it on my face.

"What?"

"Todd never got the chance to take the cyanide pill."

"They probably surprised him."

"Right, and if they tortured him and he gave up your name, it stands to reason that he gave up Malcolm's name too. They probably sent men to Vero Beach. But Malcolm was already gone. He came up here to this cabin. The house would have been empty. But these guys don't quit easily. They'd just found their first clue in six years—they weren't about to just let it go. They would have asked questions and pored through personal records. Even if this land was still in his late wife's name, they may have found this place."

I thought about all those tire tracks outside.

"He's dead," I said, looking down at the bed. "He chose to kill himself, and judging by the lack of decay, he did it very recently. Why?"

"Oh God." Jed saw it now too. "Because Minor's guys found him."

As he said those words, I heard cars pull up. It was so clear now.

Minor's men had been here already. Malcolm Hume had seen them coming and taken matters into his own hands.

So what would they do about that?

They'd have set a trap. They'd leave someone behind to stake out the house in case someone else showed up.

Jed and I both rushed to the window as the two black cars came to a stop. The doors opened. Five men with guns came out.

One of them was Danny Zuker.

Chapter 34

The men kept low and spread out.

Jed reached into his pocket and pulled out a pillbox. He opened it and tossed the pill inside to me.

"I don't want this," I said.

"I have the gun. I'll try to hold them. You try to find a way to escape. But if you can't . . ."

From outside we heard Danny call out. "Only one way out of this!" he shouted. "Come out with your hands up."

We had both ducked down to the floor.

"You believe him?" Jed asked me.

"No."

"Me neither. There's no way they're going to let us live. So all we're doing right now is giving them time to set up." He started to rise. "Find an escape route out the back, Jake. I'll keep them busy."

"What?"

"Just go!"

Without warning, Jed knocked out a windowpane and started to pull the trigger. Within seconds, return gunfire raked the side of the house and took out the rest of the window. Shards of glass fell on me.

"Go!" Jed shouted at me.

No reason to tell me a third time. I commando-crawled toward the back door. It was, I knew, my only chance. Jed started firing blindly, keeping his back against the wall. I headed into the kitchen, still moving low across the acrylic. I reached the back door.

I heard Jed let out a celebratory shout. "Nailed one!"

Great. Four to go. More gunfire. Heavier now. The walls were starting to give way, the bullets weakening and now penetrating the wood. From where I was, I saw Jed get hit once, then twice. I started back toward him.

"Don't!" he shouted at me.

"Jed . . ."

"Don't you dare! Get out now!"

I wanted to help him, but I could also see how foolhardy that would be. It wouldn't help him. It would just be suicide. Jed managed to stand. He was heading for the front door.

"Okay!" he shouted out. "I surrender."

Jed had the gun in his hand. He looked back at me, winked, gestured for me to keep going.

I glanced out the back window, preparing to make a break for it. The house was right up against a wooded area. I could go into those woods and just hope for the best. I didn't have another plan. At least nothing that would help immediately. I took out my iPhone and flipped it on. There was service. I dialed 911 as I looked out the window.

One of the men was in the back on the left, covering the door. Damn.

"Nine-one-one, what is your emergency?"

I told her quickly that there were shots being fired and at least two men hit. I gave her the address and put the phone down, keeping the line open. From behind me, I heard Danny Zuker shout, "Okay, throw the gun out first."

I thought that I saw a smile on Jed's face now. He was bleeding. I didn't know how badly he was hit, if his current injuries were mortal or not, but Jed knew. Jed knew that his life was over no matter what he did and with that, there seemed to come a strange sense of peace.

Jed opened the door and just started firing. I heard another man call out in pain—maybe another one of Jed's bullets had found its mark—and then I heard the hollow pop of automatic gunfire tearing into flesh. From my vantage point, I saw Jed's body fly backward, arms dangling overhead as though in a macabre dance. He fell back into the house. More bullets hit him, jerking his lifeless body.

It was over. For him and probably for me.

Even if Jed had managed to kill two of them, three would still be alive and armed. What chance did I have? I calculated the odds in nanoseconds. Almost zilch. I had one chance, really. Stall. Stall until the police could get there. I thought about how far out we were, about that drive up the dirt road, about not seeing any municipal-type buildings within miles of this place.

The cavalry wouldn't be arriving in time.

Still the Minors may want me alive.

I was their last chance to get information on Natalie. I could tap-dance a bit that way.

They were approaching the house. I looked for a place to hide. Stall. Just stall.

But there was nowhere to go. I stood up and looked out the back door window. The man was there, just waiting for me. I sprinted across the kitchen and back into the bedroom. Malcolm hadn't moved, but then again I hadn't expected him to.

I could hear someone enter the cottage.

I threw open the bedroom window. What I was counting on here—and really it was my only shot—was that the man in back was watching the door. The bedroom window was on the side toward the right. From where the guy had been standing when I saw him from the kitchen, he wouldn't be able to see this window.

From the main room, I heard Danny Zuker say, "Professor Fisher? We know you're in here. It'll be worse for you if you make us wait."

The window shrieked when I opened it. Zuker and another henchman ran toward the sound. I saw them as I rolled out the window and started to sprint for the woods.

Gunfire erupted behind me.

So much for keeping me alive. I didn't know if it was my imagination or reality, but I could swear that I felt bullets nipping at my side. I kept running. I didn't turn around. I just kept . . .

Someone tackled me from the side.

It must have been the guy who'd been out back. He hit from the left, knocking us both down. I prepared a punch and delivered it hard to his face. He rocked back. I reeled back to deliver another one. Again it landed. He went slack.

But it was too late now.

Danny Zuker and the other henchman stood over us. They both pointed their guns down at me.

"You can live," Zuker said simply. "Just tell me where she is."

"I don't know."

"Then you're worthless to me."

It was over. I could see that now. The man who'd tackled me shook his head. He stood and grabbed his gun. There I was, lying on the ground, surrounded by three men, all with guns. There was no move I could make. There were no distant sirens coming to my rescue. One man stood on my left, the other—the one I had decked—stood on my right.

I looked up at Danny Zuker, who stayed a step back. I threw up one last Hail Mary: "You killed Archer Minor, didn't you?"

That caught him off guard. I could see the befuddlement on his face. "What?"

"Someone had to quiet him," I said, "and Maxwell Minor would never murder his own kid."

"You're crazy."

The other two men exchanged a glance.

"Why else would you try so hard to find her?" I asked. "It's been six years. You know she'd never testify."

Danny Zuker shook his head. There was something akin to sadness on his face. "You don't have a clue, do you?"

He raised the gun, almost reluctantly now. I had played my final card. I didn't want to die like this, on the ground beneath them. I stood up, wondering what my final move would be, when it was made for me.

There was a single gunshot. The head of the man on my left exploded like a tomato under a heavy boot.

The rest of us turned toward the sound of the gunshot. I recovered the fastest. Letting the lizard brain take over again, I dived straight toward the man I'd already punched. He was closest to me, and he'd be weakest from my earlier blow.

I could get his gun.

But the man reacted with greater speed than I anticipated. His lizard brain at work too, I guess. He stepped back and took aim. I was too far away to reach him in time.

And then his head exploded in another crimson haze.

The blood splashed me in the face. Danny Zuker didn't hesitate. He leapt behind me, using me as a shield. He wrapped his arm around my throat and put the gun against my head.

"Don't move," he whispered.

I didn't. There was silence now. He stayed close to me, moving us back toward the house to keep himself protected.

"Show yourself," Zuker shouted. "Show yourself or I'll blow his brains out!"

There was a rustling sound. Zuker jerked my head to the right, making sure to keep my body blocking his. He turned me more toward the right—to where the rustling had originated. I looked out into the clearing.

My heart stopped.

Coming down the hill, gun still in her hand and aimed at us, was Natalie.

Chapter 35

Danny Zuker spoke first. "Well, well, look who's here."

My body had gone numb at the sight of her. Our eyes met—Natalie's and mine—and the world exploded in a thousand different ways. It was one of the most powerful experiences of my life, this simple act of looking into the blue eyes of the woman I loved, and even now, even with a gun to my head, I felt oddly grateful. If he pulled the trigger, so be it. I had, in this single moment, been more alive than any time in the previous six years. If I were to die now—and, no, I didn't want to, in fact, more than anything else I wanted to live and be with that woman—I'd die a more complete person, have lived a more complete life, than if I had died just a few moments earlier.

With the gun still trained on us, Natalie said, "Let him go."

She never took her eyes off me.

"I don't think so, sweetheart," Zuker said.

"Let him go, and you can have me."

I shouted, "No!"

Zuker drove the muzzle of the gun into the side of my neck. "Shut up." Then to Natalie he said, "Why should I trust you?"

"If I cared more about myself than him," she said, "I wouldn't have revealed myself."

Natalie kept her eyes on me. I wanted to protest. There was no way I would allow this exchange, but something in her look told me to keep still, at least for now. I thought about it. She was almost willing me to obey, to just let this play out the way she wanted.

Maybe, I thought, she wasn't here alone. Maybe there were others. Maybe she had a plan.

"Okay then," Zuker said, still hiding behind my body. "Put your gun down and I'll let him go."

"I don't think so," she said.

"Oh?"

"We bring him out to his car. You put him in the driver's seat. The moment he pulls away, I put the gun down."

Zuker seemed to be thinking that over. "I put him in the car. You drop your weapon and he drives off."

Natalie nodded again, still looking directly at me, almost willing me to obey. "Deal," she said.

We started toward the front of the house. Natalie kept her distance, staying about thirty yards back from us. I wondered whether Cookie or Benedict or some other member of Fresh Start was nearby. Maybe they were waiting by the car, armed, ready to take Zuker out with a single bullet.

When we reached the car, Zuker took an angle so that the vehicle and my body were still shielding him. "Open the door," he told me.

I hesitated.

He pressed the gun against my neck. "Open the door."

I looked back at Natalie. She gave me a confident smile that reached into my chest and crushed it like an eggshell. As I slipped into the driver's seat, I realized with mounting horror what she was doing.

There was no plan to save us both.

There were no other Fresh Start members who were going to intercede. There was no one hiding, waiting to pounce. Natalie had kept my attention, had offered up this hope in her eyes, so I wouldn't fight back, so I wouldn't make the sacrifice she was about to make for me.

To hell with that.

The car started up. Natalie began to lower her weapon. I had a second, no more, to make my move. It was suicide. I knew that. I knew that there was no way the two of us could survive this. That had been her thinking. One of us had to die. In the end, Jed and Benedict and Cookie had been right. I had messed up. I had stubbornly followed some love-conquers-all inner mantra, and now here we were, exactly where I was warned we would be, with Natalie facing death.

I wouldn't let that happen.

Once I was in the car, Natalie stopped walking and turned her attention to Danny Zuker. Zuker, understanding that it was his turn, moved the gun away from my neck. He changed hands so that the weapon was too far away from me, sitting as I was, to make any kind of foolish move.

"Your turn," Zuker said.

Natalie put her weapon on the ground.

Time was up. I had spent the seconds planning my exact move, the exact calculation, the element of surprise, all of it. Now I didn't hesitate. Zuker would have time, I was fairly sure, to take a shot at me. That didn't matter. He was going to have to defend himself. If he did that by shooting me, it would give Natalie the time to either run or, more likely, pick her own gun back off the ground and shoot.

No choice for me now. I wasn't driving off, that was for sure.

Without warning, my left hand shot up high. I don't think he expected that. Zuker had figured that if I did anything, I'd go for the gun. I grabbed his hair hard and pulled him toward me. As I predicted, Danny swung the gun in my direction.

With my left hand, I pulled his face closer to mine. He expected my right to go for the gun.

It didn't.

Instead, using the right hand, I jammed the cyanide pill Jed had given me into Zuker's mouth. His eyes widened in terror as he realized what I had done. That made him hesitate—the realization that there was cyanide in his mouth and that if he didn't get it out, he was a dead man. He tried to spit it out but my hand was there. He bit down hard, making me scream out, but my hand stayed still. At the same time he fired the gun at my head.

I ducked away.

The bullet hit my shoulder. More agony.

Danny started to convulse, taking aim for another shot. But he never got that one off. Natalie's first bullet caught him in the back of the head. She fired twice more, but there was no need.

I fell back, my hand on my throbbing shoulder, trying to stop the blood. I waited for her to come over to me.

But she didn't. She stayed where she was.

I had never seen anything more beautiful and crushing than the expression on her face. A tear ran down her cheek. She just slowly shook her head.

"Natalie?"

"I have to go," she said.

My eyes went wide. "No." Now, finally, I could hear the sirens. I was losing blood and feeling faint. None of that mattered. "Let me go with you. Please."

Natalie winced. Her tears came heavier now. "I can't live if something happens to you. Do you get that? It's why I ran the first time. I can live with you heartbroken. I can't live with you dead."

"I'm not alive without you."

The sirens were growing closer.

"I have to go," she said, through her tears.

"No . . ."

"I will always love you, Jake. Always."

"Then be with me." I could hear the plea in my voice.

"I can't. You know that. Don't follow me. Don't look for me. Keep your promise this time."

I shook my head. "Not a chance," I said.

She turned and started back up the hill.

"Natalie!" I called out.

But the woman I loved just kept walking out of my life. Again.

Chapter 36

ONE YEAR LATER

A student in the back of the room raises his hand. "Professor Weiss?"

"Yes, Kennedy?" I say.

That's my name now. Paul Weiss. I teach at a large university in New Mexico. I can't say the name of it for security reasons. With all the dead bodies at the lake, the powers that be realized that I'd be best off in witness protection. So here I am, out in the west. The elevation still gets to me sometimes, but overall I like it out here.

That surprises me. I always thought I'd be an East Coast guy, but life is about making adjustments, I guess.

I miss Lanford, of course. I miss my old life. Benedict and I still stay in touch, even though we shouldn't. We use an e-mail drop box and never hit the send button. We created an e-mail account with AOL (old-school). We write each other messages and just leave them in the draft section. Periodically we go in and check it.

The big news in Benedict's life is that the drug cartel that was after him is gone. They were wiped out in some kind of turf battle. In short, he is free at last to return to Marie-Anne, but when he last checked her Facebook status, it had changed from "in a relationship" to "married." There were photographs of her wedding to Kevin all over both their Facebook pages.

I'm urging him to tell her the truth anyway. He says he won't. He says he doesn't want to mess up her life.

But life is messy, I told him.

Deep thought, right?

The rest of the pieces of the puzzle have finally come together for me. It took a long while. One of the Minor henchmen that Jed shot survived. His testimony confirmed what I had suspected. The bank robbers known as the Invisibles broke into the Canal Street bank. In Todd Sanderson's box, there were both last wills and testaments and passports. The Invisibles had taken the passports, figuring that they could be resold on the black market. One of them recognized Natalie's name—the Minors were still actively looking for her, even after six years—and reported it to them. The box was in Todd Sanderson's name, so Danny Zuker and Otto Devereaux paid him a visit.

You know where it went from there. Or you know most of it.

But a lot of things didn't add up. I had raised one with Danny Zuker right before his life ended: Why were the Minors so consumed with finding Natalie? She had made it pretty clear that she wouldn't testify. Why stir that up, flush her out, when the end result could very well be her running back to the police? I had at one point surmised that it was really Danny Zuker behind it all, that he had killed Archer Minor and wanted to make sure that the one person who could tell Maxwell Minor that fact was dead. But that didn't really add up either, especially when I saw the befuddlement on his face when I accused him of the crime.

"You don't have a clue, do you?"

That was what Danny Zuker had said. He'd been right. But I'd slowly started putting it together, especially when I started to wonder about the central question left here, the incident that started it all:

Where was Natalie's father?

I figured out the answer to that almost a year ago. Two days before they sent me to New Mexico, I visited Natalie's mother again at the Hyde Park Assisted Living facility. I wore a cheesy disguise. (Now my disguise is simpler: I've shaved my head. Gone are the unruly professorial locks of my youth. My dome gleams. If I wore a gold earring, you'd mistake me for Mr. Clean.)

"I need the truth this time," I said to Sylvia Avery.

"I told you."

I could see people needing new identities and vanishing because they'd been accused of pedophilia or had upset members of a drug cartel or had been battered by brutal husbands or had witnessed a mob hit. But I didn't see why a man involved in a college cheating scandal would have to vanish for life—even now, even after Archer Minor was dead.

"Natalie's dad never ran away, did he?"

She didn't reply.

"He was murdered," I said.

Sylvia Avery seemed too weak to protest anymore. She sat there, still as a stone.

"You told Natalie that her father would never, ever, abandon her."

"He wouldn't," she said. "He loved her so. He loved Julie too. And me. Aaron was such a good man."

"Too good," I said. "Always seeing just the black-and-white."

"Yes."

"When I told you that Archer Minor was dead, you said, 'Good riddance.' Was he the one who killed your husband?"

She lowered her head.

"There's no one who can hurt any of you anymore," I said, which was only partially true. "Did Archer Minor kill your husband, or was it someone his father sent?"

And then she said it: "It was Archer himself."

I nodded. I had figured that.

"He came to the house with a gun," Sylvia said. "He demanded that Aaron give him the papers that proved he'd cheated. You see, he really did want to escape his father's shadow and if word got out he cheated . . ."

"He'd be exactly like his father."

"Yes. I begged Aaron to listen to him. He wouldn't. He thought Archer was bluffing. So Archer put the gun against Aaron's head and . . ." She closed her eyes. "He smiled when he did it. That's what I remember most. Archer Minor was smiling. He told me to give him the papers or I'd be next. I gave them to him, of course.

Then two men came by. Men who worked for his father. They took Aaron's body away. Then one of the men sat me down. He said if I ever told anyone about this, they'd do horrible things to my girls. They wouldn't just kill them, he said. They'd do horrible things to them first. He kept stressing that. He told me to say that Aaron ran off. So I did. I kept the lie up for all those years to protect my girls. You understand that, don't you?"

"I do," I said sadly.

"I had to make my poor Aaron be the bad guy. So his daughters wouldn't keep asking about him."

"But Natalie wouldn't buy it."

"She kept pressing."

"And like you said, the lie had darkened her. The idea that her father had abandoned her."

"That's a horrible thing for a young girl to think. I should have come up with another way. But what?"

"So she pressed and she pressed," I said.

"She wouldn't leave it alone. She headed back to Lanford and talked to Professor Hume."

"But Hume didn't know either."

"No. But she kept asking questions."

"And that could have gotten her in trouble."

"Yes."

"So you decided to tell her the truth. Her father hadn't run away with a coed. He hadn't run away because he was afraid of the Minors. You finally told her the full story—that Archer Minor had murdered her father in cold blood while smiling."

Sylvia Avery didn't nod. She didn't have to. I said good-bye then and left.

So now I knew why Natalie was in that high-rise late that night. Now I knew why Natalie had gone to visit Archer Minor when no one else would be around. Now I knew why Maxwell Minor never stopped looking for Natalie. He isn't worried about her testifying.

He's a father who wants to avenge his son's murder.

I don't know this for sure. I don't know if Natalie shot Archer Minor with a smile on her face or if the gun went off accidentally or if Archer Minor made threats when she confronted him or if it was self-defense. I don't even ask.

The old me would have cared. The new me doesn't.

Class ends. I start across the commons. The Santa Fe sky is a blue like no other. I shade my eyes and keep walking.

That day a year ago, with the bullet still in my shoulder, I watched Natalie start to walk away. I shouted, "Not a chance" when she asked me to promise not to follow. She wouldn't listen to me or stop. So I got out of the car. The pain in my shoulder was nothing compared with the pain of her leaving me again. I ran toward her. I wrapped my arms, even the one aching from the bullet wound, around her and pulled her close. Our eyes squeezed shut. I hung on to her, wondering if I had ever felt such contentment before. She started to cry. I pulled her even closer. She lowered her head into my chest. For a moment, she tried to pull away. But only for a moment. She knew that this time I wouldn't let her go.

No matter what she might or might not have done.

I still haven't let her go.

Up ahead, a beautiful woman named Diana Weiss wears a wedding band that matches mine. She has decided to teach her art class outside on this glorious day. She moves from student to student, commenting on their work, offering guidance.

She knows that I know, even though we've never talked about it. I wonder whether that was part of her leaving the first time, if she felt as though I could never live with the truth about what she'd done. Maybe I couldn't back then.

I can now.

Diana Weiss looks up at me as I approach. Her smile shames the sun. Today my beautiful wife is glowing even more than normal. I may be thinking that about her because I'm biased. Or I may be thinking that because she is seven months pregnant with our child.

Her class ends. The students linger before slowly drifting away. She takes my hand when we're finally alone, looks into my eyes, and says, "I love you."

"I love you too," I say.

She smiles up at me. The gray has no chance against that smile. It vanishes in a wonderful haze of bright color.

HARLAN COBEN

"Coben is simply one of the all-time greats."

—Gillian Flynn, bestselling author of *Gone Girl*

For a complete list of titles,
please visit prh.com/HarlanCoben